THE HOUSE OF THE RISING SON

*When adolesce   collide
– the result is a delightful blend of dark comedy and pathos,
that moves at warp-speed towards a scintillating climax.*

Ardal O'Hanlon (actor, author, comedian)

*A funny, touching book that rings horribly true for anyone
who has ever felt the impossibility of getting parenting/
marriage/career/health/ even death – right.*

Imogen Stubbs (actor, writer)

*Captures the cruel irony of the male midlife crisis colliding
with teenage angst. This wry, funny, unexpectedly touching
tale has a nail biting finale peppered with some brilliantly
hilarious moments.*

Jan Ravens (actor, comedian)

*Gershfield manages to find humour in the darkest places.
The storylines bob and weave in compelling fashion –
there's not a dull moment from beginning to end.*

Bill Dare (producer, screenwriter, author)

A comic tour de force via pathos and humour from beginning to the finish line as one desperate man hilariously (and pathetically) tries to re-connect with his teenaged son. If you loved About A Boy... boy, you're in for a treat.

Paul McKenzie (producer, screenwriter)

It's quite a feat to make a serious novel so funny (or a comic novel so serious) but Gershfield pulls off this literary legerdemain with commendable brio in his captivating debut. And as a screenwriter/director of some note, it is no surprise that his dialogue nails the characters so assuredly and wittily, whilst totally involving us in Alex's family dynamics. From the very first quite startling paragraph I was hooked! The action never stops. This would make a terrific contemporary TV series.

Paul A Mendelson (screenwriter, author)

The House of the Rising Son riotously depicts the catastrophic impact that a teenager's hormones can have on his father's run-of-the-mill mid-life crisis. It's a suburban tale of sex, drugs and rock n'roll...with some kidnap thrown in for good measure. Deliciously written with enormous heart, Gershfield puts his protagonists through hell and back for our exquisite pleasure. Buckle up for one helluva ride!

Paul Kaye (actor, screenwriter)

THE HOUSE OF THE RISING SON

JONATHAN GERSHFIELD

Copyright © 2025 Jonathan Gershfield

The moral right of the author has been asserted.

Apart from any fair dealing for the purposes of research or private study, or criticism or review, as permitted under the Copyright, Designs and Patents Act 1988, this publication may only be reproduced, stored or transmitted, in any form or by any means, with the prior permission in writing of the publishers, or in the case of reprographic reproduction in accordance with the terms of licences issued by the Copyright Licensing Agency. Enquiries concerning reproduction outside those terms should be sent to the publishers.

The manufacturer's authorised representative in the EU for product safety is Authorised Rep Compliance Ltd, 71 Lower Baggot Street, Dublin D02 P593 Ireland (www.arccompliance.com)

This is a work of fiction. Names, characters, businesses, places, events and incidents are either the products of the author's imagination or used in a fictitious manner. Any resemblance to actual persons, living or dead, or actual events is purely coincidental.

Troubador Publishing Ltd
Unit E2 Airfield Business Park,
Harrison Road, Market Harborough,
Leicestershire. LE16 7UL
Tel: 0116 2792299
Email: books@troubador.co.uk
Web: www.troubador.co.uk

ISBN 978 1836282 433

British Library Cataloguing in Publication Data.
A catalogue record for this book is available from the British Library.

Printed and bound by CPI Group (UK) Ltd, Croydon, CR0 4YY
Typeset in 11pt Minion Pro by Troubador Publishing Ltd, Leicester, UK

For Max and Dan – my own two rising sons – and for the adolescents they themselves may one day spawn.

SUMMER

CHAPTER 1

LIFE AND DEATH

Alex Feinstein was not an impetuous man, so of course he'd considered all the options before finally deciding to hang himself. Getting hold of a gun, for example, was always going to be a challenge – and besides, the mere thought of other people having to clear up his mess made him feel slightly queasy. High buildings were out of the question because of his vertigo and plastic bags were equally off-putting because of his mild claustrophobic tendencies. Pills, poisons and pesticides seemed too unreliable somehow, his Rangemaster oven was electric and there was a hole the size of a ring-pull in the Saab's exhaust. So hanging, on balance, seemed by far the safest bet.

The old beech tree in the back garden was the obvious setting. In full leaf, he'd be more or less invisible to prying neighbours and its sturdy limbs had been stress-tested countless times over the years. That swing he'd rigged up for Fred's tenth birthday had once borne three kids in one fell swoop, so it would have no problem with Alex's hefty frame.

There *was* another problem, however. Tonight's torrential rain and gale-force winds would make *any* kind of swinging virtually impossible out there. Or at the very least, highly unpleasant.

Thankfully, he had a contingency plan. Someone in his line of business usually did. The wooden beam that bisected the living room of their large Victorian semi was a non-structural relic from the previous owners which Alex had always regarded as an affectation. His ex on the other hand thought its rustic charm was 'to die for'. Now it seemed she was right. The ropes from Fred's swing could be looped over it, bound together and fashioned into a noose with a good workable drop. In any case, at the end of the day, his living room was a lot more congenial than the garden. Some mellow music, a fine wine and the eco log-fire would give him the send-off he deserved.

Such practical considerations certainly helped distract him from the enormity – the finality – of the act he was about to commit. Because despite the glibness of his gallows humour, it was not a decision Alex had taken lightly. He just knew that if he didn't take charge of his emotions, they would whirl and howl like tonight's storm, and blow him right off course.

The only thing affecting his course right now, was all the Malbec he'd already quaffed. It was meant to act as a gentle anaesthetic, dulling the jagged edges of his pain. In the event though it had just made him squiffy. And maudlin. And tormented by the same nagging questions that vexed him when sober. Like why had it all gone to shite? And who was *really* to blame? Him? Her? Or the institution itself? In his more forgiving moments, he'd tended to plump for the latter. Back in ancient Mesopotamia, where they first popped the question, people rarely lived beyond the age of thirty five, so its durability was seldom tested. Whereas he and Ally had been hitched for coming up to a quarter of a century. Maybe humans simply weren't designed to stick together that long? Even the strongest of glues, after all, lost their adhesive qualities eventually, especially if conditions changed. And the same could be said of a marriage. All those tiny tectonic movements. Work issues, money issues, family issues, health issues, sex issues, ego issues, temptation issues… so many fucking issues, it's a wonder any couples stuck together beyond their first few shags.

Ally had never been a fan of Leonard Cohen. 'Music to top yourself to,' she once said – and Alex had to concede she had a point. So with the Grim Crooner's mournful tones rasping out of his mini-speaker, Alex closed the living room curtains and teetered back to check on his handiwork. He'd fixed it to the centre of the beam, right there where in happier times he'd hung the mistletoe. Thankfully he'd had the foresight to rig it up *before* he'd opened that second bottle. *Fail to prepare, prepare to fail.* That had always been his mantra. His family used to tease him mercilessly for it, but he didn't care. They could stick it on his gravestone if they wanted. In fact he nearly suggested that in the goodbye note he'd left by his bed, then decided against it. They probably wouldn't see the funny side.

Of course the break-up of his marriage had been distressing. And the collapse of the career he'd once loved. And, most of all perhaps, the disintegration of his relationship with Fred. But somehow he'd managed to struggle on – until last week.

In a rare moment of self-pity, a single tear trickled slowly down Alex's cheek. And then a sudden burst of sound brought him abruptly to his senses. At first he wondered if Leonard Cohen had gone rogue, until he recognised it as his ringtone – the Mission Impossible theme tune. But who the hell could be calling at this time on a Friday night? He delved into the pocket of his Chino's and... *Jesus Christ!...* there she was, beaming serenely up at him from his iPhone, the last person he wanted to speak to.

Pressing 'reject' gave him a brief frisson of satisfaction. Like she was finally getting a taste of her own medicine. Although to be fair, when the test results came through, Ally was the first – the *only* – person he wanted to share them with. Still, what bloody good would it have done? She was no longer the shoulder he wanted to cry on. The soulmate for his innermost secrets. Confiding in her would merely make an agonising situation more intolerable. So after the consultant's confusing diagnosis, he'd confided in the internet instead – and Doctor Google confirmed his worst fears.

He had no intention of following his father's torturous crawl towards oblivion. Of observing his own disintegration in slow motion. Of watching his faculties fester and cease to function one by one. Not for him, the grisly, dehumanising roll-call of wretchedness that his dear old dad had endured. He was damned if he was going to let Nature 'take its course'. In the inimitable words of his least favourite ex-politician, he intended to 'take back control'. To negotiate an exit on *his* terms. Which made talking to Ally doubly pointless. Given her strong moral stance on such matters, she'd only turn her persuasive powers on him, and talk him down.

As if spurred on by the tacit threat, he clambered, a little unsteadily, onto the dining-chair he'd used earlier to secure the gibbet, and raised himself up to his full five foot eleven.

Bollocks. His ringtone again. Why couldn't she just leave him in peace? Back in the day, Ally's dogged determination was one of the qualities he'd admired most. Now it just pissed him off, big time. Besides, he wasn't too wasted to know he was too wasted to speak to her. So, clinging on to the rope for dear life with one hand, he cancelled the call with the other. But as soon as the phone was back in his pocket – it was ringing again. Surely it was obvious he wasn't about to pick up? Hadn't they been together long enough for her to know she didn't have an exclusive on bloody-mindedness? He pressed 'reject' yet again and carefully eased his head into the noose.

The Godfather of Gloom was onto 'Closing Time' now – a track which Alex had earmarked as his perfect 'outro'. Swaying precariously, he glanced around at the kaleidoscope of memories that surrounded him – the family photos; Fred's childhood trophies; the painting Ally bought on their honeymoon. But, no, he refused to get mawkish. Of course it would be upsetting for Fred to come home and find his dad's corpse dangling from the living room ceiling. But one short sharp shock would be less traumatic by far than watching him necrotise, day after day, as Alex had to do with *his* dad.

He pulled the slip-knot tight around his throat and felt the rope's rough fibres scouring his skin. Then, filling his lungs one last time, he readied his foot to kick the chair from under him and the life from out of him… when the sharp ping of a WhatsApp froze him to the spot.

Whatever Ally wanted to say was entirely irrelevant now. And yet for some perverse reason Alex felt compelled to take a look at her message. With a long-suffering sigh and both feet planted firmly on the chair, he pulled out his phone one last time.

'*Hallo from Glasto,*' it said. '*We have your son. But hey – don't sweat it. Hes in safe hands. And for a mere £200K in readies – we guarantee to get him back in one peace. Deets to follow.*'

Alex didn't have a clue what this meant. He just knew he had to call.

Ally picked up on the first ring. 'Did you read it?' she rasped, clearly in no mood for pleasantries.

'The text?'

'No. Fifty Shades of Grey.'

For a clergyman's daughter, Ally did a good line in sarcasm. Which was something her dad couldn't abide. If he only knew about her other indiscretions, he'd certainly turn in his pulpit.

'I'm sorry Al,' she added. 'I'm beside myself with worry.'

'Who sent it?'

'Freddie.'

'*Freddie?*'

'Well obviously *not* Freddie, but it came from Freddie's phone. And so did this...' She put herself on speaker and read out a second message, her voice now trembling with emotion. '...You have one week to find the dough. But breathe a word to anyone and you can kiss him goodbye forever.'

Right now *any* kind of breathing was a challenge for Alex. And as he struggled to loosen the knot from his windpipe, his right foot slipped off the chair edge. For a split second, the entire weight of his body was hanging by his throat.

'What was that?' Ally asked, in response to the blood-curdling splutters.

'N... nothing,' Alex gasped as he recovered his footing. 'Just... a... pappadum got stuck.'

'OK. So? What are we going to do?'

Alex grimaced as he ran a finger along a part of his neck that seemed to have lost several layers of skin.

'Don't worry,' he said, taking special care to separate his words so they didn't bump into each other. 'It'll be some stupid schoolboy prank. Or else his phone's been nicked again. Fred's not at Glasto anyway. He's at Center Parcs with Ollie and his mum. For Ollie's birthday.'

'He's not,' Ally said, audibly choking back tears. 'I just spoke to Ollie's mum. Ollie's at the cinema with his sister. And his birthday's in March. And in any case, I just got sent a photo.'

'What photo?'

'Of Freddie. In a sea of tents. Next to a banner that says 'drop acid not bombs."

'Oh,' was the best Alex could come up with. And then 'shit.'

Ally hated him swearing almost as much as she hated him drinking. But a Class C expletive seemed perfectly reasonable under the circumstances. And – *fuck it* – what Ally hated really didn't matter any more.

Or shouldn't.

'How does he look?' Alex added.

'Wet,' she sobbed. 'And traumatised. Do you have any idea who he could've gone with?'

'Erm…'

That wasn't the kind of intel teenage boys tended to share with their fathers. Not Fred anyway. Not when he was meant to be at Center Parcs with Ollie.

'I feel so utterly helpless,' Ally blurted.

The anguish in her voice was making Alex melt, despite his despair and despite all the misery she'd caused him. Still, one of them needed to hold it together.

'Where are you?' he asked gently.

It was a risky question. If she was off on some romantic weekend, he really didn't want to know.

'Rotterdam,' she said. 'The armpit of Europe. On a conference.'

Alex tried not to sound too relieved. 'Have you tried calling?'

'Of course.'

'And?'

'Just goes straight to voice-mail.'

'Did you leave a message?'

'What's the point?'

'I dunno. Get a dialogue going I suppose. If he really

has been… you know…' *Kidnapped*? *Abducted*? Whatever the word was, Alex couldn't get his mouth to form it. '… we have no idea how dangerous they are. How unstable.'

'Exactly. So the main thing is not to antagonise them.'

'You're right.' Alex pondered for a moment. 'We need to call the police.'

'Are you *mad*? You heard the warning.'

'I'm not saying we turn up with the flying squad. Just…'

'For god's sake Alex, *no!*'

Like most relationship counsellors, Ally was a study of composure – most of the time. But like anyone, when her own back was against the wall, she struggled to keep her emotions in check.

'If anything happens to him, we'd never forgive ourselves. Or at least, I wouldn't.'

'What's *that* meant to mean?' Alex snapped.

It was true his relationship with Fred had been on life-support ever since Fred's voice dropped an octave and his impending pubescence was announced in warbling baritone like an acne-ridden town crier. If women were from Venus and men from Mars – adolescents were from another galaxy altogether. But that didn't mean Alex wouldn't do anything – *anything* – in his power to protect the boy if he was in danger. And now, with his own life hurtling towards the buffers, he had absolutely nothing to lose.

'OK,' he said, suddenly infused with a visceral urge that he'd never experienced before. 'I'm on my way.'

'Where?'

'Glastonbury.'

'*What?*'

'Shouldn't take more than a couple of hours this time of night.'

Ally snorted with derision. 'You're crazy. They'll never let you in without a ticket. And even if they do, how on earth do you expect to find Fred amongst a quarter of a million mud-soaked ravers?'

Maybe she had a point. Maybe he *was* being rash. There again, next to hanging himself it actually seemed pretty restrained. And for reasons he couldn't quite fathom – he wanted to prove he still had the... what? *Bottle? Guts? Balls?* Not just to Ally either. Not just to Fred. But to himself.

'And let's just say you *did* manage to track him down. What then?'

'I dunno,' he shrugged. 'We could... swap places maybe.'

Given everything that had happened over the past nine months, this was a pretty magnanimous gesture. He'd have thought even Ally would acknowledge that.

'Have you been drinking?' was what she acknowledged instead.

'I can't bloody win, can I?' Alex raged. 'You spend twenty-four years complaining about my lack of spontaneity. My aversion to risk. My obsession with planning. Then as soon as I propose something *spur of the moment*, you go mental.'

'And of all the times to start improvising, you choose this one. Great!'

'You're right,' Alex said. 'I'm sorry. Next time Freddie gets kidnapped, I'll insist they put it in writing at least two weeks in advance, so I can plan a more measured response.'

Oh yes, he could do sarcasm too, when push came to shove.

Alex ended the call, eased himself out of the noose and clambered down from the chair. Then, lurching into the hallway, he grabbed his car-keys and flung open the front door – only to be virtually blown off his feet by a ferocious gust.

Undaunted, he snatched a flimsy pac-a-mac from the coat-hook, barrelled out into the deluge, and bundled himself into the Saab. Sure, the old rust-bucket had seen better days. But appearances weren't everything. It was an indestructible old warhorse, specially constructed for adverse conditions.

Whether that could also be said of its owner remained to be seen.

AUTUMN

(NINE MONTHS EARLIER)

CHAPTER 2

PISSING ON THE PETUNIAS

The teenage psyche needs to feel independent in order to flourish. That was Ally's contention at any rate. And when it came to psychology, no-one could say Ally didn't know her onions. So the Feinsteins' basement was upgraded from junk room to chill-out space and on the morning of Fred's fifteenth birthday, the key to its external door ceremoniously handed over.

'At last, the pearly gates are all yours!' Alex proclaimed, with a wry glance at Ally. He seldom missed the opportunity for a gentle pagan dig at her conflicted beliefs, and the inevitable eyebrow was duly raised.

Fred was far too stoked to notice. For him, the door was a rite of passage – quite literally. And with its own private access to the front garden, his mates could now come and go as they pleased.

There were other benefits too. Alex had always been the lightest of sleepers, so two floors of separation between their bedroom and a bunch of boisterous teens would make tonight's party perfectly bearable. And in truth, he was feeling rather pleased with himself. The basement make-over had been his idea. His brother Joe, the finest scenic artist in London, had painted it to his brief, like an Arabian-themed opium den. Its lurid images of eye-rolling, pipe-toting sultans and their nubile concubines, lounging catatonically on kilims and ottomans, provided the perfect setting for a bunch of middle-class kids to chillax in. All the trappings of depravity without the risks. If anything was going to cement that special father-son bond, this was it. Not to mention the hundred quid he'd chipped in for pizza and pop.

Unfortunately, the feeling wasn't exactly mutual. Secretly, Fred didn't much like the mural, and when his mates pitched up later that evening, neither did they. Sure, Uncle Joe had done an awesome job, but the basic concept had been his dad's. And in his opinion, the end result was borderline weird.

'Pervy,' was how Felix put it.

'Pretentious,' was Mikey's assessment. 'Your old man'd be a whole lot cooler if he didn't try so hard to be cool.'

Fred had to agree. The problem was, when the Feinstein genes were handed out, the cool ones all went to Uncle Joe. His dad meant well, of course, but as his mum once told him, the road to hell was paved with good intentions.

Somewhere along that same road, Ollie had bought a bottle of Red Square toffee vodka and Fred had smuggled some booze from his dad's drinks cupboard. 'Normal rules don't apply on your birthday,' Mum had said.

Alright, she never actually *said* it. Fred just read between the lines.

Ally didn't like the mural either, for different reasons, although it had taken her a while to say so.

'What a fine example to set a bunch of impressionable adolescents,' she sniped, once the party was in full flow and she and Alex were getting ready for bed.

'Credit them with a bit of intelligence Al,' Alex said. 'It's a pastiche. Not an advert for opium.'

'It's not just the opium. Haven't the past few years taught you *anything*?'

'What do you mean by that?'

Ally refused to elaborate. But a while ago, when that vile film producer was convicted, she'd made the inevitable jibe about their surnames. *Feinstein / Weinstein.* Now it seemed less of a joke.

Perhaps something else was bugging her though? Perhaps the maternal urge to mollycoddle her son whilst simultaneously giving him wings, was causing her some kind of meltdown? Or perhaps it was the abusive husband she'd seen today? She'd always found it hard not to bring her work back home, and Alex had noticed a tendency of late to project her male clients' least attractive traits onto *him*. As if sharing a gender made *him* a toxic misogynist too. But wasn't that like someone assuming she drunk rum and smoked ganja – just because her parents were Jamaican?

It wasn't bigotry per se. Or even feminism. Sure, Ally was a feminist, but then so was *he*. It was more – an excess of *empathy*. Her uncanny ability to relate to other people's feelings and experiences was one of the first things he fell in love with. It was something she'd been famous for, even as a kid. According to her mother, Ally's dolls were the most cherished and pampered objects in Christendom. So when Freddie was born six weeks premature and spent the first month of his life in an incubator, that super-protectiveness naturally transferred onto him. Not being able to breast-feed, or even hold her beautiful baby in her arms, would have been traumatic for any new mum. For Ally it was devastating. Its impact still affected her, fifteen years on. And by extension, it affected Alex too.

Still, he'd learned to roll with the punches. And this evening he let Saturday night TV lift the mood. Until the chirpy chat-show banter was interrupted by the doorbell. Alex checked his watch. 10.15. Bit late for a Jehovah's Witness or an ex-offender selling tea-towels.

When he padded downstairs and peered through the spy-glass, a hollow-cheeked woman was standing on the porch in her dressing gown. It was Anna Boston, their next-door neighbour. A retired coroner, she looked even more austere than usual in the penumbra of the porch-light.

'Is your son having a party?' she enquired as Alex opened the door, her voice cold as a coffin.

You'd have thought the head-banging bass booming out from Fred's new speakers would have offered a clue, especially to someone in her line of business.

'He might be,' Alex teased. 'Do you have an invitation?'

'I'm in no mood for wisecracks Mr Feinstein,' she replied haughtily.

In all the years they'd shared a postcode, Alex had never known Mrs Boston in that kind of mood. He'd once made it his new year's resolution to get her to crack a smile. In fact, along with developing a six-pack and learning Mandarin, he still regarded it as a personal challenge. And one that was no less attainable.

But Mrs Boston's grievance had nothing to do with decibels.

'I've just seen three boys urinating on my flower-beds from my bedroom window,' she said, with a face like a squeezed lemon.

An august officer of the law she might have been, but syntax was clearly not her strong point.

'What makes you think they're Freddie's friends?' Alex asked.

'I watched them skulking back to your basement,' she huffed. 'Giggling like half-wits.'

*

All Fred's crew were giggling now, as they watched Jake, Finn and Mikey do *The Piss Artist Challenge* on Ollie's Galaxy S-8. Which was 24 karat video-gold. Everyone cheered as Ollie dished out the dosh. Jake and Mikey were psyched, and Finn was bouncing around like he'd netted the winner in the Champions League Final. Or just had a BJ off Izzy – that girl he'd been chasing since Christmas.

The grin quickly disappeared when Ollie sent Izzy the vid.

'You've betrayed me! You've betrayed me!' Finn warbled in falsetto, like some half-crazed Shakespearean heroine.

'Sorry man,' Ollie shrugged, pulling a typed sheet of A4 from his pocket. 'Check the small print!

Ollie – or *Ollie-garch* as they called him because his dad was Russian and minted – was the school's self-appointed patron of the arts. A nailed-on media tycoon in the making.

'I own the broadcasting rights,' he gloated. 'I can post it on TikTok or YouTube. I might even send it to Sky News.'

Mikey gave Finn a consolation pat on the back. 'Don't worry dude,' he said. 'I heard Izzy's really into golden showers.'

*

'*Boys* huh? What are they like? I can only apologise, Mrs Boston.'

Alex was doing his best to close the door along with the conversation, but a fur-lined slipper planted staunchly on the hall mat, was making it difficult.

'When you've worked in criminal justice as long as I have Mr Feinstein,' Mrs Boston crowed, 'you learn that apologies are worthless. Perpetrators need to be identified – and punished.'

'Oh. Well… what kind of punishment did you have in mind?'

Her face was rigid. Implacable. Like a coroner's.

'My garden needs a thorough hosing,' she said. 'To wash away the impurities.'

Alex could understand her being upset, but he had no intention of turning his son's fifteenth birthday into a glorified ID parade.

'OK, I'll have stern words with Fred tomorrow. And maybe he can…'

'*Now*, Mr Feinstein. They'll have disbanded by tomorrow won't they? The culprits will have got off Scot-free. And some of my plants may have perished.'

Her lifeless eyes drifted across to the house sign next to the doorbell. *Fein Mess*. OK, it wasn't the greatest gag ever, but it managed to raise a smile from most visitors. Not Mrs Boston. Her look was so withering, it made Alex feel like he'd committed a crime against humanity.

He *so* wanted to tell her to piss off. Ally would have, that's for sure – in her own refined way. Despite her aversion to swearing, she had no issues with controlled confrontation. And his brother Joe would have unleashed a torrent of abuse so savage that the old crone would never dare set foot on the doorstep again. Or even venture off hers. But Alex was cut from different cloth. Face-offs weren't really his bag. And what was the worst that could happen anyway? The three miscreants got their knuckles rapped; sluiced down her herbaceous borders; and returned to watch their number of Instagram followers soar to an all-time high?

*

Everyone was still gathered round Ollie-garch's phone, wide-eyed and open-mouthed at the golden shower montage he'd downloaded off the internet. *Eew! How could anyone find* that *a turn on*, Fred wondered. His mates would probably be thinking the same – but they were too damned spineless to say so.

And so was he.

The show was brought to an abrupt end by a shaft of light, appearing from above like the Ten Commandments.

'Quick!' someone hissed. 'Code nine!'

Ollie shoved his phone under a cushion as they flung themselves back on their bean-bags.

Fred felt more angry than guilty. The bunker was an adult-free zone. At least, that's what he'd been promised. And now it was being invaded. By his dad and a witch in a burgundy bath robe.

Alex stopped half way down the steps and peered into the murk. The wall of sound and the fug of smoke made it hard to identify a soul, although he could just make out someone necking a Bailey's – nicked, as he was later to discover, from his own booze cupboard. Along with three Cuban cigars and a bottle of Freixenet.

Alex was well aware he had a duty of care to Fred's mates, most of whom were still only fourteen. So drinking and smoking were not to be encouraged. On the flip side, no self respecting father wanted to come across as an old fart, especially on his son's big day.

'Sorry to butt in fellas,' he said, raising an apologetic hand.

Mercifully, someone dialled down the volume from *deafening* to *very loud*.

'This is our next-door neighbour, Mrs Boston. And I hate to piss on your parade, but I'm afraid she's just seen three of you doing just that on her petunias.'

Alex's attempts to curry favour didn't impress Mrs Boston. He could feel her bristling on the step behind him. Still, without kids of her own, how could she know that to get their co-operation, you first had to get them onside? This was something that came instinctively to a veteran with countless tours of duty under his belt.

Although that's *not* how Fred saw it. His dad clearly thought he could talk the talk. Win them over with some deep-pan pizza and a half-baked joke. But the boys could see right through him. If he wanted to gain their respect, he should try acting *his* age – not theirs. In the event, a snide comment that Alex couldn't quite catch was followed by a burst of barely muffled laughter. And if there was one thing Alex couldn't abide, it was insolence.

'It's no laughing matter,' he said. 'There's a perfectly good toilet upstairs.'

As he jabbed a desultory thumb at the floor above, Mrs Boston's face was a picture of horror – like an Edvard Munch. The draught had now cleared the smoke away from the mural, and to someone with a sense of humour bypass, the debauchery Joe had so graphically depicted, must have seemed like a brazen attempt to turn their suburban semi into a den of iniquity.

'It's a pastiche,' Alex offered meekly. 'Like Hogarth?'

Hogarth was buried in a churchyard just up the road, so for a snob like Mrs Boston, he was bound to carry some weight. Or so Alex hoped.

As it turned out, she looked like she'd never even heard of Hogarth.

Actually she looked like she was having a seizure.

In a desperate attempt to dodge CPR, Alex continued the inquisition. 'So who was it…?' he demanded, drumming his fingers on the bannister, '…who was it that thought Mrs Boston's garden needed watering?'

Fred looked on as his dad scanned the room. Eyes narrowed. Fingers twitching. Like the baddie in some lame spaghetti western.

'Your dad's a proper wanksta!' Mikey muttered under his breath.

And after fifteen years of believing the sun shone out of his father's arse, Fred was starting to think his bestie had a point.

Maybe it was the giggling that set Alex off. Or some deep-seated need to show Mrs Boston that, despite appearances to the contrary, his moral compass was fully-functional. Either way, before he knew it, he was corralling Fred and his guests towards the basement door, marching them out into the cold night air.

Some were blitzed enough to find it funny. But for Fred it had gone well beyond a joke. The witch's poodle (now barking itself into a frenzy behind her frosted front door) weed on her flower-beds every time she took it for a walk. Did she ever feel the need to sluice *that* down? Did she hell. And what's more, it was starting to rain – Nature's own way of dealing with these things. But when Fred tried to point this out, the old bat just brushed him off and continued uncoiling her hose.

'This is not cool Dad,' he murmured.

Alex knew it wasn't cool. He could feel the groundswell of indignation bubbling up around him. He could see the expression on Freddie's face, dour and brooding in the light-spill from Mrs Boston's porch. Such was the fickleness of the teenage ego, that he could sense fifteen years of filial respect, ebbing away in an instant.

And yet he felt incapable of stopping it. He wasn't

a natural disciplinarian – far from it – but for some unfathomable reason he *needed* to show Fred and his mates who was boss. *Needed* to prove to Mrs Boston that he had what it took to control a bunch of boisterous adolescents.

Freddie implored him to relent. '*For god's sake Dad, this is crazy,*' he whispered.

It didn't take eight boys to wash down a small front garden. Yet his father made them take it in turns, like some dickhead party organiser forcing a bunch of six year olds to pass the parcel. And at a stroke, the dad who wanted all his son's mates to adore him, became the dad they all cast as a loser.

CHAPTER 3

COTTON WOOL BALLS

When Alex returned to the bedroom, the TV was switched off and Ally was at the dressing-table, removing her make-up in the three-leafed mirror. Her skin was still as smooth as the day they'd first met, and her hair no less lustrous, but after the four inches she'd had lopped off last week, she now regarded herself as 'officially middle-aged'. Perhaps that had affected her mood. Either way, she'd apparently been listening to the drama unfold. With a face like thunder. In triplicate.

'Why did you do that?' she simmered.

'Do what?' Alex said, taken aback at the uncharacteristic harshness of her voice.

'Humiliate Freddie in front of his friends? Can you imagine how that must have made him feel? On his birthday?'

'Mrs Boston insisted…'

'Oh right. So you suck up to that desiccated old prune and fall out with your own son into the bargain?'

'Some of his friends…'

'…Weed in her garden, yes I heard. And if you'd had a quiet word I'm sure they'd have apologised. You went too far Alex.'

Alex knew she was right – he *had* gone too far. He would have admitted it too, but Ally was on a roll.

'And then, after forcing them to dance to her tune, you broke up the party and packed them off home. *Why?*'

OK. It had been a stupid thing to do. Alex wasn't sure how to explain it, even to himself. But he was going to give it a bash.

'Freddie was out of order.'

'What do you mean, *out of order*?'

'One of his friends insulted me and he just… sniggered.'

'What do you mean, *insulted you*?'

'Called me… a name.'

'What name?'

Alex realised this was going to sound odd, so he clammed up. But Ally was like a dog with a bone.

'*What name?*'

'Erm… Mr Burns?'

'*Who?*'

'Mr Burns.'

'Who the hell is Mr Burns?'

'The evil power plant boss in The Simpsons.'

Ally spun round from the mirror and fixed him with an icy stare.

'A cartoon character?'

Alex shrugged.

'Is this the kind of example you want to set for your son? The type of dad you want to be? The kind of role model?'

'I can't have him undermining me in front of his friends.'

'*Undermining*? Who do you think you are, Donald Trump? They're *his* friends Alex, not yours. And you've made yourself a laughing stock. They'll have gone away thinking what a puffed-up petty dictator Freddie has for a dad!'

Again, she had a point. But at the end of the day, even a puffed-up petty-dictator had the right to defend himself.

'Why is it,' he said, slumping on the bed to remove his socks, 'that whenever Freddie and I have a disagreement, you always end up taking Freddie's side?'

'Because he's still a kid Alex. And you're an adult, allegedly, and you ought to know better.'

She grabbed her dressing gown and stomped out of the room, flinging her cotton-wool ball at him with such venom, that had it been made of anything else, it would have split his skull.

*

Fred was lying on his bed, fully-clothed, night-light on, shit-faced. There was a knock on the door and it opened before he could shove his toffee vodka under the duvet. Or his one-eared teddy. But Ally wasn't about to judge him. He and Teds went back a long way. They comforted each other in times of stress – and this was one of those times.

She understood that. So she just sat on the edge of the bed and gently touched his wet cheek with her soft hand.

'Are you OK sweetheart?' she murmured.

'I'm fine thanks,' he said, sniffling back a tear.

'I'm sorry about tonight.'

'It's not your fault.'

'Dad's sorry too.'

'Whatever.'

'I know he can be a bit of a pillock sometimes,' she said, stroking Fred's arm.

Pillock? His mum never used language. Not in front of him. Pillock was as strong as it got. He tried to summon a smile – but toffee vodka did funny things to your face.

'He's going through a tough time at the moment,' she added.

'Why?'

Ally shrugged. 'He's not the big cheese he used to be. It takes its toll.'

Fred tried to look sympathetic, but he couldn't pull that off either. Perhaps it was time for people like his dad to step aside and let the *smaller* cheeses have a go? The cheeses that hadn't passed their sell-by date. Right now though, he just wanted to sleep. His mum took the empty bottle from his hand and kissed him tenderly on the forehead.

'Sweet dreams darling,' she said. 'You'll feel better in the morning.'

*

Alex picked up the cotton-wool ball and placed it back on the dressing table. Even happy marriages had their flash-points, didn't they? And he'd always regarded their marriage as happy. Especially as he'd chosen her out of a catalogue.

That had been their little joke for the past 24 years – and it was actually true. Ally was signed up to a TV extras agency and Alex had picked her out as 'Lab Assistant 2' for a nasal spray ad he'd been directing. The moment she'd sashayed onto set in her lab-coat, he was smitten. From some angles she had the beauty of a young Halle Berry. From others the grace of Iman. From *any* angle, she was so damned distracting that (as much for his own focus as the viewer's) he asked wardrobe to put her in a pair of safety goggles, then tucked her away at the back of the set.

At coffee break, when he engineered a brief conversation, it was her intelligence he found disarming. At tea-break, her wit. So he spent the entire final session wondering how to overcome his natural diffidence and set up another meeting. He seized the opportunity on wrap. She'd told him earlier in the day that she was working as an extra to help subsidise her MBA, so on the pretext of wanting to find out more about her course for a 'friend', he invited her out for a drink. He had no expectation at all that she'd say yes – but she did. And from that very first date, their relationship took off like it was fuelled by NASA. So much so, that Alex renamed the wine-bar *Grape Canaveral* – and back then in those heady early days she even thought it was funny.

Their first few weeks were spent in a state of sexual delirium. When they finally emerged, blinking and dizzy, both sets of friends agreed they were made for each other – although Ally reckoned this had more to do with them both answering to 'Al' than any perceived commonality.

Alex's parents were less effusive, though they could hardly have been surprised when a son of theirs announced he was 'marrying out'. *Chutzpah*, the family's non-kosher Jewish restaurant on the Holloway Road, was after all, more of a gimmick than a credo. And beyond it, the two Feinstein boys had experienced less than a foreskin's worth of Jewish culture in their entire lives.

There again, a woman so conspicuously proclaiming her *shiksa* status by dint of the colour of her skin, could never be 'passed off' as a nice Jewish girl. For Morris and Miriam, this was unacceptable. Or 'beyond the pale' as Joe indelicately put it. For Alex, it was non-negotiable. The simple fact was, that he and Ally had fallen madly in love and nobody was going to talk them out of spending the rest of their lives together. Not even his parents with their unutterable (and to be fair, unuttered) prejudices. In any case, Ally eventually seduced them both with her charm, warmth and sunny disposition, just as she seduced everyone she ever met.

The only unshakeable naysayer was her *own* father, who as a Baptist minister, was dismayed to see his cherished daughter consorting with a lapsed Jew. Actually, a Jewish son-in-law worried him far less than a *lapsed* one. He never said so of course. But when they eventually got married – in a registry office in Westminster, not Linval's beloved church in Catford – it was as if the very pillars of his faith had been dismantled brick by brick.

As far as Linval was concerned, Alex's heathenism

was entirely to blame for his daughter's subsequent inability to conceive, and he had a litany of bible quotes to prove it. He conveniently refused to address the fact that non-believers had babies too. When Ally did finally get pregnant, it had nothing whatsoever to do with those gruelling years of IVF, and everything to do with the fact that Linval had persuaded Alex to celebrate Advent at his church.

Perhaps he was right. How should Alex know? He was an atheist for god's sake.

The IVF undoubtedly did one thing for Alex and Ally though. It totally screwed up their sex-life. Almost overnight, intimacy had become a results-based exercise for both of them. So the birth of Fred and the death of sexual pleasure went hand in hand.

Fred's arrival in the world marked a pretty big sea-change in other ways too. Inspired by the course of therapy she'd embarked on for post-natal depression, Ally changed her mind about a career in business and retrained as a relationship counsellor. Which suited her down to the ground. In the space of a few years, she'd soared to the top of her trade. Although in a cruel twist, her *own* relationship took a bit of a hit in the process.

A quick glimpse of his reflection in the three-leafed-mirror jerked Alex back to the present. The ever-expanding bald patch, the darkening shadows under his eyes, the deepening parentheses on either side of his mouth and the dusting of salt and pepper on his sideburns – incontrovertible proof that he wasn't getting any younger. Ally blamed their recent spats on his 'late-mid-life crisis'. Of course she did – she was a therapist. It had to be down to some kind of syndrome, complex or trauma and nothing whatsoever to do with a simple difference of opinion or a bolshie son.

If, on the other hand, she meant Alex was more irritable because his work had dried up, then maybe she had a point. Still, he wasn't beating himself up about that. The industry had changed for starters. Everyone was a director these days. Twenty years ago, ad agencies were queuing up to work with him. Not the high-end creative ones, granted. He'd always been too risk-averse for them. But if an organised, dependable safe pair of hands was needed – someone fluent in *client-speak* – Alex Feinstein was their man. So he'd cornered the market in detergents, pet-foods and pharmaceuticals and although he may not have won a sack-full of gongs, he did at least win almost every job he pitched for. And built a busy company on the back of it.

Things were different now. Very different. Alex's win-lose ratio had got so bad, that his brother had renamed him *Pitch Bitch*. Some of the wannabe's he found himself up against were only too eager to waive their fee, merely to get on the map. And talking of maps, being London-based was no longer even a bonus. He was just as likely to lose a gig to someone in Copenhagen or Cape Town, as Covent Garden.

It didn't help when the creatives who wrote the ads and gave out the jobs were less than half his age, talked in a language he barely understood, played music he couldn't bear and referenced TV shows he'd never even heard of. So it was hardly a surprise that after nearly three decades of more work than he knew what to do with, his devoted production team went freelance last month, and he was forced to close the office.

That's not to say the show was over. Far from it. It was just that *Very Fein Films* no longer operated from a lavish suite on Golden Square, but a room the size of a postage stamp, in a Hammersmith semi.

If Alex's star was fading, Ally's was on the rise. She was flooded with referrals and struggling to cope with the work-load. More than that, after two highly praised essays in *Therapy Today*, she was now regarded as a leading authority on self-harm.

'Would you say you're at the cutting edge?' Alex couldn't help asking the other day, which hadn't gone down at all well. He had a tendency to be a bit crass sometimes, but Ally never used to mind. Something had apparently changed.

By the time she returned to the bedroom, Alex was in his PJ's, ready for bed. But she was in no mood for a cuddle. She snatched her eye-mask and ear-plugs from the bedside cabinet, shoved her memory-foam pillow under her arm, and bustled towards the door.

'Where are you going?' he asked.

'The spare room,' she said in a voice like a glacier.

CHAPTER 4

THICKER THAN WATER

'So how would *you* handle it?' Alex asked, keen to get an impartial steer on the situation before his brother's brain addled.

Joe leaned back on his bishop's throne, took a deep contemplative drag on a super-sized spliff, and watched the smoke curl laconically upwards, into the vaulted ceiling. Alex should have been used to it by now, but he was still slightly unsettled by the weird ecclesiastical vibe in the apartment. When Joe bought it last year, his self-proclaimed mission was to create a Cathedral of Hedonism – and the stained glass kitchen partition, confession-box music-centre, wooden altar dining table and embroidered prayer cushion footstools certainly contributed to the desired effect. There was a row of giant church candles too which he lit on 'special occasions' – although that obviously didn't include a visit from his brother.

As confidantes go, Joe was hardly the obvious choice. He had no kids of his own, was resolutely single, and had never held down a romantic relationship for more than a few weeks. It's true that he *was* married once, to Alesia, a Sicilian actress every bit as volatile as Mount Etna, but their union barely out-lasted the honeymoon. There was a question-mark too when it came to integrity. Ever since Joe's own puberty, a constant dabbling in illegal substances and a catalogue of school expulsions, bore testimony to that.

In fact, if the Bayswater penthouse, vintage Mustang and designer wardrobe were anything to go by, then at some stage the dabbling had clearly turned into something more. You don't make that kind of dough as a scenic artist, however good you are. And Joe was coining it well before he embarked on his chosen career-path. The court took that into account when it sent him down 'to pleasure her Majesty', as he put it, for a string of drug-related offences, including supplying and resisting arrest.

'This is a turn up for the books, bro,' he said finally, his handsome sun-tanned face breaking into a broad smile. There was a hint of gloating in his voice too, as if seeing his brother on the rack was a source of comfort. But Joe was right. This *was* an unfamiliar dynamic. Normally *he* was the one in crisis, and Alex the one offering wise counsel.

Joe stretched his arm across the wooden church door which served as a coffee table, and held out the spliff. Alex was actually quite partial to the occasional joint, but not at 11 o'clock in the morning. At that time of day his drug of choice was caffeine. So he declined, and took another sip of his macchiato to prove the point. Joe grunted and toked on his reefer, as if the brain-cogs required it.

Smoking, Joe gloated, was a form of weight-training for him. And he probably had a point, given the chunky Boho rings that adorned every finger (and thumb) of his smoking hand. People laughed when he called them his knuckle-dusters, but Alex had a suspicion it wasn't altogether a joke.

Joe had always been proud of his 'scholarship' at Feltham Young Offender's, from the age of sixteen. He still dined out on how it cost twice as much as Eton, yet was paid for by the state. His own relationship with their parents had already disintegrated by then, but it was still a huge blow when it happened.

And yet, despite all his foibles and quirks, and despite Alex being away at Uni by the time Joe hit his teens, they shared a surprisingly strong brotherly bond. In Alex's head, Joe's own tortured adolescence made him the ideal person to discuss these issues with. Apart from Ally of course, who did this kind of thing for a living, but who for obvious reasons, ruled herself out.

'You need to give the poor bugger a break,' Joe said, closing his eyes and emitting a solid cylinder of smoke from each nostril like the dual exhausts of his V8 engine. 'He's a fifteen year old kid, oozing testosterone. It's perfectly natural to want to give authority's arse a good kicking – and guess what? You're that authority.'

'Sure, but it's not like I rub it in his face.'

'Maybe not. But it's no good trying to be his best buddy when as far as he's concerned, you're just a cunt.'

'Thanks,' Alex said, 'that's heartening.'

However used to it he was – Joe's turn of phrase could still give him a nasty jolt.

'Well you asked me and I'm telling you. I've been there, as you know.'

Oh, he'd been there alright. Joe was around Fred's age the first and only time he worked at their dad's restaurant. Which by a cruel twist of fate, happened to be the night the Evening Standard's food critic showed up. As a fully paid-up member of the *tribe*, there were high expectations for a five-star paean. But Joe got hopelessly drunk, mixed up the orders, and spilled an entire *kugel* all over her lap. Her poisonous review almost certainly triggered *Chutzpah's* decline, and when Joe refused to apologise, their father refused to let him in the restaurant ever again.

'You need to apologise,' Joe said, without a hint of irony.

'Why the hell should I apologise?' Alex protested. 'I've done nothing wrong.'

'You've treated him like a child.'

'He *is* a child.'

'I rest my case! You've patronised him. Belittled him. Emasculated him.'

'No I haven't.'

'Course you fucking have. You're his dad for fuck's sake. It's what dads do.'

Joe had a thing about dads. A kind of inbuilt aversion. Fuck the Patriarchy and all that. And theirs wasn't the only dad he fell out with either. When Freddie was born, Ally insisted on having him blessed at her father's church. Alex wasn't thrilled to let Linval get his Baptist mitts on their little cherub, but he finally gave in, on one condition. That Joe could be godfather.

To an extent, he was stamping his atheist feet. His parents would certainly boycott any religious ceremony that didn't take place in a synagogue, so there was no risk of an unwanted encounter with their wayward son, whom they'd recently excommunicated. Ally was resistant at first. For all his charm and sex-appeal, Joe wasn't exactly your standard godfather material. But as it happens, the Baptist church didn't recognise godparents anyway. Officially he would merely be Freddie's *'sponsor'* – a role that required him to do nothing more than stand by while the pastor recited a short blessing or dedication. So she eventually consented.

They should have known that Joe was never going to be a bit-part player – certainly not with half a gram of coke up his nose. In response to Linval's question: 'Will you uphold this family in the Christian nurture of this child?' which was anyway addressed to Ally and Alex, he just couldn't help himself.

'In all honesty, man, that's not my bag,' he interjected. 'But I'll definitely show him how to have a fucking good time.'

There was a spontaneous gasp from the pews. Several congregants, including Ally's mum, started hyperventilating. Linval himself was so aghast, he nearly dropped the baby.

They'd kept Joe at arm's length after that. But as Linval still believed it was a deliberate act of heresy, Alex's own relationship with the in-laws, already shaky, had been on life-support ever since.

So yes, Joe could be a liability. But he was still his brother. And still the most charismatic and colourful man Alex knew. Even Ally would agree with that. No-one could deny he was outrageously funny, outrageously good-looking and an outrageously talented artist. A talent – strangely enough – which Freddie seemed to have inherited. But it was more than that. Because although Joe had had no long-term relationships of his own, he'd had more than his fair share of short-term ones. Which meant plenty of first-hand insight into things going horribly wrong.

Alex took another long contemplative sip from his macchiato. 'OK… So… you think I should say sorry?'

Joe pursed his lips. 'Fraid so.'

'And give up trying to be Freddie's best friend?'

'Yep. That way you won't get all bitter and twisted like you are now.'

'I'm not bitter and twisted. I'm just… you know… maybe not as *chilled* as you.'

Joe emitted a weed-induced guffaw. Alex waited for it to subside, before asking how he thought he should handle Ally.

'What d'you mean?' Joe asked.

'Well she's… I dunno… she seems kind of hostile towards me these days. And she…'

'… thinks you're a cunt too?'

'No of course not but…'

'Have you stopped having sex?'

'No. I mean yes. Actually I don't know. Maybe. Should I confront her, or just hope it blows over?'

Joe shrugged. 'You been married a long time dude. If you dunno how to handle your own wife by now, I'm afraid I can't help.'

Out of nowhere, the theme to *Pulp Fiction* piped up. Joe delved into his pocket and pulled out his mobile.

'Yo! Wassup?' he boomed.

And then his Zen-like countenance shattered.

'Don't take any shit Tommy,' he snapped, rising unsteadily to his feet and grinding his roach into a brass collection bowl. 'We ain't a fucking charity. They want a discount, they'll need to buy a shed-load more than that. Gimme half an hour, I'm leaving now.'

He ended the call and snatched his brown leather flying jacket from a tall free-standing crucifix.

'Sorry bro,' he shrugged. 'Duty calls.'

'No worries,' Alex sighed, grabbing his raincoat. 'These scenic painting gigs get more demanding by the day.'

'Tell me about it,' Joe grinned. 'When will people finally realise – quality doesn't come cheap?'

CHAPTER 5

FAMILY OUTING

Being forced to apologise to his fifteen year old son for being a 'pillock' was not something Alex found easy. Especially when his drinks cabinet had been raided and along with several bottles of booze, his presentation box of Cohibas had been prised open and three were missing. But maybe Joe had a point. Maybe he *did* need to cut the boy some slack. And if that's what it took to get his marriage back on track, it was a small price to pay. Because Ally still meant the world to him, despite their minor disagreements about parenting. And gender politics. And swearing and murals and god and the afterlife. And despite their once cherished 'chemistry' now being reduced to the occasional clockwork bonk to avoid 'abstinence' becoming a 'thing'.

Fred accepted the apology with the most grudging handshake he could muster, while Ally deigned to move back into their bedroom. But for a while, their once lively, fun-filled home resembled little more than a monastic retreat. Ally – as Mother Superior – had managed to weaponise silence, while on the rare occasions he was seen outside his bedroom, Fred was the surly young novice. This change in his son's behaviour upset Alex far more than he let show. It was a stark contrast to the sunny-natured boy who used to live there. The Freddie he'd taught to ride a bike. Climb a tree. Kick a ball. The smily, cheeky, sparkle-eyed child who beguiled everyone he met with his cheery demeanour and his sing-song conversation.

At dinner these days, the only eye contact Fred made was with his phone. And as soon as he'd finished eating, he was back in his bedroom, door shut. Sure, he knew he was living the cliché. But at the end of the day he was being *himself*. And apparently that's all that mattered.

The cold war raged for a week or two, until Ally finally held out an olive branch. Fred had just left for school, barely managing a neanderthal grunt as he trudged out of the front door.

'Puberty does funny things to boys, doesn't it?' she sighed, stirring the porridge. 'Do you remember our white water rafting?'

'Remember it?' Alex said, surprised and relieved as a prisoner suddenly released from solitary confinement. 'I've still got the bruises!'

He started to dare to believe he'd served his penance. Although he was still confused. That trip to Wales was four years ago, long before Fred's puberty had reared its ugly head.

'Hurtling down the rapids at breakneck pace,' Ally went on, 'no idea where we were heading or where we'd end up.'

The same could be said of her analogies, though they

were seldom as random as they first appeared. A bit like her father's sermons, but without the sanctimonious undertones.

Alex poured frothy milk into Ally's coffee mug, and placed it in front of her. 'Freddie reckoned it was the best day of his life,' he said, still baffled but trying not to show it.

'It was exhilarating alright,' Ally conceded. 'But scary too. I don't know about you but I had an overwhelming sense of being out of control of my own destiny.'

'Let's just say I was glad I was wearing brown trousers.'

Ally unleashed one of her signature grins. The kind that would light up any dull grey morning.

'You were wearing your pink Paul Smith swimmers as it happens. I still have the photo on my phone. But there was also a real sense of camaraderie, wasn't there? A sort of united front against forces so much bigger and more powerful than us.'

She ladled out two bowlfuls and continued her treatise – or whatever it was – with characteristic authority.

'The main difference between white water rafting and puberty, is that with puberty, no-one hands you a helmet, a life-vest or a paddle. Or even a raft. It's just you, isn't it? Battling your way down-river as best you can, hoping and praying you make it over the rapids unscathed.'

Ah! *Now* he could see where this was heading. Ally passed him his porridge and spooned a generous dollop of molasses onto hers. A last remaining nod to her cultural roots.

'What's more,' she continued, sliding onto the stool beside him. 'With rafting there are often long stretches of calm between the turbulence. To help you relax and catch your breath before the next onslaught. Whereas with puberty, the entire journey is a white-knuckle ride of curlers, cartwheels and god-knows-what-else.'

'I take your point,' Alex said, resolutely dribbling buckwheat honey into his bowl. 'Perhaps I *was* a bit tough on him.'

Ally tried her best to conceal it, but she'd earned the right to look smug.

'Tell you what,' Alex added. 'Let's do a family outing. We haven't had one for ages.'

'Sounds like a plan,' she said.

'This weekend?'

'If Freddie's up for it. Though I draw the line at rafting.'

'So how about the zoo?'

Ally shook her head, emphatically. 'He's *fifteen* Alex.'

'Everyone likes the zoo.'

'Yes but we used to take him there when he was five. So he's hardly going to see it as acceptance of his new grown-up status. And anyway – I'm sure he'd prefer something more… interactive.'

*

Fred had no intention of playing Happy Families just to make his dad feel better. But with his new Ray-Bans masking half his face, and his noise-cancelling headphones clamped over his ears, there was no risk – god forbid – of any actual *engagement*.

Ally glanced at him in the rear-view with a rare flicker of irritation that Alex found strangely consoling.

'If you can't beat'em – join'em,' she sighed, riffling

through the CD's in his glove compartment. 'What we got? Leonard Cohen. Bob Dylan. Paul Simon. Mark Knopfler. Oy vey!'

'Do you have a problem with ageing Jews, *Mrs Feinstein*?' Alex said archly.

'Not at all! But didn't I lend you some of mine?' Ally checked the recess under the arm-rest. 'Ah! Now we're talking. Whitney… Tina… Beyoncé… Come to Mama!' She grabbed the CD's and hugged them to her bosom.

'Bit of a theme there too, right?' Alex said.

'Get with the programme Honky. It's the age of diversity!'

'OK – so let's *have* some diversity.'

'Fine – then you choose the damned toons.'

'Alright – I will!' Alex reached into the door pocket and pulled out his Lenny Kravitz CD. 'There ya go. Jewish *and* black. That's two boxes ticked.'

'And peace in our time!' Ally beamed. 'That's three.'

Alex popped it in the player and skipped to track 3.

'Ah, ya old softie,' Ally purred.

And they nodded along in perfect sync, just as they'd done in those Halcyon pre-Freddie days, when nothing and nobody could ever come between them.

'*You are the flame in my heart,*' Alex trilled.

'*You light my way in the dark,*' Ally trilled back.

'*You are the ultimate star,*' they trilled together.

'Cheesy or what!?' Ally blurted.

'You never used to think so back in the day.'

'When I was young and naive!'

Alex laughed, although deep down, he couldn't help feeling slightly crestfallen.

*

They'd been there over an hour now. Squatting on their little camping stools. Slathered in factor 30. Dangling their rods. Alex eager. Ally bored. Fred perched between them, grumpy. Interactive it certainly wasn't. There were lone anglers dotted around at regular intervals – all male, all white, and – judging by their reactions to the three new arrivals – all keen to keep it that way. Apparently the lake was teeming with carp, bream, roach and tench, but it was eerily quiet. And so far no Feinstein had had so much as a nibble. Whereas the old boy on the next peg had already filled three buckets.

'Are you sure you brought the right bait?' Ally whispered.

Alex nodded. 'The website said sweetcorn – so that's what I got.'

Fred didn't give a toss about the bait. He had no interest in fishing. And he was pissed off about having to leave his headphones in the car, because he now had no protection against the *serious conversation* his father seemed determined to have.

'So, Fred…'

That's how they always began.

'…Looking ahead… I was wondering if you've had any thoughts about what you might want to *do*?'

His dad was talking in that super-cringe voice he usually reserved for Easter Sundays at Grandpa's church.

'What d'you mean – *do*?' Fred muttered, the Ray-Bans barely hiding his contempt.

'I mean… for a living?'

'Give him a break Alex,' Ally cut in.

The old man on the nearby peg wheeled round and glared.

'Well – you know what they say,' Alex whispered. 'Fail to prepare...'

They don't effing say that, Fred thought. Or at least, he'd never heard them. His *dad* did though. All the time. *Preparing* was his shtick. Everything had to be organised, worked through and mapped out – ideally years in advance. Every possible outcome pre-planned like some military operation. He'd have prepared this too, whatever 'this' was. Any moment now he'd be breaking out the power-point. Or a fully developed story-board.

'...And don't forget, Freddie, Mum and I have *contacts*. Not just in advertising and counselling. I'm talking law, medicine, architecture, engineering – whatever floats your boat.'

Ally rolled her eyes. Behind his shades, Fred was almost certainly doing the same. And who could blame them? Alex's eyes would be rolling too if he let them. Because he couldn't help thinking how much like his *own* dad he was sounding. In his defence though, this wasn't about being a pushy-parent. It was about being a supportive one. About fixing the bond. Getting the fam back together.

'Seriously, if you ever want to shadow someone,' he continued, 'you know, for a day or two, to help you plan a career-path, just let us know and we'll do our best to set it up.'

Fred just about managed a tight-lipped 'thanks'.

'No worries,' Alex said cheerfully. 'It's all part of the...'

As he caught Ally's eyes rolling again, he tailed off.

Trailing some old fart around an office, law-court or hospital was the last thing Fred was ever going to agree to. He was on the verge of saying so too, when a better idea popped into his head.

'…Actually – there *is* a career I've been thinking about,' he said, with what seemed like genuine enthusiasm.

'Excellent,' Alex said, with a discreet wink at Ally. 'What is it?'

'Scenic artist.'

Ally gazed out at the lake, her face set like concrete, as Fred went in for the coup de grace.

'So… maybe I could shadow Uncle Joe?'

The interminable silence that ensued was torpedoed by a sudden commotion. They spun round to see a large fish wriggling and thrashing on the end of the old boy's line.

Alex was wriggling too. 'Oh. I don't… I don't…'

The fish finally gave up the fight – and so did Alex.

'…I don't see why not,' he said, meekly. 'I'll sound him out if you like.'

Fred smiled triumphantly. 'Thank you.'

Ally said nothing. She just flared her nostrils and slapped the lake with her rod.

CHAPTER 6

APPROPRIATE ADULT

Uncle Joe had never been the hands-on kind of godfather. So Fred was secretly stoked to be spending the afternoon at his studio. And secretly terrified. It felt more like an audience with the Pope than his favourite uncle.

'*I'm shocked they're allowing you near me,*' Uncle Joe had texted. '*What if I lead you to eternal damnation? Which FYI I have every intention.*'

That's maybe where he and the Pope parted company. Or maybe not.

Fred was a bit shocked too. Joe had never been invited to any of his godson's birthday parties. Never included in family dinners. Rarely even mentioned in his presence. 'A dangerous liaison,' is how his dad had described him last Christmas, after Fred received that special delivery. There was no actual proof it was from Joe, but who else would have sent him a first-aid box full of hash brownies? Which (of course) mysteriously vanished before he'd had a chance to sample just one.

Fred followed his maps app out of London Bridge station, along a row of old railway arches and past an exotic assortment of stalls, where hordes of hungry punters were gorging themselves on Taiwanese egg-waffles, miniature French pastries, Brazilian chorizos, Japanese dumplings, Alpine raclettes, duck frites and gourmet chocolate truffles. Fred was salivating alright, but even the most awesome street food he'd ever seen couldn't compete with what was on *his* menu today. He turned out of Rope Walk and into Tanner Street, towards an old brick warehouse with hard rock blasting out of the top floor windows. It took a while before anyone answered the buzzer, but eventually the heavy metal door creaked open and a female face peered out.

'Hey!' she said – a little breathless.

Guessing women's ages wasn't one of Fred's specialities, but he reckoned her to be around twenty. And the spontaneous tightening around the crotch of his Levi's provided *boner fide proof* – as Mikey would say – that she was seriously peng.

'Hey!' he replied. 'My name's… I've come… my uncle said…'

Why was he always such a loser in the presence of *Perfection in Female Form*? They were just human beings after all. And he'd had plenty of first-hand experience. His own hand, admittedly, with some help from the internet, but even so.

'It's lovely to meet you Freddie,' she smiled.

The PFF knew his name! How cool was that?

'I'm Izzy. I work with your uncle.' She gestured to her paint-splattered overalls. 'No shit Sherlock, right?'

Fred followed her up a creaky old staircase, struggling to avert his gaze from her bum which, despite the baggy overalls, was doing its best to hypnotise him. At last, on the fourth floor, the stairs opened out to a loft space as big as a barn, with polished floorboards, brick walls and light streaming in from all sides. Right in the middle, beneath a V-shaped ceiling, two massive canvasses hung on chains from the hefty wooden beams. Splattered across one – an explosion of random graffiti. Across the other – a trippy collection of circles and swirls. Psychedelic – like the music pumping out from the speakers.

A tall dark-haired figure stood on a platform between them. Strutting his stuff, singing along at the top of his voice. Spray-gun in one hand, jumbo-sized spliff in the other. Two matching snake tattoos curling round his sun-tanned calves and up into a pair of sawn-off denims.

He spun round and shot Fred a big fat grin. 'Welcome to the pleasure dome dude,' he said in a voice rough as sandpaper.

'Thanks Uncle Joe.'

Joe's grin quickly morphed into a steely glare.

'Don't *Uncle* me,' he rasped. 'Makes me feel like some kinda freak. Or worse… an *appropriate adult*!'

'Appropriate' was something Joe could never be accused of. Perhaps that's why he was Fred's all-time favourite rellie. To be fair, there wasn't much competition, but Joe would have won hands-down regardless. He looked a bit like Johnny Depp, only taller and hencher. Or Khal Drogo in Thrones, without the make up. And his personality too, so different from his brother's, it was hard to believe they were related.

'I said he was posh, didn't I?' Joe drawled, as two more *PFF*'s emerged from a backroom. 'This is my team – Izzy, Sasha and Raki.'

'Hey Freddie,' they chorused, like a scene from Barbie.

'Pleased to meet you,' Fred said, trying not to sound like an over-excited puppy. Or a privately educated dick. And failing miserably on both counts.

Rays of sunlight poured in through a row of tall arched windows, glinting off Joe's rings as he drew on his reefer.

'Make yerself at home,' he winked. 'Grab whatever you want from the pig-trough.' He pointed at a table groaning with pastries and cakes.

'Amazing. Thank you!'

'You're welcome. It's hungry work – painting. Leonardo had pizzas on tap when he did the Last Supper. Written into his contract.'

'*Really*?'

'Sure. American Hot was his fave. Whereas Rembrandt was hooked on stroopwafels. Each to his own eh? Personally I prefer these.' Joe took another deep drag from his spliff. 'Your dad tells me you're a bit of an artist yourself?' he added.

'Not really. Though it's probably my best subject.'

'Art's not a *subject* dude. It's a passion. An obsession. A way of life. Not something you squeeze into a fucking timetable once a week along with RE and Latin.'

'No I mean it's…'

'That's the trouble with schools. Exams. Uniforms. Detentions. Bollocks. Their only goal is to snuff out any spark you might have – to stop you burning down everything they stand for.'

Fred nodded earnestly. 'I know what you mean.'

'Yeah, but are you gonna *do* anything about it?'

'Erm...'

'Question for another day perhaps. In the meantime...' He gestured to the cluster of paint cans on a wooden trolley. '...Let's see what you got.'

Fred looked blank. He'd assumed *shadowing* meant hanging around in the shadows. He had no wish to make a tit of himself.

Joe spotted the hesitation. 'Every tom-cat needs to mark his territory,' he said. 'Or have you just come to ogle my girls?'

'Course not, but...'

'No, you're right. No-one does their best work sober.'

He stooped down over the platform's guard-rail and held out the joint. Fred was a rabbit in headlights. Sure he'd smoked joints before. But never in broad daylight. And never with actual grown-ups.

'Come on man,' Joe said. 'It ain't fucking Novichok.'

Fred shuffled forward, tentatively took the joint, slid it between his lips, and – desperately trying not to splutter or cough – filled his lungs, held his breath and...

...Woah! Everything went fuzzy. Just like that time the dentist gave him gas and air to take out a molar.

'You got some catching up to do,' Joe said, as Fred tried to hand it back. 'Pop yerself over there and finish it off.'

By the time he'd toked the whole joint, Fred could have had *all* his molars removed without flinching. The only thing he wanted now was to stuff his face with those sick-looking pastries. But he could feel Joe's eyes burning into him. Waiting to see what his godson-cum-nephew could do – now he could barely walk.

Fred's rattle-can experience was limited. He'd seen a couple of tutorials on YouTube. And he'd once helped Mikey pimp up his grandfather's garden shed, after the old man's stroke. But his can-control was shaky at best and he'd have backed out for sure if he hadn't already been high as a kite.

As it was, he was ready to spray like a tom-cat.

The left-hand canvas was a mishmash of mantras and graphics, like some epic toilet-wall graffiti designed by the world's greatest taggers. He wheeled the squeaky trolley of paints to a section at eye-level, covered in base colour only, and within moments, was lost in a whirl of drip, flares and funk.

'Not too shabby!' Joe said, as Fred stood back to survey his handiwork.

And he was right. It wasn't too shabby at all. Even in his current state Fred could see that. They'd covered Michelangelo in double-art last week, so what he'd painted were two hands – like God and Adam's – in crazy fluorescent colours. Except *his* God had a big chunky ring on each finger. And his Adam – a jumbo-sized spliff.

'Y'know what they say,' Joe grinned, smacking Fred on the shoulder with his knuckle-duster. 'Blood is thicker than spray paint. You're welcome to borrow my gear whenever you want – just as long as it's for a worthwhile cause.'

CHAPTER 7

ARBEIT MACHT FREI

As it happens, Fred had a worthwhile cause lined up already. Because that very week, in his capacity as a future media mogul, Ollie had launched a search for West London's answer to Banksy. Or put another way, someone who could 'enhance' the school's hideous new science-block. It was a challenge that would excite any wannabe artist. But what made the cause especially worthwhile, was the £100 prize that went with it. So, with his uncle's support and encouragement, Fred arranged to meet Mikey and Omar by the gap in the railings at 8 o'clock sharp on Thursday evening. The place would be deserted by then.

At a few minutes past, a blue van pulled up and Izzy leapt out, fit as a Ninja. Actually, with her shaggy blonde hair, long slim legs and eyes like saucers, she was more like a Manga princess.

'Hey handsome,' she said, breezily planting a big sloppy kiss on Fred's cheek and leaving Mikey and Omar slack-jawed.

'Gimme a break guys. This is my uncle's assistant. She's like, family – OK? Plus we're on special ops tonight so get a grip!' is what Fred *would* have said – if he hadn't gone slack-jawed too.

Izzy yanked the ladder out of the van, breaking the spell.

'I'll be back in an hour boys, OK? Nine o'clock. If you're sure that's long enough?'

'Perfect,' Fred said, grabbing a big sack of spray paints. 'Thanks so much.'

'You're welcome,' she smiled. 'I used to do this in my teens. Bridges. Tunnels. Disused buildings. But always in a balaclava. And never on my own patch. So please don't get caught – OK?'

'Don't worry,' Fred smiled. 'We won't.'

*

Dear Mr and Mrs Feinstein

I'm sorry to have to inform you of a significant disciplinary issue involving your son. I arrived at school this morning to discover that the new science-block wall has been spray-painted in large block letters with the words: Arbeit Macht Frei. On close examination of footage from the CCTV installed only last week, I'm afraid there is incontrovertible proof that your son was one of the three boys responsible.

The school takes any kind of vandalism very seriously, and in view of the deeply offensive reference, I'm afraid we have no option but to put him on a week's exclusion. In consequence, he will not be permitted to return to school until Monday 29th October. Please ensure he is properly supervised during his time away. Exclusion is a punishment – not a recreational opportunity. And it goes without saying he will be expected to catch up in his own time with any work he misses.

If there is anything you would like to discuss about this or any other matter, please get in touch.

Yours sincerely
Dr James Fogerty, Deputy Head

Ally was often at home on a Friday afternoon, and when the email came through she was up to her elbows in cake-mix. Alex read it aloud from his phone.

For a few moments, both were lost for words. Ally was the first to regain her composure.

'*Whatever* he's done,' she said, engaging her counselling skills, 'it's our job as parents to make him feel secure. Secure, loved and fully supported.'

'That goes without saying,' Alex said, 'but…'

'…And this would never have happened,' she added, 'if you hadn't suggested he spend time with Joe.'

The long, slender, flour-coated finger of blame was apparently pointing at *him.* Alex was incredulous.

'Hang on a second,' he said. '*You* encouraged it.'

'Yes but only after *you* suggested it. And you'd have lost him forever if you'd backtracked.'

Alex couldn't tell if this was genuine compassion or unadulterated bullshit.

'Having said that,' she added as his eyes narrowed, 'multi-generational bonds outside the nuclear family can often be beneficial.'

'Oh sure,' Alex said, brandishing his phone. '*Very* beneficial!'

Ally's attitude to his brother had always baffled Alex. It was almost as if she found a perverse fascination in Joe's lack of respect for so many of the principles she held dear. And yet whenever Alex did the slightest thing in contravention of those same principles, she was down on him like a ton of bricks.

'So… what are you saying exactly?'

'What I'm saying is that we *all* bear some responsibility Al. Of course it was a stupid thing to do. But we need to put it in perspective. It's not like Fred's gone in with an AK47 and mown down half his classmates.'

'That's true,' Alex said, adopting Ally's upbeat tone. 'We should be thankful for small mercies. Although comparing St Josephs to a Nazi concentration camp does seem a bit extreme. Either that or they owe us a rebate.'

'Why does it always boil down to money?' Ally said, seizing the opportunity to change the narrative.

'It was a joke for god's sake.'

'Yes. Like Arbeit Macht Frei!'

All mothers were tigers when it came to defending their cubs. But Ally was next level. She was a genuine sabre-tooth.

'All that aside though,' she said, parking herself at the breakfast table and adopting a more reasonable tone, 'who's going to look after Freddie next week?'

'Oh. Didn't you say you were taking a few days off work?'

'I am. I mean I was. But that's… no… that's not going to fly.'

Ally gently stroked her right eyebrow with two fingers of her left hand, leaving a thin trail of flour across her temple. It was a thing she did, whenever her mind was elsewhere, as if her right brain needed calming.

'I have wall-to-wall meetings,' she explained. 'For the charity.'

As if she didn't have enough on her plate, Ally was helping set up a therapy centre in Shepherd's Bush for traumatised refugees. It was an excellent cause, and one Alex fully supported. The problem was that for the first time in months, he was up to his eyeballs too. Because *Pitch Bitch* had finally pulled. OK, it was a script so naff that every other director had no doubt turned it down, but a gig was a gig. And sure enough, next week he'd be holed up on a sound-stage in West London, trying to turn Huff's Menthol Tissues into a household name.

But Ally was indomitable. And if anyone could transform a problem into an opportunity, she could. Especially when Fred was involved.

'Why don't you take him to your shoot, Al?' she said. 'It'll be a rare treat for him to see you in action and I'm sure you'll find something useful for him to do. He's very adaptable.'

Alex couldn't think of anyone *less* adaptable than Fred. Or anything less *feng shui* than having him mope around set, scowling and grunting and wishing he was somewhere – *anywhere* – else. The basic requirement for the most menial of gofers was a winning smile and an easy-going, nothing's-too-much-trouble attitude. But making the clients feel special, the actors feel loved and the crew feel looked-after was well beyond Fred's capabilities these days. He was more likely to prompt a mass walk-out.

As Alex racked his brains for an alternative plan, a key slowly turned in the front door.

'We got an email from Dr Fogerty,' he said as Fred sloped into the kitchen, looking subdued. 'If it's not a stupid question, what exactly were you trying to prove, beyond your own hare-brained immaturity?'

Ally flinched, but said nothing.

'We were just… making a stand,' Fred said in a voice that somehow managed to sound sheepish and defiant at the same time.

'Making a stand about what exactly?'

'Oppression.'

'*Oppression*?' Alex all but spat out his tea on the kitchen table. 'You're an over-privileged middle-class schoolboy Freddie. And about as oppressed as Lord Fauntleroy.'

Fred had no idea who that was, but he got the gist. 'I may be over-privileged and middle-class,' he parried, 'but I know what it's like to live under the bloody Fuhrer.'

This was the first time he'd ever had a proper face-off with his dad. And it went down like Sieg Heils at a Bar Mitzvah. Even Ally was taken aback.

'Don't talk to your father like that,' she snapped. 'Please apologise *now*.'

To give him his due, Fred knew he'd crossed the line.

'Sorry Dad,' he said. 'I didn't mean it. Been a bit of a day.'

Alex took a few seconds to gather himself.

'Ah well,' he replied eventually. 'At least you didn't go in with an AK47 and mow down half your classmates.'

Ally fixed him with a Gorgon look.

'So… where did you get all the gear from?' Alex asked, as moderately as his brimming anger would allow.

Fred looked shifty. 'I borrowed it from… from someone at school.'

'Who?' Alex persisted.

'Why on earth does that matter?' Ally cut in like the defence in a courtroom drama. 'Paint's not an illegal substance as far as I know.'

'We have every right to know the facts,' Alex insisted, determined to keep the cross-examination going.

The defendant's face tightened, with the muscles on either side of his jaw working overtime. His mum and dad knew the signs only too well. The flood gates were about to burst open.

'Come here,' Ally said, opening her arms. 'It was an incredibly stupid thing to do. But we still love you.'

'Love you too Mum,' Fred mumbled. 'I'm gonna have a bath now though, if that's OK?'

'You do that my darling. We can talk later.'

Fred ambled towards the stairs, just about managing to hold it together, and relieved to have got away without the major bollocking he'd expected. A tad disappointed too, that his act of sedition hadn't caused more of a stir. How would Che Guevara have felt, if he'd returned home after the revolution, to nothing more than a wagging finger from his dad and a sympathetic hug from his mum?

Alex shook his head dejectedly. Actually it wasn't just his head that was shaking.

'I never thought I'd hear the race card being used to

put a wedge between me and my own son,' he said, once he heard Fred's bedroom door click shut.

'What race card?'

'He called me the Fuhrer. Next thing I know I'll be a white supremacist.'

'We all say and do things in the heat of the moment that we later regret Al. He said he was sorry.'

Alex strongly disagreed with letting Fred off the hook. But right now, there was a far more pressing issue to deal with.

'How about we send him to your parents next week?' he said. 'It's a while since they've spent any quality time together.'

Ally shook her head emphatically. 'We can't.'

'Why not?'

'We'd have to explain why he's not at school and Dad would just put that down to the usual.'

'What's the usual?'

'You know – an abdication of moral guidance.'

'Oh. You mean he'll blame *us*?'

Ally's silence said it all. Of course he wouldn't blame *them*, plural.

'OK,' Alex sighed. 'Then we'll have to press the emergency button.'

'I hardly dare ask what that is,' Ally said.

'My mum.'

This was not something Alex suggested with any real conviction. His mother was in her late eighties – although that in itself wasn't the reason. She was actually as fit as he was, with a voracious appetite for life. And like any Jewish matriarch, she totally doted on her only grandson. But her cooking was flaky at best, and imposing Fred on her for an entire week would be risky.

In any case, Miriam had her hands full these days, having recently taken up with a retired Greek shipping insurance broker, four months her junior, whom she'd met last year on a Mediterranean cruise. Her *toy-boy* as she called him. Add to that, her uncompromising passion for lawn bowls (she was the current Elstree and Borehamwood veteran ladies champ) as well as her twice-weekly stint for an old people's charity helpline, and she really didn't have time for *in loco parentis*.

Ally summed up all the above with a single raised eyebrow.

'OK then,' Alex said, thinking on his feet. 'How about a nanny?'

The *double* raised eyebrow said it all. And to be fair, he *was* fifteen. Besides, their last nanny was summarily sacked when Freddie was five, after she managed to lose him in Covent Garden. He was picked up by the police, wondering around the Piazza, bawling his eyes out. Since when, the very idea of having him looked after by a non-family member, was like proposing to send him up a chimney.

'It'll be good for Fred to see his Dad lead the troops into battle,' Ally said. 'It'd certainly help balance things out, after his day shadowing Joe. You never know – it might even inspire him to consider directing as a career choice.'

The Art of Persuasion. Ally had it mastered alright. In any case – they were fast running out of other options. And home alone certainly wasn't one of them. Fogerty's email made that crystal clear. So the production team would have to find Fred something useful to do. Even if it was just making tea.

*

Two days later, on Sunday evening, Alex was in his study, doing some last minute tweaks to his shooting-board, when the phone rung. It was Laura Houston, his producer.

'We're screwed Al!' was her opening salvo.

'What's the matter?' Alex said, trying not to sound too alarmed. Staying calm in a crisis was his USP after all. And Laura had a tendency to panic.

'I just had a message from Sophie,' she said, in a voice that sounded like she was about to announce Armageddon. 'Jayden's got glandular fever.'

Sophie was their casting director and Jayden the seventeen year old boy they'd cast for Huff's. So for the first time in twenty years, Laura's voice of doom was entirely justified.

'Fuck!' Alex exclaimed, his USP shot to pieces.

To lose an actor on the eve of a production was a major blow. What made this especially serious, was that Jayden was literally the only boy on the casting tape the clients liked. For one reason or another – too handsome, too plain, too tall, too short, too white, too black, too quirky – they'd rejected all the others. If the mum, the dad or either of the two girls they'd cast as daughters had got glandular or dengue or any other godforsaken fever, there'd be plenty of back-up. But for the son, there was none.

Of course they should have arranged another session to find an understudy. But there were so many other things to deal with in the run-up to a shoot – and who could have predicted this?

Sure, they could ring around the stage-schools in the morning. But the earliest they could hold new auditions would be Tuesday. And given they were filming on Wednesday and they'd need client sign-off – that was far, far too tight. So Houston, they did indeed have a problem. Laura wondered if they could lose the boy altogether and give his dialogue to one of the sisters. But Alex assured her that the mere suggestion would be enough to push an already-jittery agency over the edge. They might even pull the plug on the whole bang shoot which, from every point of view – not least his bank balance – would be an unmitigated disaster.

In a moment of sheer desperation, Alex's mind turned to Fred. Like so many TV ads these days – the Huff's family was inter-racial. And Fred just happened to be the right ethnic mix. He wasn't a bad actor either. In the school production of Bugsy last year, he had the audience eating out of his hand. Granted, that was before he turned into a ball of angry hormones. And admittedly he was playing Tallulah. And OK – he was fifteen not seventeen – and his voice was still breaking. But who knows – the client might see that as a positive. It could even add a touch of 'memorability' to an otherwise unremarkable ad. It was worth a punt.

But first he had to sell the idea to Fred.

CHAPTER 8

WHERE'S THE HUFF'S?

'So they're gathered round the table, much like we are now.' Alex prised open the foil containers of their Sunday evening takeaway. 'Chatting amongst themselves, about to eat dinner. And outside the window it's pouring with rain.' He spooned some pilau onto Fred's plate. 'The boy comes in – soaking wet, muddy track-suit, filthy football boots flung over his shoulder – and sneezes. He grabs a tissue from the box on the side-board. But when he realises it's a 'bargain' tissue, he stops in his tracks and says: 'Mum! Where's the Huff's?"

Fred looked puzzled. 'Mum! Where's the Huff's?'

'Yes.'

'That's it?'

'That's all the boy has to say, yes.' Alex crunched on a pappadum. 'So? What d'you reckon?'

Fred regarded him blankly, like he'd explained the whole thing in Serbo-Croat.

'Why does he care what kind of tissue he sneezes into?' he said, upending the Korma onto his rice.

'Well, because Huff's tissues are menthol and a lot more…'

'No. I mean, like, he's a teenager, right? Why would he give a toss about that kind of thing?'

'Erm… because it's a commercial and they're paying him to?'

Fred nodded inscrutably and dug his fork into the Bhindi Bhaji. 'And it's all in period costume?'

'No. It's contemporary,' Alex said, trying to hide his exasperation. 'Why would it be in period costume?'

'I dunno. Because it's so… out of date and old-fashioned?'

Alex's head sunk momentarily, but he couldn't afford to give up. There was too much at stake.

'OK, OK, I'm not expecting it to win any awards Freddie,' he said tersely. 'But I very much doubt it'll ruin your acting career.'

'Plus you'd get paid, wouldn't he Al?'

This was Ally, joining the pressure group. And effortlessly hitting the sweet-spot.

Freddie glanced up with a glint in his eye. The first in weeks. 'How much?'

Alex hesitated for a moment. The boy had just committed a serious act of vandalism and got himself suspended from school. A school that he and Ally were paying a king's bloody ransom to keep him at. It really didn't feel appropriate to reward him with…

'Two hundred and fifty pounds.'

By any measure he knew it was wrong. But if Fred could get him out of this mess, it was worth a lot more than that.

'OK. What do I have to do?'

Even grumpy adolescents had their price, it seemed. So after dinner they headed upstairs and recorded several takes of Fred entering the study, sneezing, and saying the line. With a range of different inflexions and moods. And – OK, maybe Alex was cheering himself up – but he wasn't at all bad and he told him so.

There was another bridge to cross however.

'Now then,' Alex said, wondering how to broach the subject. 'We need to stick an ID on the front. And – nothing personal – but it's probably best if, erm, no-one knows you're my son. Is that alright with you?'

'Whatever.'

'Great. So you can be *anyone* – other than Freddie Feinstein. OK?'

Fred considered this for a moment. To be anyone other than Freddie Feinstein was something he'd dreamt about a lot.

'Clark Kent,' he proclaimed finally, straight down the lens.

'Hmmm. They may not buy that.'

'OK. Kent Clark. Final answer.'

*

By Monday evening, there was a fervent thumbs-up from the client. They agreed that acne and a breaking voice could add a touch of 'verisimilitude' to the proceedings.

So two days later, Alex was in the trenches, shooting his first commercial in over five months. And the morning went like clockwork. The kitchen was warm and welcoming, the rain-effects looked great, the lighting was soft and painterly, and most important of all, the Mum, Dad and two girls looked almost like a real family. They even managed to make the stilted dialogue sound vaguely convincing. And when Zoe – the ad agency's feisty new CEO – declared that it was all looking 'spectacular', the entire team visibly relaxed. Her three execs breathed a communal sigh of relief; their two clients stopped twitching; the young creatives sank back in their canvas chairs; and Tess – the super-uptight agency producer – almost cracked a smile. There was a genuinely positive vibe on set that Alex wasn't expecting.

Fred was relieved that his dad hadn't wanted to drive him to the studio. Apparently he wasn't in the first few set-ups anyway, so his call-time was later. Which meant he could have a nice long lie-in before the top-of-the-range Lexus picked him up at 10am. It certainly beat school.

A *PFF* in a very short skirt greeted him at reception, introduced herself as Holly, and showed him to his dressing room.

'I'm afraid breakfast finished at nine, Kent,' she said. 'But I got them to hold one back for you.'

She returned moments later with a full English, which Fred guzzled appreciatively in front of MTV – despite having already had breakfast at home. Then another *PFF* in an even shorter skirt breezed in and introduced herself as Polly. Fred shook her hand delightedly. Holly and Polly – you couldn't make it up! Polly led him down a long corridor to meet Lance the costume designer, who dressed him in track-suit and trainers, complimented him on his muscle tone, and said he looked like a brown-skinned

Poldark. Next up was Rio, an Asian make-up artist with a rose tattoo and a nose-ring who covered his spots with concealer and gave him a complimentary neck rub.

Eventually Fred met his 'new family' in the green room. He had a white mum, a black dad and two bi-racial sisters – Tiana and Kylie – both younger than him, and both very sweet. Or they *were* – until they started listing their various credits. Films. Dramas. Shorts. Ads. It was obviously how you measured your worth in this world.

Tiana went straight for the jugular. 'So how about you Kent? What else have *you* done?'

'Erm… Not all that much…'

'Awwwww,' she said, like his puppy just got run over.

It was one thing to feel inadequate. Another thing entirely to be pitied.

'…Except… Bugsy Malone,' he added quickly.

'Jinx!' Kylie shrieked. '*I'm* doing Bugsy this Christmas. At the Palladium. I'm playing Tallulah. Who were you?'

'Erm… Bugsy,' Fred lied. No way was he going to own up to playing Fat Sam's girlfriend.

'Coo-wool!' she whooped. 'Where was it on?'

'Oh – just my school,' were the words his mouth was struggling to form. But what came out, inexplicably, was: 'Broadway.'

Tiana and Kylie were still on their iPhones, furiously googling Kent Clark, when they got called to set.

'Hey *Kent*,' his *real* dad said stiffly when Fred turned up. 'I'm Alex. The director. Thanks for jumping in at such short notice.'

'Sure,' Fred said, a little spooked.

Beyond his dad, there was a row of people on canvas chairs, in front of two giant monitors, like X Factor judges. From their detached, aloof manner and smart clothes, Fred assumed they were clients. His dad certainly seemed keen to impress them.

'This is *Kent*,' Alex said, with heavy emphasis on the *Kent*.

Yeah yeah I get the message Dad. I'm not a total bozo.

The woman closest to him had pink spiky hair. Fred felt like he'd seen her before. And sure enough, his dad introduced her as Laura Houston, his producer. Fred had known her most of his life, on and off, although the last time they'd met, her hair was orange. It was nice to find a familiar face amongst a sea of strangers.

'Hey Laura!' he said, stooping to give her the two cheek salute.

'Hey *Kent*,' she said. With heavy emphasis on the *Kent*.

His father's glare shook him back to his senses. *Don't kiss women you're not meant to know,* it was saying. *This isn't Love Island.*

Shit. He needed to cover his tracks. Demonstrate that he was just *a touchy feely* kinda guy. So he moved down the line, shaking hands with the men and kissing the women. And repeating his spiel like some smarmy American jock.

'Hey. I'm *Kent*. Pleased to meet you. Hey. I'm *Kent*. Pleased to meet you.' With heavy emphasis on the *Kent*.

OK, maybe he *was* a total bozo. But he'd got away with it. Just.

'Alright Kent,' Alex said, once Fred had finished manhandling his clients. 'Let's get to work.'

He placed a firm hand on Fred's shoulder and steered him briskly away.

'This is Kent everyone,' he said as they walked onto set.

'Hey Kent,' everyone chanted in unison.

'Hey everyone,' Fred said, completely overawed, but trying not to show it.

His new Huffs family were already at the kitchen table. Fred waved, although the girls were still buried in their iPhones.

They rehearsed the action a few times, to get the mechanics right, and then they were ready to roll. The DoP took a light reading. The VFX guys lined up the rain bar. The boom op climbed his ladder. The prop man titivated the tissue. The gaffer tweaked a lamp. The grip pumped the dolly's hydraulics. The focus puller took some measurements. The wardrobe guy wetted the track suit, applied some mud, handed Freddie his boots. The make-up assistant spritzed his hair and face. The home economist brought plates of piping hot food to the table. The 1st AD yelled 'turn over'. The camera assistant held up the board, marked it: '8 Take 1' and snapped it shut. Alex waited for her to leave frame and settle, and then called: 'Action.'

Fred lumbered into the kitchen, soaked to the skin, with the muddy boots slung over his shoulder. He sneezed, grabbed a tissue from the box on the side-board, and stopped in his tracks.

'Mum! Where's the Huff's?'

'And cut there,' Alex said.

The assistant cut the camera, the grip rolled it back along the rails to its first position, the VFX guys killed the rain.

'Thanks Kent. Very nice. Could we try one now with *attitude*?'

Attitude? Christ. That was something he never thought he'd hear coming out of his father's mouth.

They lined up for take two. Alex called action and they went through it again. The door. The sneeze. The tissues. The line.

'Mum! Where's the Huff's?' Only this time with *attitude*.

'And cut there. Very good. But pull it back a bit Kent. The sneeze was a bit panto. And the line sounded like you actually wanted to murder your mother?'

There was a ripple of laughter. His dad was clearly scoring points at his expense. Or at least that's what it felt like.

'You said you wanted *attitude*?'

'Yeah – but all Mum did was buy the wrong tissues. It's not a capital offence. OK?'

'OK.'

'Great. Let's give it another go.'

They gave it another go.

And another.

And another.

Faster.

Slower.

Sharper.

Softer.

With more weight on Huff's.

With less.

And each time Fred got muddied and wetted again, the *attitude* was more authentic.

Alex knew there was a risk of over-compensating – of being tougher on *Kent* – because he was his son. But at the same time, his clients were spending a great deal of money. They had the right to demand thirty seconds of perfection. And even if you achieved perfection on take one, you were expected to keep going – to cover a range of alternatives. As far as they were concerned, if you didn't shoot a minimum of ten takes on every set-up, you didn't *care.* No, *safety first* was the mantra. That's why they'd hired a safe pair of hands, and that's what he was contracted to deliver.

Fred, however, was becoming increasingly agitated. They were on take sixteen now, which was insane. Like he was being made to look stupid, for everyone else's entertainment.

'OK Kent. Let's try one now where your voice cracks a bit. Give us a hint of those hormones.'

Fucking hell.

'Right, I've had enough of this Dad!' Fred exploded. 'You want hormones? Then see what you can do with these…'

With a surge of ferocity, Fred flung his boots at the box of Huff's and sent it crashing to the floor. The clients looked on in horror, as he stomped past them, ranting under his breath.

'*Fucking… arsehole… bastard… cunt!*'

Into the long corridor. Past the green room. Past make-up. Past wardrobe. Out through the studio doors.

'*I hate you. I hate you. I hate you!*'

And then he remembered. He was still in his muddy tracksuit. With a radio mike taped to his chest.

The sound recordist quickly nixed his audio-feed, but not before everyone with a set of cans heard Fred's Tourette's-on-speed in hi-res. Every pair of eyes was now transfixed on Alex, watching, waiting to see how he'd respond.

But Alex was *incapable* of responding. He felt like he'd been tasered. Or machine-gunned with an AK-47. It took Zoe, the CEO, to break the silence.

'We need to talk,' she declared in a voice as severe as her pinstripes. 'In private.'

CHAPTER 9

TALKING BOWLS

By the time Holly and Polly emerged, Fred was already cowering in the Saab's footwell, courtesy of its broken lock. He could see them in the wing mirror, scanning the car-park and shrugging their shoulders, before tottering back in, defeated.

And then he remembered. His keys, cash and phone were still in his jeans – and his jeans were still in the dressing room, along with the rest of his stuff. But no way could he go back in to fetch them. There again, no way could he be in the Saab when they wrapped. His dad would go mental.

Ha! Who was he kidding? His dad would go mental anyway. The only get-out-of-jail card was his mum. As long as he got to her first. But how was he going to get *anywhere* without his phone or his bus-pass?

*

Alex led Zoe behind the scenery flats to a small prop store at the back of the stage. A startled chippie fluttered out like a scolded hen, but before Alex could close the door, two clients, three account execs, two creatives and the agency producer had barged in, taking up positions like enemy snipers, between crates, boxes and surplus set-dressing.

Zoe fired the opening shot. 'So… is he *actually* your son?'

Alex eased himself behind a table that bore a dozen boxes of Huff's, each carefully primped and prepped with the requisite tuft of tissue. If things got out of hand, they could prove a useful shield. Directors were dispensable, but the product certainly wasn't.

'I'm afraid so,' he said weakly.

The agency producer could smell blood. 'Then why the hell did you…?'

'I'll deal with this thanks Tess,' Zoe commanded with an imperious sweep of the hand.

Tess shrank back into the gap between a pine dresser and a winged-back chair as her boss continued the inquisition.

'So why the hell did you pretend he wasn't?' she fumed.

'I suppose I just… wanted… to avoid any whiff of nepotism,' Alex burbled, struggling to cling to the tattered shreds of his directorial authority.

'Avoid it – or cover it up? And did you not consider it a risk to cast him in our ad? Or *any* ad for that matter? Given his… combustible nature?'

In a last-ditched bid for clemency, Laura Houston popped out from beneath a fringed standard lamp.

'Freddie doesn't have a combustible nature,' she pleaded. 'I can personally vouch for that. What we just saw – and heard – was totally out of character. He's a lovely boy. It's just... the pressure must've got to him.'

Zoe was still staring at Alex as if battling a natural urge to let the firing squad finish him off. In the end though, after a rueful mea culpa, he managed to convince her that – with some skilful editing and dubbing – a reshoot would not be necessary. But one thing was certain: regardless of whether Walters, Wigmore and Wahldrom had a blacklist, there'd be no repeat business any time soon.

*

Thanks to some loose change in the Saab's glove compartment and the 72 bus, Fred did manage to make it home before his dad. But his mum was still out, so getting inside without a key was going to be a challenge. He could have broken in through their small conservatory, but he decided that if she got back to find him perched outside on a plant pot like a garden gnome – cold, wet and miserable – it might just help his cause.

And he was right. Ally's maternal instincts went into hyper-drive.

'I'm so sorry darling,' she tizzed once she'd made a hot chocolate, wrapped him in a warm towel, and he'd finally stopped shivering. 'I can't believe Dad would have belittled you like that.'

'He made me feel like a dick!' Fred blurted. 'He's obviously still punishing me for the graffiti thing.'

'I'm sure he's moved on from that. We both have.'

'It's not like I even wanted to be in his stupid advert.'

Later that evening, when Alex arrived home with all Fred's clothes, Ally and Fred were curled up in front of the TV. It was clear from their body language that he'd been tried *in absentia* and that judgement had been passed. And he was far too shattered, mentally as well as physically, to lodge an appeal. So he ate his dinner alone in the kitchen, then trudged upstairs to bed.

It was gone eleven by the time Ally joined him, and he was almost asleep.

'It's not working Alex,' she said.

Her voice was so calm, he assumed she was referring to the shower or the hairdryer.

'What's not working?' he mumbled, his eyes barely half-open.

'*We* aren't.'

She sat on the edge of the bed, folded her hands demurely on her lap and adopted that compassionate yet detached gaze she'd no doubt finessed for her counselling sessions. Slightly pious, slightly Christian, like the one her father adopted at the pulpit.

Alex was bolt upright now.

'I know you're going through a crisis,' she went on. 'Your career's in free-fall. You're confused and frustrated. You feel you still have a lot to offer, but that feeling is no longer shared by the people who hand out the work.'

'That's blatantly untrue. What about…?'

'Huff's? You wouldn't have touched it with a ten foot pole two years ago. And yes of course that leads to self-esteem issues. I understand that. But I've had enough of you taking it out on Freddie – it's hardly his fault.'

'That's a crazy thing to say. For a start…'

Ally raised a hand, determined to finish.

'I simply can't manage your anger any more Alex,' she said.

'*My* anger…?'

'Yes! It's doing my head in. So I'm afraid we need to…'

'…Alright, alright.' Alex sensed an urgent need to stop her completing the sentence. 'He's a teenager. I get that. I know it's their job to be a pain in the arse. And OK, maybe I struggle to make adjustments sometimes. But I did nothing wrong today, I promise. Not by anyone's standards. And we can't let Fred fuck up our marriage. It's too much of a burden to place on his shoulders.'

Ally didn't answer. This seemed to be an angle she hadn't considered.

'*OK*?'

Alex could feel the cogs whirring as Ally slipped quietly under the duvet. There was still a vast tract of permafrost between her side of the bed and his. But the clear and present danger had subsided.

For now.

*

To sit and watch a bunch of octogenarians, dressed head to toe in white, heaving large balls up and down a strip of manicured grass, was hardly Fred's idea of a good time. It certainly wasn't what he had in mind when he signed up for Ollie's science block project. But that's how things panned out. Because he'd now been granted the *special privilege* of attending Bubby's bowls competition – with private access to the club-house veranda, where smart phones were strictly verboten. It was a bit like a school detention, only worse – because he couldn't play *GTA* or *Hitman*.

'Well! Wasn't that fun?' Bubby giggled as she reversed out of the bowling club car-park, missing the concrete gate-post by a whisker. 'I knew you'd enjoy it.'

She squeezed Fred's knee with her arthritic fingers and he let out a squawk. Not because it hurt, but because the star of David dangling from her rear-view was lurching precariously to one side. A horn blared and Bubby grabbed the wheel in both hands again, dodging an oncoming van.

'Those crazy white-van drivers!' she cried. 'They should all be knocked up!' Bubby may have lived in the UK for the best part of eight decades, but her English went to pot when she was stressed. When she was *very* stressed, it sometimes converted to Yiddish.

'Meshuggah!' she said, tutting and shaking her head vigorously. 'Got hit aundz!'

Fred shook his too – in total disbelief at his grandma's driving. And her phenomenal ability to shift blame.

But she quickly regained her composure.

'Unfortunately the next part of our day won't be so jolly,' she said. 'I have an appointment. But don't worry Freddie. Marta is also a friend. She won't mind you being there.'

Fred assured her he was perfectly happy doing homework in the garden or watching TV in the bedroom. But Bubby wasn't up for that.

'Your mama told me you need to be supervised,' she said. 'And a mama's word is always final.'

So while Bubby had the corns scraped off her gnarly old trotters, Fred slumped in the tatty armchair, doing his best not to look. The photos on the dresser were a useful distraction. Bubby and Zeyde at their wedding – like something out of a museum. Bubby and Zeyde with Dad on his first day of school. Mum and Dad at *their* wedding, gazing nauseatingly into each other's eyes. Fred himself as a toddler – straddling his dad's shoulders. Huge creamy ice-cream in his hands. And all over his face.

But none of Uncle Joe. Not one. Is that how it worked? The family black sheep got dumped, deleted, *cancelled*, like he never even existed? Could that ever happen to *him,* Fred wondered? Could he end up as his mum and dad's *Joe*?

The more he avoided Bubby's bunions, the more the chiropodist tried to hook him back in. Droning on about her teenage daughter. How charming. How pretty. How gifted at physics and cello. *Bloody hell.* If he didn't know better, he'd say he was being set up.

Eventually Marta packed away her instruments of torture and Bubby saw her to the door.

'Guess what I'm cooking this evening?' she beamed when she shuffled back in. 'Kugel! Your favourite!'

Fred's heart sank. Bubby was famous for her dreadful cooking, and the last time he had her egg and potato casserole, he'd spent two hours hugging the toilet. She was six when she first came to Britain and her foster mother never let her go near the kitchen – or so she claimed. Perhaps that's why she married Zeyde. When they started a family, Jewish food was all they ever ate at home. Not because they were kosher, but because Zeyde could cook Jewish food with his eyes closed. And on his one day off from the restaurant, that's precisely what he did. Every Monday night, the fridge would be groaning with kneidlach, borekas, gefilte fish and chopped liver. And when he died, Bubby had been determined to 'carry on the tradition'. So these days, it wasn't just the fridge that was groaning.

The problem was, today was parents' evening at Fred's school. Which meant he wasn't being picked up till later. So there'd be no hiding place from Bubby's cooking.

'And Stavros is coming!' she announced gleefully.

Stavros was Bubby's 'toy-boy' as she called him. Given he was fat and hairy and breathed through his mouth, it's possible she was being ironic, but Fred somehow doubted it. They'd only met once, and when Stavros finally stopped groping Bubby, he'd spent the rest of the afternoon boring Fred rigid about shipping insurance.

'I've invited someone else too,' Bubby added with a mischievous dig in his ribs.

*

Marta's daughter far from lived up to the hype. She wasn't pretty. She wasn't charming. She wasn't even a teenager. In fact she was barely *twelve*. Plus she wouldn't shut the fuck up for one second. Even now – as they polished off a bowl of shop-bought chopped-liver and those big queen olives on cocktail sticks – she couldn't stop banging on about longitudinal sound waves.

While Stavros bent Fred's ear about the cost of premiums.

And Bubby talked bowls.

'I'm just gonna wash my hands,' Fred said, grabbing the last olive as Bubby ushered them into the dining room.

As soon as he was inside the toilet, Fred popped the olive in his mouth, placed the sharp end of the cocktail stick on the tip of his thumb – and pushed it in until blood started to ooze. Then he smeared it all over his nostrils.

By the time he'd staggered back to the dining room, he looked like he'd had a haemorrhage.

'*Oy vey iz mir!*' Bubby cried, launching herself out of her chair. 'What happened?'

'Nosebleed,' Fred sniffed. 'I get them sometimes.'

'You poor thing! Come, sit down.'

Stavros and Lena looked on, speechless at last.

'No thanks Bubby. I need to *lie* down. In a darkened room. It's the only way of making them stop.'

Once her *kvetching* subsided, Bubby guided him to her bedroom, lay him down on the bed, and passed him some tissues.

'Where's the Huff's?' he gibbered.

'I'm sorry?'

'Oh… nothing. I might be a little delirious.'

'Get some rest *bubala*,' Bubby said as she turned off the light. 'We'll save you some Kugel.'

*

School parents' evenings weren't everyone's cup of tea, but Alex actually enjoyed them. Or used to. Fred had always been a hard-working, confident child, and from his very first day at St Joseph's, his teachers had been lavish with their praise. They all agreed that he was diligent, smart, and eager to learn. How could any parent *not* find that a deep source of pride?

This year though, the prospect filled Alex with trepidation. If it hadn't been for Ally's three-line whip, he'd have bunked off for sure. He'd just spent a long hard day in the cutting room, digging himself out of a large, Fred-shaped hole. What's more, he and Ally were barely talking. And Fred had just been suspended for a tasteless prank which the entire school community would know about. As they did the walk of shame past the new science block, the faint outline of Fred's handiwork still served as an indelible testament to his disgrace. There would be nothing pride-inducing this year, that much was certain.

To be fair, dads were not responsible for the sins of their sons. No-one blamed his *own* dad, after all, when Joe blacked out in RE after drinking a bottle of Ouzo. Or singed the lab-assistant's beard with a Bunsen burner. Or let down the Headmaster's tyres.

Even so, this year's parents' evening was a sobering experience. Like a set of well-briefed politicians, Fred's teachers all toed the party line:

'Fred is talented, creative and smart, but he lacks discipline and focus.'

'Fred has a gift for words, but he also has serious issues with authority.'

'Fred shows great insight into the subject, but he does need to rein in his rebellious streak.'

As it happens, Alex wasn't entirely against Fred's

rebellious streak. No father wanted an anodyne child after all. In his own formative years, Alex himself had been far too deferential to authority. Who knows what he might have achieved if he hadn't been so restrained by convention. Kubrick, Scorsese and the Coen Brothers never had to bear that cross.

Still, when Fred's history teacher declared that 'he really needs to control his propensity for insurrection', Alex felt vindicated.

'You see?' he said, as they emerged, 'it's obviously not just me!'

Ally ground her teeth and marched off towards their next appointment.

By the time they hit Geography, all Alex could think about was a bubble bath and an early night. But when the new Geography teacher greeted them at her classroom door, he somehow got his second wind. She was by no means a beauty in the conventional sense of the word. And a faint filigree of tell-tale lines around the mouth suggested she was well past her first flush of youth. But as she stood there, dramatically backlit by the evening sunshine, her mane of copper-coloured hair glowed like a halo. And through the translucence of her blue pencil skirt, a fleeting glimpse of thigh tattooed itself onto his retina. Alex knew he'd succumbed to the *male gaze*, but he couldn't help it. He was male for god's sake. His only hope was that no-one else noticed.

Ms Banks sat down elegantly in front of a photographic display of the natural wonders of the world (where to an adolescent boy she may not have looked at all out of place) and launched into her own assessment of Fred's progress.

But Alex was so taken by the curl of her lip and the ebb and flow of her soft Aussie burr, that he hardly registered a thing. He rarely experienced these kind of stirrings any more, and when he did, they took him by surprise. So at the end of her monologue, when she asked if there was anything they wanted to ask or add, he was literally stumped for words.

Ally was less than impressed. 'That was quite possibly the most mortifying five minutes of my life,' she vented as they left the room.

Despite the frostiness in her voice, Alex was pleased they were actually talking. 'Why do you say that?' he asked.

Ally shook her head but said nothing. Keeping the line of communication open was clearly down to him.

'I have no idea what you're on about,' he continued. '*Why* was it mortifying?'

By now Ally was walking at such a clip, it was hard to keep up.

'You know bloody well,' she said. 'You were ogling so hard I thought your eyes would pop out of their sockets.'

'Don't be ridiculous.'

'Ridiculous? Ha! That's rich! You were *so* ridiculous I actually lost track of which adolescent we were talking about.'

As they strode down the endless corridor, the parents of one of Freddie's friends emerged from another classroom, arm-in-arm. The stout ruddy-cheeked mum opened her mouth to greet them, but Ally's next volley of vitriol stopped her right there.

'Jesus Christ Alex,' she bristled, 'if you're going to

cream your jeans over another woman – have the grace to do it when I'm not around and preferably not at your son's school.'

Alex threw the couple a cheery wave which (he hoped) said: '*Don't worry – just some jolly marital banter*'. In perfect unison, they both pretended not to notice them – and sailed on past.

Beyond the double-doors at the end of the corridor, the quad was already bustling with parents and staff. As soon as they were outside, Alex stopped and gently touched Ally's arm. She turned, tears in her eyes.

'Read my lips Al,' he said. 'I have no interest in any other woman. End of.' He took a step towards her, partly to emphasise his point, partly to prevent anyone else from overhearing. 'I know we have our moments, but I still consider myself a happily married man.'

Ally stood there, implacable, hands on hips. He moved his own to the crook of her elbow, discreetly, tenderly. It was the first proper physical contact they'd had in weeks, and after an initial tensing, she softened under his touch.

'I only have eyes for one woman,' he persisted. 'And if I *did* ever have an interest in another – I assure you it wouldn't be one of Fred's teachers.'

Ally was far too astute to believe his empty declarations of innocence. But it was clear she *wanted* to. She paused for a moment, blinking through a curtain of tears, then gently leant in and kissed his lips.

'Let's get out of here,' she said, grabbing his hand and marching him towards the exit.

CHAPTER 10

THE ELEPHANT IN THE BEDROOM

They could have seized the moment. They could have gone home (via Borehamwood, of course, to pick up Fred), ripped off each other's clothes, and for the first time in months, properly tested the springs on their Hypnos mattress. But would that really have moved things forward? Would it really have had the turbo-charged effect their marriage was crying out for? The presence of Fred, in the next bedroom, his pillow less than a foot away from theirs, was hardly an incentive.

To be fair, that never used to be an issue. The mellow tones of Tracy Chapman or Katie Melua, the whiff of a scented candle, the creak of the bed or a squeak of one of its occupants – none of these would have entered the consciousness of a pre-pubescent child. Nowadays, however, just one such tell-tale clue would be irrefutable proof that his parents were 'at it'.

Why should that matter? Without 'it', after all, Fred wouldn't even exist. And two consenting adults were entitled to do what they wanted in the privacy of their own bedroom. Aside from that, what Alex and Ally got up to these days barely justified a PG-rating.

It wasn't something they'd actively discussed. Conversations about sex were so prevalent in Ally's professional life, that they got next to no airtime at home. But Alex was sure she shared his compunctions. She probably felt them even more acutely. On the rare occasions that they'd actually *had* sex over the past year, she'd been silent as a proverbial church mouse. Whereas when they first met, she'd been one of the most vocal lovers he'd ever been with. The IVF played its part of course. And after that, the last flickers of marital passion had been gradually smothered by the fire-blanket of parenthood. Since Fred's adolescence – all but extinguished. If good sex was an affirmation of a special bond – an endorsement of everything that was right in a relationship – then bad sex could expose everything that was wrong. Ally would know this better than anybody, which was maybe why she preferred not to go there. But Alex also knew that urgent action was needed if he wanted to resuscitate their increasingly moribund marriage.

'I've had an idea,' he said, as they hit the North Circular on the way to Borehamwood. 'Let's go away for the weekend. Just you and me. Somewhere romantic.'

Ally reacted like she'd been invited to Guantanamo Bay. 'What about Freddie?' she asked incredulously.

Alex tightened his grip on the steering wheel, and managed, wisely, to moderate his thoughts before they converted into words. 'I wondered if maybe he could stay with your parents. They haven't seen him in months. And we have nothing to feel guilty about this time. Do I?'

Ally pursed her lips. 'I don't think he'd be up for that.'

'Why not? He'd kill for your mum's jerk chicken.'

'I know, but the internet's rubbish and he's allergic to the cat. Not to mention Dad's church.'

'Fine. Then I increase his data allowance. We dose him up with Piriton. And he tells your dad he has homework to do. Job done.'

'Homework on a Sunday? You know that's a cardinal sin.'

In the end they reached a compromise – which Alex chalked up as a victory. One night in a hotel, after all, was half the price of two. And one night, he felt sure, was all they needed to get things back on track.

Fred wasn't happy about being palmed off with Grandma and Grandpa Pinnock, having barely survived a day with Bubby Feinstein. But the fifty quid from his dad towards a new guitar helped sweeten the pill. Along with the solemn promise that he'd be picked up well before church on Sunday morning. And that Bob Marley would be shut in the kitchen.

'And another thing,' Ally added, as she kissed him goodnight. 'Grandma's got two tickets for a matinee.'

'She does know I'm not five any more, doesn't she?' Fred said sulkily, remembering all the pantos and puppet shows he used to get dragged to.

'Of course she does darling. It's a new play at the Churchill. She even asked if you'd be comfortable with 'adult themes'. Grandpa would have gone too, if he didn't have a sermon to write.'

Fred grunted, and turned over to cuddle his teddy.

*

Thelma and Lewis contained adult themes alright. It opened in an old-age home, with a pair of wrinklies rolling around on a bed, semi-naked. Fred had to bite his own knuckle just to stop himself gagging.

'The good Lord must have known,' Grandma tutted as they snuck out at the interval. 'Which is why he stopped Grandpa from going.'

'Why didn't he stop me too?' Fred protested.

'He'll have his reason,' she assured him. 'The good Lord always have his reason.'

All the same, from now on – Fred decided – he'd be sticking to puppets and panto.

*

The moment they entered the hotel's reception, Alex could see why there was plenty of last-minute availability. Still, the fusty decor, surly staff and wilting flowers were minor issues. He hadn't booked it for its grand public spaces. And the bedroom boasted glorious views over rolling Kent hills – as well as a large four-poster. So he was happy enough.

Dinner, however, was a stuffy, joyless affair. Sepulchral, almost. The quiet clink of glasses. The soft baroque muzak. The restrained susurration of voices.

'It's like Aunty Aubrey's funeral,' Ally murmured once they'd placed their orders. 'Only gloomier.'

'And several shades paler,' Alex mused.

Ally glanced around at the other diners. Sure enough, apart from a junior waiter on the other side of the room, Ally's was the only non-white face there. And with the exception of a young couple canoodling at the table next to theirs, everyone was well over fifty.

'Actually it's more like that lake,' she said. 'Without the hats and the buckets.'

'Well let's just hope we get something this time!' Alex said.

'And that we're still talking to each other at the end of it!'

'I'll drink to that!'

Ally raised her tumbler of Highland Spring to meet his glass of Merlot. Then reached across the faded damask tablecloth to give his hand a gentle squeeze. 'Don't beat yourself up Al,' she said. 'We all make mistakes.'

Alex drew her hand up towards his face and kissed it tenderly.

After fifteen years of full metal parenthood, this already had the feel of a second honeymoon.

*

'Gracious god. We have sinned against thee. And we are unworthy of thy mercy. Pardon our sins. Bless these mercies for our use. And help us to eat and drink to thy glory. For Christ's sake. Amen.'

For Christ's sake indeed. Gracious god surely hears quite enough of Grandpa's voice on a Sunday, Fred thought. But grace was trotted out before every meal in the Pinnock household. And ever since he learned to talk,

Fred had mumbled along. To be fair, it was a small price to pay for the serious bean-feast that followed.

Grandpa peered at him beadily, over his wire-rimmed specs. He was a gaunt, humourless man, whose faith in god seemed to come at the expense of his faith in human beings. A tough upbringing on a sugar plantation outside Kingston must have drummed it out of him.

Thankfully Grandma more than made up for it with her kindness and her world-beating jerk chicken.

Their previous house was a three-story terrace in Catford, right opposite Grandpa's church. The front room had been lined with crosses, books, framed quotes from the bible, photos of Baptist bishops, a blow-up picture of the Windrush. Grandpa's stuff. And the back room was crammed with Grandma's stuff. Colourful paintings of fruit and beaches, a big Jamaican flag, and a photo of Grandma and her gospel choir, posing with Usain Bolt of all people.

But last year, because of her knees, they'd moved to a bungalow in Bromley. It was about half the size, with all their possessions now squashed in one room. And when he beseeched god to pardon their sins, Grandpa's eyes weren't the only ones drilling into Fred. Above his chair, three stern-looking Baptist elders were wagging their fingers and shaking their heads judgementally.

Grandma did her best to lighten the vibe.

'What are you drinking Freddie?' she asked as soon as grace was over. 'There's some Red Stripe in the fridge if you fancy.'

Good old Grandma. She was obviously taking his new grown-up status to heart. Up till now, the strongest drink he'd been offered at their place, was ginger beer. Or *Grandma beer* as he used to call it.

'Just help yourself,' she said.

'Cool,' he said. 'Thanks.'

But Grandpa had other ideas.

'He's *fifteen* putus. He isn't ready for the Red Stripe yet.'

'He's had a traumatic afternoon Linval. We both have. One little beer won't hurt him.'

'That's how it start Dorothy. Didn't we learn our lesson with Alison?'

Fred looked bewildered. 'What do you mean?' he protested. 'Mum never touches booze.'

Grandpa gazed at him intensely. 'We all like sheep have gone astray,' he said. 'Isaiah chapter 53 verse 3. Your mother weren't much older than you when she…'

'*Linval!*' Grandma rarely raised her voice or dropped her smile, but everyone took notice when she did. Especially Grandpa.

He stared at her for a few seconds, recalibrating.

'So… how you getting on at school these days?' he asked finally, picking up the jug of Grandma beer and filling Fred's glass to the brim.

*

By the time they'd finished dinner, Alex and Ally had made a reconnection of sorts. They held hands as they left the dining room and even snatched a quick kiss in the lift – just like old times. When they got back to the bedroom, Cupid had already done the groundwork. The lights were dimmed, the sheets turned down, and either side of an elaborate towel swan, two heart-shaped chocolates had been placed on the plumped-up pillows. If ever there was a time for 'rekindling', this was it.

But Cupid could be a rascal sometimes. In a cruel twist of synchronicity, Ally emerged from the ensuite (looking sensational in the hotel's fluffy white bathrobe) at exactly the same moment as a burst of activity in the bedroom next door. Not a half-deaf guest with the radio turned up loud, or a drunk one bellowing into his mobile, but an amorous couple (presumably the token Gen Z's at dinner) doing some 'rekindling' of their own, moving swiftly through the gears from tender to steamy to torrid.

Alex and Ally stared at each other, unsure how to respond. After such a long period of abstinence it was as if someone was trying to provide them with a crude refresher. And far from dispelling their inhibitions, it made them both more self-conscious than ever.

Unable to suppress the tension, Ally started giggling – and they were soon both helpless with laughter.

'Just ignore them,' Alex whispered, finally pulling himself together and beckoning her to the bed.

Ally retied the cord around her waist like a chastity belt.

'There's no way I'm competing with *that*,' she said. 'Be like having group sex. With people I can't even see.'

'Right!' said Alex, stomping across the room in his boxers.

'What are you doing?' she hissed.

'I'm gonna shut them up.'

He raised his fist to the wall like a hammer.

'Don't do that!' Ally snapped. 'You can't stop people having fun.'

Her expression was tough and intractable. Just like the night when Alex broke up Fred's party.

'What about *our* fun?' he said, trying unsuccessfully to avoid sounding desperate.

Ally shrugged. Their fun was clearly not a priority.

Alex pondered for a moment. A compromise was called for. Again. He unclenched his fist and grabbed the remote.

'OK. They won't last long at that rate. Let's watch some TV.'

They settled down on the bed to watch Strictly. But it wasn't easy to appreciate even the most flamboyant of tangos with such a bravura performance going on next door.

'My pulse is racing – my heart is pumping,' one of the judges raved as he held up a 10. 'What a scintillating expression of zipless erotica!'

It was interrupted by a buzz on the bedside table.

'Is it Fred?' Alex asked as Ally scrolled through a text.

'No… just… a work thing,' she said, gently stroking her right eyebrow.

'At 9.45 on a Saturday night?'

'One of my clients. Bit of a crisis.'

'I didn't know you offered round the clock service?'

'I don't,' she said, earnestly typing out a reply. 'But needs must.'

It was hard for Alex not to feel miffed. Sure, Ally struggled to leave her case-load in the surgery sometimes, but she had firm rules about her work/life balance, which her clients respected.

There was another buzz. Then another. Then another.

'I'm sorry,' she said. 'Bit of an emergency.'

Ally made a point of never discussing her clients or their issues, not even obliquely. But by the time she'd finally switched off the phone, her professional karma had been replaced by a tight-lipped testiness. It was almost as if, once again, Alex was being blamed for the bad behaviour of someone else's husband or partner.

Still, next door's carnal activities showed no sign of abating. Far from it. Alex had given up counting climaxes and the bar had now been raised to such dizzying heights, that the prospect of their own 'rekindling', was now totally out of the question.

*

'So what you gonna do about it bro?'

Joe dipped a celery stick into his Bloody Mary and stirred contemplatively.

'About what?'

'The elephant in the bedroom.' He popped the dribbling leafstalk in his mouth and sucked on it salaciously, before returning it to his crystal highball. 'Because I have to tell you, I wouldn't put up with it for one second.'

Given Joe saw life as one long bonkathon, this point of view wasn't altogether surprising.

'When room service drops off,' he continued with almost evangelical fervour, 'it's time to check out – and book yourself into another hotel.'

He winked, to make sure Alex fully appreciated the subtext. Although Joe's subtexts never needed much elucidation.

'That's Versace, right?' Alex said, in a bid to move the subject away from his painful relationship issues.

Joe looked surprised. 'What is?'

They were perched, or in Joe's case, sprawled, at either end of a sky-blue Chesterfield at Bertie's, the exclusive private member's club where Joe apparently brought all his dates. He looked the part too, with his dark purple shirt, peeping discreetly out from beneath a grey velvet Mao suit. Alex, by contrast, who didn't get the memo, was sporting a baggy jumper and jeans. Joe had to slip the receptionist a tenner just to smuggle him in.

'Your aftershave. I used to wear it too, back in the day. Ally bought gallons of the stuff.' Alex gazed into the middle-distance. 'Turned her on big time,' he added wistfully.

Joe stiffened. 'I got it from Betsy.'

'Who's Betsy?'

'Just – someone I met on Tinder. Swimwear model.'

There was something dismissive, evasive even, about the way Joe said it, and a tinge of paranoia flickered through Alex's consciousness. Those hotel texts had apparently unsettled him more than he thought. But for god's sake – *Ally and Joe*? The very notion was insane – and he gave it the short shrift it deserved.

'Well Betsy obviously has *some* good taste then,' he joked. 'At least when it comes to men's aftershave.'

Joe smiled. He'd been dating like a dervish for years now and there was hardly an app, website or introductions agency to which he hadn't, at some point, subscribed. If his claims were true, he'd been outrageously successful, although in his restless quest for five star room service, he'd usually moved on to his next play-mate before Alex had a chance to meet the last.

'You should get yerself online, bro,' he said. 'Don't be a dinosaur. If you sign up now, by this time tomorrow there'll be a bunch of babes queueing up to meet you.'

'Aren't you forgetting one small detail?' Alex said.

'Objection overruled,' Joe snorted. 'Ally doesn't need to find out. And so what if she does? It might even make her…'

He trailed off, distracted by something over Alex's shoulder.

Alex followed his gaze to an elegant young man in a tartan frock coat, framed in the doorway. A large diamond ear-stud sparkled under the rococo chandelier as he nodded, turned on his Cuban heels and strutted off up the corridor.

Joe scrambled to his feet. 'Back in a minute,' he said, following the man to the rest-room.

Alex could think of only two possible reasons why a man would follow another man into a toilet – and given Joe's proven track record, one of those seemed highly unlikely. When he returned, less than a minute later, patting the inside pocket of his jacket, Alex had narrowed it down to just one.

'Sorry dude,' Joe said, slumping back down on the Chesterfield. 'Designers are so demanding these days!' He chuckled to himself and resumed his celery ritual.

'Christ J! Didn't eighteen months at Feltham teach you anything?'

'What the hell's that meant to mean?'

'You know damn well what it means,' Alex murmured. 'You'd get a lot more than eighteen months if they ever catch you again. Is it really worth the risk?'

Joe's eyes flashed. 'Don't get all paternal on me, bro. I didn't take it from the old man, and I certainly won't take it from you.'

'I don't want to see you getting banged up again, that's all.'

'You wanna Daddy someone, Daddy Fred. That's the whole point of kids, right?'

Alex *was* Daddying Fred as it happens – or trying to – and he could do without other people sticking their oars in. The graffiti incident, for example, had Joe's fingerprints all over it, and he was on the verge of saying so when the barman rocked up with two more Bloody Marys.

'Grazie mille Luigi,' Joe purred in his best Italian.

At least he'd learned something from his brief union with Alessia.

'Prego, signor Feinstein,' Luigi purred back.

Alex was grateful for an excuse to take stock. In truth, there was more than enough family strife going on already, and he could really do without adding Joe to the list.

'Just off for a pee,' he said, rising to his feet.

Joe frowned. 'Didn't you go when we got here?' he asked, glancing at his brother's two Bloody Marys, both virtually untouched. 'You might wanna get that checked out. Remember what happened to the old man.'

'Ha!' Alex smiled wryly. 'Now who's Daddying who?'

Although he couldn't deny Joe had a point.

*

When Alex got back home, Ally was in the kitchen in her pink dressing gown. Her face set hard.

'I've been having a think about things,' she said.

'What things?' Alex removed his shoes and placed them neatly on the mat next to hers.

She took a long deep breath. 'I've decided it would be good for us both – all three of us actually – if we had a bit of a break.'

'That's a lovely idea. Let's do it. Paris? Prague? Penzance?'

'I meant from each other Alex. I need you to move out for a while.'

WINTER

CHAPTER 11

DISCOMFORT ZONE

Alex always thought of himself as being pretty plugged into his feminine side, but right now, he felt utterly incapable of confronting his emotions. It wasn't so much *denial* as *self-preservation*. Because despite the occasional ups and downs and tiffs and disagreements that surely characterised all marriages, it never once occurred to him that *his* wouldn't last the distance. And even now, the prospect of *not* sharing the rest of his life with Ally was something he just couldn't contemplate. She *was* his north, his south, his east and west – and every time that bloody poem tried to insinuate its way into his consciousness, he had to stifle it.

Mercifully, he did have a flimsy distraction in the form of the Pampers ad he'd just been asked to pitch for. And although the script was indeed a steaming pile of what the product itself was designed to contain, it somehow represented a vain hope that – despite the Huffs debacle – his career might not after all be in free-fall.

In the event, that hope proved short lived. After forcing him to leap through more hoops than an old-style circus, the ad was finally awarded to a twenty-eight year old Vietnamese transgender called Rokkit. Alex was determined to avoid getting bitter and twisted, but when he checked their showreel online, it was hard *not* to jump to the obvious conclusion. On the other hand, perhaps the *real* nod to 'diversity' was the inclusion of an ageing straight-white-bloke in the bidding process?

Either way, swapping a penthouse suite in Golden Square for a suburban semi in Hammersmith hadn't helped his cause. In fact it was one of the reasons the agency gave for not choosing him. But like it or not – this was his new HQ. And it was on that basis that he turned down Ally's ultimatum.

'I'm afraid our home is now my place of work Al,' he declared. 'So moving out would deprive me of my livelihood – or what's left of it. And seeing as *you're* the one who wants a break, I really don't see why I should suffer any more than I already am.'

Ally wasn't giving up of course. It wasn't in her nature. But short of strong-arming him off the premises and changing the locks, she knew she had to bide her time. So she decided to move in with her parents. They had no room for Fred in their little bungalow, and Bromley was anyway too far away from his school. So father and son were left to battle it out on their own – like two cage-fighters without a ref. Which, considering their fraught relationship was the given reason for Ally wanting out in the first place, seemed utterly mystifying to both combatants.

Alex tried everything to change her mind. He conceded that he'd found Fred's adolescence hard to handle and admitted he was sometimes prone to over-reacting. But he also insisted he'd never knowingly been anything other than a devoted husband.

Ally begged to differ. He was angry, she said. Short-tempered, curmudgeonly, chippy, impossible to live with. He had a habit of turning every drama into a catastrophe. But if that were true – or even half-true – how could she justify leaving Fred with him on his own?

No, something else was going on. Had to be. Those texts at the hotel, for example. What were *they* all about? And who the hell were they from? The very thought that Ally, with all her integrity, empathy and principles, could be having an extra-marital… no he couldn't even bring himself to say the word. There was no earthly point in confronting her anyway. She'd only deny it. And the whole ugly situation would only get uglier.

With no prospect of work on the horizon, the practical challenges of running a home would have to provide his escape from insanity. Alex was no stranger to shopping or washing or ironing, but he certainly hadn't inherited his own father's culinary skills. So Ally's effortless five-star home-cooking was quickly replaced by a series of take-aways and ready meals, bolted down in front of the telly, to avoid any actual conversation. And as a result, Alex's quality of life, and Fred's too, took a major dive.

Day-time distractions were one thing, but when Alex lay awake at night staring into the darkness – a common affliction even at the best of times – his mind just refused to be shackled. And its meditations were a constant source of torment. It was Ally's presence, he realised, that he missed more than anything. The electric smile that lit up the room when she opened her eyes in the morning. The sweet little dimples in her cheeks. The trill (and thrill) of her singing in the shower. The way she hooked her legs over his when they were watching TV. It was only now she'd gone that it became clear how viscerally he loved her. If only he'd told her. All those things he should have said and done, as Elvis put it, but just never took the time.

*

Still, if Alex felt wretched, Fred felt even worse.

'Can I ask you something Mum?' he murmured as they sat munching popcorn in the back row of the Shepherd's Bush Vue, the Sunday after she left. They'd *FaceTimed* every day of course, often more than once, but that was no substitute for a proper convo – IRL.

'Anything you want,' she said.

'Is it something to do with me?'

'What's that darling?'

'You moving out?'

'Don't be silly.'

'So why did you go?'

Ally mulled for a moment. 'Marriage is tough,' she said eventually. 'All relationships are. If they weren't, I'd be out of a job!'

'I know that, but…'

'I mean obviously I struggled with you and Dad

constantly at each other's throats. Apart from anything else, it dredged up memories of my own teenage years. But that's hardly *your* fault.'

'What memories?'

'Oh, doesn't matter now. Water under a very old bridge.'

Fred looked puzzled.

'I know it seems odd,' Ally added. 'Moving back in with Mumma and Puppa to avoid reliving my teens. But Grandpa's far less controlling these days. More chilled. And Dad will be too one day, you'll see.'

'Maybe. But in the meantime I have to live with him. Without you to smooth things over.'

'I'm always here for you darling. Just a phone-call away. And it's only for a few weeks, I promise.'

Ally squeezed his hand reassuringly as the houselights dimmed and the opening music crashed in.

Spiderman: Into the Spider-verse. A movie far better than its title. About a mixed-race kid called Miles Morales with a mega-controlling dad and a hyper-cool uncle who taught him to break rules and do graffiti, until he got bitten by a radioactive spider and ended up saving the world. Super-far-fetched, sure, but for Fred, it was like watching his own life-story, in cartoon form. Except maybe the bit about saving the world.

The plot twists were hard to follow though, what with everything going on in his head and the bunch of lairy kids farting about in the row in front. The boy at the end kept trying it on with the girl beside him, over and over again. And like a mechanical toy on repeat, the girl kept shrugging him off.

Fred was praying his mum didn't get involved, but she'd always been incapable of staying neutral when someone was being bullied or harassed. And true to form – just as Miles was paralysing Kingpin with his venom blast – she tapped the boy hard on the shoulder.

'Why don't you leave her alone!' she hissed. 'She's clearly not interested. And some of us are trying to watch a movie.'

The boy wheeled round, furious.

'Why don't you fuck off?' he seethed.

And then, clocking Ally's steely expression, proceeded to fuck off himself.

*

'I still don't think you should've said anything,' Fred grumbled, once they'd ordered their burgers.

'I had no choice,' Ally said. 'She made it clear she didn't want his attentions.'

'She could have moved if she didn't like it. There were plenty of empty seats.'

'That's not how it works, Fred. She probably didn't want to make a spectacle of herself.'

'So *you* did it for her?'

Ally shrugged, but Fred knew she had a point. The truth was, he didn't have a clue how these things worked. How was a boy meant to know if a girl was interested or not, if she didn't say what she meant? Especially when he was fifteen, went to a single sex-school and the only women he knew were his mum and two grandmas. As it happens, with the school's Christmas bash coming up fast, this was something Fred had been pondering. A lot.

'Trust me,' Ally said, reading his mind. 'Girls have had to wait thousands of years to be allowed to make the first move. And now they can, maybe it's best just to let them?'

*

The last time Alex had a heart-to-heart with his *own* mother was when Ally was pregnant. Yet now, for some peculiar reason, he had a powerful impulse to tell her about their split. Perhaps human beings were genetically programmed to share these life-defining moments with their mums? So on the evening of Fred's school disco, and on the pretext of sorting out her Sky-box – something he'd been promising to do for a while – he invited himself over.

There were a few obstacles to deal with first – her *toy-boy* being one of them. Once they'd finally finished fondling and petting each other (a show Alex believed was put on for his benefit, even though it turned his stomach over) Stavros took advantage of a fresh pair of ears, to catalogue the vessels he used to insure, along with their risk assessments, premiums, claims, profits and losses. Alex tried tactfully to display his disinterest, but like most bores, Stavros was oblivious to the signals.

The only thing that shut him up was a sudden howl of anguish from the kitchen. Alex bowled in to find his mother safe and sound, but her meatballs burnt to a crisp. Secretly relieved, he assured her he wasn't hungry anyway. But lack of appetite had never been a good enough excuse for not eating her food. She grabbed a Tupperware tub from the freezer and shoved it in the microwave.

The men returned to the dining room, to be followed minutes later, by a steaming pile of sludge, thinly disguised as 'stuffed zucchini'. Alex did his best to look enthusiastic, but in truth, incinerated meatballs would have been far more palatable.

Still, Stavros rose to the challenge.

'Nostimo!' he gushed as he chowed down the first mouthful. 'Delicious!'

A keen appreciation of Miriam's cooking was clearly the price you had to pay for any kind of relationship with her. Though judging by his waistline, the concept of quality control was already an alien one to Stavros. In that sense they were the perfect match.

Alex, however, had made no such Faustian pact and his gut was a lot more discerning. So when he stared down at the bilge on the plate in front of him, he knew straight away that evasive action was an absolute necessity. It was the paper napkin tucked between the top two buttons of Toy Boy's tight white shirt, that gave Alex his Eureka moment.

*

Ministry of Sound had nothing to worry about. There was a strict ban on booze, the DJ was a nerdy prefect in a tie and, at the end of the day, the school dining room was still a school dining room. But they had at least made an effort. The fairy lights were flashing. The speakers were bulging. The glow-sticks were glowing. The usual stodgy pasta and dodgy bakes had been replaced by copious trays of mince pies and pigs in blankets. And a hundred over-excited girls had been bussed in from St Mary's.

The Year 10 Christmas bash was arguably the biggest event in the school calendar – for kids in Year 10 at any rate. But at last year's do, two couples were discovered having sex in the cricket pavilion, so *both* sets of staff were now prowling around like cops at the Notting Hill Carnival. Deep mistrust barely hidden beneath smarmy laid-back smiles.

They must find the whole thing pretty bizarre, Fred thought. Take dress code for starters. How could the words *smart casual* mean so many different things? Omar, for example, looked like he'd just stepped out of a Boden catalogue. Felix was like a pimp in his pointy shoes and shiny-shirt. Jake had clearly borrowed a beige sports-jacket off his dad. Fred, for his part, had been intending to double-down and have *Arbeit Macht Frei* printed on a hoodie. In the end though, he went with *Never Mind the Bollocks* on a T shirt. Along with torn jeans and trainers. Distressed, to match his mood.

The girls were a lot more festive. High heels. Short skirts. Buckets of glitter. Plenty of flesh. And thick layers of war-paint. Fred couldn't help feeling slightly intimidated. Blood red lippie and eye-lashes like centipedes were a terrifying combo. Throw orthodontic headgear into the mix and you got Hannibal Lecter in drag.

For the first hour or so, the space was split into two equal halves. One reeking of Lynx Africa. The other Katy Perry Purr. Two armies peering across at each other from the trenches. The dance-floor itself a disputed territory, land-grabbed by a squad of screaming girls when Dua Lipa came on. Re-occupied by a bunch of boisterous boys when Drake did his Hotline Bling. Only with Jason Derulo's Swalla did the two sides finally mingle.

Most of Fred's crew were already fully embroiled. Rory and Felix checking out some girls from the 72 bus. Jake and Omar flirting with a pair of hyperactive elves. Finn mobbed by what looked like a deputation of god-squadders, gazing up at him in awe like he was the second coming. Or else their first *actual* encounter with an *actual* boy.

Fred was perched on a window-sill well away from the dance-floor, scoffing mini-cheese balls. The Christmas disco was clearly the perfect time to pull. He and his crew had discussed it for months. But something was putting him off. Perhaps it was that pep-talk from his mum? Perhaps his parents' split had affected him more than he thought? Or perhaps he just hadn't spotted anyone he was prepared to make an arse of himself with.

The same could not be said of Quentin. The smallest boy in the class was now slow-dancing with a leggy redhead a good nine inches taller. At first it looked more like a dare, or a TikTok opportunity. But it soon ramped up into a full-blown snog. Quentin on tip-toes. The redhead half-stooping, half-squatting. Sucking each other's souls through their Dementor-like mouths.

*

Alex returned to the dining room, to find his mother's toy-boy pawing her under the table, blissfully unaware they could be seen in the reflection of the old mirrored sideboard.

'Why do you keep going to the toilet Alex?' Miriam asked, shrugging off Toy Boy's attentions and discreetly rearranging her dress. 'Is everything OK?'

It was partly a bid to cover her embarrassment. And partly genuine angst. When Morris first got his diagnosis, she would literally bar him from having a wee, as if making him hold it in would somehow reverse the condition. And ever since he died, Alex's trips to the toilet had been monitored too. In fairness, it had barely been five minutes since his previous. But this one had nothing to do with waterworks. His sole objective was to dump the zucchini that he'd managed to conceal in a napkin.

'Everything's fine thanks,' he said. 'More or less'.

'*Oi vey*! What you mean 'more or less'? Have you had an S.P.A. test?'

Some people trembled when they got anxious. Others went red in the face. But stress for his mother had always expressed itself through some kind of linguistic malfunction. And her dyslexia was never more pronounced than now.

'Did they do rectal probe?' she continued. 'What the doctor say?'

'I don't need rectal probe Mum,' Alex assured her. 'I'm perfectly OK.'

Miriam hadn't finished her *own* probing however. 'Why you say 'more or less' then?' she enquired, eyes like lasers.

Alex glanced across at Stavros. He'd fully intended to

confide in his mum this evening, but it wasn't easy with Stavros fondling her at every opportunity or funnelling gunge into his bloated face.

'Is it work?' she persisted.

'No, work's great. Well not *great* exactly. I mean there's not much around at the moment. But…'

'Stavros will get you job, won't you Stavros? Stavros very well-connected.'

Stavros ingested another mouthful and blotted his chin.

'Thanks for the offer Mum,' Alex said, 'but it's a bit late to start a new career now. And besides, I have no intention of giving up on commercials.'

Stavros's relief was as blatant as Miriam's displeasure.

'So what's the problem?'

'Well if you must know… Ally and I are…'

Her fretful face broke into the broadest of grins.

'Having another baby? Mazel tov!'

After so many years of lobbying for a second grandchild, Miriam had obviously forgotten that Ally was now fifty-three. With tears in her eyes, she pinched her son's cheek so hard that he now had tears in his too.

'That's wonderful news. Stavvy – fetch that bottle of Asti please. It's in the fridge.'

Stavvy heaved to his feet.

'No Mum,' Alex insisted. 'Ally and I are not having another baby…'

Stavvy stopped and turned.

'…We're splitting up.'

It was hard to tell if it was the zucchini or this new piece of information that his mum was struggling to digest. Either way, the grin slowly disappeared and she finally responded with a terse:

'*Why?*'

Alex shrugged. 'Ally wants out.'

Miriam clearly now felt the same about her zucchini. She slid it away, unfinished, and leant back pensively in the chair.

Toy Boy sank back in his too. 'The captain of a cargo ship I used to insure…'

'*Shut up Stavros!*' Miriam snapped, scything the air with her bingo wings.

*

Two girls dressed in Sexy Santa outfits, were scoping out the dance-floor. Fred watched them from the safety of his distant window-sill. One pale and chubby, like a pre-diet Adele. The other sleek and brown-skinned like Beyoncé. Suddenly they were tottering towards him, wreathed in toothpaste ad grins.

'Hey there,' Adele said jauntily, struggling to be heard over Ariana Grande. 'D'you fancy some of this?'

She fumbled in one of her pockets and pulled out a shiny green hip-flask with 'Comfort and Joy' embossed in fancy red lettering.

'Oh. That's… thank you,' Fred said, a little hesitant. 'What's in it?'

She leant forward and put her mouth to his ear. 'Grey Goose. Forty percent proof.'

Cracks were starting to appear in Fred's *nothing-fazes-me* mask. He glanced across to where Mr Mantle was still rummaging through the handbags at the entrance.

'How did you manage to smuggle it in?' he asked.

'We went trad,' Beyoncé said. 'Down the chimney.'

Both girls collapsed into fits of giggles. They'd clearly been at the Comfort and Joy themselves.

Beyoncé was the first to pull herself together. 'What's yer name then? Johnny Rotten?'

Fred was impressed. Most kids their age had never even heard of the Sex Pistols.

'Freddie. Freddie Feinstein.'

'Hey Freddie. I'm Chanel.' She did an elaborate curtsy. 'And this is my bestie – Hestie.'

Hestie curtsied too. Then hiccupped.

'Pleased to meet you,' Fred smiled, instantly fretting that he'd come over as some middle-class muppet – and then realising that *all* the muppets there were middle-class.

'So Freddie,' Hestie said, passing him the hip-flask. 'This could be your lucky day.'

'Why's that?' he said. 'Is it laced with Rohypnol?'

That was more like it!

'Haha! Not *that* lucky!' Chanel pointed to the plastic cup on the sill beside him. 'But maybe orange juice is more your speed?'

It was as if Fred's credentials as a red-blooded male were being challenged. He turned to the window, away from prying eyes, lifted the flask to his mouth and took a hefty swig.

Euuwwcchh! Battery acid would have tasted better. And by the time the feeling returned to his face, both Santas were wetting themselves.

'Chanel wants to know if you fancy *her*,' Hestie said, retrieving the flask.

Chanel wiped away a tear and pouted seductively. Fred was looking at her through Grey Goose goggles now, but *of course* he fancied her. Who wouldn't? She was the sexiest girl there by a mile. What's more, she'd made the first move. Not that he needed his mum's approval but still, his mum would be happy he'd passed the consent test. So he nodded – a tad too enthusiastically perhaps. Although it didn't put them off.

'You can kiss her if you want,' Hestie said.

Was this for real – or a wind-up?

'Are you like... her manager or something?' Fred asked.

Chanel edged closer till her boobs squished up against his chest. 'She's my designated driver.'

Hestie was right. It *was* his lucky day. *All* his lucky days rolled into one. So why was he pulling away?

'Should we... maybe... go for a walk?' he suggested.

Chanel frowned. 'Where to?'

'Outside?'

'*Why?*'

'Just... you know... get some air.'

Hestie scoffed. 'Are you kidding? It's freezing out there. And look at what we've got on. We'll catch hypochondria.'

Which was a cue for both girls to crack up again.

It was undoubtedly true that their skimpy Santa outfits were not designed for Lapland, but the prospect of kissing a girl with her best friend breathing down his neck made Fred feel weird. Plus, despite all the cred-points on offer, he had no interest in putting on a floorshow for the whole of Year 10.

What made the entire sitch even more intense, was that Fred hadn't actually 'been' with anyone before. And the thought of getting marks out of ten from his mates was putting him right off his game. Across the room, Felix and Finn were already observing his every move.

'OK Fred,' Hestie huffed, shoving the flask back in her belt. 'It's your loss. C'mon ChaCha. Let's find someone who appreciates us.'

*

'Jews and Jamaicans have only one thing in common,' Miriam declared as she dolloped lumpy lokshen pud into Alex's bowl. 'That's what your father used to say.'

'*And*? What is it?'

'The letter J.'

'That's not true. Ally and I have plenty in common.'

'Such as?'

'The letter P. We're both people. And parents.'

'You know perfectly well what I'm saying.'

'No I don't. What *are* you saying?'

'Your history. Your backgrounds. Your…'

She managed to stop herself using the R word. Religion cut no mustard with Alex and she knew it.

'OK – well as it happens our history's similar too,' he said.

'Oh really? How do you work that out?'

'Ally's people were persecuted and so were mine. We're both second generation migrants. Her dad on the

Windrush. You on Kindertransport. But at the end of the day, it's got nothing to do with history.'

'OK – so what *is* it to do with?'

There was no point in dressing it up.

'For whatever reason, Ally's not happy.'

'*Happy*? What's *happy*? I was married to your father fifty-five years. Was I *happy*? Of course not. Imagine being married to your father fifty-five years! Happiness isn't the point. Marriage is the point. A marriage is for life – not just for Chanukah.'

Oddly enough, in spite of the fervour with which Miriam now defended Alex's union, she'd never been Ally's greatest fan. And nor had Morris. It was never referred to of course, the colour of Ally's skin. But right from the start there'd been subtle references to being born and raised a Baptist. Coded remarks about 'events in her past'. Dark allusions to problems their kids might encounter: identity crises; being spurned by both communities; feeling 'neither one thing nor the other'. *How many mixed race kids did they actually know?*

Eventually though, Ally's warmth and personality won them over. And for the first few years, they welcomed her into the fold. But when Freddie was born – the most beautiful baby ever, despite being '*neither one thing nor the other*' – the old prejudices started bubbling to the surface. It all came to a head, so to speak, when Ally refused to have him circumcised. The poor little thing had been through enough trauma in the first few weeks of his life, she insisted. And Alex agreed. Morris and Miriam, however, were scandalised. So what, if they hadn't been inside a synagogue for years? This was a total repudiation of their legacy. And that of their ancestors.

Who knew an uncircumcised grandson could be the source of such shame? It was almost as bad, apparently, as a son being sent to a young offender's institution for eighteen months. Or filing for divorce just a few weeks after his wedding. But for her *other* son to get divorced – her *ershtgeboyrn* – the apple of her eye? That would condemn the family to a disgrace of such epic proportions, that she would never be able to show her face again in public.

'So you go back and tell Ally you're not accepting this,' she said sharply.

'I have to Mum. I don't have a choice.'

'Enough already. Of course you have a choice. You must to be doing something to upset her. Or *not* to be doing something to cheer her up. So, whichever it is – very simple – either stop it. Or start it. End of.'

*

'You absolute bell-end,' Felix said at their Saturday morning debrief in the park. 'Chanel Fairfax! The hottest girl at St Mary's. What the hell's wrong with you Fred?'

'Maybe he bats for the other side?' Jake chipped in helpfully.

'It's the only possible explanation,' Finn agreed.

The entire crew found this highly entertaining. What made it even worse, was that every single one of them had pulled – with the exception of Freddie and Ollie. And Ollie had the squits, so he was officially exempt.

Mikey slapped a consoling hand on Fred's shoulder. 'Don't worry about it dude,' he said. 'We're off to Nando's later, with our new GF's. Tag along if you like. You might learn something.'

End of term could not come fast enough for Fred.

CHAPTER 12

THE ANTICHRIST

A question-mark bigger than the Star of Bethlehem was still hovering over Fred's Christmas. Ally made it clear he'd be spending it with her, but so far nothing was planned.

'Let's do an adventure,' she said. 'To cheer us both up. A last minute trip somewhere nice. The Canaries. The Alps. The Caribbean maybe.'

They ended up in Merthyr Tydfil.

The deacon of a local church, whom Grandpa had known since their time at the South Wales Baptist College, had invited him to give a sermon. Grandma and Grandpa would be staying at his house, and Ally and Fred were invited to join them.

'I know it doesn't sound thrilling,' Ally said, 'but you'll be *amazed* how much there is to do there. Castles. Funfairs. Bike rides. Plus we're only half an hour from the sea.'

Fred was amazed alright. The house reeked of damp. The deacon's wife had dementia. His bedroom was full of dead flies and the door didn't shut. And because Grandma's cat-sitter had let her down, Bob Marley spent the night on his bed. When he woke up on Christmas morning, his face looked like it had been bitten by a radioactive spider.

On the plus side, being rushed to A & E would at least mean skipping church.

Or so he thought.

As it turned out, within less than an hour of the injection, his allergic reaction had subsided, so they made it there just in time. And Grandma had saved two seats on the front pew. *Hallelujah*!

If there'd been a prize for the dullest, most holier-than-thou sermon ever, Grandpa's would have been right up there. The theme itself was relatable enough – the ups and downs of family life. Or more precisely, the pain, hurt, grief and trauma that kids can inflict on their parents. And judging by all the nodding, the congregation fervently agreed with its sentiments. Not a surprise, perhaps, given an average age of seventy-plus. There was no reference, of course, to the hurt, pain, grief and trauma that parents could inflict on their kids.

Fred could feel Grandpa's stare, boring into him throughout, as if he himself was being blamed for his parents' break-up. If only he could sneak out, like at the theatre. But there was no chance of that. The only escape route was falling asleep, which, with all the antihistamines coursing through his veins, would have been easy enough. But Grandma was a vigilante, and every time his eye-lids started to flicker, he got a dig in the ribs for his troubles.

If god really did exist, Fred thought, why the hell was he torturing him like this?

There were nine around the table for Christmas lunch, most of whom were proper geriatrics, so the central heating was sky-high. By the time the food arrived, Fred was more basted than the turkey. In a desperate attempt to conjure another allergic reaction, he tried to coax Bob Marley onto his lap, but the furry bastard refused to play ball.

As for the chat – *Thelma and Lewis* sparkled by comparison. And half way through, the torture reached a whole new level when out of the blue, without previously exchanging a word, the deacon's wife leaned across the table, and in a surprisingly loud and disinhibited voice, asked Fred if he practised safe sex.

The room was plunged into silence.

'He's fifteen dear,' the deacon piped up eventually.

'Don't be naive Ifan,' the woman cackled. 'They're all at it these days. He'll have had more sex than you. Though that won't be hard. Who *is* he anyway?'

'I told you Megan. He's Linval's grandson. Ally's boy. You remember Ally?'

Megan frowned as she rummaged through her derelict memory bank. Then brightened.

'D'you mean the one in all the papers? The one who nearly brought the Baptist Union to its knees? Haha! Of course I remember Ally.'

At first Fred assumed this was just more crazy-talk. But everyone round the table looked shifty, as if she'd somehow struck a chord. The deacon, for his part, was mortified. Ally exploded into a major coughing fit. Grandma looked like she was about to have a seizure.

'The Lord our God is merciful and forgiving,' Grandpa intoned solemnly once Ally had rushed from the room. *'Even though we have rebelled against him.'*

*

'It's a long story,' Ally said as they inched back across the Severn Bridge in her Corsa. 'And not one I'm particularly proud of.'

Fred glanced out at the boxing day traffic. 'I think we've got time Mum. And you definitely owe me.'

Ally sighed and put Aretha on mute.

'Fair enough. Well I was seventeen at the time. Grandma and Grandpa were away at a retreat, and I was home alone. Looking after Marcus Garvey and revising for my mocks.' She paused, as if dredging up something painful. 'But I was also seeing… this boy. On the quiet.'

'Why on the quiet? You were *seventeen*.'

'Sure, but Puppa was strict. Very strict. And *very* protective. If Brian had been a Baptist it might have been OK. Or Jamaican. But he wasn't either of those things.'

'*Brian?*'

'Yes.'

'What was he then?'

Ally hesitated before confessing: 'A punk.'

'A punk?'

'Yes. With a pink mohican.'

'Ah!'

'And lead singer in a band called The Antichrist.'

'You're kidding, right?'

'I wish I was.'

'Wow! I can see why Grandpa might not have approved.'

'If I'm honest – that was the main incentive. Maybe even the only one at the time. Anyway, it was a Friday evening and the band had been booked to do their first ever gig – in Maidstone – an hour's drive away. They were meant to be travelling in the drummer's camper van, except he couldn't get the old banger to start and they didn't have the money for a taxi. So Brian asked if they could borrow Puppa's car. Actually he didn't *ask*, he *pleaded*.'

'Awkward! What did you say?'

'Obviously I said no! If Puppa found out I'd lent his precious Mondeo Estate to The Antichrist…'

'…there'd have been hell to pay!'

'Exactly. Although in spite of the name and the haircuts, they were a perfectly nice bunch of lads. And they were distraught, poor things. The drummer himself was in tears. So eventually I gave in…'

Fred looked at her, incredulous.

'…on one condition,' she continued.

'What was that?'

'That they took me with.'

'Ha! My mum – the Antichrist's groupie! Were they any good?'

'They were very… *loud*. But the gig went well. *Too* well in fact. By the end they were totally hammered. All of them. The drummer could hardly *walk* let alone drive.'

'So you had to abandon the car?'

'We couldn't. Mumma and Puppa were due back in the morning.'

'Shit.'

'So I had to drive. There was no alternative.'

'Had you passed your test?'

Ally looked deeply uncomfortable. 'I'd had some lessons,' she said, 'and I felt pretty confident.'

'But the test?'

'Erm, no. I hadn't taken it yet.'

'Jesus Mum!'

'I did say I wasn't proud.'

'Did you get back in one piece?'

'Well it was very late and we got horribly lost. But we eventually made it back to Catford, yes.'

'Phew!'

'Except… the story doesn't quite end there.'

Large drops of rain were starting to blob on the windscreen. Ally flicked on the wipers and snatched a sidelong glance at Freddie.

'Go on,' he said. 'I'm listening.'

'OK.' She took another deep breath. 'Well the guys were all squashed in the back like sardines, and the idiot drummer – I forget his name – had his legs stuck out of the window. Next thing I know, there's a blue light flashing behind us. And I suppose I must have panicked.'

'Driving without a licence? I'm not surprised.'

'It wasn't just that. I'd… had a couple of drinks too.'

'Oh my god. What did you do?'

'The stupidest thing I've ever done in my life. I tried to shake them off.'

'*Bloody hell Mum!* I thought graffiti'ing the science block wall was bad!'

'Like I said. We all make mistakes.'

'So what happened?'

'Well back in those days, Puppa's church had a carpark behind it. For some reason I thought it would be a good idea to pop the car in there until the police gave up. But it was dark and wet and... you know the side of the church where the wall juts out? Well I took it a bit too tightly.'

'No!'

Ally nodded gravely.

'You crashed Grandpa's car. Into his own church?'

She nodded again.

'Was anyone hurt?'

'A few bumps and bruises – nothing serious. Although the car was a write off. The police heard the crash and followed us in, sirens blaring. I was breathalysed and they threw the book at me.'

'Which book?'

'A hefty fine and three months community service. Only it was worse than that. Because one of the locals raced out in his dressing gown – with a camera. And a few days later it was all over the papers. A minister's daughter being led away from his own church in handcuffs. The Antichrist wrenching drums and guitars out of his smashed up car. A boy with a pink mohican being sick beside a *Jesus Saves* poster.'

'What did he say?'

'Grandpa? It was the only time I ever heard him swear. He was angry for weeks. *So* angry, Mumma said, it nearly cost them their marriage. I was grounded till I made it to Uni. And banned from seeing Brian again. It was also the last time I ever touched a drop of alcohol. Though to be fair, that was *my* decision.'

Fred looked at her, utterly gobsmacked.

Ally shrugged. 'Show me an adult who never did something wild in their youth and I'll show you a boring old fart. Or a liar!'

She smiled and unmuted Aretha.

Respect indeed*!*

CHAPTER 13

FIRST MOVES

The words 'Alex Feinstein' neatly penned on an envelope in Ally's elegant handwriting, would have once made his heart skip a beat. And it had the same effect today, for different reasons. As if to illustrate the point, a week's worth of dirty cereal bowls tumbled from his grasp as he stooped to grab the letter from the doormat. His hands were trembling, even before he clocked the words '*Without Prejudice*' at the top of the preternaturally tidy blue missive. Here it was. Five days into the new year, the Basildon Bombshell. Leaving a small puddle of porridge congealing on the hall carpet, Alex headed off to the kitchen to read it.

Dear Alex

It's now over six weeks since we split, and high time we re-organised our lives in a more balanced manner.

As I'm sure you'll agree, it's completely unfair that I'm banished from my home, isolated from my son, and forced to move into the box-room of my parents' bungalow. Let's be honest, quite aside from my own privations, Freddie is at a vulnerable age. Your relationship with him is parlous to say the least, and I think you'll agree that he still needs his mum. What's more, as you rarely work these days, your contention that our home is now your office and that moving out would be detrimental to your livelihood – is entirely spurious.

I still hold out hope that at some point in the future we may be able to mend bridges, but for the time being, it's obvious that we are incapable of living together. So I am formally requesting that you find alternative accommodation within the next two weeks, to allow me to move back in. You will of course still have access to Freddie whenever he's happy to see you. And in an attempt to preserve lines of communication, I would be happy to arrange a family dinner once a week, as a gesture of goodwill.

I have taken legal advice on this, and if you don't agree to these entirely reasonable requests, I shall have no alternative but to file for divorce. In that eventuality, we would be forced to sell the house, so none of us would be living in it. Which, I'm sure you'll agree, would be far more 'final' than any of us might want at this stage?

Please think carefully about this Alex and try not to allow your calm, considered and rational side to be ambushed by your righteous indignation.

Ally x

Alex stared incredulously at the letter. Surely a relationship counsellor worth her salt would know that if there was one thing guaranteed to provoke a person's *righteous indignation*, it was being warned against expressing it. So Alex decided to defy his natural aversion to confrontation and type his response straight away, whilst his *righteous indignation* was fully revved up. Popping his own *Without Prejudice* at the top for good measure.

Dear Ally

Thank you for your letter and the warm sentiments expressed – namely that I'd be welcome to eat in my own home once a week and see my own son whenever he deigns to grant me an audience. How comforting. I feel I need to remind you that the decision to separate was, and still is, unilaterally yours. As far as I'm concerned, you are welcome to move back in whenever you like. More than welcome in fact. In spite of your 'entirely reasonable' stance on this matter – not to mention my own 'righteous indignation' – I really miss you and still really want you back in my life. The door is always open (and even when it's closed, you have the key!) But if you genuinely can't bear to share a roof with me, then I'm afraid I genuinely can't see an alternative beyond continuing as we are.

Of course I understand that living with your parents is no picnic. But imagine how much worse it would be for me if I moved in with my mother. At least you don't risk food-poisoning every time you sit down!

Nor, FYI, do I intend to rent a squalid bedsit in some run-down neighbourhood. And yet the bitter truth is that if I'm going to keep shelling out on our mortgage, health insurance, cars and living expenses, not to mention the small matter of Freddie's school fees – then a squalid bedsit is all I could afford. The only other viable option, would be to take Freddie out of school and stick him in the local comp. I'm fine with that in principle – but the run up to his GCSE's is probably not the ideal time to switch.

In summary, I'm afraid I have zero intention of moving out. If you persist in insisting – then sadly I have no alternative but to respond with that tired old cliché... 'I'll see you in court'.

Alex x

To be fair, Fred's education was mainly paid for out of money his grandfather had left in trust. Which, because he was a minor, had been put in Alex's name. But most of that had gone towards the purchase of their home, so the same principle applied, and Ally knew it.

In any case it was several days before Alex got a response, and again, it wasn't what he was expecting. Instead of the lawyer's letter, it came in the form of a barrage of calls and messages from mutual friends – 'caring but objective' voices who claimed to have the family's best interests at heart. All of them employing their own personal tactics to prod, urge, coax and cajole him into '*seeing reason*'. The only people who Ally hadn't press-ganged, it seemed, were Miriam (a lost cause); Joe (too immersed in his own pursuits to join a pressure group) and Fred (who ruled himself out for obvious reasons).

During the first few conversations, Alex was politeness personified. Channelling the very best version of himself, after all, was a subtle and effective way of demonstrating Ally's unreasonableness. But by the time he got the call from his father-in-law, his patience was shot to pieces. To be fair, he wasn't proud of telling an ageing Baptist minister to get stuffed, especially whilst trying to persuade him that Ally's point of view was utterly unfounded. On the plus side, any future interaction with the sanctimonious old prig would now be minimal. And if a reconciliation with Ally became less tenable as a result, so be it.

*

'Wow!' Joe exclaimed, decadently flicking a pistachio shell into the roaring log-fire. 'I know everyone gets divorced these days, but I really thought you and Al would buck the trend.'

He was reclining on a chaise longue in Bertie's cosiest snug, like one of the sultans in his harem mural. Alex was perched rather more stiffly on a Louis XVI lyre-backed chair, clearly not chosen for its comfort. And the same could be said of the blue double-breasted suit he was wearing, originally bought for his wedding when he was considerably leaner and fitter. On the plus side, there was no problem signing him in this time.

'Anyway, I don't want to spend all evening discussing my break-up,' Alex said, harpooning an olive and popping it into his mouth. 'How's it going with the swimwear model? Betty wasn't it? Or Bethany?'

'Betsy.'

'Betsy, that's it.'

Joe casually flicked another shell into the fire. 'Betsy's toast.'

'Oh dear. What went wrong?'

He shrugged insouciantly. 'Nothing lasts forever.'

'That's a shame. I was looking forward to meeting her.'

'I can give you her number if you like. You never know, she might welcome the safer, older model.'

'Nah, you're alright.'

Joe glanced up as the barman arrived with reinforcements.

'Grazie mille Luigi!' he said.

'Prego Signor Feinstein.'

Alex raised his Bloody Mary. 'Here's to old, free and single then!'

Joe snickered and lobbed another husk on the fire. 'So… what was it you wanted to talk about bro?'

Alex sucked hard on the straw, then dabbed his mouth with the napkin. He still hadn't talked to Joe about Fred and the science block wall. But right now he had other things on his mind.

'I was hoping for some advice. About dating.'

*

They'd met at the school disco. Or rather, *almost* met. She'd spotted him from afar, perched on the sill, mean and moody in his Sex Pistols T shirt. Dead ringer for Poldark, she'd thought, with his black curly hair and high cheekbones. Except with lovely chestnut brown skin. And she was on her way over to ask him to dance, when out of nowhere, Chanel Fairfax jumped the queue.

It had taken nearly three weeks to forgive him. But on New Year's Day Fred got a text asking if he fancied meeting up. He had no idea who she was. And anyway, what kind of name was *Viola*? But he couldn't pretend he wasn't slightly intrigued. Not to mention a little bit flattered.

Viola – or Vi – wasn't beautiful exactly, or even pretty, but there was definitely *something* about her. She had big eyes, a big face and big hair that she called cranberry blonde. And a big brain too, from what he could tell. In fact Mikey's cousin, who was in her maths set, reckoned she was a genuine egghead. Not that Fred was looking for an algebra buddy, but he couldn't deny he found a high IQ sexy.

So on the last day of the school holidays, they'd met in the park for a waffle – her shout. Fred went for the *nothing-fazes-me* vibe he'd been working on for a while, and it seemed to be going OK – although underneath, to be fair, he was bricking it. This was, after all, his first-ever first-date. So, he decided to follow his mum's advice, and let Vi make the first move. She seemed on the verge of it too, when her waffle collapsed, covering her in whipped cream and syrup. And that put her right off her stride.

A few days later, they met up after school for a coffee at Starbucks. They were both more relaxed this time, but again, nothing happened. It didn't help that Mikey and his mum were sat at a nearby table. Mikey was wearing a surgical boot, having spent all day in A & E after 'some bastard' had broken his toe. And unfortunately that bastard was Fred. It was a perfectly innocent tackle of course, but Mikey's mum didn't see it like that – judging by the evils coming Fred's way through her tortoiseshell glasses.

Still, none of this seemed to put Vi off. Because the next day Fred got a text to see if he was up for a walk.

It was nearly dark when they met, and so cold they could see their own breath. On the plus side, Vi looked older and cuter with her mascara and lippie.

'Suits you better than whipped cream and syrup,' he joked.

'Maybe,' she said, 'although it doesn't *taste* as good.'

While they circled the pond talking shizzle, it occurred to Fred that since *she'd* asked *him* out, she'd sort of ticked the consent box already. So maybe it was up to *him* to make the first move. But what *kind* of move should he make? Slide a sly hand into hers? Hook a nervous arm round her waist? Or go straight in for a big fat kiss? There was no playbook for this kind of thing. And nothing on YouTube or TikTok. So how were you meant to know what to do?

Vi put him out of his misery. 'I've been thinking,' she said. 'Shall we have sex?'

*

'At fucking last!' Joe cried. 'Welcome to my world!'

Dating was, after all, Joe's specialist subject. He settled back on the chaise-longue and launched into a detailed overview, listing the wealth of websites on offer, describing their characteristics and demographics, outlining how to write impactful messages, decoding user-names and buzzwords, extolling the virtues of singles nights, explaining the importance of tactics.

'Just don't be too keen bro,' he said. 'Women like their men to be enigmatic, mysterious and hard to pin down!'

'So... if I *were* to dip my toe in the water,' Alex chipped in as he paused to draw breath and wet his whistle, 'which site do you think I should try?'

'Your *toe*? I had no idea that was your thing. But no worries, there's an entire website for foot fetishists.'

'Very funny!'

'I dunno man. Tinder. Grinder. SugarDaddy.com. All depends on what you're into. I don't have a type as you know. But if you want a well-read, left-of-centre, socially-aware career-woman like Ally, then Soulmates is the one for you. Or else if your tastes have changed and you now have a thing for heels, Botox, labradors and kids at boarding school – try Encounters. Or sign up to both for three months. It won't break the bank.'

For Alex, the prospect of finding a new partner felt unnatural enough, even without an algorithm. But perhaps it would somehow lessen the pain of losing the woman who until a few weeks ago, he'd always thought of as his *own* soulmate. He grabbed a biro from his rucksack to make some notes on a napkin. But the bloody thing was out of ink.

Joe plumbed the inside pocket of his black Nehru jacket and produced a sleek blue ballpoint.

'Cheers,' Alex said. 'OK.... so... Encounters and Soulmates...'

As he jotted them down, he noticed a name and crest embossed on the side of Joe's pen.

'Ha! That's amazing!'

'What is?'

'La Sanctaire Hotel, Corsica. I've stayed there!'

'Oh really?'

Now it was Joe's turn to look uncomfortable.

'You never told me you'd been to Corsica?' Alex said.

'I haven't.'

'So... who did you nick this from then?'

'I dunno. Could have been Betsy,' Joe shrugged. 'Ah well, she'll be happy it's found a good home!'

Joe's explanation would have been entirely plausible but for one tiny detail. La Sanctaire, a small converted olive press near Calvi, had first opened its mahogany portals a few months before Alex and Ally had stayed there. Fred would have been about nine at the time, and they'd farmed him out with Ally's parents. The first – and until that ill-fated weekend in Kent – the last time they'd been away without him. It was a beautiful place which, less than a month after they left, was burnt to a cinder by Corsican separatists. Unsurprisingly, its Parisian owner promptly removed all her investments from the island. Which made a branded pen like this as rare as a Dropa stone. Ally kept hers neatly sheathed in the old leather pouch of the mini-Filofax she still used. So it seemed far more likely that this belonged to her, as opposed to 'Betsy' who may or may not have visited Corsica several years after La Sanctaire ceased to exist.

Alex pondered all this for a moment. Joe was wearing Ally's favourite scent and carrying her pen. Yet he'd studiously avoided any mention of having seen her. So it was hard to avoid the obvious conclusion. He tried to blot it out of his mind, but grotesque, fractured images of Joe and Ally acting out the Karma Sutra on Joe's altar-table were already violating his consciousness.

His wife and his fucking brother.

How long had it been going on? Who seduced whom? How could a woman with 'integrity' and 'principles' – the daughter of a Baptist minister no less – accept Joe's total disregard for all the values she claimed to espouse?

Alex could feel that *righteous indignation* burning inside him like magma. He drew hard on the straw, preparing himself for a showdown – when Joe's phone pinged.

'Shit!' he cried, leaping to his feet. 'Sorry dude. Gotta run.'

'Why? What's happened?'

'I completely forgot. I have a… date of my own. She's outside my flat now.' He signalled across to the barman. 'Mettilo sul mio conto Luigi!'

'Certo signore,' the barman replied.

Outside the club, when they'd said their goodbyes, Joe folded his tall slim frame, like a Brompton, into his bright red Mustang, and revved off into the night.

Quite why Alex should want to inflict even more torment on himself now, he had no idea. Perhaps the monster you could see was easier to handle than the one you couldn't? Whatever the reason, he felt a sudden unassailable need for certainty.

*

Should we have sex?

A question like that undoubtedly deserved some kind of drum-roll, but Vi dropped it into their conversation like she was suggesting a spin on the roundabout.

'Sure,' Fred replied, trying to match her for matter-of-factness. 'Like, when did you have in mind?'

In a year or so, when it's legal, was the response he half expected. Half hoped for even.

'How about now?' was the one he got. 'I've brought these so we're all set.'

Vi rummaged around in her satchel and pulled out a packet of multi-coloured condoms.

Fred had never imagined his first ever shag to take

place in a park, and to be honest, he wasn't all that up for it. No-one could accuse him of being a woos or a snowflake. He didn't need soft lighting or a well-sprung mattress. It's just that… it was pretty exposed out there. What if someone caught them at it? Couldn't they arrest you for that sort of thing? What if a dog came snuffling around? Worst still, what if he couldn't get a hard on? This wasn't like being alone in his room with his laptop. And someone he hardly knew – someone he hadn't even snogged – how could he expect *her* to know what to do?

'They lock the gates at five thirty,' he said, trying to make this sound like an insurmountable problem, as opposed to the perfect excuse.

Vi checked her watch. 'That gives us twenty three minutes,' she said.

Twenty three minutes? Was that enough? Some of the scenes on Pornhub went on for like, hours. Although Mikey said they got paid by the minute on there, with a back-up team of fluffers, first-aiders and physios to help keep them going. Even so, twenty three minutes from a not-yet-standing start? It did sound indecently quick.

'If they lock us in we'll just jump the railings,' Vi grinned. 'I'm a wicked climber.'

'But… what if… my crew shows up?' Fred babbled, ditching the *nothing-fazes-me* vibe altogether. 'We'd be all over social like a rash.'

Vi's grin slowly ebbed away.

'OK no worries,' she shrugged, popping the condoms back in her satchel. 'You're right, it's a rubbish idea.'

'Ah, no, don't be like that!' Fred pleaded. 'It's not a rubbish idea.'

Before he knew it he was holding her hand. Or more accurately, her thick woolly mitten. And it felt good to be *almost* connected.

'I'd love to have sex with you Vi,' he said, with a candour that shocked even him. 'Just… not in a park. Because… well… it's cold and muddy. And it's about to rain.'

Vi's big green eyes were dancing again. And her bright red lips were curling up at the corners, moving slowly, unswervingly, towards Fred's.

So they kissed – a full-blooded no-holds-barred deep-dive – and it felt *amazing*. And when they did finally come up for air, everything seemed… somehow different. Like he'd finally gained access to a club he'd spent years on the waiting-list for.

'Let's go back to mine,' he whispered, nuzzling her neck. 'I've got a free yard.'

Which was true, because his dad had SMS'd to say he was off for a drink with Uncle Joe.

But Vi shook her head.

'Why not?' Fred asked.

'I dunno,' she said. 'I just… wouldn't feel comfortable.'

Comfortable? Gimme a break, Fred thought. His room was a darn sight more comfortable than a bloody park.

There again, he knew exactly why she'd said it. Still super salty about his foot, Mikey had gone round telling anyone who'd listen – including his cousin – that Fred's dad was a psycho. And that no house-guest was safe now his mum had moved out. Fred knew it was crazy. His dad was a lot of things, but a psycho wasn't one of them. From the look on her face though, Vi had made up her mind.

'How about yours then?' he said.

'No chance. I share a room with my sis.'

'OK.' He grabbed Vi's mittened hand and led her briskly off towards the park gates. 'I have an idea!'

CHAPTER 14

REVERSE COWBOY

The first thing Alex noticed as his Uber rounded the corner, was the navy blue Corsa parked behind Joe's Mustang. It had a visitor's permit in the windscreen and (just in case he was still in any doubt) that little extravagance he'd bought Ally for her landmark birthday – the '*AF 50*' reg plate.

Rather less familiar was the sudden surge of something uncontrollable welling up inside him. Whatever it was – outrage? jealousy? hatred? – Alex felt an instant, visceral urge to express it, and his fingers spontaneously tightened around the keys in his pocket. And then he remembered that Ally's motor insurance was still in *his* name, so if he *did* key her car, *he'd* be the one paying the excess. What's more, as crimes of passion went, it was pretty pathetic.

Yes, he could do better than that. Far better.

As he climbed out of the Uber and stood in the shadows of an overhanging plane tree, Alex noticed two other things. The first was a silhouette, moving around in the flickering candle-light of the penthouse flat. The second was that all five floors of the building's white stucco facade were covered in scaffolding – daring him, goading him almost, to take retribution.

Five floors of scaffolding was a daunting prospect for a man of a certain age who suffered from vertigo not to mention a life-long aversion to risk. Especially at night. But the rage burning inside him – and those industrial strength Bloody Marys – made almost anything possible. So, with scant regard for his well-earned reputation as a safe pair of hands, Alex stepped briskly out of the shadows, hopped onto the low wall, reached up for the rail and jumped.

For several seconds he was suspended mid-air – every muscle straining, every sinew stretched. Then, with a bionic thrust that threatened to burst every blood-vessel in his face, not to mention the buttons on his double-breasted suit, he raised his knees to his chest and swung – first one leg, then the other – onto the wooden decking. As he lay there inert, hyperventilating, body in shock, he could sense someone moving directly below him.

He peered gingerly over the edge to see a very small dog doing a very large poo on the pavement. An old lady in a blue plastic rain-hat stood beside it, mumbling words of encouragement. Job done, she stooped arthritically to scoop up the deposit, painstakingly enclosing it in a green plastic bag, before tottering on.

The first floor facade was bathed in an eerie glow from the red nightlight attached to a scaffold tube. Alex scrambled unsteadily to his feet, edged stealthily towards a steel ladder at the end of the platform, and clambered up.

There were peels of raucous laughter coming from the flat on the second level, and he could just make out four people having dinner through one of the windows. He dropped onto his stomach, commando-style, and crawled to the ladder at the other end. His wedding suit would be ruined, but so what? In a funny kind of way that felt somehow right.

He had no idea what he'd do once he'd reached the top. It would be hard to control his emotions if he caught them in flagrante. In fact the very thought made him sick to the stomach. But if he could keep his cool, stay out of sight, and record it through the window on his iPhone – who knows? It might even help in the fight for Fein Mess.

Even if adultery was not a 'crime' per se, a court of law couldn't ignore it – and nor would Linval. Regardless of how he might feel about a lapsed Jewish son-in-law who'd told him to get stuffed. For his own daughter to transgress with the very man who'd blasphemed at his grandson's blessing? Her *brother-in-law* no less? It would surely be excommunication at best.

By the time Alex reached level four, the threatening clouds were finally dumping their payload. And the Bloody Marys were taking their toll on his bladder.

But the fourth floor flat was dark and the wooden deck well shielded from the street. Alex edged over to the wall, unzipped, took aim and fired. The flow was slow but the relief exquisite. He watched in fascination as it dribbled down the white stucco wall, puddled on a plank and drip-dropped through a crack to the floor below. Sure, he'd given Fred and his mates a serious bollocking for doing the very same thing in Mrs Boston's garden. But hey. A world without hypocrisy – as someone once said – would collapse like a house of cards.

Alex stared back at his reflection in the darkened window. His hair was fringed by a halo of red back-light from the night-lamp, and for one insane flash-frame – he was a rockstar, axe in hand, rain sweeping behind him in sheets, crowd cheering his every hip-shake and crotch grab. Until a crack of light inside the room gave way to a baying, snarling creature, like a beast from Hades, baring its teeth and hurling itself at the pane.

Alex had never been known for his bravery around dogs, but he stuck resolutely to the job in hand whilst shooing the little demon away with the other. And then a second angry, red-tinged face loomed into view. He recognised the blue rain-hat in her gnarly hand as her knuckles rapped sharply on the window.

'Get avay you pervert,' she shrieked. 'I am going to call ze police.'

'I'm so sorry,' he shouted, tucking himself back in and hurtling away at a rate of knots. 'I'm not a pervert – I promise. I was just…. aarrghhh!'

Suddenly, the tip of his pointy shoe caught a wooden plank and sent him scudding across the deck. As the unstoppable force of his skull met the immovable object of a scaffold-joint, the pain was both immediate and searing. For a moment there were *two* vicious dogs, *two* outraged old Hausfraus. But with the barking and shrieking at fever-pitch now, and the prospect of the Old Bill hurtling around the corner, sirens blaring, he had no option but to abort. He staggered to his feet and crashed back down the ladders like a fireman on speed.

On terra firma once again, Alex staggered off into the night, as the rain washed rivulets of blood down his face. By the time he made it to Bayswater station, every part of him was drenched. But at least he'd kept his powder dry – for now.

*

Vi was less than enthusiastic when Fred pointed to the Saab. Granted, it wasn't ideal that it was parked in the drive, but its tinted rear windows meant no passing snooper could see in. Plus his dad would be gone for hours, he assured her – and even then he'd be far too pissed to even *think* about driving it. With the rain now coming down in buckets, Vi finally caved.

The bottle of Benedictine that Fred 'liberated' from his dad's booze cupboard certainly helped break the ice. And it was anyway warm as toast beneath the duvet he'd grabbed from his bedroom. In a matter of minutes, even the Saab's *un*-tinted windows had steamed up. Off came the shoes and the mittens and the blazers and the sweaters and the shirts and the trousers and the skirt and the socks.

'*And?*' Vi giggled, mischievously tugging at his red tartan boxers. 'What are *these?*'

'Same as *these*,' Fred parried, pointing to her black bra and pants.

'OK – I'll race you,' she said.

Within seconds her bra was pinging against the windscreen and slithering down to the dashboard. And her pants were swishing against Freddie's face. He yanked off his boxers and flicked them at Vi.

'I win!' she crowed. 'So I get to choose.'

She reached into her packet of condoms and pulled one out.

'Turquoise' she said. 'My favourite colour.'

*

When Alex finally made it back home, it felt like he'd been away hours, although it was only just gone 8.30pm. He could see the light in Fred's window as he opened the gate. He should be able to sneak upstairs unseen, but what if he couldn't? What if they met on the landing? How would he explain the hole in his trousers? The clotted blood in his hair? His resemblance to a half-drowned rat, attacked by bunch of stray cats? How would he act out the role of 'responsible parent' when 'jilted husband' and 'betrayed brother' were the only roles he could play convincingly right now?

The gash on his head felt ugly under his cold wet hand. The blood had congealed, but it was still throbbing like hell. And he had the mother of all headaches. He was definitely in need of some medical attention and with luck, the all-night pharmacy on Brompton Road would provide it. The alcohol would have worn off by now, and a spin in the Saab with the stereo on at full blast was never not therapeutic.

*

There was an online survey last week, Vi said, on women's favourite positions. And *Reverse Cowgirl* came out on top.

So that's where she was now. On top. Steadying herself on a headrest.

'Give it to me cowboy!' she whooped, as the Saab's backseat squeaked like a gate in a hurricane.

Fred found himself thinking about Mrs Boston – hoping to god she had the telly on loud. But those thoughts soon disappeared as he got more and more carried away. And with every squeak and every squawk… with every gasp and every whoop… he was slowly building to the most powerful, the most intense, the most incredible…

'*Fuccccckkkkk!!*'

Viola suddenly nose-dived to the floor, twisting Fred's turquoise joystick into a mutant balloon animal. It was utter agony and he was about to say so, when the driver's door clunked open and a bedraggled figure in a shabby blue suit clambered in, slumped behind the wheel, sighed deeply, flicked on the headlamps and fired up the engine.

The opening chords of The Animals classic on his 60's compilation had the desired effect as Alex reversed out of the drive. By the time he'd hit the Great West Road, Eric Burden's gravelly tones had calmed him right down. It was the perfect stress-buster. Far more effective than meditation or a power-nap – especially whilst driving. Physically, though, he was still a bloody mess. His stomach was in knots, his head was spinning, and there was every chance he had mild concussion. On the far side of the dashboard, for example, lay a dark stringy object that his brain was trying to convert into a bra!

Even more inexplicably, when he hooked it in for closer inspection, it was exactly *that* – a bra – black, lacy and underwired! It certainly didn't look like one of

Ally's and anyway, what would Ally's bra be doing on his dashboard? Far more likely was that, thanks to the broken lock, someone had been using his car as a changing room. There was a peculiar smell in there too. Sweet and herby, like some kind of liqueur.

'... *it's been the ruin of many a poor boy, and God I know I'm one*'.

Burden was growling his heart out now, but the magic had gone. And as they approached Hammersmith roundabout, Alex became increasingly aware of a *presence* behind him. He squinted myopically into the rear-view and a pair of disembodied eyes blinked back at him out of the darkness.

'*WHAT THE FUCK?*'

A taxi lurched alongside, honking its horn. Alex veered back into his own lane, waving the black lacy bra apologetically. The cab window lowered, and a furious face leaned out.

'Fucking maniac!' it yelled, before crashing straight through a red light.

Alex jammed on the brakes and squealed to a halt. Then, dropping the bra onto the seat beside him like a hot potato, he turned to face his demons.

Fred managed a feeble wave. 'Hey Dad.'

Vi heaved herself back on the seat, covering herself with the duvet.

'Hello Mr Feinstein,' she said. 'Nice to meet you.'

No twenty-first century dad wanted to be seen as an old fart. Alex certainly didn't. But sex in his car was *not OK*. In fact, given Fred's age – and presumably the girl's too – sex *anywhere* was not OK. Wasn't it statutory rape or something, even if it *was* consensual? As a responsible parent, Alex knew it was his duty to point this out – or at least ensure they took necessary precautions. As it happens, Eric Burden himself was urging him to tell his children 'not to do what I have done.'

In his current debilitated state though, the only precaution Alex felt able to invoke, was that they put their seatbelts on please.

CHAPTER 15

AMOROUS INTENT

Fred's 'peccadillo' – or whatever the hell he wanted to call it – did at least have some positives. That's what Alex told himself anyway once the dust had settled. It was, after all, an important milestone in any teenager's personal development. Of course it was still incumbent on him as a dad to take him to task, but that would have to wait. Because all he could think about at the moment was Ally and Joe.

What he couldn't get his head around, was how did it happen? What on earth could have drawn her to a man who embodied all the things in life she couldn't abide? A womaniser, a stoner, a narcissist with little or no respect for the law – or *anything* beyond his own self-gratification. And so *what* if he oozed sex-appeal? She was hardly the most highly-sexed woman on the planet these days. Nor had she *ever* been the kind of woman to swoon at a man's feet, however devastatingly attractive he might have been.

Perhaps it was a kind of release. Her own little act of defiance. Maybe the strait-jacket of a strict Baptist upbringing, together with the pressures of motherhood and a job that demanded exemplary behaviour at all times, had finally got the better of her. Perhaps the forbidden fruit represented some a kind of liberation.

Of course, he could destroy her professional reputation at a stroke if he wanted to. But how would making *Ally* feel worse make *him* feel better? Forcing her to face up to her guilt might be a better approach. Only, what if she didn't *feel* guilty? He'd merely be fuelling his own misery. And there was every chance it could get messy with Joe. Seriously messy. The fact they were brothers was completely irrelevant. So were Cain and Abel. And neither of *them* had a coke-habit.

*

'*Embarrassing*? For fuck's sake Fred, it was far worse than *that*,' Vi sobbed when he called the next day to apologise. 'I trusted you. And you just, like, totally abused my trust. All you bloody cared about was getting your end away.'

'If that was true,' Fred protested, 'we'd have done it right there in the bloody park!'

'We *should've* done it right there in the bloody park,' she screeched. 'Mikey was right. Your dad *is* a psycho. And a lech. And on top of that – he stinks.'

Fred couldn't argue with the last one. But that was hardly *his* fault. And how was *he* to know his dad would come back early from a night out with Uncle Joe? He wasn't bloody Nostradamus.

'Well at least you got a lift home!' he pointed out, trying to take the sting out of his first lovers' tiff.

And he managed it too, in a manner of speaking. Because there was a very long silence – and then the phone went dead.

*

A few days after his own world fell apart, Alex was in his dressing-gown, half-listening to a radio debate about the destruction of everyone else's, when the doorbell rang.

It wasn't the ab roller and resistance bands he'd ordered off Amazon to counteract his increasingly sedentary lifestyle.

It was Ally.

'I know I could've let myself in,' she said, brandishing the front door key, 'but I worried I'd give you a shock.'

It was already a shock just to see her there on the doorstep. And even more of a shock that, in spite of everything, his heart did a somersault when he spotted the suitcase beside her.

'I called several times,' she added, 'but you didn't pick up. And as I took the morning off work, I thought I'd come anyway.'

Of course he'd rejected her calls. Acting as if everything was normal, was well beyond his capabilities. And yet to see her standing in the porch, her smile lighting up the hallway for the first time in weeks, made him feel totally euphoric. If he'd been a dog, his tail would be wagging so much it would probably have fallen off. How mad was that?

'I bought Fred some trainers,' she went on, holding up a JD Sports bag. 'Also, I need to pick up a few bits and pieces.' She pointed to her suitcase. 'OK to come in?'

Alex's invisible tail-wag was swiftly replaced by a silent howl of disappointment.

'Sure,' he said, stepping aside to let her pass, then retreating to the kitchen.

For a few minutes, the radio discussion and the threat of universal extinction, felt strangely consoling. And then, out of nowhere, a tsunami of *righteous indignation* swept him out into the hall, propelling him upstairs.

When he barrelled into the bedroom, Ally was by the open wardrobe, adding another dress to the three already draped over her arm. She swung round, startled.

'Oh yeah – he'll like that one,' Alex snarked.

'I'm sorry?'

'Purple. It's his favourite colour.'

Ally's eyes narrowed. Puzzled or panicked – he couldn't tell which.

On the wall behind her, there was a photo of the two of them by the banks of the Seine, the day he'd proposed. Ally in a beret. Alex in a necklace of onions. Both wreathed in smiles. How times had changed.

'Do I have to spell it out?' he asked.

'I'm afraid you do,' she said coldly.

'OK. Let's just say – *I know.*'

'You know *what*?'

'About you and Joe.'

Before he met Ally, Alex had always imagined that one of the benefits of black skin, along with requiring less sunscreen, was that no-one would know you were blushing. That honky hypothesis had been disproved many times over the years, but never more so than now. Ally's face, normally a rich mahogany, had flushed the colour of his dressing gown – a deep maroon. And yet she wasn't going down without a fight.

'Not for the first time in your life, Alex,' she said scornfully, 'you've put two and two together and made nine hundred and forty six.'

'OK. So why don't you set me straight?'

He lowered himself onto the corner of his bed. *Their* bed. One half unslept in, the other more Tracey Emin. A graphic commentary, if ever one was needed, on the state of their marriage.

'I'm not even going to flatter that insane allegation with a denial,' she seethed, scrunching up her dresses and tossing them into the open suitcase. 'I actually find it incredibly offensive.'

'*Offensive?* You know what *I* find offensive? Spending twenty-four years with a woman I *thought* was decent and principled, and then finding out that I couldn't have been more wrong. I saw your car outside his flat the other night.'

Ally stood there motionless, poker-faced, doubtless deciding whether to fold or raise.

'As it happens,' she said finally with a sangfroid that took him by surprise. 'I was there for entirely professional reasons.'

'Ha! Counselling? At his own home? Surely you can come up with something better than that?'

'Who said anything about counselling?'

'Oh... so... what? He's teaching you how to paint?'

'I don't need to explain myself to you Alex. Apart from anything else, different rules apply when couples split. But as a matter of fact, Joe's doing some work for my charity.'

'*Joe?* Give me a break! He's never done anything charitable in his entire life.'

'I didn't say he was doing it for free. You're welcome to check it out if you don't believe me. In the meantime, if you don't mind, the sooner I finish packing, the quicker I'll be out of your hair.'

*

After a flood of unanswered texts, calls and FB messages, it was clear to Fred he'd been *cancelled*. Somewhat less clear was why, a week to the day after their disastrous date, he'd decided to revisit the park, and trudge round the pond with *Blinded by your Grace* on repeat.

It did nothing whatsoever to cheer him up, of course. And nor did those weird noises he could hear as he skirted the playground. At first he put it down to some kind of interference on Spotify. But when he took off his cans the noises got louder. Muffled whimpers, like an animal in distress. And now, as he peered hard into the gloom, he could see a strange lumpen shape moving around on the roundabout, which, as his eyes adjusted, turned into two people, snogging each other's faces off. A girl with big hair and a blazer. And her partner wearing… Jesus Christ… a surgical boot!

Fred was beyond horrified. To be dissed, dumped, cancelled and cheated-on straight after his first ever first date – felt properly rubbish. Part of him wanted to race over and beat the crap out of both of them. Instead, he rushed to the gates, barely fighting back tears.

*

The mural was, frankly, spectacular. There was no other word for it. A vibrant montage featuring people of all ages, colours and creeds – baggage balanced on their heads or under their arms, misery etched on their faces, trudging towards a Big Ben that glowed like a beacon of hope.

'Do you believe me now?' Ally scoffed.

They were standing in the middle of a tatty old hall with a heavily-stained carpet, tables and chairs stacked around the edges, and a smell of stale beer. Along one wall there was a wooden bar (devoid of its bottles and glasses) while the two on either side boasted a fusion of wood-panels and flock wallpaper – half faded Victoriana – half high-street curry house. But the room's focal point was Joe's magnificent artwork on the wall opposite.

'Why didn't you tell me?' Alex asked.

'I didn't know I had to.'

'OK, why didn't *Joe* tell me? He went out of his way to avoid mentioning it. What's the big secret?'

Ally gently stroked her right eyebrow. 'If you must know, changing the usage from working men's club to refugee centre is upsetting a few of the members. So I've been asked to keep it under wraps until all our loose ends are tied up.'

Alex followed her gaze towards a half open door. A bald-headed man with black rimmed glasses was pacing up and down in a side-office, in the middle of an intense phone-conversation.

'Who's that?' Alex asked.

'Our principle donor,' Ally replied, sotto voce. 'A guy with a big pile of money and an even bigger heart.'

'Does he have a name too?'

'Not one he wants bandied around.'

Right on cue, the guy glanced up, instantly softening as his eyes met Ally's.

'Can I ask you something?' Alex asked as Ally steered him gently towards the exit.

'Sure, go ahead,' she said.

'If there's nothing going on between you and Joe, why have you walked out of our marriage?'

She glanced over her shoulder and lowered her voice again.

'You seem hellbent on casting yourself as the victim in all this, Alex. Do you think it's easy for me? Moving out of my own home? Leaving Freddie. Leaving *you*? You've known me long enough to know I don't take my responsibilities lightly. This is by far the biggest decision of my life. Bigger even, than deciding to get married in the first place. Because this time it's not just you and me who are affected.'

'So why have you done it? All marriages go through peaks and troughs. And I love you.'

She shook her head dolefully. 'We don't connect any more Alex. I accept that's a two-way thing, but believe me I tried. Over and over and over again. It's almost as if your advancing years and your declining career have scooped out all the substance and left me with the shell of the man

I married. I've done my best to big you up. To boost your ego. Bolster your self-esteem. Because god knows all men need that. But it's a lost cause. The only thing that seems to validate you is your work. And now that's dried up – so have you. And you blame everyone for that – except yourself.'

'That's completely unfair.'

'No it's not. We all have faults, but you're incapable of recognising yours. And whenever I've tried to gently point them out, you just push back. Well I've reached the point where more self-sacrifice feels futile. Why should I let you take me down with you? There was no mention of that in our marriage vows.'

She gently opened the door. Alex stood motionless on the threshold for a moment, looking at her in disbelief. Then he shook his head disconsolately, and stepped out onto the bustling high street.

*

He still had nagging doubts about Joe. Yes, it was possible that their meeting was entirely innocent. That the sole purpose of Ally's visit to his flat had been to vet the designs for his mural. That he'd pocketed her pen at a previous encounter. And that the after-shave was a present from Betsy after all.

But in practical terms, it didn't change a thing. The bottom line was – she'd gone. He'd lost her. And in the interests of sanity, he had to find a way to channel his despair. In the past, he'd found solace in hard graft. The day after his dad's funeral, for example, Alex was on set, directing an ad for fabric conditioner. And as some wag wrote on his condolences card – at least it provided some *Comfort*!

This was loss of a different kind though. If anything, his grief was more acute. And with no work this time to soften the blow, the only hope was to create his own diversion. He still had little or no interest in meeting someone else, but perhaps a date would cheer him up? It might even help restore what was left of his battered self-esteem.

The shredded wedding suit was still dangling from a hook on the bedroom door. It was clearly beyond repair, but Alex refused to consign it to the dustbin. The symbolism would have been far too painful. Instead, he reached into a pocket to retrieve the notes he'd jotted down during his last conversation with Joe.

Encounters. Bumble. Soulmates. All Joe's tips felt tainted now. But he did find a website called *Amorous Intent* which quoted plenty of satisfied customers. Alex poured himself a large glass of Merlot and started scrolling through the extensive collection of fifty-somethings. And even to a half-hearted sightseer like him – some were surprisingly attractive. But how could he be certain they weren't airbrushed or photoshopped or ten years out of date? Or of someone else entirely? They could be in their seventies by now.

There again, if he targeted a younger age-group he'd be displaying the very ageist tendencies he despised. Someone who'd been round the block a few times was probably a far better match for him anyway. Someone who'd actually *heard* of Dire Straits. Someone too busy worrying about her crow's feet and grey streaks to notice his rapidly expanding bald patch and waistline.

Either way, to communicate with the likes of *SunnySideUp*, *DomesticGoddess* and *SweetDreamer21*, you had to sign up and pay. But first you had to engage those weapons of mass seduction – a not-too-unflattering photo and a few bon-mots. Before that though, in the interests of due diligence, a sneaky peek at the opposition might be in order. He clicked on the Men-Looking-For-Women page and a pageant of raw masculinity swaggered across the screen. Men with massive motor-bikes. Fast cars. Giant fish. Gargantuan paunches. Spectacular beards. Hideous tattoos. Glittering medallions. Come-hither grins. *'Have some of this darling,'* the unspoken refrain. It was a full-on testosterone-fest which made him feel both inadequate and bilious at the same time.

Perhaps his own understated version of manhood would be regarded by some as a breath of fresh air? There was a photo of him on his laptop, looking tanned and chilled, with Calvi harbour bathed in golden sunshine, working its magic. He uploaded it onto the form, then moved to the bit that asked for a headline. With another large glug of Merlot, he settled for *'Buy now while stocks last!'* Hardly the most original sales pitch – but as a pithy nod to what he did for a living, it felt kind of apt.

Next up you had to choose a 'username'. He plumped for Alan Smithee, the alias directors use when they want to disown their own movie. Not the sexiest, granted, but it amused *him*. And he was the customer, right?

The following section required a little white lie. Or a 'suspension of disbelief', as Alex preferred to see it. To qualify for a slightly lower age bracket, his DOB would need a tweak. He was fifty-three when that Calvi photo was taken, so it seemed the appropriate number to go for.

Finally you had to list the qualities you most admired in a woman. Alex listed all the attributes he could think of, and then realised he'd just described Ally. He promptly deleted them all and typed:

'*Has a pulse*'.

*

'4 – 5 – 6 – 7…'

Mikey had spent the whole week scoring points at Fred's expense and Friday morning was no exception. He was entertaining the lads before art-class, playing keepie-uppie with a ping-pong ball.

'…15 – 16 – 17 – 18…'

Everyone was counting in unison. Everyone that is, except Fred. Sure – keepie-uppie with a surgical boot was no mean feat. But he had no intention of helping to boost Mikey's already inflated ego.

'What about you, Fred? How long can *you* keep it up?'

Callum Jackson's trademark leer confirmed he wasn't talking footie.

'He has no idea,' Mikey sneered. 'His Dad always comes in half-way-through!'

From the eruption of laughter, it was clear the entire class was in on the joke.

'Which is lucky for you,' Fred responded, quick as a flash. 'Or she wouldn't have looked at you twice. Not even playing the disabled card…'

The class bleated 'oooooooh!' – like a flock of pantomime sheep.

'...Unless you paid her of course. And I wouldn't put that past either of you.'

Hoots, hisses and peels of laughter echoed round the studio. The only one *not* laughing was Mikey. He hobbled towards Fred, his face set like concrete.

'*What. Did. You. Say?*'

Fred stood his ground. Surely even Mikey wasn't stupid enough to start a fight in his current condition.

'You heard.'

More whoops. And several voices baying for blood.

'Whack him Mikey!' shrieked a voice from behind. 'Show the mongrel what a pedigree can do!'

As Fred wheeled round to see where that sickening comment had come from, Mikey's knee slammed into his crotch like a piston.

He doubled up, gasping for breath.

A huge cheer rang out and Mikey windmilled, milking the applause like a gameshow host.

But this was no gameshow. It was a declaration of war.

Slowly, painfully, Fred stood up straight. Un-cupped his still throbbing gonads. Wiped the tears from his eyes. And placed the tips of his fingers on Mikey's chest.

Mikey recoiled, tripped and toppled backwards, smashing into an easel – which in turn cannoned into the one behind. Within seconds – six went down like skittles, and Mikey went tumbling after them like a drunken stunt man. There was a piercing scream as he sprawled on the floor with paints, brushes and easels crashing down on top of him.

'Aaargghh – my foot!' he yelled. 'My fucking foot!'

But the foot he was clutching *wasn't* the one in the boot.

*

'Is that Mr Feinstein?'

Alex was busy checking his first set of *Amorous Matches*, but he always answered the phone, even with *No Caller ID*. The freelancer's curse. It was invariably someone offering to help him claim for a recent road accident or PPI. But this time, unusually, the woman at the other end pronounced his name correctly.

'Alex Feinstein, yes.'

An extremely fetching Asian lady – *Living the Dream* – was smiling beguilingly out from the webpage. He placed the phone on speaker, so he could scroll through her profile as he talked.

'I'm calling about your son,' said the voice – its muted, measured tone less than reassuring.

Alex immediately stopped scrolling. 'Freddie? Is he OK?'

He glanced at his watch. It was 5.20pm and Fred wasn't back from school yet, although that was pretty standard these days.

'No,' she replied, after a lengthy pause. 'He's far from OK.'

Her manner was neutral, restrained, as if holding her emotion in check. But if she was trying not to alarm him, it hadn't worked.

'What's happened?'

There was another long ominous silence, and then: 'He's a disgrace, Mr Feinstein,' she said, her restraint now in tatters. 'A total disgrace. And I intend to take the matter to the police.'

'What matter? Who *is* this?'

'I'm Michael Oberman's mother.'

'Oh, hello. I don't think we've…'

'*Shut up!*'

Her brittleness exploded into full-blown Banshee, forcing Alex back in his chair like a bomb blast.

'I'll do the talking if you don't mind! For the second time in three weeks, Michael has spent the day in A & E. The first time he fractured his foot playing football. After a reckless tackle. By your son. And now he's fractured his *other* foot. After a brutal assault. By your son. What kind of monster would attack a disabled child in front of his class-mates?'

'I'm really sorry Mrs Oberman. I can understand you being upset, but…'

'*Upset*? I'm a lot more than upset. I'm hopping mad.'

Alex was half-tempted to try to lighten the mood by cracking the obvious joke, but – wisely – he thought better of it.

'Look – Freddie's not back from school yet,' he said instead, 'but I honestly can't believe he'd do something like that. It's just not in his nature.'

'It obviously *is* in his nature,' she retorted. 'Because twenty-three other boys saw him do it. The simple truth, Mr Feinstein, is that your son is a sociopath. The sooner that's recognised, the safer it will be, for everyone.'

Freddie? A sociopath? No way was he having that.

Adolescent, sure. Gauche, hormonal, volatile, fair enough. But *sociopath*?

'I don't like your tone Mrs Oberman,' he said. 'I know my son and I'm sure there was no malice involved. Whatever the case, it's a slanderous accusation and if you ever repeat it in public, I'll be forced to take legal proceedings.'

'You're clearly in denial Mr Feinstein. Which doesn't altogether surprise me. From everything I've heard, the apple doesn't fall far from the ...'

Alex couldn't press *end call* fast enough. And as he did, another voice piped up behind him.

'Nice one Dad!'

He lunged for the keyboard and managed to minimise *LivingTheDream* a split second before Fred appeared at the study door.

'Oh – hi,' Alex said. 'That was Michael's mother on the phone. Mrs Oberman.'

'I heard,' Freddie said. 'She left off the 'D'.'

'Come again?'

'The 'D'. In doberman.'

Alex was now in no mood for puns. 'How much of what she said is true?'

'Well I don't know much about apples. I'm pretty sure I'm not a sociopath though.'

'I know that. But did you do it?'

'What?'

'Break both Mikey's feet?'

Fred shifted awkwardly on his. 'No. I mean yes. Kind of. But...'

His stuttering defence was cut short by the ping of an incoming email. Alex scanned it in silence.

Dear Mr and Mrs Feinstein

I'm sorry to have to inform you of another significant disciplinary issue involving your son. This morning there was an altercation in the art studio which resulted in Michael Oberman fracturing a bone in his left foot. The incident was witnessed by everyone in 4A, and Freddie has admitted responsibility. This is particularly unfortunate as barely three weeks ago, Michael fractured a bone in his right foot, for which Freddie was also responsible.

The first may have been an accident but there seems little doubt this latest incident was intentional, and I'm afraid the punishment must reflect that. The school has a duty to protect its students, and we take all events of a violent nature very seriously. You should be aware that in view of Freddie's poor disciplinary record, we did in fact consider expulsion. But I understand from other boys that there may have been an element of provocation, and for that reason, I am prepared to reduce his tariff to a week's exclusion.

In consequence, he will not be permitted to return to school until Monday 4th February. Please ensure he is properly supervised during his time away.

Yours sincerely
Dr James Fogerty, Deputy Head

'Do you have any idea what it costs to send you to St Joseph's?' Alex said, inadvertently brushing the lap-top's track pad as he spun round to face his son.

Fred's attention was now fully focussed on the webpage that had just popped up in front of him. 'Why does it always boil down to money?' he said.

Alex was aghast at the impudence. 'Maybe it's because I work my bollocks off to pay the fees?'

Fred jabbed a scornful finger at the screen. 'Is *that* what you call working your bollocks off?'

Alex spun back to see *LivingTheDream* pouting up at him. With lightning speed he slammed the lid shut – but the damage was done. And being caught with a photo of a woman who wasn't Fred's mum felt distinctly uncomfortable. Of course it was a minor transgression compared with what Ally herself might – or might not – have been up to. But Fred didn't know that – and Alex had no intention of telling him.

'OK, let's stick to the matter in hand,' he said, struggling to regain his parental authority. 'Why don't you tell me what happened?'

Fred's grip tightened around the door handle. Considering he and his dad had barely exchanged a sentence in months, opening up now would feel more than weird. At the same time, there was so much emotion bubbling up inside him, he literally couldn't hold it back any longer.

'Viola dumped me,' he said, struggling to make it seem like he didn't give a shit.

'Oh dear,' Alex said. 'I hope that had nothing to do with what happened the other night?'

Fred blinked at him. 'Of course it did.'

'I'm sorry fella,' Alex added, tenderly. 'I truly am.'

It hung there for a moment, the apology, slowly infiltrating Fred's defences. The jaw muscles were going and the bottom lip starting to quiver.

'Jesus Freddie. Come here.'

Fred held back until, without warning, the mask shattered. He collapsed, sobbing, into his father's embrace, and it all spilled out. Everything.

'I'm not having this,' Alex said, taking charge again. 'I'm writing to school to demand they reverse their decision. We're gonna make that little bastard apologise. And we're gonna find out who it was that called you... that word.'

Fred stiffened and pulled away, wiping his eyes with the back of his hand. 'Please don't!'

'Why not?'

Yes, why not? Why should his school-record get mullered over this? Why should Mikey have the last laugh? Why should he put up with a vicious racist slur?

The answer, of course, was that Fred couldn't face seeing *anyone* right now, least of all his so-called 'mates'. But there was a limit to how much vulnerability he was prepared to reveal in one go.

'I've got revision to do,' he sniffed. 'So I'm better off staying at home.'

'I'm sorry Fred. It's a total miscarriage of justice. And as your dad I'm not gonna stand by and...'

'*For fuck's sake Dad – no! This is my life. Why do you have to control it every step of the way?*'

And he thundered out, shaking the house to its very foundations as he slammed the door.

CHAPTER 16

AN EMBARRASSMENT OF RICHES

'His *foot*? If you ask me, dude, cunt got off lightly. I'd have gone for his knee-caps.'

Fred mustered a laugh – his first in days – and burrowed deeper into the bean-bag.

'What's so fucking funny?' Joe snorted. 'Just say the word and I'll sort it. That's what a godfather's for, right?'

'No thanks Unc…Unc…'

'Say again?'

'I meant… no thanks… Joe.'

'So why the fuck are you phoning?'

Fair question. Why the fuck *was* he phoning? Perhaps he'd hoped his exclusion from school would somehow bolster his bad-boy rep and strengthen his bond with his uncle.

'Look on the bright side dude,' Joe continued, in the absence of an answer. 'You've earned yourself a week off school. That's a result in anyone's book. So make the most of it.'

*

Alex was reconciled to the fact that unless you were the Pope or a president, pushing sixty was unlikely to enhance your career. But for a bloke with his own hair and teeth, it was apparently no impediment to online dating. Within hours of pressing send, there was a steady trickle of 'consumers' keen to '*buy now while stocks last*', or at least, check out the merchandise. Within days – an absolute deluge. Women from all walks of life and all parts of the country, with only one purpose in mind.

For Alex, it was fast becoming a full-time occupation. Sifting through photos, profiles and mission-statements; fielding messages; composing responses; adding to his own steadily growing archive of 'favourites'; lobbing nods, winks and short cheeky notes into the ether like flirt-grenades – was certainly an effective way of putting grief to the back of his mind.

Sure he felt bad about Freddie, especially after last week's meltdown. But the less interaction they had these days, the better they seemed to get on. And no-one could accuse him of neglecting his paternal duties. Fred was downstairs in his own space, with smoothies and Cheerios on tap. And, curtesy of Ocado, the kitchen fridge was chock-full of ready-meals. So if as Ally said, encouraging the teenage psyche to feel independent was key, he was being an exemplary dad.

*

Fred tried to take his uncle's advice. To make the most of his week of freedom. But by Monday he was bored. By Tuesday, down in the dumps. And by Wednesday, depressed. He'd had it with *Fortnite,* and he'd had it with Drake and his self-referring bollocks.

On Thursday though, everything changed with a ping.

'*Hey man,*' the SMS read. '*I feel bad I got u in trouble. I was an a-hole. Im at the hospital now – waiting to get my 1st boot removed. Can I pop over later – say sorry? PS – I split up with Vile.*'

*

Things were improving for Alex too. Three hot new contenders had landed in his overnight inbox, all expressing guarded interest. *LipstickFeminist* – a yoga teacher from Gerrard's Cross; *BrownEyedGirl* – a PR exec from Islington; and *MoJo69* – a picture restorer from Camberwell. None would have Ally's charm or grace, he knew that. And yet to his bleary pre-caffeinated peepers, they all looked bloody gorgeous.

How did it work though, he wondered? What was the protocol? Was it OK to flirt with three women at once? Like in house-hunting, say, where you could make offers on as many as you liked until one was accepted? Whatever the case, by Thursday mid-morning, there was a flurry of online banter – with all three.

*

'I'm sorry mate,' Mikey said, lowering himself, gingerly, onto a bean-bag. 'I was a dick and you were right to push back. Peace pipe?' He pulled a ball of resin out of his pocket.

'Cool,' Fred beamed.

After what happened on his birthday, the chances of his dad venturing down to the basement were close to zero. Still, it made sense to be careful. So as Mikey produced some Rizlas and a packet of Silk Cut, Fred opened the outside door for some fresh air, placed a wet towel along the foot of the internal one, and taped a plastic bag over the smoke alarm – like on a YouTube vid he'd once seen.

Then Mikey lit up and the weight of the world lifted from his shoulders.

'Let's do Call of Duty,' Mikey said once they'd sucked the living daylights out of their third blunt and most of their Vile-bile was spent.

'I have a better idea,' Fred said, launching his iPad. 'A far far better idea.'

*

MoJo69 was the first to suggest a proper old-style phone-call and within seconds of exchanging numbers, Alex's ringtone was blaring.

'I thought I'd strike while the iron's hot,' she trilled. 'In case you change your mind. Or *I* do!'

She had a cheerful, upbeat voice and a refreshing sense of frivolity. She was also the first woman Alex had chatted up in nearly quarter of a century. So of course it felt weird. But he was determined to push through.

'There's no risk of that,' he replied. 'Me, changing my mind, I mean.'

Joe would have said this was far too eager. But it didn't put her off.

'So as Paul Simon might say,' she continued, 'can I call you Al?'

Alex explained the Alan Smithee thing and she liked the joke.

'Gimme a creative any day,' she chuckled. 'Far more fun than the banker-wankers I usually meet on this site.'

'Not as well-heeled though, sadly!'

'Lucky for you I'm no gold-digger then!' she laughed.

'You have no idea how true that is! So… how about 'MoJo69'?'

'Well that's less of a mystery. My first name's Maureen and my middle one's Joanna.'

'Ah ha. And the 69?'

'The year of my birth,' she said. 'As well as one of my favourite hobbies!'

'We're kindred spirits then,' Alex said.

Her laughter was intoxicating. 'Shall we meet up and find out?'

'Great,' Alex said, struggling to curb his enthusiasm. 'How about some tapas?'

He'd fully intended to kick things off with a cautious cappuccino or a cheeky glass of Sauvignon. But fuck it, life was short.

'This Sunday? Early evening?'

'You're on,' she said.

'Brilliant. I'll book somewhere between my place and yours and email the deets. I mean details.'

'I know what deets are Mr Smithee! I may not have a teenage son, but I'm not a dinosaur.'

'I'll bear that in mind,' he said.

*

'Is that him?'

'That's him alright! My mum used to have that photo on her desk.'

Having set up a false ID and ticked the over-eighteen box, Fred and Mikey were having a good old rummage around *Amorous Intent.* And sure enough, there was Alex, grinning sleazily out from the new member's section. All orange skin and gleaming teeth.

'So who the hell's Alan Smithee?'

Fred shrugged. 'No-one uses their actual name on these things, do they?'

'"*Buy now while stocks last!*" That's a pretty fucked-up way of selling yourself.'

'Whole thing's fucked-up man,' Fred said. 'He's even taken six years off his age!'

'Ha! I bet he's added three inches to his dick too. Let's have a look.'

'We can't.' Fred pointed to the small print. '*Full access – 40 quid.* That's how they reel you in.'

'Splash the plastic then,' Mikey said. 'If your old man's anything like mine – he'll never notice.'

'My dad notices when a ten pence piece disappears from the back of the sofa. Anyway – I've got a better plan.'

Fred typed *AlanSmithee* into the login page.

Mikey shook his head. 'No chance. The passcode has a minimum of eight characters made up of letters and numbers. That's a billion permutations at least.'

'Don't be so sure,' Fred grinned.

He'd once seen his dad tracking an Amazon delivery, and the first half of his password was FEIN. Why would he bother to change it? The rest would most likely be four numbers with some kind of personal significance.

So Fred tried the year he was born.

The year his dad was born.

The year his mum was born.

The year his mum and dad got married.

The year England won the football world cup.

The rugby world cup.

The second world war.

The battle of Hastings.

'How many goes before they lock you out?' Mikey asked.

'Sky's the limit by the looks,' Fred said, doggedly typing in a quartet of digits from his dad's mobile number.

His mum's mobile number.

His own mobile number.

Their postcode.

'If it was easy they'd all be doing it,' Mikey said helpfully.

'They *are* all doing it,' Fred smiled.

But he was on the verge of giving up when something else popped into his head. 7-6-4-3 were the last four digits of Bubby's landline and – being old school – that's how she still answered her phone. And his dad phoned her every day, so they'd be indelibly etched in his memory.

Sure enough, Alan Smithee's profile opened up like the Enigma code.

'*Yes!*' Fred cried, leaping into the air and landing dangerously close to Mikey's foot.

'Put me in A & E again dude,' Mikey glared, 'and my Mum will cut off your balls with her chicken shears. Just sayin.'

'I'll bear that in mind,' Fred said, as he scanned the impressive collection of nods and winks in the inbox. 'Jesus! Look at this! What do they see in him? He's like – ancient.'

'Yeah, but so are they!' Mikey said. 'And desperate.'

'Maybe they're plants. You know, to push up the numbers?'

Mikey clicked on the chat.

'Haha! Check this out! '*I live with my 15 year old son. Not the easiest housemate in the world but we rub along."*

'Bastard!'

Mikey curled his fingers into a pretend microphone and shoved it towards Fred's mouth. 'So – Frederick,' he pronounced in posh BBC. 'How does it feel to play such a key role in your father's seduction technique?'

'Fuck off!'

They scrolled down to the final entry, timed at… five minutes ago.

'*Sunday 7pm. El Toro. Westbourne Grove.*' Fred grinned. 'Looks like he's got himself a date!'

*

Alex was pleased with his choice of venue. If he was going to grab the bull by the horns, *El Toro* was the perfect place to do it. There were candles on the table, flamenco on the stereo and padrón peppers on the menu. Bring on la corrida!

In truth though, he felt more like a matador with stage-fright, waiting for his first adversary to rampage into the ring, horns akimbo. A lot had changed, after all, since his *last* first date and the quandaries were endless. Should he kiss her when they meet, for example, or would that look predatory? Perhaps shaking hands was a safer option? Does the man still choose the wine, or was it cooler to let her do it? And when the bill came, should they split it, or did that particular privilege remain his?

The wine dilemma was duly sorted when he spotted a card propped up against the olive oil, offering 50% off a bottle of Rioja if ordered before 7pm. It was now 6.58pm, so he quickly hailed the waitress. A bottle was brought over, uncorked and poured – and despite being pretty sure that etiquette still required him to wait until his date arrived – a long soothing glug to calm the nerves was exactly what was needed.

Only it didn't. It just jostled them around a bit, ushering in a fresh set. MoJo69 may have sounded lovely on the phone, but say she had five o'clock shadow and halitosis? What then? And what if she was six inches shorter than advertised, even in heels? Or six inches taller? Or looked nothing like her photo and they failed to recognise each other?

The sudden urge to pee seemed more urgent than usual, but any thoughts of a quick bathroom dash were promptly scuppered by a violent bursting open of the restaurant door. With a fluttering of tablecloths, a guttering of candles and a muttering of diners, a tall elegant woman in a shiny yellow raincoat and wedge shoes, stepped in from the gusting wind and heaved the door shut.

She scanned the room, flashed a smile and strode towards Alex.

'I like a dramatic entrance,' she announced as she reached his table.

'That was more than dramatic,' he said, struggling to his feet, 'it was biblical!'

She popped her bum-bag on the floor and wriggled out of her raincoat, revealing a lithe figure, wrapped in a blue fluffy cardigan and jeans – well-preserved, like the pictures she restored for a living. She draped her coat over the empty chair and plopped down by the window, with Westbourne Grove providing a wild and windy backdrop.

'Looks like I've got some catching up to do!' she said, gesturing to his wine glass.

'Yeah, sorry about that,' he said, hurriedly filling hers. 'I needed a bit of Dutch courage!'

She looked at him, askance. 'Really?'

'I told you I'm out of practice!'

'OK. Well... to Amorous Intent then!' She raised her glass, sipped, swallowed and purred: 'Mmmm. Good choice!'

'Glad you approve,' Alex said, discreetly nudging the '50% off' promo card onto the floor.

She reached across and touched his hand. 'Lovely to meet you Mr Smithee!'

'Lovely to meet you too... Ms 69!'

He liked her already. Was that a bit *previous?* Indiscriminate? Like falling in love with the first house you clapped eyes on? Her manner was so relaxed that his angst quickly disappeared – although the urge to pee was no less acute. And now that a decent amount of time had elapsed, he was ready to excuse himself.

MoJo beat him to it.

'Back in a sec,' she chirruped, retrieving her bum-bag from the floor. 'Would you keep an eye on my coat?'

'Oh... sure,' he said, crossing his legs. 'I'll guard it with my life.'

She grinned and glided towards the Ladies. Alex caught himself discreetly checking the rear-view. Was that acceptable behaviour these days? Either way, he liked what he saw. Who'd have thought, after a lay-off of a quarter of a century, that getting back on the bike would be so straight-forward?

He took a small sip of wine and gazed smugly out of the window to where a woman was wrestling with a large orange umbrella. When she finally brought it under control, she turned and peered in. Their eyes met and she waggled her fingers. Alex glanced round, assuming she was waggling at someone behind him. But all the other diners were minding their own business. And by the time he turned back, she was through the door, furling her brolly and beating a path to his table.

'Hey!' she said brashly, thrusting out a hand.

'Hey,' he said, taking it in his, uncertainly.

'Sorry my paw's a bit damp! There's a tempest out there. How're ya doing?' She was tall, fair and American, with cherry-red lips. 'Gotta say, I don't normally meet a guy without talking first, but since you have an aversion to phones... well... nothing ventured nothing gained, right?'

Aversion?

She was too busy taking off her aviator jacket to notice Alex's bewilderment – but what she did now notice was the yellow raincoat draped over the back of the empty chair. And the second glass of wine on the table. Her big broad smile quickly morphed into an even broader frown.

'Have I got the right night?' she said.

'Erm... I think you might be mistaking me for someone else?'

'Oh. Sorry. Are you not *Alex*?'

'Erm, yes, but...?'

As he was struggling to come to terms with his obvious amnesia, an attractive brunette appeared in his peripheral vision. She too seemed to be making a beeline for his table.

'Sorry I'm late Alex,' she smiled, leaning over and kissing him warmly on both cheeks. 'I just spent ten minutes looking for a parking space. You must've had the same problem, right? Or did you leave the Ferrari at home?'

Ferrari?

Only then did she spot the other woman.

And the yellow raincoat.

And the two glasses of wine.

She was almost as baffled as Alex.

And then the penny dropped. This was *BrownEyedGirl* from the website! Alex glanced across at the American and... *shit!* ... those cherry-red lips! That aviator jacket! This was *LipstickFeminist*! But what the hell were they doing there? He'd only arranged one date with one woman, and that was *MoJo69*. The same *MoJo69* who was now returning from the Ladies, a picture of utter confusion.

As the piped flamenco built to a climax like some specially composed film-score, the background chat faded to a murmur. Every punter on every table was staring at Alex, slack-jawed – like he was a participant in some reality dating show, about to deliver his verdict. In the event, he was in no position to deliver anything other than an abject apology.

'I'm... I'm... so sorry ladies,' he babbled, gazing out of the window in an attempt to avoid eye contact. 'There's obviously been some kind of technical malfunc...'

He broke off, distracted by something in his line of vision.

Outside the pub opposite, two shady figures in hoodies were huddled together on a bench, holding their phones up towards him, convulsing with laughter.

*

Faking his dad's identity on a dating site was *already* the most fun Fred had had since... well, ever. He never imagined that either of the women would actually fall for it. For *both* to show up was insane. Even more insane was that he and Mikey now had a perfect mosh-pit view of the headline act. Only they were laughing so much, it was hard to hold their camera-phones steady.

'*Shit! He's seen us!*' Fred hissed, knocking his lager to the ground as he leapt to his feet. '*Run!*'

By the time Alex made it across the road, dodging a black cab going one way and an old man on a mobility scooter going the other, the two boys had disappeared down a narrow alleyway skirting the side of the pub. It was the ideal escape route – or would have been – had it not been for the surgical boot. When Fred made it to the other end and glanced back, Mikey was flat on his face, groaning, beside a large stack of beer-crates. Fred was about to dart back and drag him out, like in every war-film he'd ever seen, but his father's silhouette was already looming at the entrance.

There were various options open to him. Pleading ignorance was one. Pleading for mercy another. Fred briefly considered both...

... then pegged it.

*

Alex too was considering his options. Fred's friend was easy prey. Lay a finger on him though, and Mrs Doberman would rip him to pieces. Besides, he needed to get back to his dates. He owed them all a very big apology. There again, now that she knew he was blameless, perhaps there'd be a chance of winning MoJo round and salvaging some self-esteem? Or failing that, his *North Face* jacket.

There was a new challenge to deal with first however. As he stood on the kerb, waiting for a gap in the traffic – still closely observed by a cluster of open-mouthed spectators through the restaurant's window – a large damp patch was slowly but conspicuously spreading around the crotch of his chinos...

SPRING

CHAPTER 17

A RUDE AWAKENING

A faint orange glow burned through the darkness. It flickered, strobed and ignited into the reassuring outline of his mother, tenderly stroking his hand. Her eyes were misty, her voice quiet, concerned.

'*Vas mahkstu?*' it murmured.

Alex pondered for a moment. How *was* he feeling? Interesting question. He had a pounding headache, his breathing was shallow, his lips dry as parchment, and Joe had just pulled off the head of his Action Man Astronaut and chucked it down the toilet.

'Nothing lasts forever,' he'd said, laughing in Alex's face. 'Mum and Dad'll get you another one anyway.'

Even now, his mind was playing tricks. A thin plastic tube was emerging from the hand that his mum wasn't stroking. And as he followed it, swivel-eyed, to a bag of clear fluid dangling from a metal gibbet above him – it all came flooding back, like an intravenous memory transfusion.

'How long was I out?' he asked, his voice feeble and hoarse.

His mother glanced at her watch. 'Three hours.'

Hours? It felt more like decades.

'The surgeon came in while you were sleeping.'

'What did he say?'

She gave him a fervent thumbs up. 'He said it went well.'

What did that mean – *well*? Right now all Alex really wanted to know was *had he spared the nerves?* – but she wouldn't have asked that of course. His sexual functionality was of little importance to his mum, nor for that matter, to *anyone* these days – except Alex. He had zero intention of staying single for the rest of his life, but how the hell were you meant to get a girlfriend when you couldn't even get an erection? What would you put on your profile? *'Man with dysfunction seeks woman with dysinterest?'*

Alex had known for a while that something was wrong with his waterworks. But just as he'd always tried to keep mechanics away from his car, he preferred to keep medics away from his body. Once they had you in their grasp, who knew where you might end up?

The flex and slap of a GP's rubber glove – that's where! The eye-watering probe of her finger… the tests… the scans… and the inevitable biopsy with its grisly urological side-effects. Never in the history of medicine could a nether region have been so exhaustively expunged and explored. And at the end of it – alas – the dreaded referral.

There were plenty of things Alex was perfectly happy to inherit from his dear departed dad. Prostate cancer wasn't one of them.

In an attempt to present the diagnosis in the least threatening way, the insensitively named Mr Seaman made it sound more like the removal of an ingrown toenail than a tumour. He may have conducted more than five thousand radical prostatectomies in his time, but this was Alex's *first,* and no amount of understatement was going to make him feel less terrified.

A stack of pamphlets on everything from pelvic-floor exercises to incontinence pads had done nothing to relieve the stress. Nor did the special diet or the hospital seminar where he was the only patient without a partner. To be fair, Ally's compassion had gone into overdrive since the diagnosis, and she had offered to accompany him. She'd even promised not to evict him till he'd got the all-clear. 'The healing power of cancer,' Alex had quipped darkly. Even so – whether she was shagging his brother or not – it hadn't seemed right to be sat there discussing penile rings and vacuum pumps with his ex.

And now, as he explored the two tubes plumbing his nostrils, he became aware of another one tugging his groin. *Jesus Christ, he had more tubes in him than the Piccadilly Line!*

'Thanks for coming Mum,' he murmured – suddenly feeling quite emotional.

His mum smiled warmly. 'I brought you some Rugelach!' she said.

Alex smiled too. In spite of evidence to the contrary, his mum had always believed that her sickly version of the Jewish pastry was a miracle cure for every known ailment – far better than anything modern medicine could provide. So when a plump nurse appeared from behind a screen, wheeling a large piece of medical apparatus, Miriam seized her opportunity.

'I've made Mr Feinstein some special pastries,' she said, removing the lid from a large Tupperware container and thrusting it under her nose. 'See?'

'Very nice,' the nurse said, 'although…'

'….But Mr Feinstein is stubborn as a donkey, so would you please make sure he eats it?'

'I'm afraid I need to…'

'And one other thing. He will say he's happy with English tea. But he prefers it with a small slice of lemon if possible.'

'I try not to get involved in the catering,' the nurse answered sweetly. 'And all being well, he'll only be here another hour or two. Then he'll be taken to his own room. He'll have a different team looking after him down there.'

Miriam ploughed on regardless. 'Oh and one last thing before I go,' she said, delving into her faux-Hermès handbag and producing a framed photograph – the one of Alex on his first day of school, flanked by his doting parents. She glanced around in vain for a surface to put it on, then thrust it into the nurse's hands.

'Mr Feinstein needs a bedside table please. I know the NSH has no money but…'

'Mum – the nurse already explained I'll be…'

'Shhh Alex,' she said, pressing a red taloned finger-tip against his parched lips. 'Get some rest! Eat your Rugelach. I'm going to the shops. I'll call you later. *Zay gezunt.*'

*

Of course Fred was sympathetic. It couldn't be easy, losing your hair, your wife and your 'prostrate' – even if he had no clue what or where a 'prostrate' was, and no intention whatsoever of googling it up. So today after school, he was off to visit his dad. Which in itself was a pretty big deal. The last time he'd set foot inside a hospital, he'd had a major meltdown. Totally inconsolable, his mum said – hysterical. In fact the midwife had to gave him a slap.

And it wasn't *just* hospitals. On his first vaccination at the age of four, Fred had bolted, terrified, out of the doctor's surgery and into the high street with his ageing GP in hot pursuit. He'd never been able to eyeball a needle since then. Or an episode of Holby.

But today he was on a mission. After the events of the past few weeks, his social life needed a reboot. His mum would've been fine with him having some mates over, but sadly she didn't get a vote these days. And even if she did, his dad would over-rule it. The slightest whiff of a party would trigger emergency measures. Barbed wire encircling the house. Maybe even a moat.

Sure, Fred felt a bit queasy about taking advantage of his dad's dodgy health. This was their home after all. The crib. The sanctuary. The castle. But his mates were all perfectly civilised. They had homes of their own. They respected other people's. So where was the harm in a low-key Friday night get-together?

Uncle Joe agreed. He was at the airport when Fred called, on his way back from a job in Istanbul. 'It's an unwritten rule,' he said. 'Any teen with a free yard has a solemn duty to use it.'

'Yeah, but if Dad finds out…'

'See that's the problem with dads,' Joe snorted. 'They spend years imposing their rules. Dominating your life. Controlling your world. Treating you like a bloody child. And maybe that's OK when you *are* a bloody child. But it's not OK once your balls have dropped. Capeesh? I'll sort you out some special entertainment if you like. Belated birthday present. Just let me know.'

So armed with his uncle-stroke-godfather's blessing, Fred spread the word. And in the spirit of goodwill – he also sent an invite to Vi. Mikey was dead against it at first, but this was a chance to prove he was a grown-up, Fred said. Plus Chanel and Hestie would be coming, along with some other girls from St Mary's. And as none of the crew's Christmas hook-ups had survived beyond Valentine's Day, there'd be plenty of *Opportunities to Pull*.

As it happens, Fred had his own *OTP*. Which, if he was being honest, was the main reason he wanted a party.

He'd first clapped eyes on Priyanka at the Queensway ice-rink and they'd met up three times since then – but always with her best friend in tow. Nisha, or the *Siamese twin* as Fred called her.

Fred liked Pri a lot. And he had a feeling the feeling was mutual. But as Uncle Joe put it: 'attraction needs feeding or it curls up and dies.' Pri's family were ultra-conservative, but she'd told them she was staying at Nisha's on Friday night, so if ever there was a time to feed that mutual attraction – this was it! Which made his hospital visit more than a matter of mere life and death.

*

The old man in the bed looked nothing like his dad. He was pale and gaunt with sticky up hair and two plastic tubes up his nose. And yet the label on the door said 'Alex Feinstein', and the photo on the bedside cabinet confirmed it. Fred tip-toed in, pulled up a chair, and sat down stiffly. He'd never seen his dad looking so weak and vulnerable, and he couldn't deny it struck a nerve.

'Hey Dad,' he whispered. 'How you feeling?'

Alex took a few seconds to open his eyes, and a few more to focus.

'A million dollars,' he said, his voice still feeble and shaky. 'Actually – make that Venezuelan Bolivars.'

Fred's knowledge of international exchange rates was limited, but he got the picture. 'Maybe this'll cheer you up?' he said, pulling a padded envelope from his rucksack.

Alex frowned and shifted painfully in the bed to fumble it open.

'How cool is that!' he said, genuinely touched.

There was nothing intrinsically special about a black baseball cap, though the gesture itself was a surprise. The main reason for the lump in his throat was the bold white lettering on the front. '*Papa*'. It was the first actual word Fred had uttered as a toddler, and it's what he'd continued to call Alex until he was ten. It was only jettisoned when a schoolfriend reliably informed him that calling your dad *Papa* was '*gay*'. To Alex, however, it represented a golden age when his son adored him unconditionally. When he was in his prime. When his career was booming. When he and Ally were in love. When he was happy.

'I'll wear it on all my shoots from now on,' he said. 'It'll hide my bald patch…'

He popped it on his head, with its peek pointing forwards, then backwards, then sideways, hoping these whacky antics would hide the tears now welling in his eyes.

'...The creatives will think I'm part of their tribe. Where on earth did you find it?'

'Oh. Just – y'know – off the internet.'

Fred *hadn't* found it as it happens. His mum had.

'Guaranteed to put a big fat smile on Dad's face,' she'd said.

'Guaranteed to make him look like a plonker,' was Fred's response.

As it turned out – they were both right. His dad *did* look like a plonker. A plonker with a big fat smile on his face.

'Suits you!' Fred lied.

Alex was struggling to hold it together. 'Thanks fella,' he gulped. 'I'll treasure it.'

Fred glanced around the small grey room. 'I see Bubby's been,' he said, pointing to the Tupperware tub.

'However did you guess? Help yourself.'

Fred hesitated. He'd once chipped a milk-tooth on one of Bubby's sugar-bombs. Still, in the interests of keeping things upbeat, it made sense to take one for the team.

'Not bad,' he said, chewing vigorously. 'Less concrete than usual.'

'Be thankful for small mercies,' Alex grinned. 'How was school?'

'OK. I saw Ollie's mum at the gates. She sends her regards.'

'Thank you.'

'And she...' Fred's chair squeaked as he shifted uneasily. '...she invited me over to stay.'

'That's nice,' Alex said. 'Pity you're sorted.'

'That's what I said. But then I thought – Bubby would obviously prefer to stay at her own place. Given a choice.'

'Don't be daft. You know how she needs to be needed. She'll be back at ours now, preparing one of her Michelin star specials!'

Fred's chair squeaked again.

'Alright. I'll brave it tonight. But tomorrow I'll go to Ollie's and Bubby can head back to Stavros.'

Alex shook his head. 'Stavros is staying with his niece on the Isle of Wight. So Bubby's thrilled to have someone to cook for.'

This was a major set-back. But Fred had no intention of taking it lying down. The stakes were too high.

'Thing is Dad,' he said. 'Ollie and I are forming a band. So we need to, y'know, make a plan.'

That was it. The magic word. If anything could get his dad onside, it was a 'plan'. Especially a plan that involved Fred's inner Mark Knopfler.

'You should've said so fella!' Alex grinned. 'I'm sure Bubby'll understand.'

Fred popped the rest of the pastry in his mouth, triumphantly.

'She'll probably stay anyway,' Alex added. 'She's got an indoor bowls match in Ealing on Saturday. It'll save her a journey. And anyway, she wants to look after me when I come out.'

Fred swallowed and the Rugelach sunk like a stone.

'But I'm glad about the band,' Alex beamed. And as he reached across to give Fred's arm an affectionate squeeze, Fred glimpsed the thin plastic tube sprouting out of his dad's hand. His revulsion and inevitable recoiling set off a chain reaction like a Rube Goldberg machine. Alex yelped and jolted violently forwards as if he'd been poked with an electric cattle-prod, thrusting one hand under the covers and the other frantically towards the floor.

Fred's eyes followed it down to a plastic bag containing amber liquid discreetly attached to the edge of the bed. Some kind of isotonic drink, he assumed. Who knew they put that straight in your veins?

He sank to his knees and crawled under the bed to where the connecting tube had got itself wrapped round a wheel. It was only when a second bag containing a strange cranberry-coloured liquid brushed against his cheek, that the grisly truth hit him.

These were not isotonics.

They were his father's bodily fluids.

Fred could feel the Rugelach threatening to make an unexpected reappearance. If he didn't get out *now*, there was going to be a....

'*Uuurrrrrggggghhhh!*'

*

'Hey handsome! How ya doing!?'

It took Fred a while to realise the shout-out was for him. After the chaos of the past few minutes he'd completely forgotten the arrangements.

He waved and hurried gingerly over to the blue van, parked by the hospital gates.

'I'm... fine. Thank you,' he said.

It was a bare-faced lie of course. He wasn't fine at all. Plus there were traces of sick down his blazer.

But Izzy seemed oblivious. 'There ya go,' she said, unceremoniously dangling a Tesco bag out of the window. 'Compliments of your fairy godfather!'

'Awesome,' Fred said, trying to sound grateful.

He glanced around furtively, then stuffed it in his rucksack.

'Thanks so much!'

'Don't thank me Fredster! Thank Joe. He wants you to have the best party ever!'

Fred didn't have the heart to tell her that the best party ever was cancelled.

*

The emergency that greeted the staff nurse when she burst into Alex's room, was not one she'd been trained for – but in any case her response was telling. Because it wasn't Alex whom she'd rushed to help. Not her *actual patient,* doubled up on the bed, with his catheter spiralising his penis. It was the teenager *under* the bed, puking his guts out.

'Fuck you old man,' she might as well have said. 'You're *so* last century. And your penis is no longer relevant.'

OK, perhaps the morphine *had* made him paranoid. And perhaps he *was* sometimes guilty of catastrophising. But how could he *not* regard the entire incident as an Oedipal assault on the damaged relic of his poor misbegotten manhood? An unconscious attack on the very instrument that helped bring Fred into the world.

By the following day he was at least feeling *physically* stronger. The tubes in his hand and nose had been removed and he was sat up in bed, washing down some Rugelach with a cup of coffee and a dose of daytime TV. He'd already done the soft-shoe shuffle up the corridor, like some disability catwalk model, cutting a dash in his kick-ass poly-cotton smock, loosely tied at the back, and wheeling his IV drip-stand before him like a badge of dishonour. And most importantly, Mr Seaman had proclaimed that he had indeed saved the nerves.

'Onwards and upwards!' he'd joked to the amusement of his disciples and the deep appreciation of his patient.

But it wasn't long before Alex's afternoon snooze was rudely interrupted by another visitor.

'How's it going bro!?' boomed a voice that could have awakened the dead, let alone any post-op patients hoping for some quiet R&R.

Alex put Bargain Hunt on mute so Joe could moderate his volume.

He didn't.

'I see Mum's been,' he brayed, grabbing a Rugelach from the tub and testing it between his teeth like a gold nugget. 'What doesn't kill you makes you stronger, right?'

He stuffed it in his mouth, chewing contemplatively, like a judge on the *Great British Bake Off*.

'So?' he grinned. 'Had a wank yet?'

Alex looked at him, stony-faced.

'You still can though, right? And I heard it's spunk-free. So you'll save a small fortune in Kleenex.'

Alex shook his head, lost for words.

'So what's it like, losing your prostate?'

'I wouldn't recommend it.'

'Y'know, that's kinda how I feel about this!'

Joe spat the masticated pastry into Alex's glass of water where it landed with a splash.

'I'll pass on your compliments.'

'Thanks. And talking of compliments, I hear you liked my mural.'

'Oh. Ally told you?'

'Of course.'

Alex wondered if she'd also told Joe *why* he'd gone to see it. Hopefully not. Joe was clearly in a belligerent mood and Alex in no fit state for a row.

'Here,' Joe said, interrupting his train of thought and yanking a crumpled bag from his document case. 'I got you this from Istanbul.'

He smacked it down hard on the tray-table, triggering the inevitable falsetto yelp.

'Jesus man, what's wrong with you?'

'Nothing. I'm fine,' Alex said, reaching inside the bag and pulling out a polished stone object, shaped like a phallus.

'They say it has magic powers. I thought you could do with some.'

A bit rich, Alex thought, to be gifted a virility symbol by the man he'd suspected of shagging his wife. Still, he did his best to look grateful.

'Thank you, that's…'

'Weird!'

'What?'

Joe was staring at the photo on the bedside cabinet.

'Oh, *that*. Mum brought it in.'

'Yeah, I didn't imagine *you* did. That really *would* be weird. Look at them – beaming from ear to ear. What are they so fucking proud of?'

'It's just a happy family snap,' Alex said, refusing to rise to the bait.

'If you say so bro,' Joe sniffed.

He was doing a lot of sniffing. It could have been a chill he'd picked up on the plane, but the dilated pupils and hyper-active behaviour suggested otherwise.

'I see you've been at the marching powder,' Alex said, biting the bullet.

'You know me too well! I had to go cold turkey in Turkey. I'm getting my eye in again. And my nose. Fancy a toot?'

'No ta.'

'Why not? You've got every other drug in here. At least you don't have to take it intravenously.'

Joe grabbed the family photo and lay it face up on the tray table. Ignoring his brother's protests, he produced a small plastic pouch from his document case, and with a speed and dexterity that came with years of practice, sprinkled a mini-pyramid of white powder onto the photo's glass front.

'Don't do that!' Alex hissed, eyeing the door like a petrified look-out on a bank raid. 'A nurse could come in any moment!'

'And? What's she gonna do? Handcuff me to a defibrillator? Call matron? We'll just say it's medicinal.'

'No way!'

'Objection overruled!'

Derision, along with an itchy nose, had now turned Joe's sniffing into a concert. Using a credit card, he cut the pile into four equal lines and proceeded to ingest the first through a tightly-rolled Turkish bank-note.

'That's what I'm talkin' about!' he bellowed. 'Y'know, there's something fun about powdering your nose on your brother's perfect childhood! C'mon!' He held out the bank-note. 'Let's wipe the grins off their smug little faces!'

Joe's own face was now so close to his, that Alex could smell his coke-breath.

'You really are something else,' Alex said.

Joe pulled back his lips and rubbed the left-overs into his gums. 'I do hope so!' he said. 'I'm not that big on toeing the line as you know. I'd far rather snort it! Incidentally – just for the record – she's not my type.'

'Who?'

'Ally.'

'I'm glad to hear it,' Alex said, struggling to pretend it didn't matter. 'Although you always said you don't have a type.'

Joe stooped over the tray table, picking up where he left off.

'You got me bang to rights there bro. But just so's you know – it wasn't me. I guess she was so horny after her sex-starved marriage, she'd have jumped anyone's bones!'

Alex didn't need to look at the monitor. He could feel his blood pressure rising. 'OK, best you toddle off now,' he said. 'Visiting time's over.'

'Don't patronise me bro,' Joe said, poking the coke-flecked end of his tightly furled bank-note into Alex's forehead. 'I didn't take it from Mum and Dad and I'm fucked if I'll take it from you.'

Alex gripped the sides of the bed, desperately trying not to flinch. But he'd finally lost the capacity to turn the other cheek.

'Get out!' he said. 'And take your fucking fairy dust with you!'

'You can have that on me,' Joe sniffed. 'But there is one thing I wanna do before I go.'

He picked up the stone phallus, turned it round in his hand, and brought it crashing down on the happy family photo. A loud crack reverberated round the room.

'You have no idea how good that felt!' he said.

An anxious face appeared at the observation window.

'What's happening this time?' the nurse said as she pushed open the door.

'Sorry Kaya. My brother and I were having a trip down memory lane. He's just leaving.'

Joe fixed him with a look of unadulterated, cocaine-fuelled rancour, then spun round and staggered out, elbowing Kaya out of the way.

A moment later, he was filling the doorframe again.

'Incidentally, on the subject of Fred…'

He hovered at the door for a moment, then thinking better of it, wheeled round and lurched off up the corridor.

Kaya regarded the shards of glass, the specks of white powder scattered all over the bed and floor, the family photo with its shattered frame, the stone phallus, lying prone beside it on the tray table. Then she looked back at Alex, as if expecting some kind of explanation.

'Turns out memory lane has some very sharp bends,' he shrugged.

CHAPTER 18

BOLLYWOOD GODDESS

Miriam lumbered in from the kitchen with her bushtucker trial on a tray – and her eyes misted over.

'Ah, *vunderlekh*!' she sighed, popping the tray on the table, spreading her bingo wings and clicking her arthritic fingers. 'We used to play this every night at *Chutzpah*. Did you know that? *Every night*! Our customers – they went *meshuggah* for it!'

She did a frisky pirouette, got dizzy and steadied herself on the back of her chair.

Of course Fred knew that. Why else would he have searched for it on Spotify? *Hava Nagila* was hardly his groove! But this evening he needed Bubby's full cooperation – conscious or unconscious. Ideally the latter.

'Ah!' she said, gazing wistfully out of the conservatory window, 'those were the days!'

Steam billowed as she removed the lid from a Pyrex dish. Fred eyed the slimy brown gunge and couldn't imagine anything less appetising. But tonight he was on full smarm offensive.

'That looks amazing Bubby!' he gushed. 'What is it?'

Bubby beamed proudly. 'Matzoh lasagne!'

'Matzoh lasagne? What's that?'

'It's lasagne. Made with matzoh.'

'Mmm.' Fred shoved a forkful of the steaming gunge in his mouth. 'Incredible!'

Inedible was nearer the mark. In fact his Nike Airs would probably have tasted better. And as Bubby dolloped her helping onto a plate, Fred dolloped his into a napkin. It was a risky procedure but her failing eyesight made it just about do-able.

'You've excelled yourself Bubby,' he said, once he'd offloaded the lot into an empty plant pot on the dresser behind him.

'I'm happy you enjoyed it. Here – have some more!'

Fred puffed out his cheeks and patted his stomach. 'Mustn't,' he said. 'Football season.'

Bubby shrugged and carried on stuffing her face. Then she tottered off to the living room to binge on Rugelach and the *Antiques Roadshow*, while Fred cleared the plates – and the plant pot – and scooted into the kitchen to make her a tea with a small slice of lemon, just how she liked it.

Only tonight there was an added ingredient.

Six to eight Temazepams would do the job, or so he'd read. And after a lifetime of chronic insomnia, his dad's ensuite cabinet was full of them. One missing blister pack would never be noticed. So using his mum's pestle and mortar, Fred crushed them into a powder and sprinkled it into Bubby's nightcap. Of course he knew it was wrong, but according to the internet it was perfectly safe. And at the end of the day, what other option did he have?

She was sound asleep by the time Finn and Mikey turned up and it was just as well he'd arranged the extra muscle-power. Hauling her off the sofa and walking her to the door of the stairs was hard enough. Getting her *up* them was a different challenge altogether. By the fifth step all three boys were shattered.

'Why don't we just pop her in your dad's car?' Mikey pleaded. 'She'll be comfy in there.'

'Are you mad?' Fred said. 'She'd freeze.'

'How about in there then?' Mikey pointed to the downstairs loo.

'Gimme a break man. Would you put *your* gran to sleep in a bloody toilet?'

'I wouldn't put my gran to sleep full stop,' Mikey said.

'Trust me, she'll thank us in the morning. She doesn't share our taste in music. Finn mate…' Fred gasped as he thrust his head under Bubby's armpit. 'We could do with some extra grunt here.'

Finn huffed grumpily up from the hallway and spread his hands like a healer, inches from Bubby's ample rump.

'For god's sake man. I said *push*. Not take measurements.'

Finn started to push, tentatively at first, and then as if his life depended on it. Which it most likely did, given the Sumo-sized bulk teetering precariously above him.

Miriam whinnied and babbled in Yiddish. Then slowly creaked upwards, one step at a time, shimmying like an ancient belly dancer as she reached the landing.

'You have the magic touch Finn,' Mikey whispered as they fox-trotted her off to the spare room. 'Should we leave you to get to know each other better?'

Finn gave him the finger.

They removed Bubby's shoes and glasses, lowered her onto the bed and tip-toed back to the door. Fred switched off the light, locked it from the outside and trousered the key.

'Thanks dudes,' he said. 'I owe you.'

'Big time!' Finn said, wiping the sweat from his brow. 'You can get PTSD from this kinda thing.'

At around 9pm, Fred opened the door to a *PFF* with eyes like fireworks and a smile like Nicki Minaj. At first he assumed she'd come to the wrong address. Or that Ollie had booked him a strippagram. It was only when he spotted the Siamese twin, lurking in the shadows, that he realised *this was his date*.

'W*ow*!' was all he could muster.

It was the first time he'd seen Pri in full party-mode and one thing was blindingly obvious. She was totally out of his league. Mikey had told him he didn't stand a chance – and he was right. In fact he hadn't just *told* him, he'd bet him ten quid.

'Is your dad here?' she asked as Fred led them into the kitchen.

'My dad?' he turned away so they wouldn't see his hands shaking as he poured out three Toffee Vodkas. 'Ha! No, he's in hosp... he's... gone away for a few days.'

'Seriously?! Whoa! My dad would never do that.'

'Do what?'

'Let me have a party while he was away.'

'Mine neither,' Nisha said.

'Come to think of it – he'd never let me have a party at all.'

'Mine neither,' Nisha said.

'Well… different strokes for different blokes I guess,' Fred said meekly as he passed them their drinks.

Pri raised her glass. 'To your dad then!'

'To your dad!' Nisha echoed.

'To my dad!' Fred smiled.

*

Being in hospital had its compensations, especially when you had your own room. You could watch trashy TV without a conscience. You could listen to all those podcasts you'd never got round to. You could even wade through reams of bumph about your medical condition, if you had the urge. But right now Alex had other urges, awakened and stirred by the alluring assortment of hopefuls smiling out from *Amorous Intent*.

There was one called *PerfectCatch* who'd caught his eye and whom – from what he could see – more than lived up to her name. She was smart, witty and attractive, and in their first brief interchange, they'd already struck up a rapport. She remained resolutely cagey about where she hung out and what she did for a living, but Alex couldn't help thinking he recognised her from somewhere. As a matter of fact, he'd been cagey too. He may even have forgotten to mention that he was now in a hospital bed, recovering from a prostatectomy, with a high chance of incontinence and a low chance of ever being able to have sex again, unaided.

*

By 10pm, everyone Fred invited had shown up, which was awesome. Slightly less awesome were the people he *hadn't* invited. Viola's new squeeze – a motorbike courier called Nelson with a bush for a beard – had posted the party on Snapchat, and a bunch of his mates (and mates' mates) had descended on *Fein Mess* like a swarm of leather-clad locusts.

Half a bottle of toffee vodka and two of Uncle Joe's finest spliffs went some way towards easing Fred's panic, along with the need to show Pri just how cool he could be in a crisis. That's what a girl wanted, right? A bloke who wouldn't lose his shit when a herd of woolly mammoths invaded the cave?

Pri wasn't quite so chilled. 'Won't your dad go ballistic?' she fretted. 'Mine would.'

'And mine,' Nisha agreed.

'Shouldn't you… y'know… just ask them to leave?'

Of course he should. But they were bigger and older and harder than him. And there were more turning up all the time.

'Or perhaps just call the police?' Pri added.

'You should,' Nisha agreed.

Again, they had a point. But wouldn't the police just close down the party? Which would balls up Fred's chances with Pri. And wouldn't they want to speak to his dad? Which would balls up just almost everything else.

Fred's *official* guests seemed surprisingly unfazed about sharing their space with a bunch of bikers. Quite the opposite in fact. It gave the party a sense of edge and excitement. And the extra numbers made everyone feel far less self-conscious. Down in the bunker, Chanel and Hestie were leading a boisterous twerk-fest. In the hall, Jake, Finn and a couple of girls from St Mary's were inflating helium balloons. And two kids were busy snogging each other's faces off behind the living room sofa. Fred had no idea who they were, until the boy turned round, spotted him by the door, and waggled his fingers self-consciously.

Having shown zero interest in girls up till now, Ollie was the last person he expected to find in a full-blown snog. Fred winked and made the standard two-handed gesture by way of encouragement, just as Ollie's squeeze turned round and smiled nervously.

But it wasn't Freya or Izzy or Ruby or Ruth… it was Quentin! Fred quickly reconfigured his hands into a heart and discreetly reversed out.

Through the conservatory window, he could see half a chapter of Hells Angels enjoying a spliff and the bottle of Captain Morgan's that Rory had scored off his grandad. Meanwhile, two hard-looking women were locked in a titanic arm-wrestle across the hall bannisters. And at the foot of the stairs, a man-mountain with a spider's web tattooed on his shiny pate was burbling away in a foreign language. With renewed sense of purpose, Fred stepped across him and tip-toed over the collection of buckled beer-cans, discarded pizza boxes and fish and chip wrappers, scattered like an obstacle course on a landfill site.

A roar of laughter more raucous than a Harley Davidson greeted him as he approached the study door.

To knock, he decided, would put him firmly on the back foot, so he eased the door open instead. Half a dozen hairy bikers were sprawled in a circle on the floor, with Nelson amongst them, spinning a bottle, and Vi cross-legged by his side, doing tequila slammers.

The room fell silent as Fred glanced around at the arsenal of boots, zips, studs and piercings, and the cache of eyes, boring into him like skewers.

'Hey!' he chirruped. 'How y'all doin'?'

No-one said a thing. They just carried on staring.

Fred turned towards Vi. 'Erm... may I... have a word?' he asked politely.

'I'm in the middle of something,' she scowled. 'Can't you see?'

Fred hopped nervously from foot to foot. 'OK. Well I just... wanted to say... it's great to see everyone having fun.'

Vi raised a bottle of tequila. 'Cheers.'

'Thing is though... I'm afraid... it's invitation only.'

Rory's ragga jungle mix was pounding out from the downstairs speakers. Or was it Fred's heartbeat? Either way, those parts of Nelson's face not covered in facial hair had now gone puce.

'Invitation only?' he said finally.

Fred shrugged, like this was a rule he had nothing to do with. 'Fraid so.'

Nelson cracked each of his knuckles in turn, like twigs.

'Well,' he said, 'it didn't say that on *my* invitation.'

Another eruption of laughter brought Fred to his senses. It wasn't ideal, allowing this rabble to stay, but it was the option least likely to result in another trip to the hospital. And once the booze had run out, he felt sure that the bikers would too.

'You're right,' he said, stepping out onto the landing. 'I should've made that clear.'

He'd already taken the precaution of locking his dad's bedroom, thank god, but his own had no lock. He slipped inside and hurriedly made a *Keep Out* sign to hang on his door.

When he got back to the kitchen, the girls were nowhere to be seen. He waited a few minutes in case they'd gone to the loo – then set off in search.

'I thought you'd done a runner,' he said when he finally discovered Pri, cross-legged on the conservatory floor, scrolling through her Instagram feeds. It was the first time he'd ever seen her without her Siamese twin.

'Of course not,' she smiled. 'I didn't want to monopolise you – that's all.'

'I don't mind being monopolised,' he said, slumping on the floor beside her.

'That's nice,' Pri smiled. 'Did you ask them to go?'

'Not exactly,' Fred said. 'They seem pretty chilled though.'

'Oh. OK,' Pri said, though she didn't look convinced.

'Is Nisha in the loo?' he asked when he noticed Pri holding two handbags.

'Er... no!'

Pri pointed through the open double-doors to the dining room where two shapes were thrashing about under the table.

'Bloody hell! Who's the lucky boy? I mean person?'

'Can't you see?'

Fred peered at the jumble of bodies in the smoky shadows, and spotted... a surgical boot!

'Jesus!'

'I know. Honestly – I let her out of my sight for two minutes!'

'How much has she had to drink?'

Pri shrugged. 'No more than me.'

'Is that all it takes?'

'Apparently!'

Fred was already joining the dots. Without her minder – maybe Pri wasn't as untouchable as he'd thought. There again, if he waited for her to make the first move, he could be there forever. And anyway, that electric smile looked very much to him like a green light.

He leant towards her – slowly and deliberately – so she had plenty of time to get out of his way. But she didn't. And as their lips met, a hundred thousand volts jolted his body.

'*Wow!*' he gasped once they'd finally prised themselves apart.

'*Wow!*' Pri gasped back.

So what happens next? Fred had no idea. He knew what he *wanted* to happen next, but it seemed a bit forward to say so.

'Do you fancy one of these?' he said instead, delving into his pocket and pulling out a handful of the heart-shaped sweets that Uncle Joe had popped in his party bag.

Pri eyed them suspiciously. 'What are they?'

'E's.'

'I've never had one.'

'Me neither.'

'What are they meant to do?'

'I dunno. Make you all... touchy-feely?'

'What if you're touchy-feely already?'

'I guess they make you *super* touchy-feely.'

Pri frowned. Like she was having second thoughts about this whole touchy-feely thing. Until the heavy breathing behind them exploded into a series of passionate moans. Pri looked round at her bestie. Then turned back to Fred with an impish grin.

'Let's do it,' she giggled.

Within a few seconds, Mikey was in serious danger of losing his tenner. The question was – where could they go? The guest room was spoken for. The Saab cold and exposed. The bathrooms cramped and uncomfortable. There was only one place where total privacy could be guaranteed.

CHAPTER 19

GUERNICA

When Alex looked at his phone on Saturday morning to find eleven missed calls, his immediate thought was that his mum had had a fall or a heart-attack. So the first voicemail, timed at 10.23pm, came as a major relief.

'Mr Feinstein,' it said, 'Anna Boston here. I don't know what's going on, but the din from your house is unacceptable. I've rung the doorbell several times to no avail. Can you deal with it please?'

The relief promptly disappeared when Alex played the next message, timed at 10.47.

'Mr Feinstein. This is like living next door to a nightclub. My walls and floors are vibrating. And I don't know *what's* going on in your back garden. Unless this madness stops *now*, I shall have no option but to call the police.'

There was no actual voice on the subsequent messages – just a cacophony of music, laughter and screaming. Alex could actually feel his blood-pressure rising again as he listened to it.

Her final message was timed at 1.38am. She sounded worn down, on the edge of tears.

'I don't know where you are, Mr Feinstein,' it said. 'But this noise is impossible. And I just caught two of your son's friends doing something unspeakable – *unspeakable* – in *my* front garden. I'm not ashamed to say I set my dog on them.'

The lovely lady from catering, who normally brightened up Alex's day, did nothing to alleviate his palpitations.

'Hello my love,' she cried as she wheeled in his breakfast. 'And how are you feeling on this glorious Saturday morning?'

'I must confess I've felt better, Dembe,' he said.

But nothing could eclipse Dembe's sunny disposition.

'I'm glad to hear it,' she grinned, parking her trolley next to his bed, and chucking him under the chin. 'You enjoy your Full Monty Mr F!'

As soon as she'd left, Mr F called his mother.

No answer.

He called Freddie.

No answer.

He called the landline.

No answer.

It was pointless calling Ally at 7.20 on a Saturday morning. Wherever she was, she never picked up before 9. So it was time to bite the bullet and call Anna Boston. To apologise, of course, and – rather more importantly – to check his home was still standing.

Her voice was thinner than usual and a lot more brittle.

'You're not the first person in the world to have surgery Mr Feinstein,' she seethed, when Alex tried to play the sympathy card. 'And assuming you *knew* you were going to be in hospital – I fail to see why you didn't arrange to have your son properly supervised.'

The door swung open before Alex had a chance to put the case for the defence. Or find out anything about his home, son or mother.

Characteristically dapper in his pinstripes, Mr Seaman strode in with his disciples.

'Early ward-round today Alex,' he said. 'It's my wedding anniversary and I'm taking the Mrs to Prague. So – how are we doing?'

Alex quickly hung up. 'We're doing great,' he beamed, channeling Dembe, or trying to. 'In fact, so great – we were wondering if there's a chance of going home today?'

Mr Seaman pored over his iPad. 'Well, the numbers look encouraging enough. Is there someone there to look after you?'

'Absolutely. My mum and son are standing by in their nurse's outfits!'

He omitted to mention the posse of people in police outfits, presumably standing by too.

The elation Alex felt when Mr Seaman said he could come out, was tempered by the news that his catheter couldn't. *That* would need to stay put for another ten days. And the prospect of carrying it into a war-zone filled Alex with dread.

Even so – in less than an hour, he was up and dressed, with a drainage bag under his chinos, a pouch of incontinence pads under his arm, and only one thing on his mind – to get home as fast as he could.

He soon regretted saying that to the Uber driver.

'Haha! And don't spare the horses, James!' Mo warbled in his best English, hitting the pedal like Lewis Hamilton.

By the time they took the last chicane, Alex's poor misbegotten member felt like it had internally combusted. But the searing pain was quickly forgotten when they reached the chequered flag.

Everything was tumbleweed quiet, as if some seismic event had taken place. Curtains fluttered from an upstairs window. One of the bay-trees that flanked the porch was lying on its side – its ceramic planter smashed to pieces. Most worrying of all, the front door was wide open. And there were no police squad cars outside. A good thing maybe. Or a bad one. Alex wasn't sure which.

As he stepped through the front gate into a sea of cigarette butts, empties, random bits of clothing and a used condom, those palpitations were back with a vengeance. More alarming still were the drops of what looked suspiciously like blood on the welcome mat.

His outrage boiled over as he entered the house. A topless man with a huge belly was spreadeagled at the foot of the stairs like a dead sentry. Beside him, a drained cider bottle, a pile of crushed Doritos, some pizza crusts and a puddle of sick. The man emitted an emphysemic grunt as Alex stepped over his heavily tattooed torso.

The first thing to hit him as he opened the living room door was the stench. A heady blend of dope, sweat, beer, food and human effluvia. Under the dining table, two sleeping figures were clasped together like star-crossed

Pompeii lovers. Six more bodies were scattered around the room, and one or two were stirring. But Miriam and Fred were not amongst them.

An empty bottle of liqueur lay on the living room floor. Alex recognised it as a souvenir he and Ally had brought back from Corsica. Nearby, the door to the drinks cabinet had been prised off its hinges, its contents plundered. There was a big ugly Mirto-coloured stain on the rug by the fireplace, and up on the mirror, some wag had scrawled '*Our Bite-Marked Fries*' in red lipstick, next to three half-eaten chips.

There was no risk of catastrophising now. It was a nailed-on dystopian nightmare, like Guernica – only with a soundscape of groaning and retching. He shuddered to think what horrors lurked down in the basement. Maybe Fred was there, maybe not. Right now Alex was more concerned about his mother.

Climbing the stairs with a catheter was a delicate operation, and the detritus made it even more of a challenge. A discarded purse here, a pair of glasses there, fag-ends, empties everywhere. And unnervingly, more drops of blood.

On Fred's bedroom door, a handwritten '*Keep Out!*' sign had been altered to read: '*Keep fuckin ab Out*' by the same lipstick wag. Alex ignored both instructions. The room was a tip – so nothing new there. But in the bed, there was not one, not two, but *three* comatose bodies. None of them Fred or Miriam.

More droplets of blood led him back across the landing, but the door to the guest room was locked, and two things struck him as odd as he peeped through the keyhole. First, the key was missing. Second, the room was still dark.

Ominously, his own bedroom door was locked too. But he knew where the spare key to that one was kept.

A scattering of plasters, bandages, scissors, antiseptic cream and a family-sized first-aid tin lay on the floor as Alex entered the study. Beyond them, a sleeping couple huddled together beneath a tartan picnic blanket. *His* tartan picnic blanket.

Part of him – the part brimming with *righteous indignation* – wanted to shake them awake and kick them out of his house. The pragmatic part, however, was focussed on his goal. He steadied himself on the desk and quietly opened the drawer. The spare-key to his bedroom was on a fob at the back, but as he fumbled inside, the drawer slipped off its runners and collapsed onto the couple, peppering them in a hail of stationary.

A heavily bearded man sat up and clenched his fists.

'Don't touch my bike, cunt!' he growled, preparing to fight to the death.

Alex's bravado swiftly evaporated. 'I'm s… so sorry,' he stammered. 'I was just…'

He broke off as something on the carpet caught his eye. More speckles of blood.

The man's girlfriend sat bolt upright, her freckled arm shielding a black lacy bra.

'Hello Mr Feinstein,' she murmured, blinking. 'It's Viola. Remember? We met when…' She glanced skittishly at her partner and clammed up.

But Alex remembered alright. The bra. The eyes. The freckles. He was on the verge of completing her sentence for her, before she swiftly changed the subject.

'I'm sorry about the mess,' she said. 'I got attacked

by your neighbour's dog.' To prove the point, she rolled over, drew back the blanket and revealed a large surgical dressing on her left buttock. 'Nelson was gonna take me to A & E but I couldn't sit down on his bike.'

'Well let's just hope to god you don't get rabies,' Alex said. 'There's a lot of it about. Especially Jack Russells. You better get a jab ASAP.'

Terror flickered across her face as Alex stooped to retrieve the key.

His own bedroom was still dark when he unlocked the door, but a spindly finger of sunshine was pointing accusingly at a face in the kingsize bed – calm, beatific and fast asleep. It was undeniably Fred's- but Fred's as it *used* to look before adolescence took him in its pitiless grip.

Alex was unmoved. He seized the corner of the duvet, about to turf him out, when he realised Fred wasn't on his own. A raven-haired girl was curled up beside him, also fast asleep. Her shoulders were bare and – if the jumble of clothes on the floor was anything to go by – so was the rest of her.

Fred's left eye popped open, dilated, squinted, focused. And then the right one followed suit.

'Hey Dad!' he croaked. 'I didn't… expect you home… so soon.'

Alex was too incensed to speak.

'This is my… my friend… Priyanka,' Fred continued, in the hope that a Bollywood smile might somehow defuse his dad's anger.

Pri raised her head slightly, but no Bollywood smile was forthcoming. Her eyes remained shut. Her face was smudged with eyeliner. Her hair looked like she'd been caught in a monsoon. And most of her crimson lipstick was now on Fred. She mumbled, groaned, and collapsed back down on the pillow.

'Where's Bubby?' Alex snarled.

'Is she… not in her room?'

'I don't know. The door's locked.'

'Ah.'

'Did you lock it?'

'Erm…'

'Where's the key?'

'Erm…'

Fred's eyes darted anxiously to the pile of clothes.

Alex nudged assorted items of underwear to one side with his foot, reached painfully down to grab Fred's jeans, frisked its pockets, pulled out an open packet of *Trojan Magnum*s and carefully placed it on the bedside cabinet.

In a desperate bid for a decoy, Fred jabbed Pri under the covers with his elbow.

'Say hello to my Dad,' he whispered as she slowly unglued her eye-lids.

It took her a few moments to register the full horror of the situation, but she was far too wrecked to say anything. Alex was in no mood for pleasantries anyway. He plumbed Fred's pockets again and pulled out a handful of pink heart-shaped sweets, holding them up like a crime scene investigator.

'What are these?'

'Oh… just… some… love hearts.'

'OK,' he said, popping one in his mouth.

'Erm… n… no Dad,' Fred spluttered, 'best not.'

His suspicions confirmed, Alex spat it out and popped it in his pocket, along with all the others, then continued his search.

'Sorry,' Fred offered feebly as his father finally produced the spare room key.

Alex was too irate to say anything. He shuffled off, stopping briefly at the door for a parting salvo.

'We need to talk.'

'Sure,' Fred said, weakly.

'In the meantime, I need everyone out of my house. Now.'

*

'*Vos di genem*!?' Miriam muttered as she slowly came back to life.

Alex lowered himself onto the edge of her bed with a grimace. 'I was hoping you'd tell *me* that Mum.'

'I don't know,' she said. 'One minute I'm watching Antiques Roadshow. The next, my head it is spinning like a Zanussi.'

Alex took her hand in his. 'Is it possible you ate something funny?'

'What do you mean, *funny*?'

'You know, like, someone slipped something into your food or drink?'

In the space of a few seconds, Miriam's expression changed from confusion, to alarm, to panic.

She lifted the bed-cover to check she was still fully dressed. And then – two wizened hands were suddenly grasping his collar.

'Please Alex, never say this to Stavros. He is old fashioned man. He don't understand these things.'

'I won't breathe a word Mum.'

'Thank you.' She let go of his collar and patted it flat. 'What time is it?'

'9.15.'

'In the evening?'

Alex pointed to the window. 'In the morning.'

'*L'maan ha'shem*! My match is starting in forty five minutes.'

Miriam swung her legs onto the floor, heaved herself out of bed and collapsed like a sack of Zucchini.

*

'Please don't be too harsh on him ziskayt,' she pleaded when they regrouped downstairs an hour later, 'he's young.'

She was slumped at the kitchen table, surrounded by fag-ends and empties. Fred had just traipsed off with the hangover from hell to buy some cleaning products. But at least his overnight 'guests' had now gone.

Alex popped a slice of lemon into the 'World's Best Grandma' mug and handed it over. 'What he did was unforgivable,' he said.

'I know, but he did apologise. And as a matter of fact I had my best night's sleep in years.'

Alex propped himself up against the fridge. 'He could have killed you Mum.'

'*Keinahora*!' she said, slurping her tea. 'It'll take more than a few Temazepams to finish me off.'

Fred's rap-sheet didn't end with the Temazepams, but she didn't need to know about those other pills. That was a conversation he'd be having with Fred, once Ally was back in the loop.

'What worries me most,' Alex said, 'is his increasing contempt for the rules. *Any* rules.'

Miriam stared wistfully into the middle-distance. 'Well we know where he gets *that* from.'

Alex looked at her. What was that meant to mean? He'd never been a rule-breaker, not even as a teen. The only thing he'd ever done to upset his parents, was marrying Ally.

'Oh... I didn't mean *you*,' his mum said, reading his thoughts.

She wobbled her head manically, like a Zanussi on its final spin. But her eyes were no longer revolving in their sockets and she now seemed perfectly lucid. No, there was something contrived, almost theatrical about the gesture.

'Who *did* you mean then?' Alex said.

Miriam stared at her mug, as if struggling with some inner demons. 'Sit down Alex,' she said eventually.

Alex? She only ever called him *Alex* if he was in trouble.

'There's something I need to tell you – before Fred gets back.'

'I'd prefer to stand Mum,' he said. 'Sitting down's a bit... uncomfortable for me at the moment. What is it?'

'OK. Well...' Miriam placed her mug amongst the detritus, and took a deep breath. 'The last time I saw your brother was at home in Borehamwood. On Morry's seventy-first birthday. You were away, so Ally came with Joe. Do you remember?'

It was a long time ago, but as it happens, he did. He was shooting a commercial in Stockholm at the time. Ally had begged him not to do it because the dates coincided with her most fertile time of the month. But it was part of a pan-European campaign for IKEA, and turning it down would have been costly.

'Anyway,' Miriam pressed on, 'there was something going on between the two of them that evening. A lot of giggling and – yes – flirting. Morry noticed it too. And half way through dinner, Joe…'

She paused. As if she couldn't quite bring herself to say it.

'Joe what?'

'…put his hand on her leg.'

Alex frowned. 'Is that *it* Mum? For god's sake, you know what Joe's like. Anything in a skirt. Even his own sister-in-law.'

'I know. And most women would just brush him off. She didn't.'

'That's ridiculous… Ally is the most principled… There's no way she'd… And if there *was* something going on between them, she'd hardly have let her mother-in-law witness it, would she?'

'She had no idea I *did* witness it. Neither of them had. You know the sideboard in the dining room? The one with the mirrored doors? I could see it in the reflection. Clear as day. And as soon as we'd finished the meal, they couldn't wait to get away.'

'I'm sure you were imagining it Mum,' Alex said. 'They'd have been messing about, that's all.'

'As you say yourself dear, I wasn't born yesterday. I'm

telling you, there was something going on. If you don't want to believe it, that's up to you.'

Had it not been for his current insecurities, Alex would certainly have dismissed this whole story as a figment of his mum's sometimes fertile imagination. Or else the innate prejudice she'd held against Ally since the first time she'd met her. But he couldn't deny he was rattled.

'Why did you never tell me this before?' he said.

'I wanted to. But your father wouldn't let me. As far as he was concerned, a marriage is for life not just for...'

'...Chanukah.'

'Exactly. And he worried that if you ever found out – you'd want to end it.'

What Alex did want, desperately, was to dismiss this crazy allegation out of hand. But the truth was, that when he and Ally were trying to conceive, their sex-life had gone to pot. Or more accurately, reduced to a series of mechanical sessions with the sole purpose of 'engineering' a baby. Pleasure had been replaced by a series of *procedures* – injections, ultrasounds, egg-collections, embryo-transfers. In those circumstances it would not have been surprising if either of them had looked elsewhere for some physical or emotional comfort. On top of that, Ally's hormones were all over the place. She said and did a *lot* of things that were out of character.

But there was something more worrying still. Something his mother had clearly already computed. His father's birthday was in January. He'd have been seventy-one in 2002. And Fred was born in September of that year. So if there *was* something going on between Ally and Joe at the time...

...The very idea was far too distressing to contemplate, and it was anyway interrupted by Fred, traipsing back in with a mop and a large plastic bag. Alex regarded his tall slim frame, his boyish good looks and his dark chiselled features, and tried for all his worth *not* to see Joe's handsome face, smiling contemptuously back.

CHAPTER 20

PAYBACK TIME

Whichever way Fred looked at it, the whole thing had been a catastrophe. He shouldn't have had a party while his dad was in hospital. He shouldn't have put Bubby to sleep. He shouldn't have taken those tabs while his home was full of strangers. And he shouldn't have taken Pri to his father's bed.

Perhaps he'd have felt better if he'd had the major bollocking he'd expected. The old hairdryer treatment might have blasted away some of his guilt. But his dad had been uncharacteristically restrained. Detached even. Sure, he'd ordered Fred to spend the rest of the day on his hands and knees with a Brillo pad and a pair of marigolds. And to go out and buy two bouquets of flowers with his own money. But he'd never actually lost his rag.

Bubby was grateful for her flowers, and she'd insisted that no apology was necessary.

Mrs Boston, on the other hand, refused to accept hers. 'That would imply forgiveness,' she'd barked across the chain on her front door, her nasty little dog yapping and snapping behind her. 'And after what you put me through – I'm just not in a forgiving kind of mood.'

Fred didn't give a flying fart about Mrs Boston, the silly old bat. Pri was a different matter though. He really liked Pri. And from the little he could remember of Friday night, Pri really liked him too.

But everything went pear-shaped on the Saturday morning. Waking up in a strange bed with an angry man looming over her – all red faced and bulging eyes – had been the most terrifying experience of Pri's entire life, she'd said.

Fred's attempt to make it up to her with Mrs Boston's rejected bouquet, had backfired badly. It might have worked if he'd remembered to remove the gift tag. Because '*I'm sorry I kept you awake – it won't happen again,*' wasn't the ideal message for a teenage girl to receive, the day after she'd lost her virginity.

He couldn't deny that the house was a tip. There again, the gatecrashers were hardly *his* fault. By definition, he hadn't invited them. And yet his dad was insisting he paid for the damage. Fred assumed it was just an empty threat, until he woke up on Sunday morning to find an email with a detailed break-down in his inbox:

Industrial cleaners: £300
Carpet cleaners: £200
Drinks cabinet repair: £125
Drinks cabinet restock: £400
Painting, decorating, revarnishing wooden floor: £1000
Dry cleaning sofa cover: £50

Replacing 4x cushion covers: £100
Dining chair repair: £250
Glasses replacements: £100
Replanting Flower beds: £150
Grand total: £2675.

Where the hell was he going to get £2675? With his pocket money nixed and less than two hundred quid left in his savings, he'd be paying it off for like… *ever*.

Thank god for Uncle Joe.

'He can't force you to pay y'know,' he'd said, when Fred called. 'You can just refuse!'

'But wouldn't that be like declaring war? Seeing as I live in his home?'

'It's *your* home too dude. Your name may not be on the title deeds. But you still have rights.'

Fred wasn't entirely convinced. He was pretty sure the courts had bigger things to deal with. No, the best white hope – as his dad used to joke – was his mum. But he needed to handle it carefully.

It was gone eleven on Sunday morning by the time he picked up the phone. Less than two hours before they were due to meet up.

'I'm not sure I can make lunch today Mum,' he said.

'Why not darling?' she replied. 'What's the matter?'

The apparent alarm in her voice hopefully meant that his dad hadn't got to her first.

'I've been grounded,' he said dejectedly.

'Why? What's happened?'

Fred told her about the small impromptu gathering he'd had, to help get things back on track with his mates. He told her about Bubby's early night, about the gatecrashers, about his dad's unexpected return, before he'd had a chance to clear up. Oh, and about some of the damage they'd caused, which his dad was now insisting Fred paid for.

'Don't worry darling,' she said, struggling to contain her fury. 'Dad's not thinking straight, what with all the morphine he's been on. Just leave it to me. In the meantime, I'll see you at one o'clock as planned.'

Bullseye!

*

Alex was in no frame of mind to take Ally's call. His mother's comments had rocked him to the core and he needed time to work out how to handle it.

'Hey Alex,' the voicemail said. 'I hope you're feeling better. Freddie tells me you're out of hospital, which is great news. Slightly less great, I suppose, is the fact that the two of you have fallen out already. I imagine the welcome home wasn't quite what you'd hoped for, but after his recent ups and downs, I'm sure you can understand why he wanted a few of his mates over on Friday night. Yes, yes of course he should have asked your permission, but at least your mum was on hand. And he can hardly be blamed for the gatecrashers. Even so, I gather he's been grounded until he's paid for the damage they did. *What are you thinking Alex?* He's fifteen for god's sake! Where exactly is he going to find nearly three thousand pounds? Your relationship with Fred is *your* business, but if you want my advice, tithing him like some feudal serf is hardly the way to build bridges. In any case, we're due to have lunch at Mumma and Puppa's today – and grounded or not – I fully expect him to be there.'

Alex's first thought was ignore it. But then, why should *he* be cast as the villain? Fred had behaved appallingly, and he had to be punished, regardless whose son he was. And since words had little or no effect – hitting him in the pocket seemed a perfectly fair way to do it.

He had several attempts at recording a response to Ally's message, but in the end he decided to send her a text.

'*Hi Ally,*' it said. '*I'm a bit under-par at the mo so not taking calls. It sounds as if Fred's been a little 'economical with the truth'. You might want to ask him about the Temazepams he used to put Mum to sleep? Or about spending the night with an underage girl – in our bed? Or the ecstasy pills that I found in his pocket? You can see him whenever you want of course. You're his mum. And as his mum I hope you'll agree – it might be time for a bit of tough love.*'

*

'We need to talk, Fred,' Ally said, bringing the car to a standstill outside Bromley station and turning to face him.

This was it. The moment of reckoning. She'd obviously decided not to spoil Grandma's special curried goat lunch by mentioning it earlier – but she hadn't been her usual self today.

'Your father told me about some other things that happened on Friday night,' she went on. 'Things you forgot to mention.'

It was pointless Fred trying to deny them, especially as his mum was a sucker for a big fat 'sorry'. Hopefully it would come across as genuine – because it actually was. But apparently that wasn't enough. Now, *finally*, he was getting the hairdryer treatment – from the least likely of sources. He'd been reckless. He'd been selfish. He'd been totally irresponsible. He could have killed Bubby. Their home could have been destroyed while he was locked away in the bedroom. And what's more, underage sex was illegal. Fred had never seen her so enraged. But she saved the most savage for last.

'And where did you get the ecstasy pills?' she demanded to know.

Fred pursed his lips. No way was he going to rat on his uncle.

'I asked you a question,' she insisted.

'Just... someone at the party,' Fred mumbled.

'I'd like to know who.'

'I can't remember.'

Ally's hand tightened round the steering wheel.

'Listen Fred, she said. 'I back you up on most things, you know that. But we're not talking paint here. And I draw the line on drugs – of any sort. I've seen too many young lives destroyed.'

Fred gritted his teeth, bracing himself for the lecture. How psychoactive substances messed with your synapses. How they were far more addictive than you'd think. How they could totally deform your personality.

'But I'm not going to bother with the usual spiel,' she said. 'Because it turns out *that* doesn't work. There are other ways of skinning a cat though, and I'm afraid I agree with your father. You're going to have to pay him that money.'

'*How*? I don't have it.'

'You'll just have to get yourself a weekend job.'

Fred started to protest but Ally placed her finger against his lips.

'I know it's a drag,' she said. 'But perhaps, while you're bagging groceries or collecting dishes, you'll have a chance to consider the pros and cons of illegal drugs, before they totally screw up your life.'

*

Once the catheter was removed, Alex felt liberated. He could finally pee again like a normal person. And he could sit down and stand up without fear of ripping his urethra. But *suspicion* still held him in its grip. And that pain didn't come in fits and starts, like a catheter. It was relentless, tormenting him 24-7, torpedoing his sleep, sabotaging any hope of recovery.

In the middle of the night, he'd find himself poring over old photos, forensically comparing Joe's features with Fred's – their chins, their cheekbones, their eyebrows, their hairline. Alex was hardly a weak-jawed albino, but his resemblance to Fred could just as easily have been that of an uncle. Whereas Fred and Joe's similarities were not merely physical. They shared a wit, a fiery temper, an aptitude for art, and above all, a subversive reckless aversion to authority.

Still, after a spate of assiduous googling, he had at least made an attempt to move forward. Harvesting his own

DNA had been pretty straight forward. A sterile swab from the inside of his cheek and he was sorted. Fred's, however, had been more of a challenge. Alex waited till he'd left for school, and then – creeping around with a pair of latex gloves – he'd taken some bristles from his toothbrush; a blade from his razor; some gum from the underside of his desk; some follicles from his comb and a cigarette butt from his window-sill. After which, having opted for the super-fast service, he'd packaged them up in separate envelopes, popped them in a jiffy-bag, and sent them off.

Five working days later, just as the lab had promised, the email had landed. Prophetically perhaps, in his junk-box. Alex sat at his desk, gawping at the keyboard, paralysed with fear. He genuinely felt more terrified than he did in Mr Seaman's waiting room, before the results of his biopsy. Because for all the delinquent behaviour he'd had to endure over the past nine months, one thing was certain: the prospect of finding out that his son was *not* his son after all, was simply too awful to contemplate.

What was really doing his head in, however, was the *uncertainty*. He typed out the password, one character at a time, hovering over the return key in the certain knowledge that tapping it could trigger a chain of events from which he might never recover.

Perhaps this wasn't the best time to face up to a brand new demon? Maybe he should wait until he felt more resilient? When he'd fully recovered from the shock of finding his home had turned into a glorified squat, his eighty-nine year old mum unwittingly sedated, and his bedroom colonised for Freddie's drug-fuelled romps.

When he'd finally got used to being dumped by his wife, betrayed by his brother, and living without his prostate. It already seemed like progress of sorts just to mark the email with a flag, and transfer it from junk-mail to inbox.

Still, Alex was under no illusions. If it was going to sit there unopened for any period of time, he'd need another distraction to avoid going mad. And of all the contenders (Mandarin and six-pack included) only one felt like it could help fill the emotional vacuum inside him. The power of love, as Huey Lewis had put it, might just save his life.

'Dear PerfectCatch, I'm sorry for the radio silence. If you assumed I'd lost interest, met someone else or died, you'd be entirely wrong. And if you assumed I'm just a rude bastard who's clearly not worth bothering with – you'd be wrong again (although I couldn't blame you for jumping to that conclusion!) The truth is, I've been away on location the past couple of weeks. If we ever do get to know each other better, I promise I'll elaborate. In the meantime – if you haven't lost interest, met someone else or died (god forbid) – I'd love to renew our acquaintance!

Yours apologetically,
Alan Smithee.'

Within less than an hour, his laptop was pinging.

'Dear A.S. I'm encouraged to hear you haven't met someone else – and pleased you haven't died. To reduce the risk of either of these eventualities, why don't we meet for a drink next Friday? I can then make up my own mind as to whether you're worth bothering with!'

For the first time in weeks, Alex was smiling.

*

'Eighteen, capeesh?' Joe murmured conspiratorially, his five rings twinkling in the yellow street-light as he pressed the buzzer.

'Capeesh,' Fred murmured back.

To think that less than two hours ago, he'd been traipsing round Hammersmith in the drizzle, promoting his services as 'a responsible young adult – open to odd-jobs of any description,' and now he was outside a fancy member's club in Mayfair, smooth and chipper in his Abercrombie bomber and his brand new trainers. Although he still had no clue why Joe wanted to see him.

'Erm… eighteen what?'

'That's your age. If anyone asks.'

'Ah.'

Fred cleared his throat and stood up ramrod straight. As if that would make any difference. He'd always looked mature for his age, but eighteen was a stretch. And judging by the look she gave him when they stepped inside, the fit young receptionist thought so too. Uncle Joe slipped her a tenner and steered him quickly through the hand-painted hallway and up a wood-panelled staircase.

'What's the point of being a goddam member, if I can't invite my goddam godson for a drink?' he muttered.

'Too goddam right,' Fred agreed as they entered the

coolest bar he'd ever seen. 'And what's the point of being your goddam godson if I can't accept?'

'You speak my lingo, dude,' Joe grinned, thumping him roundly on the back, and rattling his rib-cage with his gaudy knuckleduster.

Joe knew how to bend the rules alright. So he didn't argue when the barman said he couldn't serve Fred alcohol. He just ordered two Bloody Mary's for himself and a Virgin for Fred, then calmly switched them round once Luigi's back was turned.

Fred was still doing his best to act eighteen, but there was something about the fruit and the mini umbrellas that made him suck on the straw like a child.

'Whoa!' he blurted, as the alcohol spritzed from his tear-ducts. 'That's... whoa... the best...'

Luigi glanced up from the bar.

'...*Virgin Mary*... I've ever tasted!'

'It just shows what a good Catholic can do!' Joe said, throwing Luigi a wink. 'He may be a raging jobsworth – but he certainly gives great cocktail!'

Luigi fluffed his feathers.

Joe stretched out on the big blue sofa, peeled a pistachio, and lobbed its shell into the crackling fire. 'I have a business proposition,' he said, popping the kernel into his mouth.

'A business proposition? I'm all ears Unc... Unc...'

Joe fixed him with one of his flinty stares.

'...Joe.'

'Good!' Joe grabbed another pistachio. 'Cos it's the perfect way to pay off your debts, and have some fun into the bargain. Interested?'

Fred was a lot *more* than interested. Inside he was jumping up and down. But as he was meant to be eighteen, it was important not to show it.

'Of course,' he said, trying to sound restrained and failing miserably.

'Great. You see the middle-class youth market's exploding,' his uncle explained. 'Or *growing exponentially* as the nerds put it. So I need someone to plug us in. Someone I can trust. With guts and a bit of nous. Someone who talks the talk and who's still at school – ideally a private one – with all the well-heeled connections that go with it.'

'I see,' Fred said, not seeing at all, but hoping the mist would clear any moment.

'And you know what?' Joe continued. 'You're just the person I'm looking for.'

'Really? Wow! Thank you.'

'You even tick the diversity box, for fuck's sake!'

'Great. But, like, I don't fully get it. What's the connection to scenic art?'

'Who said anything about scenic art?'

'Oh. I just thought…'

'No-one makes money from scenic art, dude. Don't get me wrong, it's got a lot going for it. But it's just a hobby. A sideline. Alongside my business interests.'

'Oh, right,' Fred said. 'So, like, what are *they*?'

Joe lowered his voice. 'Confectionary.'

'*Confectionary*?'

'Yeah. You know – sweeties. Moon Rocks. Scooby snacks. Love hearts. Like the ones I popped in your party bag the other day?'

'I see... I didn't... I hadn't realised it was an actual *business*.'

'No, funnily enough, we don't tend to stick it in the Yellow Pages. So – you in?'

'Well... what exactly would it entail?' Fred asked, suddenly a little hesitant.

'*Entail?*'

'Involve?'

'Yeah, I may not have gone to private school, dude, but I do know what entail means.'

'Of course, I just...'

'What it *entails* is this: we get you into a bunch of music fests over the summer. And you become a valued member of our sales team. Piece of piss. Or it will be for someone like you. And with the commission you make, you'll pay off your debts ten times over.'

Fred was beyond buzzed. The chance to work for his uncle, in any capacity, was awesome. Getting into a music fest for nothing – and earning serious dosh into the bargain – insane. And if his dad didn't like it – he could always just cancel the debt!

But there was something still holding him back.

'Can I... can I have a day or two to think about it?' he said.

Joe looked at him, incredulous. 'What is there to *think* about? I'm amazed you're not biting my hand off!'

'I am. Or I would be if... if it wasn't, you know...'

It did seem a bit wet to list his misgivings. He wanted to say yes – of course he did. But this was a step-up from graffiti on the science block wall. Or throwing a party behind his dad's back. Or sending Bubby off to the land of nod. Or having a drink, or smoking some dope or even popping a couple of E's. Sure, some of that was borderline, but as Uncle Joe had pointed out, teens weren't *expected* to be models of good behaviour all the time. And the consequences for those minor lapses were unlikely to be overly harsh. A rap on the knuckles or a detention were surely the worst that could happen. Whereas selling Joe's 'confectionary' was a whole new level. One he didn't necessarily want to get to. If his parents found out, they'd go ballistic. And OK, he was past the point of caring about his dad. But his mum was a different matter entirely.

He didn't need to spell it out. It was written all over his face. But Joe seemed to know how to handle it.

'By the way,' he said. 'Have you seen my new mural?'

'No?' Fred said, grateful for any change of subject. 'What mural?'

'The one I did for your mum. For her refugee centre.'

'I didn't even know you were doing one!'

'Really? I'm surprised she didn't mention it.'

He pulled out his iPhone and scrolled through an impressive collection of photos.

'Wow! That's amazing!'

Joe put the phone away, job done. 'I thought you'd like it. So… have a think about my proposal, dude. Only don't take too long, OK? I'd hate you to miss out.'

*

By the time he got home, Fred had received three texts in response to the flyer he'd dropped round some neighbouring houses offering his services for odd-jobs.

The first asked if he liked dogs. The second if he could babysit. The third if he cleaned cars. None of these activities would grant him free access to a music fest. Or help strengthen his bond with his uncle. Or get him very far with his debt. But nor would they put him in shit!

Or so he thought.

As it turned out, he spent most of Saturday up to his neck in it. How three small dachshunds could produce *so much* of the stuff was beyond him. Maybe that's why they were called 'sausage dogs'? And why their owner made Fred take six poo bags on his walk – 'in case of emergencies'. Not only did he end up using them all, he actually had to *re-cycle* two. One of the dogs wasn't well, and trying to scoop diarrhoea into thin bio-degradable bags was the grossest thing he'd ever had to do in his life. Even more disgusting, was that the poor little thing got covered in it. And to cap it all, before he got his £12.50, Fred was forced to wash it all off with a sponge.

But it didn't stop there. In the afternoon, he had to scrub fossilised seagull poo off a Range Rover. And in the evening, the skanky little brat he was baby-sitting, spent an hour on the toilet with the door wide open, making the most god-awful stink.

No way could he face another day like that. *Ever*!

What it taught him, more than anything, was that earning money was hard. So in his head, he now had a straight-forward choice. Tell his dad he could sing for his money and risk open warfare at home. Or sell a bit of 'confectionary' and risk falling out with his mum. There again, his mum obviously trusted Joe enough to use him for her purposes. So why couldn't Fred use him for *his*?

Nobody needed to know. He could just say he'd borrowed the money off Ollie. Or else had a win on the lottery.

'I knew you'd come to your senses!' Joe whooped when Fred called to accept. 'It's great to have you in the team. Your first gig's on May Bank Holiday. The Electric Sheep Fest in Berkshire. I'll get Izzy to give you the brief.'

CHAPTER 21

PERFECT CATCH

Beneath the suave linen jacket he'd picked up for a song at TK Maxx, Alex's heart was racing. He was perched on a cosy two-seater in the crowded bar of a swanky hotel in Piccadilly, looking out for a mystery blonde in a bright red jacket. And she *was* still a mystery. Despite his best endeavours, he had no idea where she lived, where she was from or what she did for a living. He didn't even know her real name.

Perhaps *that's* why his palms were so clammy. Or perhaps it had more to do with the still unopened email in his inbox. To be fair, it was barely six weeks since his op, and he definitely hadn't got his mojo back yet – assuming he ever had one. The problem was that if Perfect Catch looked anything like her photos, he knew he was punching well above his weight. To add insult to injury, he'd just seen the prices of the cocktails. If she turned out to be a lush, he'd need a second mortgage.

He glanced up from the drinks menu to see a blonde

in a bright red jacket, loitering in the doorway, scanning the room. She had the wide-eyed, nostril-flaring air of a gazelle downwind of a lion. Or a woman on a first date. Fit, sleek, with candy floss hair backlit by the evening sunshine, there was something about her, even from a distance, that seemed strangely familiar. And not just from her online photos. Alex's brain skittered back and forth across the still smoking battlefield of his recent past. Someone he'd worked with perhaps? An agency creative? An actress? Someone he'd seen in his dreams?

As they locked eyes, her face opened out into a radiant smile and she waved.

He waved back.

She sashayed towards him.

He scrambled to his feet.

'Hey Al,' she said, in a soft Aussie brogue, barely audible over the Friday night hubbub. 'It's lovely to meet you. I'm Sandra.'

The accent was unmistakeable. And so was the hair. They *had* met before in real life. She was Freddie's teacher – the one he and Ally had fallen out over at parents evening, shortly before their split. And now – *Jesus Christ!* – she was *his date*! Perhaps there *was* a god after all!

'It's lovely to meet you too Sandra,' he said. And not wanting his clammy paw to be their first point of contact, he ignored her outstretched hand and planted an eager kiss on either cheek. 'Mmmm. Great perfume!'

'Velvet Splendour,' she said. 'Aussie as a dingo in a cork-hat.'

'Thankfully it smells a bit better,' Alex said – and then worried he was trying too hard.

'Let's hope so, or this'll be a very short date!'

She glanced around, realised the only place to park her bum was on the other half of his pygmy sofa, threw him a look that said: 'nice work cobber!' and sat down. Alex followed suit, trying not to notice the flash of well-toned thigh as her skirt rode up, or the tease of cleavage as she took off her jacket.

'Popular spot,' she remarked, angling towards him and nudging her knees against his. 'Is this where you bring all your dates?'

'Only the slim ones,' he winked.

A playful smile flickered across her rosebud lips. 'Charmer!'

Either she was a consummate poker-player, or Sandra had no idea they'd met before. Which in a way was disappointing, though it would have been hard to make an impression from the conveyor belt of parents passing in and out of her classroom. And Alex hadn't mentioned a son in their correspondence this time. A grumpy teen wasn't, after all, the most seductive weapon in a charmer's armoury!

But all this begged another *Big Unanswered Question*. Should he come clean? Should he tell her he was Freddie Feinstein's father? It was obviously the *correct* thing to do. Except that their relationship – or whatever this was – might never survive it. No self-respecting school teacher would get into bed – metaphorically or otherwise – with the father of one of her pupils. Even if it didn't violate some Hippocratic oath, it would certainly compromise her position. And if the boys ever found out, she'd be toast. And why the hell *should* he be penalised for being

Freddie's dad – when there was now every chance that he wasn't!

Alex gazed into Sandra's deep blue eyes – sparkling as the Tasman Sea – and made an instant decision. He wasn't going to breathe a bloody word.

They ordered a bottle of Shiraz (Sandra's poison of choice) and embarked on some light-hearted banter on the pitfalls of internet dating. She'd signed up to *Amorous Intent* six months ago, she said, but had been on very few actual dates.

'There's a lot of creeps out there. So I'm exceedingly picky.'

'Then I'm exceedingly flattered,' Alex countered.

'You should be. You're only my fourth.'

'Snap!'

'Seriously?'

'God's honour!'

'*And*? How did they go?'

Alex was on the verge of explaining that his previous three had all sort of overlapped – until he realised there was no way of doing it without mentioning Fred.

Sandra sensed his reticence. 'Don't be shy!' she teased.

'I'm not. It's just that now I've met *you*, I've erased all the others from my memory!'

She laughed and proceeded to describe her own encounters with '*the name-dropper*', '*the dribbler*' and '*the octopus*' – each less appealing than the last.

'How will you describe *me* I wonder? When you've moved on to date number five?'

'Why? You dumping me already?' she said archly.

'No, I just…'

'Only teasing! What would you suggest?'

'You want me to write my own epitaph?'

'You said you were creative.'

'Hmm. OK. Then I'll settle for '*the charmer.*"

'Perfect! So c'mon...' She jabbed his ribs with her elbow. '...let's hear some more about *you* Mr Charmer!' She adjusted her position so they were now almost joined at the hip. 'What was the shoot you were doing?'

'What shoot?' Alex asked innocently, distracted by the warmth of her body next to his.

'The one that made you forget I existed for almost a month?'

Dammit! In his fervour to spin this new line, he'd completely forgotten his previous one.

'Ah *that* shoot. Nothing too exciting. Just... a bank ad. In Istanbul.'

'Istanbul? Sounds pretty exciting to me. I'm an Aussie. I love to travel. Fossil-hunting in Folkestone is the best I can manage these days.'

There was no way out. If he didn't want to come over as a self-obsessed prick, he *had* to ask.

'So... what... exactly do you do for a living?'

'I'm a geography teacher.'

'A geography teacher?'

'You sound surprised?'

'Yes. No. Well maybe a bit...'

'We don't all wear corduroy trousers and elbow pads you know!'

'If I ever had a geography teacher like you,' he said, reaching for another compliment to get him out of trouble, 'I'd never have dropped geography! Where do you teach?'

Alex realised his blunder as soon as it was out of his mouth. But there was no going back.

'St Joseph's,' she said. 'Do you know it?'

The path to righteousness – or the gates of hell? There was no doubt which one she was leading him down. Warm and intelligent but with a sense of fun that was more intoxicating than the Shiraz, he was already well under her Siren-like spell.

'St Joseph's? Nope, can't say I do.'

'It's an independent day school for boys.'

Alex wiped the pearl of sweat from his forehead before it trickled conspicuously down his face.

'Incidentally,' Sandra continued, 'you never talk about your son. How old is he?'

'How… do you know I have a son?' Alex asked, bracing himself for the moment of truth.

'It says so on your profile. Was it meant to be a secret?'

'My profile? Oh. Right!' Of course! The dreaded questionnaire! Body Type. Ethnicity. *Children.* 'It's so long since I filled it out I'd forgotten.'

'So?'

'Oh. F… F… Fifteen.'

'Ha! My sympathies!'

'Thank you!'

'What's his name?'

'Erm. F… F… Kent.'

'Kent? Cool. The garden of England. Where does Kent go to school?'

'Erm… Nowhere you'll ever have heard of.'

'Try me,' she said. 'I may be a foreigner, but I know most of the schools in West London.'

'Well... he... he doesn't actually live in West London. He... he lives with his mother. In Bromley.'

It was another barefaced lie, the kind he'd normally associate with his brother. Which in a weird kind of way, was quite heartening. Until now, he'd characterised Fred's transgressive tendencies as having all the hallmarks of Joe. But if Alex *himself* was capable of dishonest, self-serving, unscrupulous behaviour, then he could still be Fred's dad after all.

'Bromley huh? Isn't that *in* Kent?' Sandra mused.

'Oh – um – yes I think you're right. I'd... never actually thought about that.'

'Takes a geography teacher, right?'

'Right!'

'Break-ups are always painful Al,' she said, giving his clammy hand a comforting squeeze. 'Especially when kids are involved. Phil and I never had any, so I guess it was easier.'

'How long have you been apart?' Alex asked, seizing the opportunity to move as far away from Kent as he could.

'Well that's the thing. We're not actually apart yet.'

'Oh?'

'Don't worry. We separated months ago. But he's still hanging around in the spare room. Like a bad smell.'

Maybe he was clutching at straws, but Alex found her reassurance encouraging. Didn't it imply he was in with a shout, despite all that sweating and lying? She certainly seemed invested in their conversation. Impressed, when he mentioned the *Vegemite* ad he once made. Thrilled, when he told her *Muriel's Wedding* was in his top ten favourite movies. By the time they'd finished the bottle and a couple of whiskey sour chasers, the connection was palpable.

Both slightly fuzzy, they kissed goodbye outside the hotel, with an intensity that belied their age – or *his* at least.

'In case you're in any doubt, Mr Charmer,' Sandra said, leaning out of her Uber window and grabbing the hem of his jacket, 'I'd love to see you again.'

'That makes two of us,' Alex said gleefully.

After months of wandering around in a loveless desert, the land of milk and honey was within his reach again.

The harsh practicalities didn't hit him till later. The fact was that however suave and charming he might be, he still had a major issue *down there* which was destined to rear its head if he ever got lucky. Or rather – *wasn't!*

The only consolation, if you could call it that, was that Sandra still lived with her ex, and Alex with Fred. So getting to that stage was a long shot.

*

'May Bank Holiday? That's the weekend after next.'

'Yes. It's half term. Ollie's parents have invited me. And I've never been to a music fest before, so I said yes.'

Any sighting of Fred on a Saturday morning was a rarity. Yet here he was, in the kitchen, actually striking up a conversation. It looked for all the world like a charm offensive – and in normal circumstances, a moment to be savoured. But there was a strange mix of friendliness and defiance in his manner, as if he was covering all bases. And the ulterior motive was all too obvious.

To buy some time, Alex parked his spoon in his bowl and wiped the porridge from his lips with a piece of kitchen roll.

'What part of being grounded do you not understand?' was what he wanted to ask. But Saturday week was his birthday. A *highly significant* birthday. And even though it seemed irresponsible to let Fred swan off to a music festival, especially after his recent transgressions, the prospect of having the house to himself was suddenly rather appealing.

CHAPTER 22

A STIFF PROPOSITION

A lanky male nurse entered the room, clutching a clipboard. He seemed edgy and self-conscious, although that might have been due to his severe alopecia, as opposed to the ordeal that lay ahead for them both.

'My name's Peter,' he said. 'Is it OK to call you Alex, or would you prefer Mr Feinstein?'

'No, no, Alex is good.'

'Good. Good. Well, before we start – Alex – I need to ask you one more question. Would you feel comfortable if a trainee sits in on our session?' He cleared his throat. 'A male trainee of course.'

'Sure,' Alex said, doing his best to put the guy at ease with a genial sweep of his hand.

Although *he* was the one, surely, who needed putting at ease. Still, the end would hopefully justify the means. According to Mr Seaman, this was by far the most effective way of dealing with 'issues of functionality arising out of radical prostate surgery.' Or – put another way – his best hope of getting a hard-on.

In any case, he had no expectations of 'feeling comfortable' today, whoever sat in, and regardless of their gender. An erection, after all, was quite a personal thing. Or *his* were, at any rate. Until now, they'd only ever been shared with one person at a time, and that person – invariably female and for the last twenty-four years, *exclusively* Ally – was generally prepared to bare all too – them were the rules! So flaunting his tumescence in the presence of not one, but *two* total strangers, both fully dressed and fully male, was not something he was ever likely to 'feel comfortable' about.

And yet, despite his Ashkenazi roots, Alex was a Brit through and through. He could usually marshal a stiff upper lip, even if other parts of his anatomy remained stubbornly flaccid.

The door opened and a sallow young man shuffled in, introduced himself shyly as Jurek, and pulled up a chair to make a cosy threesome.

'OK, let's get going,' Peter said, opening a drawer behind him, and casually producing a large fibreglass penis.

'Ooh Matron!' Alex warbled in a vain attempt to lighten the mood.

His joke failed to raise either a smile or an eyebrow, although to be fair, Jurek probably didn't understand it, and Peter didn't *possess* an eyebrow.

Peter put the penis to one side, took a collection of carefully wrapped objects from a small box and proceeded to show Alex how to break off an ampoule; how to draw the solution into a syringe with a long green needle; how to expunge air-bubbles and then how to switch to the shorter yellow one. And finally, grasping the fibreglass penis again, how and where to inject. His manner was detached and pragmatic – more suitable, Alex felt, for injecting sealant into the inner tube of a car tyre than a blood-flow stimulant into the most sensitive part of a man's anatomy.

At the end of the demo, Peter glanced up and made eye-contact for the first time.

'So. Is all that clear Alex?'

Alex nodded and shifted uneasily in his chair. In a normal world, the last thing you'd want to do, would be to put a sharp object anywhere near a sensitive area, let alone an erogenous one. Yet that was precisely what he was being asked to do, under Peter's watchful eye.

And Jurek's.

Four watchful eyes, peering unblinkingly at his privates.

Alex laid out the instruments of torture with precision. But as he held the ampoule in his left hand, drawing the solution into the syringe with his right, the needle jolted and pricked the tip of his finger.

'*Owwww*!' he yelped as blood oozed.

Jurek reached for a plaster, visibly relieved to have a role beyond that of voyeur.

'You'll be more comfortable on the bed,' Peter said, once Alex had recovered and the syringe was locked and loaded.

'I bet you say that to all the boys,' Alex quipped, again without so much as a flicker of appreciation.

They were a tough crowd alright, but he did as he was told. With a stoical grimace he lowered his kecks to half-mast, perched on the edge of the bed and gently took himself in hand.

Jurek's sallow face was now red as a pepper.

Peter remained matter-of-fact, as if checking the tread on a Goodyear radial.

'Somewhere in that area,' he said, pointing his little finger at the base of Alex's penis. 'And try to avoid the veins.'

That in itself was a challenge, given how much Alex's hands were now trembling. He took a long deep breath to steady himself, then carefully lined up the needle and slowly pushed it home, his face contorted in anticipated agony.

In the event, it was remarkably pain-free.

'Well done,' Peter said.

On what? Alex wondered. On not bolting for the door? On not hitting a main artery? But he thanked him just the same.

'Jurek and I will step out now,' Peter added. 'So you can massage yourself in private.

Massage himself? Jesus Christ! There'd been no mention of *that* in the booklet!

'We'll be back in ten minutes. You should have a result by then.'

'Touch wood,' Alex said. But again the joke fell on unappreciative ears.

When the two men left, he shuffled over to the window to check the venetians were closed. Then returned to the bed. It wasn't easy to think of anything even mildly erotic in this brightly-lit room. If Trip Advisor had a page, he would definitely post some suggestions. Access to the internet, for example. Scented candles. A Barry White playlist.

After a while, with his mind fully-trained on PerfectCatch, there was a gradual stirring 'down there'. And by the time the Chuckle Brothers returned, Alex did have something to present.

Peter nodded his approval, like the King, proudly inspecting his Home Guard. Then, from the same drawer, he produced a plastic ruler, mounted with four rubber buttons. Were you meant to kneel while it was ceremoniously placed on your shoulder, Alex wondered? Or stand, so it could be pinned to your lapel like a medal? When Peter explained that it was a way to measure 'erectile strength', he duly pressed number 3: *'firm enough for penetration but not completely hard'*. There was plenty of room for improvement of course, but hey – not bad for starters!

Still, this qualified success was tempered with a health warning. If his erection lasted more than an hour, he was to run vigorously up and down some stairs. If it lasted two, he should take a cold shower. Three, grab an ice-pack. Four, call an ambulance.

With those cautions ringing in his ear, Alex quickly got dressed, took his going-away present with five injection kits inside, and said goodbye to the two men with whom, despite everything, he now felt a strange connection. Then he headed off to the tube, grateful that he'd had the foresight to wear boxers and loose-fitting trousers.

CHAPTER 23

RENEWABLE ENERGY

This was more like it! *This* was the kind of *shit* Fred could get used to. The endless green fields. The beautiful cloudless sky. And DJ Koze's punchy groove fizzing through his headphones. It was the inaugural Electric Sheep Fest near Hungerford, and Fred was travelling first class. The upgrade only cost five quid and Uncle Joe had offered to pick up the tab.

So yes, of course he was psyched. Not just because some of his favourite UK artists were in the line-up. But also because a load of extra tickets had been released last week and he'd managed to talk some of his mates into grabbing them. On top of all that – Chanel and Hestie were going to be there, and they'd asked if he was up for sharing their tent.

'*Does the Pope shit in the woods!*?' he'd texted back.

And to think he was getting paid for his troubles! According to Uncle Joe, by the end of the weekend, he could pocket five hundred quid. *Five hundred quid!* You didn't get that, walking dogs or washing cars.

The only drag was having to hang around in the B & Q car park for more than two hours in the scorching sunshine, waiting for Uncle Joe's candyman. The guy overslept – or so he said – and as a result Fred missed a lift from Mikey's sister. So by the time he made it to Hungerford, the rest of his crew would be trashed. There again, it shouldn't take long to catch up. And to be fair it was a small price to pay for an awesome Bank Hol.

*

'I hope you're not trying to take advantage!' Sandra said, clinking the bottle of Malbec with her half-empty glass and unleashing one of her trademark smiles.

'Wouldn't dream of it,' Alex said, topping her up again.

He'd lost count of how many glasses she'd had, but they were half way through their second bottle, and he'd been going slow, for obvious reasons. Sandra could certainly hold her drink, but she was a lot more 'relaxed' than when she first arrived.

And yet, with her little red dress and her four inch heels, her copper skin and her beacon eyes, she still looked bloody fantastic. Five-and-a-half feet of pure Aussie sunshine.

The real question, was what did she see in *him* – a sexagenarian with health issues, desperately clinging to a career in an industry that venerated youth, and a home from which his estranged wife had vowed to evict him, that he shared with a moody adolescent who may or may not be his son? The fact that she was blissfully unaware of all this, only served to heighten his stress-levels.

He'd certainly felt devious, scurrying around the living room, hiding all Fred's photos. And Ally's too – in case she'd made more of an impression at parents' evening. But if you were going to weave that tangled web, you had to weave it properly. For much the same reason, he'd decided not to tell Sandra that today was in any way special. He didn't want her thinking she'd been lined up as some kind of birthday conquest. And having inadvertently 'mislaid' six years along the way, it seemed safer all round not to bring up the subject of birthdays. But that hadn't stopped him preparing an epic dinner. He'd learned how to do Coquille Saint Jacques and rack of lamb at a half-day cookery course Ally had bought him two Christmases back. The fact that they were still pretty much the *only* things he could cook, was something else he would keep to himself.

Up till now it had all worked a treat. Or at least, Sandra seemed to be having a good time. At the end of the meal, he steered her through to the living room, where the lights were low, the candles lit and Leonard Cohen growling mellifluously from the Bose minispeaker. She waltzed past his two armchairs and spread herself out on the sofa.

'Nice to share a couch that wasn't made in Lilliput!' she purred, patting the cushion enticingly.

'Hold that thought!' Alex smiled. 'I'll be back in a sec. Nigella can entertain you in my absence!'

He passed her Ally's favourite coffee-table book and disappeared upstairs. If it were just for a pee and a quick splash of aftershave, the downstairs loo would have done the job. But Alex had another agenda.

OK, maybe it was a bit forward. This was only their second date after all. But the mood seemed right and the signals positive. And given their respective housemate situations – who knew when there'd be another opportunity?

He pulled Peter's going home present from the ensuite cabinet, laying out the ammunition with military precision. Such field manoeuvres had been carried out on several occasions since his induction, but this was the first time he'd be engaging in actual armed combat. He attached the needle to the syringe, removed its plastic cap, snapped open the ampoule and ingested its solution. But once again his hands were trembling, once again he impaled his finger, and this time his yelp was so loud that not even Leonard Cohen could cover it up.

'What the hell are you doing up there?' Sandra hollered.

'Nothing…' Alex hollered back. 'Just… my teeth.'

'Well try and leave some in!'

Alex could see his face refracted in the single glinting pearl of liquid now quivering on the needle's point. One-part trepidation, three-parts fervour. Six decades of masculinity, hanging in the balance.

'Hey – have I frightened you off?'

It was the Aussie interrogative again. Alex mustered a laugh, lowered his boxers, steadied his hands, aimed the needle carefully, ineluctably, towards its target – engaged, inserted and squeezed the trigger.

There was no going back now, the soufflé was in the oven. But he did have around ten minutes before it rose, so plenty of time to get things going again.

'At last,' Sandra sighed as he returned to the living room, flushed with vim, vigour and two milligrams of phentolamine mesilate. 'I thought you'd done a runner!'

With an imperious toss of the head, she kicked off her heels, leant back against the cushions, and hooked her long sleek legs across his grateful lap.

'Now where were we?' she enquired coquettishly.

'Erm. I think we were discussing your dissertation on renewable energy.'

'Were we? How dull.'

Alex could think of no obvious transition from renewable energy to the interchange of bodily fluids. He'd always found that gear-shift a challenge, even in his prime, and it felt no easier now in this brave new #MeToo world, especially with no actual bodily fluid to contribute. So it was to his enormous relief that Sandra seized the initiative. With Leonard urging her to *Dance Me To The End Of Love,* she swayed to her feet and danced Alex to the end of the living room.

Within moments, the eco log-fire had transported him to the natural wonders of the Antipodes. He had a willing tour-guide too. By the time they were *A Thousand Kisses Deep*, their clothes were scattered on the shag-pile, and Sandra's legs clamped around his trunk like a koala's. She reached down, grasped his now fully renewed energy in her soft warm hand, and was starting to guide it home… when Alex heard the front door click open.

The moment he stepped inside, Fred could tell something was up. The reek of Lynx Africa in the hallway. The woman's coat draped over the bannister. The two silhouettes scuttling around the living room, leaping onto armchairs, slapping on fake smiles.

'Hey Dad,' he said, struggling to take it all in. 'Is that my Lynx Africa?'

'Jesus Christ Fre... Fr... for goodness sake,' Alex stammered. 'Why aren't you...?'

'I didn't go in the end. The car was full.'

OK – so that wasn't entirely true. And yes of course he should have tucked the stash down his pants like Uncle Joe had told him. In fact, for most of the journey, he had. But by the time he got to Hungerford, his package had started to chaff. No-one was that well endowed anyway, not even on Pornhub. So he'd transferred it to a secret pocket in his rucksack, which as it turned out, wasn't that secret. After another major bollocking, the jobsworths at the gate had snagged the lot and ordered him to 'bugger off back home to mummy and daddy.'

Sandra's shock had morphed into pure unadulterated fury. Alex could feel it radiating from every pore. And who could blame her? He found his *own* behaviour repugnant.

'You should've... let me know you were *coming to stay*,' he told Fred. 'I would've... made up the bed.'

Fred glanced around the semi-lit room. The underwear on the floor. The flickering fire. His dad, stark-bollock naked, perched on the edge of a chair, holding a large book over his crotch. His surprisingly fit-looking friend – a dead ringer for Fred's geography teacher – clutching bits of clothing to her equally naked body.

Bloody hell! It *was* his geography teacher. The one member of staff every boy fancied the pants off, was now in his house with her pants *actually* off.

'Hello Miss Banks.'

Miss Banks! The name itself a gift to smutty schoolboy rhymesters. Fred's fingers were twitching like a gunslinger's, itching to whip out his phone and start filming. It would have been a nailed-on TikTok chart-topper, a video-viral of global proportions. The problem was he didn't have his phone. He'd gone and left the bloody thing on the train.

'Hello Freddie,' she replied.

Who knew what was going through her head as she sat there with her dress in one hand and his father's chinos in the other, covering her modesty like an exotic dancer with stage-fright.

Fred stared at his father in disbelief. How did this even happen? Had he pounced on her at parents evening? Stalked her on the school-intranet? Ambushed her riding home on her pink Vespa? It was all so horribly sleazy.

Still, it would be lame not to use it to his advantage.

'Erm, I haven't had a chance to do my essay I'm afraid. What with one thing and another.'

'What essay?'

Her voice was devoid of its usual swagger. In fact it was barely audible over the music.

'The one on climate change?'

Climate change? Alex glared at him. His biological cock was ticking and they were talking *climate change!*

'Oh, that's... don't worry about it,' she murmured.

Boom! Miss Banks never let you get away without doing your homework. *Ever*! Even if you had leprosy. Or your house had fallen into a sinkhole. Or you'd spent the night in a rat-infested police-cell. She was a stickler for homework, Miss Banks.

'You mean I don't have to do it?'

'On this one occasion.'

'Cool. Thanks!'

So that's how it worked! Your dad shagged your teacher and your teacher let you off your homework. Get in!

'So… why didn't you call?' Alex asked, finally emerging from his coma.

Fred shrugged. 'I couldn't.'

'Why not?'

'My phone got… stolen.'

Alex knew he was lying. But sitting naked in an armchair, with Nigella Express his last line of defence, was a weak position from which to exert paternal authority. And yet, *something* needed to be done. Sandra's professional reputation was now at the mercy of a spotty teenager with all the integrity of a chat-room troll. If this were to get out, her job would be untenable.

'That's a bummer,' Alex said, brain cogs whirring. 'But don't worry, I'll get you a new one.'

'Thank you.' Fred was playing it cool, but inside he was elated.

'On one condition,' Alex added.

'What's that?'

'That you never breathe a word to anyone. And I mean *anyone*. *Ever*. Is that understood?'

'Breathe a word about what Dad?' Fred said, like butter wouldn't melt.

To say a weight had been lifted from Sandra's sun-kissed shoulders would be an understatement. It would also be a lie. Her fixed smile had transmogrified into a death-mask. It was clear Alex would have his work cut out now. But hey, he'd never been a quitter. And having successfully negotiated the NDA, he now needed to get Fred out of the house, ASAP. Before the prospect of providing an involuntary tent-pole for the paramedics' blanket became all too real.

He reached over to rummage in the pockets of the chinos that Sandra was still clutching to her bosom.

'Here Freddie,' he said, handing him a twenty pound note. 'Go buy yourself something to eat. And keep the change.'

'Thanks Dad. Will do. Bye Miss Banks. Nice to… erm… *see* you!'

'I'm so sorry Sandra,' Alex said, as soon as Fred was out of the door. 'If I'd thought there was the slightest risk of…'

Sandra silenced him with a look so withering he was surprised it didn't turn him to stone. And then, with *That's No Way To Say Goodbye* playing in the background, she scurried around, clambering into her clothes, and stomped out of the house, slamming the door behind her.

CHAPTER 24

LOOSE TALK

'Freddie told me what happened,' Ally said, her voice warm and empathetic as a switchblade.

It was Sunday afternoon, and they were in Starbucks, at her request. Alex would never have taken her call if she hadn't hijacked him on the landline. They'd still not talked, after all, since his mother dropped her bombshell. But maybe it was time for a few home truths.

'What happened *when*?' he said.

'Last night.'

'Ah.'

'*Ah*? Is that all you can say?'

'Well I *could* say: *Jesus Christ, he didn't waste much time, the little shit.* But I'm trying to resist the temptation.'

'This is not a joke Alex. How do you think it feels for a teenager to arrive home, shattered and sad after all his half-term plans have collapsed, to find his father butt-naked on the living room floor, shagging one of his teachers?'

Alex had to admit that the optics weren't great. And any mum would instinctively defend her child, however much of a shit he may have been. Plus Ally was all too aware of the deep psychological damage that parents could do to their kids. The '*Philip Larkin effect*' as she dubbed it in one of her papers. On top of that, she was clearly feeling guilty about Fred. All her spare time had gone into the imminent opening of her refugee centre, so it was hardly surprising she felt the need to over-compensate.

But the most pressing concern for Alex right now, was that she was talking far too loud. The café was almost full and conversations were breaking off all around them, heads turning their way.

He shifted uneasily in his chair. 'Ally – do you mind…?'

'Actually I do,' she said, unconsciously twisting her wedding ring round and round her finger. 'I mind very much. I find it deeply unsettling that someone I was married to for so many years can behave in such a reckless and irresponsible way.'

'Well – as you said – different rules apply when couples…'

'Don't be obtuse Alex! I'm not talking about *us*. I'm talking about Fred. This is precisely the kind of trauma that can have a deeply damaging effect on a child's development. *Our* child's development.'

She managed to resist citing Philip Larkin but Alex could see where it was heading.

'The bottom line,' she concluded, 'is that it's not safe for him to carry on living with you. I need you out of the house by the end of the month.'

That's where.

From the corner of his eye, Alex could see three middle-aged ladies on another table, openly staring, as if this were café theatre. But trying to placate Ally in this kind of mood, was a lost cause. So instead, he tried to set an example, gently removing the Earl Grey tea-bags from the pot, methodically pouring tea into both cups, quietly adding milk and sugar.

His composure only wound her up more.

'Did you hear me?' she seethed. 'What do you have to say about it?'

Alex took a sip and returned the cup to its saucer.

'What I have to say,' he continued with the same icy calm, 'is that I admire your nerve.'

'I beg your pardon?'

'Accusing *me* of being reckless and irresponsible.'

'So how would *you* describe your sordid little fling with Fred's geography teacher?'

'Possibly the same way as I'd describe *your* sordid little fling with his uncle.'

'For Christ's sake, change the record! I already told you. It was an entirely professional arrangement.'

'And what kind of arrangement was it the *first* time round?'

'I'm sorry?'

'Sixteen years ago. What was it *then*?'

'What the hell are you suggesting?' she blustered. 'Whatever it is, I…'

'…Don't waste your breath Ally. What I'd like to know – what I *need* to know is – which one of us is Fred's father? Only it kind of makes a difference, going forward.'

Ally glanced around, dropping her voice to a whisper.

'I have no idea where you get your fake news Alex,' she said, gently stroking her right eyebrow. 'But…'

A heavily-built woman was standing close to their table, peering down over a pair of tortoiseshell glasses.

'If I were you,' she said, lowering her large ruddy-cheeked face between theirs, like a lunar eclipse, 'I'd keep your voices down when you're out in public. You never know who might be listening.'

And with the most synthetic of smiles, she ambled off to join her two companions at the exit.

*

Sod's law. First up after the Whitsun break was double geography. Fred actually considered bunking off, until it occurred to him that it must be ten times worse for Miss Banks. He wasn't the one, after all, prancing around in the buff, shagging an OAP.

Not surprisingly, Miss Banks didn't so much as glance in Fred's direction for the entire lesson. And at the end – as she waltzed round collecting their essays – she deliberately missed him out.

Felix poked him in the ribs with a pencil. 'Why didn't she ask for yours Fred?' he hissed.

'Oh that's… because…'

Back at her desk, Miss Banks turned and eyeballed him.

'…because I've already handed mine in.'

Felix seemed happy enough with that, and so did Miss Banks. Fred, too, was pleased to have kept his side of the bargain. Until morning break, when his mates started bleating on about the Electric Sheep Fest. The best weekend ever. The best sounds. The best vibe. Fred knew they were bigging it up for his benefit, but when Rory launched into a blow-by-blow account of his steamy nights with Chanel and Hestie, Fred had had enough.

He was in the library, leafing through Viz and minding his own business, when Mikey rocked up, grinning from ear to ear.

'How's it going hombre?' he said, flopping down on the bench beside him, and thrusting his big round face into Fred's airspace.

Fred could feel himself bristling. 'If you're gonna bore me rigid about Electric Sheep, *hombre*,' he said, 'you can flock off.'

'I have no intention of boring you rigid,' Mikey said.

'So what's *that* all about?'

'What?'

'The stupid grin?'

'I wish I could tell you.'

'No worries then,' Fred said, happy to get back to Buster Gonad.

'Aren't you just a teeny bit curious?' Mikey said.

'Not really.'

'Well, what if I said it was about your mum and dad?'

Fred swung round to face him again. 'What about them?'

'Ah – *now* he wants to know! What's it worth?'

'What do you mean *what's it worth*?'

'I mean if I was to let you in on this piece of hot goss – what do I get in return?'

'You're out of luck mate. I'm skint.'

'This is far too precious to give away for nothing, even to a bestie. But I'm open to any kind of trade-off.'

Fred folded the magazine and lobbed it onto the table in front of them. 'OK. Well if it's that *precious*... and I'll be the judge of that... I've got some super-hot goss of my own. But you'd have to swear on your life to keep it to yourself.'

They sealed the deal with a fist-bump.

'OK,' Mikey said in hushed tones, like he was about to reveal the riddle of sphinx. 'So yesterday afternoon, my mum was at Starbucks in Hammersmith...'

*

Ally insisted it was malicious tittle-tattle – of course she did. Even if he'd *filmed* her having sex with Joe on his altar-table, she'd have claimed it was AI-generated. Or that Alex had paid his VFX mates to fake it.

On the plus side, her campaign to evict him had suddenly lost all traction. Information was power – power which Ally knew he wouldn't hesitate to use when cornered. With Freddie, with her parents, or if push came to shove – in a court of law.

On the minus side, Alex genuinely didn't know how long he could bear to share his home with a son who despised him.

Especially if he wasn't his son.

The one thing he'd hoped would get him through this mess, was clearly an absolute non-starter. *Amorous Intent* had lost its allure. He couldn't even bring himself to glance at the website any more. As some wise old soul once said, you couldn't love someone else, until you loved yourself. And right now, he couldn't *stand* himself.

Booze didn't come naturally to an Ashkenazi Jew. Or it didn't to Alex at any rate. Apart from the occasional nip of Palwin No 4, no alcohol passed his lips till he was at least sixteen. But now he was making up for lost time. A bottle of Burgundy. A whisky or gin. A brandy and benedictine nightcap. And it certainly numbed the pain. But it didn't seem to help him face his demons. So those dreaded DNA results were still sitting there in his inbox, unopened, like a ticking time-bomb.

And sadly, they weren't the only thing on Alex's mind. Not after the call he'd had from his urologist's secretary, inviting him in for an urgent consultation.

*

'Is everything OK Fred?' Ally asked. 'Only you look a little... troubled.'

They were gazing out at the sunset from the 72nd floor of the Shard, clutching their two-scoop gelatos. Ally had been promising to bring him here for years. But right now Fred was far too 'troubled' to appreciate the view. To find out from a friend, that your dad might *not* be your dad after all, was always likely to be '*troubling*'. And so was being lied to, all your life, by the one person in the world you thought you could trust.

That aside though... *Mum and Uncle Joe*! Bloody hell – who knew? No really – who *knew*? Maybe no one? Maybe *everyone* except him? But of course his mum would never fess up on the phone. And although she was just as unlikely to fess up in person – at least Fred would be able see the whites of her eyes when she denied it.

'Do you mind if I ask you something Mum?' he said.

'Of course darling. Ask away.'

'It's a bit... I dunno... a bit personal?'

Ally placed a comforting hand on his arm. 'That's what mums are for – right?'

'And... like... would you promise to give me an honest answer, even if it's awkward?'

Ally was already looking awkward. More than awkward. Shifty. And doing that thing she did with her eyebrow. And as she turned back to the window to avoid Fred's gaze, her shoulder-bag swung round, knocking the ice-cream clean out of his hand. It dive-bombed his shoe, splatting it with pistachio and panna cotta. A huddle of Chinese tourists broke off from their selfies to giggle and point.

'I'm so sorry,' Ally said, stooping to pick up the smashed cone. 'I'll get you another.'

'I'm OK thanks Mum.'

'No, I insist.'

'*I've had enough,*' Fred yelled, grabbing her elbow, then letting it go on her sharp intake of breath, and gasps from the tourists. 'Sorry,' he added, 'but I do need to ask you this question.'

Ally stood rooted to the spot. Cones akimbo. 'OK darling. What is it?'

Fred's heart was beating like a bongo.

'I need to know... I need to know if Dad is *actually* my dad?'

Ally's eyes widened. 'What a bizarre question,' she said. 'Of course Dad's your dad. Why on earth would you ask me that?'

'Because Mikey told me he wasn't.'

'I beg your pardon?'

'His mum was in Starbucks on Sunday.'

'So?'

Ally was trying to look unfazed, but Fred could tell she was rattled.

'So… she saw you in there. With Dad.'

'How did she know it was us?'

'Does it matter? You *were* there, weren't you?'

'Yes but…'

'I don't know how she knew it was you. She must have recognised you from school or something.

'Ah.'

'Anyway, she overheard your conversation. And she heard Dad accuse you of…'

'It's a complete and utter lie,' Ally said.

'Do you mean Mikey made it up? Or Dad did?'

'How on earth could you think I'd have anything to do with Joe of all people? He's just about the opposite of everything I admire in a person.'

'Then how comes you got him to paint the mural for your new centre?'

'Who told you about that?

'He did.'

'OK… well… he happens to be a talented artist.'

'Right. So he's not *all* bad then?'

'Did I ever say he was?'

Ice-cream was dribbling through the smashed cone in

her left hand, but she ignored it, turning to the window and gazing out at the Lego-like structures beneath them.

'*L'appel du vide,*' she murmured.

'Sorry?'

'The call of the void.'

'What are you on about Mum?'

'You know – that feeling of being drawn towards the edge of a very high building. Some people see it as a kind of death-wish, but it's not that. It's more the sense of liberation you feel when you step out of your hermetically-sealed and predictable life. In the full knowledge you can step back into it again whenever you want.'

Fred literally had no clue what she meant. But before he could ask her to say it again, in actual English, something jolted her out of her trance.

'Oh god – look at me!' she said, finally clocking the puddle of ice-cream by her feet, and bounding off in search of a bin.

*

Having got nowhere fast with his mum, Fred had no option but to broach the subject with his grandma. And Sunday lunch at hers was the perfect opportunity. He put down his knife and fork and cleared his throat.

'Bubby, can I ask you a question?'

'Of course you can Bubala. Anything you like.'

'Except her age and weight'! Stavros said playfully, cupping a chubby hand round Bubby's chins.

If only Stavros wasn't stuck to her like a limpet. He'd even gone with to pick Fred up from the station, despite having to heave his incredible bulk in and out of Bubby's tin can. Still, at least Dad wasn't there. Or rather *Alex*. He had a conference call or some such. Which seemed highly unlikely on a Sunday. Far more likely was that he simply couldn't face all that one-to-one time with Fred in the car. Or else was too pissed to drive. Whatever. It meant Fred was free to ask Bubby anything he liked. Except her age and weight.

Bubby giggled like a schoolgirl and said something frisky which Fred didn't catch, thank god. Stavros parked his wobbly paunch on the table and puckered up. When he pulled away, there was a thin brown smudge above her mouth which made Fred feel queasier still.

'It's got nothing to do with her age or weight,' Fred assured them. 'It's about Uncle Joe.'

Bubby stiffened. 'We don't talk about him in this house,' she said frostily.

'Why not?'

She stared at her plate.

'Is it something to do with my mum?'

'Of course not,' she said defensively. 'Why would it have anything to do with your mum?'

'I dunno. I heard a rumour, that's all.'

Bubby looked flustered. 'What rumour?'

'That Mum and Uncle Joe were once... you know... that they'd had a *thing*. A *fling*... or whatever. Before I was born.'

Bubby mumbled something under her breath.

'It's just... if it's true...' Fred persisted, 'then it's possible that I'm...'

'*Arketa!*' Stavros slammed his knife and fork down

on his plate. 'Did you hear what your grandma said? She don't like the Joe talk in this house. It make her upset. If you wanna know something about Joe – go and ask to him yourself. In the meanwhile, eat up your kugel.'

*

Mr Seaman turned back from his computer screen, removed his glasses, and placed them carefully on the leather inset of his imposing mahogany desk. For a usually jocular man, he had an alarmingly serious expression on his face.

'So how are you feeling?' he asked solemnly, his forehead furrowed and his gimlet eyes boring deep into Alex, as though conducting a PET scan.

For some reason, Alex's natural tendency to catastrophise always disappeared in the presence of a doctor. Especially a doctor who looked so concerned.

'I'm feeling… fine,' he trilled. 'Top notch.'

Of course it was a brazen lie. Funnily enough, when you've just found out that your wife's had an affair with your brother and that your son might not be your son after all, the last thing you feel is 'fine'. But as it was now over three months since the removal of his prostate, and Alex had been summoned to discuss the results of a follow-up blood test, the surgeon was unlikely to be interested in his psychological wellbeing.

'Any bone pain? Fatigue? Trouble peeing?'

'No,' Alex said with an anodyne smile that concealed a growing sense of unease. 'Why?'

'Well I'll cut to the chase,' Mr Seaman said gravely. 'After a radical prostatectomy, your PSA is meant to be undetectable. And I'm afraid, yours isn't. You have a reading of four ng per millilitre, which is unusually high. Of course blood tests are prone to the occasional blip, and that's why we asked you to do a second one. But this is even higher.'

'Oh,' Alex said, suddenly plagued by aching bones, a recalcitrant bladder, and chronic fatigue, all at once. 'What does that mean?'

'Well, we can't be certain until we've investigated further, but we have to be realistic. It may mean the cancer's metastasised.'

Metastasised. The word hit Alex like a sledgehammer. He'd heard it over and over again, after the barrage of tests, consultations and therapies that they'd put his poor father through. It was the word which, for Alex, always signalled his dad's harrowing slide towards an unconscionably brutal death, and which suddenly dislodged his own already tenuous grip on reality.

Mr Seaman was still talking – or at least, his mouth was still opening and closing – but Alex was no longer listening. And aside from a few random words – *referral… oncologist… malignant… lymph nodes… life-expectancy…* he was no longer hearing either. His father's ghost flashed before him like a victim of Belsen, jaundiced, haggard, skeletal, his face contorted in excruciating pain, his sunken eyes pleading with Alex to help put him out of his misery.

Ally had always warned Alex against doing medical research on the internet. It would prey on his paranoia, she said. Exploit his hypochondria. But the moment he got home, there was no way he could stop himself. And the more he researched, the more he knew it was curtains. The only question now was how to deal with it.

*

Uncle Joe sank back in his big red throne, toked on his spliff, and passed it to Fred.

Fred watched the smoke curl slowly up to the rafters, then followed suit. 'Whoa!' he said. 'This is good shit!'

'I'm hardly gonna give you *bad* shit am I?' Joe winked. 'Even if you *did* lose me a shed-load of merch.'

'I'm so sorry about that. I stuck it down my pants like you suggested but…'

'Forget about it dude! What's gone is gone. But we need to get you back in the ring again – pronto.' Uncle J reached across for the joint, took another pull and shot a cascade of perfect O's across the room. 'You up for that?'

'Of course.'

Fred was trying to rock a proper business-like vibe, although being half-stoned already, it wasn't all that convincing. Still, Joe seemed happy enough.

'You're a good kid, you know that?' he said. 'I never wanted a kid of my own. But if I did, I'd be happy to have one like you!'

Wow. That was some compliment. Revealing too maybe.

'Thank you!'

'You're welcome.'

Joe chuckled to himself as he stubbed the roach in a large metal bowl and started rolling another.

This was Fred's opportunity. It's why he'd come after

all, and he'd soon be too baked for any kind of sensible convo. So it was now or never. But how do you pop a question like that?

'Excuse me Uncle Joe. Could you help me out with something? I was wondering... have you ever shagged my mum? Is it possible, do you think, that you got her up the duff? That you are, in fact, the Darth Vader to my Luke Skywalker?'

Possibly not. In any case, while he was trying to find the right words, Joe pulled the rug from under him.

'So, how do you fancy a weekend at Glasto?' he said.

'*Glasto?* Are you winding me up?'

Joe ran his tongue along the edge of the Rizla. 'That'd be cruel, wouldn't it?'

'I would literally *kill* to go to Glasto.'

'Well you won't have to do that. And you won't have to stick anything down your pants either. By the time you get there, the merch will be in place. You can even go commando if you like!'

Joe slipped a perfectly handcrafted reefer between his lips, lit it with a sleek black Zippo, took a long deep drag – and handed it over.

'That's *so* cool Uncle Joe. Thank you! I promise I won't let you down.'

Fred's attempt to inhale whilst simultaneously looking like a responsible eighteen-year old, triggered a violent coughing fit.

Joe grabbed a bottle of Evian from a side-table, and lobbed it over.

'It's next weekend though,' he said as Fred swigged. 'Is that gonna be OK?'

'One way or another, I'll be there. Just leave it to me!'

'Cool. Izzy will sort out your tickets and transport. There's just one thing we need to agree before you head off. And this time I'm serious.'

'What's that?' Fred asked.

'That you stop fucking calling me Uncle!'

*

Hammersmith Bridge had always been a good place to watch the sunset, especially since they'd closed it to traffic. And even from the depths of his despair, Alex could see that this evening's show was going to be a spectacle. There were gawpers dotted all along the western walkway, ooh-ing and aah-ing and pointing their phones as the big golden orb took its final extravagant bow. The river was calm as a millpond and the breeze that caressed his face, as gentle as it was warm. Which was odd, in a way, because the bridge was actually swaying. More than swaying in fact – *lurching* – like a trawler in a storm. Alex had to cling to the handrail just to stay afloat.

Or maybe *he* was the one that was lurching? The Tignanello he'd quaffed to help palliate the diagnosis had certainly taken its toll. He'd intended to stay at home and slowly drink himself into a coma until he'd been overtaken – *god knows why* – by a strange deep-seated urge to stagger out and watch the sun slowly sink over the horizon.

OK, cards on table, Alex *did* know why. A few years ago, a film director friend whom he'd always admired – had leapt to his death from a Los Angeles bridge. His career was still flourishing. He had a big fat income, an enviable Hollywood life-style and a wife and kids who adored him. So nobody knew why he'd done it, although it was rumoured he'd been told he was terminally ill.

Alex had always regarded his friend as a role model. A successful British commercials director, living the dream. But he was famously pragmatic, hardheaded and tough. So when that dream came to an abrupt end, he didn't muck about. He put an abrupt end to his life as well. And today, in the wake of this hammer blow, Alex couldn't help wondering if he had what it took to follow his lead. He leaned over the railing and gazed down into the inky river. Yes, it was still as a millpond tonight. But appearances were so often deceptive. Who knew what hazards lurked beneath. According to stuff he'd read, the Thames had a fierce undertow. All kinds of flotsam and jetsam. And it was full of e coli. As a matter of fact, right where he was standing, a small metal plaque was embedded in the handrail, honouring a soldier who'd jumped from that very spot a hundred years ago, almost to the day, to save a drowning woman. He'd survived the fall, but died two weeks later from tetanus, poor bugger. And however much Alex wanted out, that wasn't a risk he was prepared to take. No, if he was going to bail, he needed to find a different exit.

*

When Fred got home, Alex was fast asleep in a deckchair. Fred could see him there in the light-spill from the kitchen, with two empty bottles on the paving stone beside him.

He looked wasted, which was maybe just as well, because Fred was too. *So* wasted, in fact, that he failed to spot the laundry basket next to the washing machine, tripped, and careered into the ironing board, which collapsed with an almighty clatter.

Alex jerked upright.

'Jesus Christ! Fred? You nearly gave me a… a….' he trailed off, all too aware he was slurring his words.

Fred clambered to his feet and stood the ironing board against the wall.

'I didn't know you'd turned the kitchen into the Crystal Maze, did I?'

Alex had no idea what that meant. All he knew was that Fred reeked of smoke. Even in his current condition, he could smell it from there. But somehow he managed to stop himself saying so.

'Where're you off to?' he said instead.

'My bedroom.'

'So… why're you whirring your bomber?'

'I've just come back. From band practice.'

Alex knew his brain was a bit cloudy, but he also knew there were a couple of things wrong with that answer. First, it was a school night, so Fred wasn't meant to go anywhere, not even band-practice. Second, regardless of what night it was – he was meant to be grounded.

Still, Alex was is no fit state for a row. 'There's some… stuff… in the fridge… if you're hungry,' he said, sinking back into his stupour.

Fred nodded. Yes, he was hungry alright. Whacky backy always gave him the munchies. And he hadn't eaten a thing since lunchtime. But there was something he needed to do first, before Alex drifted back into his slumber.

'Oh, by the way,' he said, clinging to the garden door as if it were a life-raft. 'I'm away next weekend.'

Alex prised his eyes open again.

'It's Ollie's birthday,' Fred went on. 'So his parents have invited me and some mates to Center Parcs.'

He could have come clean of course, but not without starting World War III. Plus Uncle Joe wanted his name kept out of it. So Ollie and Center Parcs was a far safer option.

Alex preferred the line of least resistance. But while he was still here, and while Fred was still living in his bloody house, he had a duty of care. Plus it was a matter of principle for fuck's sake.

'What part... what part of being *grounded* do you not understand Fred?' he burbled. 'It's barely six weeks since you nearly destroyed our home. When're you gonna start paying me back? And how're you gonna get a weekend job, if you keep buggering off?'

Fred shook his head, disdainfully. 'You didn't mind me buggering off when you were banging Ms Banks, did you?' he scoffed. 'And anyway – who are *you* to tell me I can't go?'

This was it. The storming of the Bastille. The peasant's revolt. The Arab Spring. The attack on the Capitol. Alex felt a weird kind of solidarity with every government, every leader, every boss, every peacekeeper, who'd ever faced a braying mob. But drunk or sober – he had no intention of firing into the crowd. Over and over again, history had proved that to be counter-productive. And anyway, it simply wasn't his shtick.

And yet, *some* kind of authority had to be exerted, or else anarchy would prevail.

'Erm. How about – *your father?*'

A contemptuous little smile flickered across Fred's lips. 'Are you though?' he said, pulling the pin from the hand grenade. 'Are you really?'

Alex froze. *He knew! Who the hell told him?*

Fred didn't hang around. As far as he was concerned, that was the end of the matter. With or without *Alex's* blessing, he was going to Glasto on Friday.

SUMMER

CHAPTER 25

GLASTO

The winds that buffeted the coach all the way to Somerset, and the rain that lashed its windows, did nothing to dampen Fred's excitement. It didn't matter that he was travelling on his own. Izzy had written out a clear set of instructions for his arrival and that made him a lot more confident. What's more, everyone on board was super-hyped and super-friendly, so the three and a half hours went by in a flash.

But nothing could prepare him for Worthy Farm, where the sheep and cows had been replaced by thousands of party-animals in whacky costumes and crazy rain-hats – all hell-bent on having the time of their lives, despite the wind and the rain and the mud. In fact, if anything, that only added to the fun.

Even the turnstiles where Fred queued up for his festival wristband were jumping. And once inside, the long squelchy trek to the campsite – past an amazing collection of bars, food-stalls, jugglers, stages, a scrap-metal sculpture, a giant tea-cup and a cardboard tower – was cooler than any Disneyland theme ride.

By the time he made it to Park Home Ground campsite, the rain had eased off a little. The large lime green tent with its flying pig flag was exactly where Izzy had said it would be when she'd dropped off his tickets on Wednesday. And she was waiting inside as promised, looking properly peng in her purple fleece, woollen leggings and waterproof boots. She rushed over to greet him like a long lost hero.

'You poor thing,' she exclaimed. 'You're soaked through.'

She wasn't wrong. In his Johnny Rotten T shirt, polyester bomber and Vans, Fred was dressed for a *summer music festival* – unlike everyone else who'd clearly had the nouse to check the forecast.

'I'm fine,' he just about managed to say without letting her hear his teeth chatter.

'Well take off your jacket, so I can give you a big squidgy hug.'

The big squidgy hug alone was worth coming all this way for. And to think he was getting paid too!

'Mi casa es tu casa,' Izzy smiled, as she showed him where to leave his bedroll. Was there something seductive in her manner, he couldn't help wondering, or was she just being friendly?

After he'd towelled himself down and she'd lent him one of her jumpers, they lounged on her double air-bed, eating tofu and beetroot wraps and listening to Nirvana.

'I'd give you some happy dust,' she said, 'but I mustn't lead you astray.'

Fred would have given his right arm to be led astray by Izzy, but he couldn't quite bring himself to say so.

'Is my uncle here?' he asked instead, in an effort to stop himself drooling.

'He'll be along later,' Izzy smiled. 'And he's looking forward to seeing you. Word to the wise though. Don't call him uncle, OK?'

'Oh god, I'll try not to.'

'Good. Because, you know, he has a thing about nepotism.'

'Understood.'

'Right, so let's get you kitted up before you get too *comfortable.*'

She delved into a cool-box and pulled out a thick plastic bag full of pink heart-shaped pills, just like the ones he'd had at his party.

'There's a hundred in there,' she said. 'And they're ten pound a pop. You won't sell them all today, but if you do, just come back and I'll give you a refill. Otherwise, see you back here around eight. In the meantime…' she pulled out a map and marked it with a cross '…this is where you need to go. It's a plum position, right outside the Pyramid Stage. The Killers are on later, so there'll be plenty of action. You should be well popular.'

'OK great. But how do I… I mean how will people know that I'm… you know…?'

'Oh, we'll give you a sandwich board.'

'*Really?*'

'Sure. *Get your Class A's here!*'

Fred looked a little uncertain. Even if different rules *did* apply inside the festival compound, he couldn't help wondering if a sandwich board wasn't asking for trouble.

'Oh god you're *so sweet*,' Izzy gushed, ruffling his hair like a child's. '*I'm kidding*! You don't need to do anything. Just hang around and look meaningful. The punters'll find you, believe me. They have a sixth sense here.'

Fred felt embarrassed and relieved in equal measure – although not at all sure he liked being thought of as 'sweet' – especially by Izzy. But his 'meaningful look' must have been convincing enough, because within five minutes of arriving at his station, he'd found his first punters. Or rather, they'd found him.

A tall, willowy woman with cropped orange hair, clumpy DM's and a nose ring, approached him out of the crowd. Not exactly the kind of demographic Uncle Joe had promised, but hey – punters were punters.

'Can you help us, I wonder?' she asked, leaning into his ear, so as to be heard over the heavy metal music. 'We're looking for some entertainment in *tablet*-form. And no, I'm not talking iPads!'

'How many you looking for?' Fred enquired, doing his best not to show how super-stoked he was to get on the score-card so quickly.

She was joined by a shifty-looking specimen in his twenties, about half her size, with long greasy hair and a glass-eye.

'We're having a little tent party, babber,' he said in a high-pitched west country accent that made him sound like a comedy pirate. 'So we needs about fifty.'

Fifty? Christ! Fred suddenly felt way out of his depth. Popping a pill at a party was one thing. Pushing the stuff, especially in such large quantities, something else entirely. There again – it certainly beat picking up dog-shit. And, if they didn't get it off *him*, he told himself, they'd only get it off someone else. On top of that, there was no way he could let his uncle down yet again. Or Izzy for that matter.

'No probs,' he said, as calmly as he could. 'They're ten pounds a pop. That OK?'

'A pop?'

'A pill.'

'Yeah, that's OK,' the woman said. 'But not here.'

She was right. This wasn't the place to start counting out fifty ecstasy tabs. Or five hundred quid for that matter.

'Our tent's a few minutes away,' she added. 'We can sort it out there.'

Fred wouldn't normally allow two strangers to take him to an unknown destination. But surrounded by all these people, with all this security, it was hard to imagine they represented any danger. And once inside their tent, the transaction would be swift. He'd swap his pills for their money, there'd be a quick count, a business-like handshake, and he'd be on his way – with five hundred smackers neatly tucked into his inside pocket. Uncle Joe would be dead proud. And so would Izzy. She might even stop calling him 'sweet'.

Except that wasn't how things panned out. Their tent was in a different campsite to Izzy's. And once they'd finally got there, the woman, who introduced herself as 'Kai', insisted on doing things the 'Glasto way'.

'When you're buying a rug in Morocco,' she explained. 'You have to sit down and drink mint tea. It's a tradition. And it's the same here. Only this isn't mint tea.'

She poured a small mound of grainy white powder onto a chopping board and cut it into two equal lines with a razor blade.

'What is it then?' Fred said, now feeling distinctly uneasy.

'A mark of friendship and trust. Ain't that right Dog?'

'That's right Kai,' Dog smirked.

'And a nice little mood-lifter too.' She handed Fred a twenty pound note rolled into a tube.

Fred didn't need a mood-lifter. And, without wishing to appear rude, he didn't need a mark of friendship and trust. The problem was that Dog had somehow managed to slip the plastic bag out of his rucksack. So they now had all his merch – and he still had none of their money. So maybe it made sense to play ball.

'Go on lad,' Dog said, clocking his hesitation. 'Shall I show you how? You just closes off one of your…'

'I know how,' Fred said irritably.

Which was more or less true. He'd once looked on as Mikey and Omar did a line of coke that they'd 'borrowed' off Mikey's sister. Fred had wanted to join in of course, but Mikey said he wouldn't 'feel the benefit' as he had sinusitis at the time. To be fair, they did offer to stick some up his arse instead, but he'd politely declined.

Bottom line, it wasn't rocket science. So he'd put the tube in his right nostril, took a long hard snort and…

Holy crap on a cracker!

'Great shit eh?' Dog leered.

Fred could feel his eye-balls, rolling around in their sockets. Maybe that's how Dog lost *his*?

'Is it coke?' he murmured.

'Nah – coke's for wimps, toffs and tossers,' Dog said. 'It's donkey dust.'

Kai gestured to the second line. 'Waste not want not, as me dear ole nan used to say.'

Fred definitely wanted not. But dissing Kai's dear ole nan was a risky business. So he switched nostrils and… that's when he must have passed out.

*

The awkward silence between Alex and Fred since Monday's face-off had finally broken on Friday morning when Fred shambled into the kitchen to announce he was going to Ollie's. They had the day off school, or so he'd claimed, for revision. His shiftiness was presumably down to the fact that he was still technically grounded, although it was the continued insolence that bothered Alex more. Still, having spent the past few days in a fug of depression and alcohol, he had neither the strength nor the appetite for a show-down. And the hospital email he'd just received, inviting him in for an MRI, hadn't improved his mood.

After a grudging goodbye, Fred had trudged off into the gathering storm while Alex struggled upstairs to contemplate what was left of his future. For several minutes he'd sat slumped at his desk in a catatonic daze, until it occurred to him that (apart from a good bottle of wine) the one thing that often calmed his mind, was a *list*. It was a little quirk he'd learned as a child from his father, and one he often resorted to when he couldn't sleep, or when he faced a stressful situation at work. He'd never tried it in an emotional crisis, but there was no harm in giving it a go. It would be comforting to know that even in his darkest hour, he was capable of objective and rational thought. So – once he'd opened the statutory bottle of Malbec – he opened his laptop and created two columns.

In the first, under the heading: 'Negatives' – he typed:
1) Health
2) Marriage
3) Career
4) Income
5) Ally and Joe
6) Dating
7) Fred
8) Fred's DNA

And in the one headed 'Positives' – he typed:
1)

And that was it. He simply couldn't think of anything, not one single scintilla of hope or consolation to offset his catalogue of woes. So there it was, staring him full in the face, the answer to the question that he'd not yet dared ask himself, but which he couldn't *not* ask now.

What was the point in prolonging his increasingly miserable existence?

As a man whose career had been built on meticulous planning and detailed preparation, Alex began to consider an exit strategy. As it happens, only yesterday there'd been a debate on the radio about assisted dying, which – despite his alcoholic haze – had made his ears prick up. The trouble was, who did he have to assist him? His father had the unwavering palliative support of a loyal wife and a loving son during his gradual descent into hell. Alex would have none of that.

Dignitas was always an option, of course, but from what he'd read, an awfully laborious one. By the time you'd done your due diligence, filled out the forms, procured the required signatures from two doctors, paid your deposit, shlepped off to Zurich for the pre-assessment – who knew what your state of health would be? Not to mention your *mental* health. No, Dignitas wasn't for him. If he really was going to take arms against a sea of troubles, he needed to be bold and decisive. No prevarication. No relying on other people. It was *his* bloody life after all.

Alex took a hefty swig of the Malbec and gazed ruefully out of his study window. The rain was battering the flower-beds and a ferocious wind buffeting the beech tree, making its little wooden swing flail about like a dancer on speed. Or a corpse on a gibbet.

A corpse on gibbet. That disturbing image somehow percolated through his consciousness and gradually distilled into a plan.

As if on automatic pilot – Alex now found himself in the garden, windswept, drenched, battling the elements, untying a set of gnarly old knots, discarding the crumbling seat, and retreating inside, trailing thick wet ropes like spoils of war.

DIY had never been his forté but he'd managed to find a video on YouTube in which a man from a platform bizarrely entitled 'Survival World', meticulously explained how to make a Hangman's Knot. Alex followed the instructions to the letter. Then, clambering onto one of his Roche Bobois dining chairs, he rigged the noose to the old wooden beam that bisected the living room ceiling.

And there it hung, a memento mori, a stark, chilling symbol of his plight. Yet at the same time – an escape route, a panacea, a solution. Alex sank into his armchair, and gazed up at his handiwork with a strange mix of exhaustion, pride and terror. But for whatever reason, he wasn't ready – not drunk enough perhaps, too hungry, or just not in the right frame of mind.

Pragmatic as ever, he opened another bottle, ordered a Biryani Feast from the local Indian, and settled down to his Mission Impossible box-set. A curious choice, some might say, for a man preparing to bring his life to a shuddering close, but if Tom Cruise couldn't detonate his scruples and spur him into action, nothing would. And besides, it was one of his favourites.

Sure enough, by the time Dead Reckoning's end-credits were rolling, he was sozzled, sated and emboldened in equal measure. He switched off the TV and switched on his mini-speaker, swapping Tom's irrepressible brio for Leonard's bleak melancholia. The next few minutes went by in a kind of Malbec-induced trance. He drew the curtains, mounted his makeshift gallows and – with his heart pounding louder than his telephone's ringtone – fended off Ally's calls, placed the noose around his neck and pulled it tight against his throat, readying himself for the coup de grace.

And that's when the WhatsApp pinged, bringing him back from the brink.

Ally's terrified voice and the news of Fred's kidnap were like an electroconvulsive shock to his system. Alex knew right away there was only one course of action – that his own *impossible mission* was beckoning.

*

Somerset Welcomes You! – or so the road-sign claimed. But with a night black as the Isis flag, hailstones the size of marbles and a road full of potholes – Somerset was hardly rolling out the red carpet. Given the turmoil in his mind and the amount of wine in his tank, Alex had done remarkably well to get his trusty old Saab this far. And so had the trusty old Saab. A headlamp had packed up, a wiper was on the blink, and the side window had jammed open, dispensing rough facial scrubs through its three inch air-gap. Oh, and a seat-belt alarm had been beeping insanely since Basingstoke. In a vain attempt to drown it out, Alex had pushed Dire Straits to the max.

A bolt of lightning torched the countryside – then plunged it back into darkness. The subsequent sonic boom was so violent, the car almost dived into the roadside ditch of its own volition.

As if triggered by Nature's electro-magnetic signals, Ally's face was now beaming serenely up from the cracked leather seat beside him. In the absence of a hands-free, Alex grabbed his mobile and pressed it hard against his ear.

'Hey Al,' he said. 'Any news?'

Crazy how a mortal threat to the so-called fruit of their so-called loins could end months of civil war at a stroke.

'*Will you please turn that bloody noise down*!' she yelled.

And how quickly it could all kick off again. Ally had never liked Dire Straits. They reminded her of miners' strikes, shoulder pads and Maggie Thatcher. 'Money for nothing indeed!' she'd mock.

But now wasn't the time to fight their corner.

'Thanks,' she said once he'd put them on pause. 'And no – no news. Other than me being out of my head with worry.'

'There's been no more contact then?'

'I think that might've counted as *news*.'

Ally took a moment to blow her nose, then resumed hostilities.

'How much money did you take?'

'They won't be expecting any money at this stage.'

'OK – but just in case – how much did you take?'

Alex rummaged in his pockets. 'About... twelve pound fifty.'

'Are you kidding? Do you think these low-lives are going to set him free for twelve pound fifty?'

'No but as I said...'

'Or maybe you think they take plastic?'

'I didn't know he was going to get kidnapped, did I?'

'Couldn't you at least have gone to a hole in the wall?'

'How would that have helped? You can't draw more than three hundred quid without prior arrangement.'

'So what'll you do when you get there? Have a whip-round?'

'I dunno. Engage with them I guess. Use my powers of persuasion.'

'What *powers of persuasion*?'

'It's what I do for a living isn't it? In a manner of speaking.'

'You don't *have* a living Alex – or have you forgotten?' Ally's voice was as brittle as a hailstone.

And no, he definitely hadn't forgotten.

'Where are you now?'

'Near Shepton Mallet. About 20 minutes away if the Saab holds out. Will you send them a text?'

'What if they don't answer?'

'Then I'll just have to use the app.'

'What app?'

'Find my iPhone. It's the upside of paying Fred's bills.'

'Do you know how huge the place is? And how many people there'll be? Not even Apple would claim you have a hope in hell.'

'You'd be surprised.'

'And if his phone's out of battery – what then?'

Torrential rain and a Force 8 gale filled the ensuing silence. It was Somerset's answer to tumbleweed.

'You know who goes to Glasto every year don't you?' Ally offered finally.

Yes of course Alex knew. Joe had been going there religiously every summer for as long as he could remember. But Joe was the *last* person he'd be asking for help. In fact he wasn't about to dignify her suggestion, or whatever the hell it was, with a response.

And Ally wasn't about to give up.

'Listen Alex,' she said, now making a concerted effort to sound reasonable. 'Joe knows people there. He knows how it works.'

'Sorry Al. I'm not having anything to do with him. And if you had any respect for my feelings, you wouldn't even mention the bastard's name.'

'Christ, Alex, will you stop being so negative?'

Negative? He'd put his own liberation on hold, driven halfway across the country in the middle of the night through an actual named storm – despite being well over the limit – in the vague hope that amongst a quarter of a million mud-soaked revellers, he would somehow make contact with Fred's abductors, and persuade them to see the error of their ways. Single-handedly, without involving the cops. You could call it *reckless*. You could call it *stark-raving bonkers*. But one thing it wasn't – was *negative*.

Before Alex had a chance to respond, another flash of lightning fizzed across the sky and the line went dead. He waited a few seconds, then hit the CD.

Mark Knopfler's solo kicked in.

And the heavens replied with a drum-roll.

*

Shock-waves pummelled Fred's body. The tent bulged and flapped like it was about to take off. And the techno-beat from a nearby stage stopped dead in its tracks – as if someone had pulled out a plug. Fred tried frantically to bury his head in the manky bed-roll they'd stuck him in after his 'photo-call', but with his wrists lashed together with fishing wire and no feeling at all in his arms – his attempts were utterly futile.

Dog was freaked out too. Squatting and shaking by the lantern, his giant shadow looming on the canvas like some low-budget horror-movie. Despite his attempts to look hard, he was far more dachshund than doberman. Still, a dachshund could give you a nasty bite too.

Kai was perched on a stool by the entrance-flap. 'Pull yerself together!' she snapped.

Or should it be 'he' snapped? There was something

about the deep baritone voice and the bulging Adam's apple that made Fred wonder. Either way, he preferred to stick to his *own* gender reassignment. '*She*' felt less threatening somehow.

'You're such a fucking wuss, Dog!' 'she' sniggered.

Dog pulled his fingers out of his ears.

'I'm not a wuss,' he yapped. 'I told you before. I has astraphobia. Fear of thunderstorms. Look it up if you don't believe us.'

Dog stared at Fred with his glass eye. 'What you staring at Posh-boy?' he said.

Fred looked away. 'I'm not staring sir. I'm just…'

'Don't friggin *sir* me. I'm not your schoolteacher.'

'Sorry sir… mate… I mean Dog… shit!'

Fred wasn't trying to be a smart-ass. But he still felt like he'd been trampled by a herd of donkeys.

Things were kicking off again now. The techno-beat. The party buzz. And Dog had finally stopped shaking. He shuffled across on all fours and hovered over Fred's face till their noses were virtually touching. Jesus Christ – he smelt even worse than the bed-roll.

'You knows who you reminds me of?' he said. 'That geyser off the telly. That Poldark geyser. Except with darker skin, and a weaker chin. And a fuck-sight posher of course.'

'I'm not posh,' Fred protested.

'Yeah you are. You talks like a bloody royal. Which is weird, considering.'

'Considering what?' Kai butted in.

Dog jabbed a grubby thumb at Fred's face. 'They don't normally talk like that do they?'

'Who don't?'

'The cross breeds.'

'Don't call him that,' Kai said sharply.

'Well you knows what I mean. The half-castes.'

'I think the term you're looking for is *dual heritage*. What about Meghan then? And she *is* a bloody royal. Or *was*.'

'Yeah but she's a Yank too innit? That's different. Anyways...' Dog's acrid breath was filling Fred's lungs again. '...You don't wanna fall out with me Posh-boy. I'm the best hope you got. Kai here was all fer chopping off yer finger.'

He waggled a muddy pinkie.

'I never said that,' Kai said.

'Yeah you did. You said if his folks won't play along we'll just send'em a finger.'

'I said we'll *give'em* the finger.'

'What's the friggin difference?'

Kai's silver tongue-stud glinted in the lamp-light as she hooted with laughter.

'Y'know what Dog,' she said, 'you may be onto something.' Slowly, deliberately, she pulled a rusty old pen-knife from her boiler-suit pocket and flicked out one of its blades. 'Body-parts can be dead persuasive.'

*

According to Google Maps, Glastonbury was now within stage-diving distance. And sure enough, a giant miasma of light, like a luminous flying saucer, was hovering above what Alex assumed was the festival site. But with the rain coming down in sheets and just one working wiper swishing back and forth like a hyperactive pendulum, it was virtually impossible to read the road-signs. Even spotting one now was a struggle.

And if the clunking and grinding at every gear-change was anything to go by, the old rust-bucket was struggling too. Who knew that instead of a tank built to withstand the Swedish winter, he'd need an amphibious craft engineered to survive the British summer? On the other hand, he'd just aqua-planed past a VW Beetle semi-submerged in a ditch, and an RAC man conducting the last rites on a terminally ill Mini. So things could be worse. Plus the seat-belt alarm had finally stopped beeping, thank god.

Miraculously, he was now at the entrance to one of the festival car-parks. He'd been hoping to slip in unnoticed – under cover of the apocalypse – but a short, hooded creature in hi-vis and wellies emerged from the Portakabin, puffing on a Vape. As he hobbled towards the car, Alex lowered the music and tried to do the same with the window – but the damn thing was still refusing to budge.

'You can't park here, chum,' the steward wheezed lugubriously through the window-gap, filling the car with apple-scented smoke. 'You need a pass.'

'Oh. So... how do I get one of those?' Alex asked, holding his breath.

Two large pale Gollum eyes and a thin bony face glowed in the darkness as he took another slow, defiant puff. Then he muttered something that was totally drowned out by the downpour.

When Alex asked him to repeat it, he grunted and lowered his mouth into the gap again.

'I said… you get it off the internet.'

'Is there another way perhaps?' Alex was doing his best not to sound like he wanted to run the guy over. 'Given I'm already here?'

'You could try the main gate,' he shrugged.

'OK. Thanks.'

'They're fifty quid.'

'*Fifty quid?*'

There was another violent cloudburst, as if someone upstairs was deliberately pouring cold water on his half-baked plans.

'Waste of time though,' he declared. 'All the car-parks are full. Festival started two days ago.'

'But I only need it for an hour,' Alex pleaded.

The steward blinked, as if Alex was talking in tongues.

'I'm… just dropping something off,' Alex added. 'For my son.'

An icy smile flickered across the weather-beaten contours of the steward's face. Contemptuous. Triumphant. Like he'd finally found some collateral for a lifetime of crushed dreams. But if it was power he craved, subservience was Alex's only hope.

'Check the boot if you like. No tent. No rucksack. No sleeping bag.'

'No shit!'' the man smirked. 'But this *is* still a motor-car, right?'

Ah, a budding comedian! The next Michael McIntyre, honing his skills in a Glastonbury car-park.

Keep at it mate and one day they might give you a

guest spot – at the Damp Squib, is what Alex *wanted* to say. Instead, he took a deep, apple-infused breath and a spur-of-the-moment decision.

'Look pal, I don't have fifty quid. But I do have this.' He flicked on the courtesy light and raised his left hand to the window. 'Whaddaya say?'

As soon as the man clocked the rose gold Rolex, his round Gollum eyes were all but popping out of his hood. Alex slipped it off and passed it through the gap. The man glanced around shiftily, then proceeded to inspect it like a myopic pawn-broker.

'Cheers!' he said eventually. And if he'd added *my precious* it would have been no surprise. He quickly shoved it in his pocket before Alex could change his mind, then jabbed his Vape at the horizon. 'Stick her over there Boss, right at the back. Facing away so they can't see you don't have a car-pass.'

Alex felt a meagre frisson of pleasure when the wheels spun, splattering the bastard in Glastonbury mud. But his main consolation was that the watch was worth virtually nothing. He'd picked it up years ago for thirty dollars in a Bangkok flee-market, and it had been losing several minutes a day since he'd dropped it in the bath last Christmas. It had served its time alright.

Cruising through the quagmire, past row upon row of mud-soaked cars, like war-graves on the Somme, Alex finally made it to the boundary. And as the drumming rain forged a strident duet with a distant wailing sax, he parked up, closed his eyes, and let his head sink slowly back onto the headrest.

CHAPTER 26

MISSION IMPOSSIBLE

'Do you think Pops'll cough up if we send him an ear?' Kai said, running her thumb along the blade's jagged edge. 'Only sometimes they don't. Sometimes they try to tough it out. Show you what they're made of.' She placed her bony hand on Fred's head and gently massaged his cranium. 'The choice is yours little man.'

'What choice?' Fred squeaked.

'Which body-part you'd be happy to part with. Finger? Toe? Ear? Tongue?' She let go his head and started circling his crotch with her penknife. 'Or maybe some other part I've not even thought of?'

'Way to go!' Dog said excitedly.

A tear slowly rolled down Fred's cheek and he couldn't even wipe it away.

'C'mon boy,' she sighed. 'Don't be a fucking snowflake. It's all for a good cause.'

To prove he was no fucking snowflake, Fred squeezed out a twisted rictus.

'That's more like it,' Kai said as her boiler suit pinged.

She pulled Fred's phone from her pocket and read his mum's text out loud. "Fred's father will be there soon. What should he do?"

Kai flashed Fred a murderous look. 'Why the fuck is your old man coming?'

'I dunno,' he said meekly.

'Do you have that kind of money just lying around in your crib?'

'I dunno.'

'Friggin hell!' said Dog. 'I said we should of asked for more.'

Kai carefully placed her knife on the chopping board, fired off a reply and pressed 'send'.

Moments later, there was another ping.

"He wants to talk." Kai glared at Fred again. 'What the fuck does he wanna talk about?'

'I dunno,' Fred repeated.

'He'll never get in without a pass,' said Dog. 'What's he think this is – the 1980's?'

'There's nothing to talk about anyway,' said Kai. 'Not till we get our fucking money.'

She pinched Fred's ear-lobe between her finger and thumb.

'You have such a nice pair of cobs,' she said, squeezing so tight that he squealed. 'I'm sure they look better attached to your face. I do hope your Daddy agrees.'

*

Another bolt of lightning arced across the sky and the whole place lit up like pyrotechnics at a Pink Floyd gig.

For a split second, through the rivulets of water cascading down the windscreen, and beyond the low timber rail that edged the car-park, Alex caught his first glimpse of Glasto's famous perimeter fence.

He'd read about it once in a glossy. Fifteen feet high, god knows how many miles long and made of solid steel, it encircled the site like a rampart. They first put it up in the noughties when half the punters got in without tickets – and it worked. Nowadays only a handful of drink- or drug-fuelled kids even considered the gatecrashing option.

As if to illustrate the point, a huge Colditz-like searchlight swept across the car-park from a sinister-looking watch-tower a few hundred yards to his right. As soon as it had danced across the bonnet – Alex grabbed the phone and hit Fred's number.

'Hey Pops,' trilled a jovial voice at the other end. 'How's tricks?'

It was hard to tell if it was male or female, old or young. But one thing for sure. It wasn't Fred.

'Who *is* this?'

'Oy!' came the jaunty rebuke. 'Where's yer sense of humour?'

Alex hesitated. His sense of humour had disappeared long ago, but there was no benefit in being openly confrontational. 'I'd like to speak to my… my son please,' he said eventually.

'You're very direct Daddy-o,' said the voice. 'But that's cool. It's the middle of the night, it's pissing with rain and you've obviously come a long way. You're right to cut to the nitty gritty.'

'Thank you.'

'So I will too. Have you got our fucking money?'

'Erm – not all of it, no.'

'How much?'

'I… prefer not to say.'

'Then… why are you here?'

'To talk. Face to face.'

'I'm afraid that's not how things are done.'

'Look,' Alex said. 'I don't know how things are done. My son's never been kidnapped before. But I'm sure there's a way of sorting things out in a civilised manner.'

'There is,' said the voice. 'As I explained to your wife. You give us two hundred thou. We give you your son. Simples. How's that sound?'

Like extortion, like blackmail, like daylight fucking robbery – is how it sounded. But with Ally's plea not to antagonise still ringing in his ears, Alex managed not to say it out loud.

The voice ploughed on regardless. 'That's a modest amount for a man of your means, right?'

'I'm not a man of means,' he said quietly. 'I wish I was.'

'Pass me the violin Pops. Fred told me what you do for a living. Funnily enough I'm a trained actor myself. A good one too I don't mind saying. Plus I have quite a contemporary look. Maybe, when this is done and dusted, you could cast me in one of your adverts?'

'I don't work much these days.'

'I know the feeling. It's hard for us creative-types isn't it? That's why we need other strings to our bow. You know it's such a pleasure doing business with a kindred spirit.'

'OK listen – whatever your name is.' Alex was still clinging to the threadbare remnants of restraint – but only just. 'You've clearly got Fred's phone. But how do I know you've got Fred?'

'We sent your wife a photo. Didn't she share it?'

'Someone could've sent you that though, couldn't they?'

'You're so cynical Pops. A career in advertising can do that to a person. But like I say, I'm in generous mood. So don't go away...'

There was a long pause. Then another, more familiar voice came on the line.

'Hey Dad. How's it going?'

'Freddie!'

It was gratifying to hear the D-word again. And for the first time in months, that detached, downbeat, don't-give-a-shit tone that Fred reserved for him, had disappeared. If *anything* rang an alarm bell, that was it.

'Are you OK?' Alex asked.

'Yeah I'm fine.'

He didn't sound fine. He sounded like he'd had something to drink. Or *worse*. As if getting kidnapped wasn't enough for a father (or whatever the hell he was) to worry about.

'So who *are* these people?'

Before Fred could answer, the other voice cut back in.

'That's yer lot Pops,' it said. 'Curiosity can kill more than just cats. As you can tell – the boy's fine. For now. So let's get back to biz, yeah? That two hundred K. You got one week. That's plenty of time to sort it out. Glasto wraps on Monday – so you'll need to bring it to a different location. I'll text you where in due course. But listen to me Daddy-o. And I promise this is no idle threat. If you care about what happens to your son – don't even think of involving the rozzers.'

As the phone went dead, the giant search-light strafed the Saab's bonnet again. But what made Alex jump wasn't that. It was his Mission Impossible ringtone.

Ally was even more wired than him, but her voice cracked with relief when he told her he'd spoken to Freddie.

'I also spoke to one of his captors,' Alex added.

'And? What did he say?'

'What we already know. They want two hundred thousand.'

'So what are you going to do?'

'I don't know.'

'Did you record the conversation?'

'No.'

'Why not?'

'What's the point? You refuse to let me call the police.'

'Christ Alex. How can you be so *laissez-faire*? This is our son we're talking about.'

Alex decided to let the 'son' reference go. But he wasn't having her impugn his commitment. 'I'm not being *laissez-faire*,' he insisted. 'I'm just trying to hold it together. *One* of us has to.'

Ally took a couple of deep Mindful breaths to calm herself down.

'You need to call Joe,' she said, her voice more measured now, but still trembling. 'He's done nothing to deserve this resentment. Nothing. But even if he had, our son's wellbeing takes priority over your damaged male sensibilities. So if *you* won't speak to him – I will.'

Alex couldn't hit *end-call* fast enough. And a sudden rush of molten rage propelled him out into the storm, with nothing more than his wispy pac-a-mac for protection. By the time he'd trudged back through the Somme, past Gollum's Portakabin and down a waterlogged road to the main gate, his chinos were sticking to him like soggy parchment, and his trainers had turned into two sodden clumps of mud.

*

Alex's voice was unsettling for Fred, dredging up feelings he hadn't had for a while. He turned them round in his head as he lay cocooned in his bedroll like an Egyptian mummy, trying to decide what they were. He couldn't deny that he still felt a kind of affection towards him, a 'closeness', that he thought had vanished altogether.

Obviously his current sitch was artificial. He was under no illusion about that. He was vulnerable, frightened, cold, hungry and knackered. Which meant he'd probably have felt warm and fuzzy after *any* contact with the outside world. Even if Genghis Khan had called up, or Donald Trump or Doctor Octopus, he'd have felt grateful.

And there was no point pretending Alex didn't piss him off. He was controlling, condescending, bossy and intolerant. Uptight, old-fashioned, and in yer face. And his obsession with planning was a pain in the arse. But the man couldn't help it. He was wired that way. At the end of the day, despite all their rows and fallouts and melt-downs, Alex obviously loved him, unconditionally. Why else would he have driven all this way through a vicious storm at a moment's notice, to try and rescue him? Especially as it was totally hopeless.

*

Considering the time of night, and the fact that the festival had been up and running for two days, there was a surprising amount of activity at the entrance. A bunch of gaunt, bedraggled kids had just pitched up with their bed-rolls and ruck-sacks, looking more like refugees than ravers. A gaggle of chunky Geordie girls sporting pink see-through ponchos over their underwear, were mercilessly teasing three Welsh lads about their namby-pamby rain-jackets and multi-coloured umbrella-hats. And a group of officials were checking tickets and handing out wristbands under a large open canopy. The entrance itself was lit by a row of spots on tall slim masts, with a flashing blue-lamp from a nearby ambulance providing some token rock n roll. And the crazy cacophony of music, blasting out from god-knows-how-many venues inside, was giving the storm a major run for its money.

Away from her colleagues, beside the *Enquiries* cabin, a large moon-faced steward was tucking into a hot-dog. She looked friendly and approachable and easier to sweet-talk than her burly, surly colleagues.

'Are you 'avin a laugh darlin?' she said. 'Even the King can't come in 'ere without a ticket.'

Hmmm. That sweet-talking might be harder than he thought.

'Yeah I know it's against the rules, but the thing is… my son's… in trouble.'

'What kinda trouble?'

'He's been… he's been…'

'He's been what, my love?'

'He's been… having some serious health issues recently. So I need to give him something. It's quite urgent.'

Hot-dog lady looked him up and down, doubtless taking in the absence of a bag of any sort, not to mention the drowned rat impression.

'What do you need to give 'im, my love?'

'Erm…' He tapped the pocket of his chinos. 'His EpiPen. He left it at home.'

She shook her head and took another bite of her hot-dog.

'Kids eh? Who'd 'av'em?'

'Tell me about it.'

'What's 'is allergy?'

'Sorry?'

'What's he allergic to?'

'Erm…'

In his current state of my mind, Alex literally couldn't think of a single allergen.

'…Hot dogs,' was what he eventually come up with.

'*Hot dogs?*'

'Well, not hot-dogs per se. But… y'know… the stuff inside… the mustard.'

'Ooh that can be nasty.'

'It can be lethal.'

She nodded sympathetically. 'OK darlin'. No worries.'

'*Really?*'

'Sure. Just leave it with us and tell 'im to fetch it from Pam at Pedestrian Gate B.'

Bollocks. Never mind *Gate* B. What Alex needed was *Plan* B. He glanced across at the entrance. The turnstiles. The ticket-check. The wrist-band station. The cluster of burly border guards. It had been a while since he'd put his legs to the test – but he was a pretty nifty mover back in the day. The marshy ground and his rubbish footwear were not in his favour. Nor were the effects of those bottles of Malbec. And it was barely three months since his surgery. But at least the element of surprise was on his side. And once in, even at this time of night, it should be easy enough to lose himself in the crowds.

Find my iPhone would take over then. And after that – OK he may not have a precise plan for what to do once he'd tracked Freddie down – but he'd be there. In person. And a sixty year old grown-up would be better equipped to handle these low-lives than a fifteen year old boy. Besides, with a quarter of a million witnesses packed in cheek by jowl, there was a limit to the harm they could do.

If only he wasn't still so hard-wired to play by the rules. A strange observation perhaps, for someone who, not four hours ago, was about to top himself. But this was different. Because having chosen life – at least for now – he'd somehow reverted to type. And playing by the rules had always been his handicap, even as a teen. Some wouldn't think twice. Opportunists. Chancers. Dare-devils. Hotheads. They'd have rushed forward like lemmings, bursting into the compound in less time than it took him to formulate the thought. Joe – to name but one. They might share the same genes, parents and upbringing.

But Joe would never allow 'caution' to clip his wings. On the contrary. Ever since he learned to walk, any act that involved actual danger would hold ten times more appeal – regardless of what it was. Of course, over the years, that kamikaze streak had given him more than his fair share of problems. But at times like this, it was a streak Alex wished he could channel.

As if in answer to his prayers, a policeman and a sniffer-dog emerged from the gates, closely followed by two paramedics carrying a woman on a gurney. The poor wretch was barely conscious – eyes dilated, head lolling. Everyone looked on in morbid fascination, as she was gently manoeuvred into the ambulance.

The next thing he knew, Alex was hurdling the turnstile and legging it down a long tented corridor like Forrest Gump. Then, as he emerged into the driving rain on the other side, two pairs of hands, like massive hydraulic claws, grabbed him and frogmarched him off, unceremoniously dumping him back outside with a few choice words.

'Woohoo! Canny try!' bawled one of the Geordie girls as he staggered to his feet, covered from top to toe in Worthy Farm mud. 'Ah normally need a few Jagerbombs before ah do somethin leek that!'

*

According to the clock on the dashboard, it was 01.31am by the time Alex made it back to the Saab. And one thing was certain. He was far too shattered to drive home – or anywhere else for that matter – even if he wanted to.

Which he didn't. Freddie might be a selfish, ungrateful, inconsiderate little shit. But for now at any rate, he was *Alex's* selfish, ungrateful, inconsiderate little shit.

How the hell could he get his hands on that kind of money though? And in a *week*? There really was only one viable option.

He started tapping out the numbers – slowly, tentatively, until with his finger hovering over the third '9' – something in the distance caught his eye.

Three spindly figures – bent double against the wind and rain like a Lowry painting – were dragging a cumbersome piece of equipment towards the large looming shadow of the perimeter fence. He flicked on his one working wiper to get a clearer view. In a well-drilled military-style operation, lit only by narrow torchlight from their smart phones, a ladder was planted, fixed and extended, until its top was flush with the top of the fence. Then, one after the other, the three figures, each lugging a hefty rucksack, scrambled up and promptly disappeared over the other side.

Alex shut his eyes, then blinked them open again, fully expecting to see nothing more than rain like tracer-bullets, beating down on the empty no-man's land in front of him. But there it was, the abandoned ladder, willing him, *goading* him almost, to follow the gatecrashers' footsteps.

The Colditz beam was now arcing across the car-park, shaking him to his senses. In the time it would take him to trudge across to the ladder, it would certainly come round again. In truth, part of him was secretly relieved to have an excuse to back out.

Then out of the blue – there was an electrifying flash of lightning and a cataclysmic bang. The miasma of light above the festival extinguished and the giant search-lamp fizzled out. Ally's father would doubtless have put it down to *Divine Providence.* But the only *rational* explanation was a total power-cut.

Whatever it was – having already proved to himself that he was more than capable of defying his factory settings – this new opportunity felt too good to ignore.

It's just a fence Alex. Get over it!

So after wading through the primordial mud to the field beyond, he stepped over the short wooden rail and splashed doggedly towards the ladder. Using the torch on his phone to see where to plant his mud-soaked Nikes, he clambered cautiously up, one rung at a time, until he reached the top. There, with the wind doing its level best to take his head off, he hooked his right leg onto the 45 degree overhang… and then his left… squinting through the curtain of rain into a deep black void. As far as he could see, there were no mangled corpses splayed out on the other side. So what had become of those kids? Did they slide down the support beams? Or just use the quagmire to soften their fall?

He was in the midst of his own risk-assessment when the decision was taken out of his hands. A colossal gust of wind came howling across the carpark, sweeping him off his perch.

The ground spun, wheeled and careered towards him.

There was another massive bang.

And everything went black.

CHAPTER 27

40% PROOF

Fred had never felt so exhausted in is life. But the pounding rain, the relentless thrum of distant music, and Kai and Dog's constant bickering, meant he was miles from falling asleep. Feeling like shit didn't help with that either. His head was still spinning and his mouth still dry as sand-paper. And the events leading up to his kidnap kept playing over and over in his mind like a busted video game. Perhaps worst of all, he was starting to feel really, *really* bad about lying to his parents. Sure he could blame his hormones for some of the things he'd said and done, and his mum would certainly back him up. But if he could have turned back the clock – he would definitely un-say and un-do quite a lot of them.

If he'd had three wishes, the first would be to get out of this bloody nightmare alive. The second – with all his body-parts fully attached. And the third – to avoid having to explain what the hell he was doing there in the first place. Although he could hardly expect these scumbags not to blow his cover.

In his defence, according to Izzy, good quality E's were a lot safer than booze. And technically he hadn't actually *sold* any. But that was unlikely to get him off the hook. The long and short of it was – his mum and dad were going to go apeshit. And that more than anything, seemed destined to keep him awake.

*

With hailstones acupuncturing his skull, Alex finally opened his right eye. The night was still dark as a tomb and he had an excruciating pain above his left one – but at least he was alive. And, intact too, more or less, thanks largely to the preservative qualities of mud. Who knows – if he *had* died and sunk without trace, they might have dug him up centuries later and branded him *Glasto Man!* How wrong they'd have been!

Having said that, he genuinely didn't have a clue how long he'd been out. Maybe it *was* centuries later? He fumbled in his pockets for the phone, but it must have dropped when he fell. If it was lost or broken, he might as well go home. He scrabbled frantically around on all fours, until his fingers finally made contact with something solid, semi-submerged by one of the fence's support struts. To his relief, the screen sprang to life when he wiped off its coating of mud. And even more surprising – the clock said 1.35am. So not centuries later after all!

A spasm of pain shot through his ankle as he hauled himself up. Most likely just a sprain – but no way was that ankle going to lug fourteen stone around the biggest music festival in Europe. As if to mark this new setback, the heavens exploded again. Not lightning this time but a massive electrical surge, bouncing off the bottom of the storm clouds. Some giant generator was kicking into life. And one by one, a host of powerful sound systems renewed their booming Hallelujahs.

Alex's own elation at having scaled the impregnable fence was tempered by the sight of another one. Admittedly it was half the height of the first and constructed out of mesh, but with no ladder and a knackered ankle, it was completely insurmountable. Especially with the Colditz search-lamp catching everything in its merciless glare.

Alex recoiled as it strafed the ground yards from where he was standing – but as it passed, it lit up a hole just large enough for a man his size to squeeze through. Judging by its jagged edges it had been hacked open with a set of industrial cutters. They'd certainly done their homework, those kids. Alex didn't need a second invitation. With the beam arcing towards him again, he dragged his gammy leg towards the hole and clattered through, shredding his flimsy pac-a-mac in the process.

Bloody hell – he was in! And greeted by a spectacular light-show. Spots, flares, strobes and LED's dazzling and dancing across a cityscape of domes, cubes, towers, spires and pavilions. Alex was awestruck. Some entire nations wouldn't use this many megawatts in a year, let alone one weekend. And as if it wasn't light enough – a procession of luminous wellies, fluorescent ponchos, flashing rain-hats, coruscating rainbow wings, iridescent pom-poms, strobing feather boas, sparkly hair-extensions, light-sabres, glow-sticks, fairy wands, halo crowns, sparkling tiaras and incandescent mohicans – went flouncing past like some funky amphibious pageant.

Half-closed and pulsing, Alex's shiner looked pretty impressive on his phone-cam – as if he'd been in the ring with Mike Tyson. Add that to the rope-burn on his throat, the ripped pac-a-mac and an all-over coating of Somerset sludge – and he wouldn't have felt more out of place if he'd worn a neon sign round his neck screaming '*Freak!*' And yet – it was clearly comme-il-faut to be a freak out here. Amongst the throngs of happy people, sloshing back and forth along the flooded walkways, no-one even batted an eyelid.

A cluster of signs above his head pointed to a range of exotic destinations: *Arcadia. Shangri-La. Avalon.* And thankfully, one that said *Toilets*! Because before putting his app to the test, he had an urgent physical need to attend to.

*

Fred could normally go hours without peeing. His mum used to say he had the bladder of a camel. But the Donkey Dust had a crazy effect and right now he was literally bursting.

'Just do it in yer bed-roll,' Dog said helpfully. 'I always do. It's like a nice warm bath.'

Kai glared but said nothing.

'Well I'm fucked if I'm takin him to the bogs,' Dog added. 'It's tippin down out there.'

Kai pointed to a bottle of Fanta on the floor by Dog's feet. 'He can use that.'

Dog gulped down the dregs, then waved it above Fred's face. 'Go on – knock yerself out.'

'I can't,' Fred said weakly.

'Oh yeah. I forgot.'

Dog reached into a canvas bag and pulled out a pair of wire cutters.

Kai glared at him again. 'What are you doing?'

'He can't move his rookers can he? I'm gonna free'em up.'

'Don't do that.'

'Why not?'

'He might do a runner.'

'He wouldn't be so friggin stupid, would you boy?'

Fred shook his head emphatically, but Kai remained unconvinced. 'You'll just have to hold the bottle,' she said.

Dog looked horrified. 'Oh right! And his dick too I spose?'

'If that's what it takes.'

'Why's it always up to me to do the dirty work?'

'It's called being a team-player. We all have to play to our strengths.'

'What are *your* strengths then, if you don't mind me asking?'

Kai tapped the side of her temple, but said nothing.

'I see. Whereas I'm basically the piss-pot holder, right?'

'You said it – not me.'

'For god's sake!' Fred whimpered. 'I can't hang on much longer.'

Dog swore under his breath and snipped the neck off

the plastic bottle with his cutters. Then shoving his hand down the bed-roll, he unfastened Fred's jeans, yanked down his boxers and, grimacing like a gargoyle, held the bottle in place.

Fred's relief was indescribable.

'Friggin hell!' Dog exclaimed. 'It's a human fountain.'

'Now go and get rid of it,' Kai said.

Dog looked at her. 'You taking the piss?'

'No *you are*. As far away as possible.'

'Fuck's sake.'

Kai smiled wryly to herself. 'Just be thankful it wasn't a shit.'

*

'GPS don't like storms,' the smooth young Asian assured him. 'The signal will come back soon, you'll see.'

Alex was sheltering under the canopy of a Goan fish curry stall, trying to fire up the app. He'd used it plenty of times before to check on Freddie's whereabouts, but this time it was dead as a dodo.

'Would you like a fish curry while you're waiting?' he said. 'Or a drink?' He placed a bottle of clear liquid on the counter. 'You look like you need one!'

Was it that obvious? Alex wondered. 'What is it?' he asked.

The man glanced round to check no-one was looking, then lowered his voice.

'Feni. Traditional drink of Goa. Made from cashews. Natural anaesthetic. I promise you will like it.'

Out of nowhere he produced ice, sugar and half a

lime, and tossed them into a tumbler. Then he poured out a generous glug.

Alex examined it carefully. The absence of a label struck him as a bit dodgy, but the truth was – he could murder another drink – especially one with medicinal properties.

'Wow! That's…!'

The man's eyes lit up. '…Good yes?'

'…Strong!'

'Forty percent proof! It will make *you* strong. My name is Zozé by the way.'

He looked on happily as Alex took another sip. Then another. And another. Before draining the glass.

'Thank you Zozé. How much do I owe you?'

'It's on the house, brother. But I will pour you another which I will let you pay for.'

'No no, I'd rather just…'

'Trust me. You will feel much better. And you know the best thing about Feni?'

Alex shook his head.

'No hangovers!'

By the time he'd sunk his second glass, the storm had eased and, just as Zozé had promised, a little icon popped up on the app, showing the exact location of Freddie's phone. That was the good news. The bad news was that it was twelve hundred metres away. Which – when you were physically shattered, with a thumping headache and an ankle the size of a small balloon – was a daunting prospect. More than daunting in fact. Out of the question.

And yet he was hardly going to throw in the towel now.

'Whereabouts are we?' he asked his new friend. 'I've lost my bearings.'

'Haha!' Zozé shrugged, tapping the bottle. 'Forty percent proof!' He unfolded a festival map and pointed to the southeast section. 'We are here. The Naughty Corner. Take it if you like. I have many.'

'Thanks. So I need to get myself to… *there…*'

He cross-checked the phone's map with the printed one.

'Pylon Ground? Haha. You have a journey in front of you my friend! I think you need one for the road!'

'No way Zozé. I'm already seeing double.'

A pink plastic rain-hat was eddying around in the mud near Alex's feet. It was the kind of thing he wouldn't normally be seen dead in. But it would stop the rain dribbling down into his eye. And he was feeling quite disinhibited now.

'Suits you,' Zozé said as he fastened the ribbons under his chin.

Alex thanked him, although he wasn't sure it was meant as a compliment. Then, having paid him the £7.50, he started weaving his way through the oncoming crowds. Young, old, drunk, sober or stoned – the one common denominator was that everyone looked upbeat. As a testament to British stoicism, this had to be right up there with the Blitz. The majority were dressed in regulation rain-gear, but many were going for a big bold statement. He counted two mermaids, three lads sporting PVC traffic cones on their heads, a medieval court jester, a human bush, a fire-eater and a gaggle of girls who looked like they'd been in a mud-bath – and who greeted him like one of their own.

Even more outlandish than the outfits – was the chat.

'It was either a wank or a super stressful poo,' he heard one of the girls tell her mate.

'He thinks he's hard, not following me on SnapChat,' said another.

'Have you ever got high on Dioralyte?' a third wanted to know.

Alex had clearly led a sheltered life. But having hobbled past a slew of stages, bars and diners, each one rowdier than the last – he finally made it to his first campsite. Laid out on an incline, its lower section looked more like low-tide in Barmouth Harbour, with rows of tents like upturned dinghies, semi-submerged in a dark brown sludge. Forget the sleeping bag, you'd want a lilo and a wetsuit for a decent night's kip there. Or better still, a submersible. And apart from a girl in waders and two lads navigating their way through the flooded channels in a dugout canoe, there was little sign of life. The higher section was dryer, but its tents were pitched so close together they were virtually touching.

'How you doin' sir?'

Alex turned to see two figures in red hi-vis tabards sauntering towards him. Security officers. One male. One female. Both around forty.

'Good thanks,' he said, cheery as a children's entertainer. 'Just enjoying the view. Bit damp down there.'

The female officer pointed to his eye.

'Surprised you can see anything through that darl,' she said. 'And you've done your leg too by the looks. What happened?'

'Erm…' If he had a scent, he needed to throw them

off it, pronto. He recalled Joe once smashing his face in at Glasto. That would do. '...Crowd surfing,' he said, with the requisite amount of self-mockery.

'Jeez! What was the gig?'

Shit! The *gig*! You wouldn't forget the gig in a hurry. But Alex had no idea who was even playing this weekend. Why couldn't he have just said he fell over?

'Erm...'

Their eyes narrowed.

And then he remembered a poster near one of the stages.

'...Imagine Dragons?'

The woman smiled. 'Bad Liar!'

Underneath its mud-pack, his face was the colour of her hi-vis. 'W... why would I lie?' he stammered.

'No no. *Bad Liar*. Imagine Dragons? It's their greatest song.'

'Oh, right. Yeah. Course.' He made the cuckoo sign with his finger. 'Must be the bang on my head...'

'I'd have to be bladdered to do a thing like that,' said her colleague.

If they only knew how bladdered Alex was right now.

'You mean I should be old enough to know better?'

'Don't matter how old you are sir,' the guy said merrily. 'There's a child inside every one of us. Where you staying?'

'Erm...' Alex checked the name on his map. 'Pylon Ground?'

'D'you need any help getting there?'

For a moment he actively considered it. But rocking up with two uniformed officials wouldn't go down well with Fred's captors, or Ally for that matter. Whether he cared any more about that was a moot point. But the fact was, if anything went wrong, he'd never forgive himself.

'Oh no – I'm cool thanks,' he said. 'Steady and slow wins the race.'

He pulled down the rim of his rain-hat to hide the sweat breaking out on his forehead.

'I see you're not wearing your wristband,' said the guy, bonhomie slowly draining from his voice.

Fuck it!

'I know,' Alex covered. 'It's just... I developed this rash – so I took it off last night. I must have forgotten to stick it back on.'

'I understand sir. But rules are rules. So if you wouldn't mind coming with us. We just need to do a routine check.'

'Is it OK if we do it in the morning? I really need to rest this ankle.'

'Don't worry,' the woman said. 'HQ's just round the corner.'

There were a number of possible outcomes here, none very appealing. If they discovered he'd got in without paying, he'd be out on his ear. Or else forced to come clean about Fred. Having said that, neither guard looked very athletic. The woman was short and stumpy. The guy actually rattled when he breathed.

Before he knew it, Alex was barrelling down towards the campsite as fast as his one working peg would carry him.

'Don't be a bloody idiot!' the woman yelled as they set chase.

And she was right. He *was* a bloody idiot. A bloody

idiot for driving all that way in the middle of the night. A bloody idiot for breaking into the most fortified festival in Europe and maiming himself in the process. A bloody idiot for giving in to that Feni. And a bloody idiot for thinking he could somehow *connect* with Fred's kidnappers, when he couldn't even connect with *Fred*.

But no way was he giving up now. A row of painted oil drums doubling as rubbish bins, lined the edge of the campsite. He flung one behind him as he hobbled past and the woman went down like a nine-pin.

'Come back here yer bastard!' her colleague wheezed as he turned back to help her.

By the time they were up and running again, Alex was on the dry side of the field, skirting fly-sheets, hurdling guy ropes. And the ankle was literally killing him.

If the migrating herds were anything to go by, most of these tents would be empty. So choosing one at random, Alex tore open the flap, threw himself inside and fastened it behind him. There, in the gentle glow of a small Elvis night-lamp, he could just make out two sleeping-bags.

And – *fuck it* – two sleeping women inside them!

One stirred, peeking out from under her eye-mask.

It wasn't easy to look 'unthreatening' when you were down on all fours and panting like the Hound of the Baskervilles, but Alex gave it his best shot.

'Please don't scream!' he whispered, pointing to his eye. 'There's a psycho out there, attacking people.'

The poor woman was so traumatised, she seemed incapable of screaming. And to be fair, if Alex had been woken up in the middle of the night by a creature from the swamps with a black eye and a pink plastic rain-hat, he'd have been terrified too.

The other woman was waking up now, ripping out her ear-plugs.

'Shhhh Jen,' hissed her friend. 'There's a nutter outside, attacking people at random.'

The three of them stayed where they were, rigid with fear, staring at each other in silence until the squelching footsteps receded.

'Thanks,' Alex said, once the coast was clear. 'You saved my life.'

CHAPTER 28

FLORENCE NIGHTINGALE

The storm had passed by the time Alex finally made it to Pylon Ground, and the curtain of rain had turned into a veil of fine drizzle. The pain in his ankle had eased a bit too, thanks partly to Zozé's anaesthetic, and partly to the fact that every *other* joint and muscle in his body was now smarting or stinging or aching. It was 2.55am and – apart from a couple of zig-zagging torches and a handful of still-glowing tents – there was little sign of life. The hard-core hedonists would be out pulling all-nighters and the ones with any sense, fast asleep. Though quite how anyone *could* sleep with this din pounding incessantly away in the background, he had no idea.

According to the app, Fred's phone was now no more than fifty metres away. So Alex trudged on, into the tangle of tents, phone held aloft like a compass.

Then, at fifteen metres, the screen went black.

It wasn't the weather this time, that's for sure. And the shaking and bashing proved useless. No, there was only one possible diagnosis. That stupid bloody app had drained his battery.

By a rough calculation, there must have been around fifty tents in the target zone. Some were still lit, but most were dark. And no working phone meant no working torch. Worse than that, when Fred was fast asleep it took a lot more than shouting his name to wake him up. So even if Alex *were* to stumble into his tent, how would he know he was there? The fact was, waiting till dawn might be better. It wasn't like he was planning to use the cover of night to do an SAS swoop. And his battered old body would certainly thank him.

Close to where he was standing, there was a dome-tent with an extension porch lit by a porcelain owl lantern. If he removed the three pairs of dirty wellies from the plastic groundsheet, there'd be room to lay his head and half his torso.

On the other hand, this was, without doubt, the most reckless thing he'd ever done in his life – and that *included* trying to hang himself. But if he put the brakes on now and let the Feni wear off, there was a major risk he'd change his mind. Only one other viable course of action remained open to him.

On the assumption that thirty hobbling baby-steps approximated to around fifteen metres, Alex began his search. It was an exhausting process, and a risky one. Who knew how even the most blissed-out festival-fan would react to a pac-a-mac'd crusader, barging into their tent in the dead of night.

In the event, most of the campers were sparko. They barely stirred as Alex unfastened the fly-sheet and gently eased his newly acquired owl lantern through the flap. But there *were* some exceptions. A breast-feeding mum almost dropped her baby in shock. A bloke throwing up in a plastic bag, vomited all over his snoring girlfriend. A grotesquely obese guy playing Auld Lang Syne on a kazoo, swore at him in German. A girl in the middle of an intimate hand-wash splatted him with her soggy wet-wipe. And a woman in the throes of giving her partner a vigorous blow-job, almost did a full Lorena Bobbitt.

And yet Alex got away with it – just.

'I'm sho terribly shorry,' he slurred. 'I've totes forgot where I pished my tent.'

Nobody hit him. Nobody screamed. Three guys smoking some evil-smelling substance, even offered him a toke on their bong.

By the time the eponymous pylon hoved into view, Alex had lost count of the number of tents that he'd 'swept'. Probably about forty. He'd certainly got it down to a fine art now:

Approach entrance…

Inch forward…

Unfasten fly-sheet…

Introduce owl…

Take one small step into the tent…

When he got to the big yellow teepee, however, his one small step became a giant leap. It all happened in super slow-motion. His shin caught on something at ground level and the owl took off, swooping into the tent and crash-landing on a pile of rain-jackets.

His own touch-down was even bumpier. There was an outburst of yelping, a frenzied thrashing of arms and legs, a knee that pummelled him like a piston and a hysterical *'Get yer hands off me – pervert!'* On the other side of the tent, a small, misshapen goblin of a man with long greasy hair, leapt up from a camping stool shrieking something in a voice that sounded like he'd been at the helium. And judging by his body language, it wasn't 'make yourself at home!'

'I'm sho terribly shorry...' Alex gasped, frantically disentangling himself from the still flailing body beneath him. 'I've totes forgot... where I... pished my tent.'

'Well this in't it cunt,' yapped the goblin in a strange west-country falsetto.

'I'll be on my way then,' Alex said, staggering to his feet. 'Would you mind if I juss...'

'Stay right where you are!'

The body he'd jumped on was vertical now, blocking his route to the lantern. Tall and aggressive with cropped orange hair and a nose-ring, he hadn't a clue if it was male or female. Although from their response to his fumblings he imagined the latter. She looked him up and down, perhaps trying to decide if he was part of some drug-addled nightmare. Eventually she turned, retrieved the still luminous lamp, thrust it into his hands, and jabbed a contemptuous finger at the door-flap.

'Now fuck off.'

'How very un-Glastonbury!' Alex thought as he hobbled back out to the porch, tip-toeing over what looked suspiciously like trip-wire.

And then a familiar voice punctured his thought bubble.

'*Dad*?!'

Dog cupped a stinking hand over Fred's mouth like a muzzle.

'Shut the fuck up!' he hissed.

Now it was Alex, wondering if he was hallucinating. Cashew-based liqueurs could do that to a man, especially when his defences were down.

'Aaargh – ya friggin retard!' Dog howled as Fred bit into his thumb.

'*Dad!*'

There was no doubting it now! A strong paternal surge propelled Alex over the wire and back into the tent.

'What part of *fuck off* do you not understand?' bawled the boiler-suited sentry, flicking open a penknife and holding it up to his nose. Alex could see his own reflection in its rusty blade – the mud-smeared face, the swollen eye, the pink plastic rain-hat – more Cuckoo's Nest extra than action movie hero. And then his focus shifted to something nestling amongst a jumble of rucksacks. Something he hadn't spotted before. A manky-looking sleeping bag, with a familiar-looking face sticking out of the top like a terrified tortoise.

Fred had never been so happy to see Alex.

Or relieved.

Or gobsmacked.

How the hell did he even get in? What had he done to his eye? And why was he decked out like a clown?

'Hey Fella.' Alex said. 'Center Parcs a bit tame for you, was it?'

Before Fred could explain or apologise, Dog grabbed a razor-blade and pressed it flat against the boy's ear.

'One more step and I'll take it off!' he barked.

The psychotic goblin's hand was trembling so much he could have sliced off a lobe without even meaning to. *Do nothing to antagonise them!* Ally's counsel had never seemed so wise.

'If I'd wanted to cause trouble,' Alex said, 'I wouldn't have come dressed as Florence Nightingale.'

He held up the lamp, but the joke went over everyone's head.

'So why *have* you come?' Kai slid the tip of her penknife inside his nostril. 'Those weren't your instructions were they? Unless you've got two hundred K tucked down your Y fronts?'

'These things are best sorted out face-to-face, don't you think?' Alex managed to say without actually moving a muscle.

'What *things*?' Kai wanted to know.

'These... negotiations.'

'There's no negotiating to be done Pops. I already explained that to your Mrs.'

The flat of Dog's blade was now twitching Fred's ear. Daring him to utter a word. But Fred didn't care. He needed to say it... He was *going* to say it out loud...

'I'm... so... sorry... Dad.'

Wow. An apology. From Fred! In any other context the shock would have brought tears to Alex's eyes. But Kai's blade had already done that. In fact it had all but depilated his nostril.

'Forget about it son,' he said. 'I'm sure you didn't mean to get yourself kidnapped.'

'Aww – that's so touching,' Kai said. 'But I've gotta be straight with you. Dog and I need to know why you're here.'

'I wanted to be with my son. It may be an alien concept to you, but it's how we parents roll.'

'When do we get our money then?' asked the goblin, his own blade still tickling Fred's ear-lobe like Sweeney Todd with the DT's.

'We can discuss that later. I need to talk to my son first – if that's OK?'

'Sure. Go ahead.' Kai removed the pen-knife and lowered it to his chin. 'No-one's stopping you.'

'Thanks,' Alex said, stretching his neck this way and that to release some tension – not for the first time that night.

In truth he had no idea what to say to Fred. There was, of course, a lot he *wanted* to say. Like how the hell did he get himself into this? Where were his mates? Who were these sleaze bags? And from a quarter of a million other punters, why did they have to choose him? There must have been thousands of *actual* rich kids they could have chosen. The sons and daughters of rock-stars, hedge-fund managers, captains of industry, minor royals. Why kidnap a kid whose dad could barely pay the gas bill?

But 'how you doing fella?' was the best he could manage.

'I'm OK thanks Dad. Kind of.'

He wasn't OK at all – that much was clear. His voice was thin and fragile and his bottom lip was quivering. Just like when he was six and someone pushed him off the climbing frame at the adventure playground. Back then Alex's knee-jerk reaction had been savage. He'd grabbed the other kid by the collar and threatened to punch his teeth down his throat if he ever so much as touched his son again. And it was no less savage now.

'Touch him again,' he said, 'and I'll punch your teeth right down your throat.'

The son of a bitch snorted with derision, clearly deciding that a geriatric in a pac-a-mac and a pink plastic rain-hat was unlikely to pose much of a threat.

'Where's your humanity?' Alex added for good measure. 'He's just a boy.'

'We'll show you some humanity,' Kai said. 'When you show us two hundred big ones.'

'Too right,' Dog sneered. 'No nob'ead from London gets to push us around.'

As if to demonstrate, he squeezed Fred's ear between his finger and thumb and readied the blade.

'Down boy,' Kai commanded. 'What are you doing?'

'Just an ear,' said Dog. 'Like in the movie.'

'That's not what we agreed.'

'Yeah it is. You said so yerself. Body parts can make all the difference.'

'No Dog! We do not injure or maim unless we're forced to.'

But Dog wasn't listening. There was a demented laugh, a shriek, a gush of blood. Then everything turned to a blur.

When Alex came to his senses, Kai was lying in a crumpled heap against the tent wall. The owl lamp had exploded into a thousand shards, although its bulb was still functioning. Which was more than could be said of Dog. He teetered for a moment, his one working eye turning inwards, then collapsed onto the pile of rucksacks.

The Feni had played its part – no doubt about that. And so had Tom Cruise. But above all else, what made

Alex such a formidable adversary, was a deep primal instinct to protect his son. Or whatever Fred turned out to be.

Fred, for his part, was completely blown away. But there was no time to say so, with Kai on the charge again.

'*Watch out!*' he cried instead.

As Kai lunged, Alex wheeled round and kicked her square in the jaw. The force would have knocked her into the Naughty Corner had the mud on his shoe not acted as a baffle. As it was, she recoiled, dazed and bruised, like a boxer reeling from a wicked right hook. But she was back on her feet in an instant, jabbing her knife at his chest.

Fred swivelled round in his bed-roll like a spinning top, smashing his legs into Kai's shins and knocking her over again. Her face contorted in agony as Alex stamped on her hand.

'Now it's your turn to fuck off,' he said, grabbing the penknife and thrusting its blade at the door-flap.

Kai struggled to her feet, paused for a moment nursing her crushed knuckles, then crashed out of the tent.

As Dog slowly regained consciousness, Alex calmly unzipped Fred's sleeping bag, unwound the wire from his wrists and dragged him to his feet. Then, grabbing a fistful of loo-roll from the jumble, he tenderly applied it to Fred's blood-soaked ear. Fred gazed at him with a mixture of awe and disbelief.

'Bloody hell Dad. That was…'

'Nothing son,' Alex said archly. 'It's what Dads do. Let's get you out of here.'

Whatever it was – his dad seemed different. Very

different. More steely. More kick-ass. More... and he never thought he'd say this, even to himself... more like Uncle Joe.

Still clutching the bloody wad to his ear, Fred pulled him in for a one-armed hug.

'Seriously Dad. You were... awesome.'

It was the first physical contact they'd had in months and Alex couldn't stop himself welling up. But it was too dark, thankfully, for Fred to clock it.

'I'm just glad you're alright,' Alex said. 'Now let's get going before they fetch reinforcements.'

Fred paused for a moment. 'OK,' he said. 'Just one small thing.'

'What's that?'

'It's stopped raining right?'

'Right?'

'So would you mind losing the hat?'

There was something strangely comforting about the boy's embarrassment. As if normal service had resumed. So in the spirit of peace and reconciliation, Alex untied its ribbons and flicked it at him playfully.

Fred was all for getting out of Glasto ASAP, but after what happened at Electric Sheep, he couldn't allow Joe to think he'd run off with the stash. The problem was, he couldn't send a message, because he didn't have his phone. So he was going to have to take a small detour.

Fred wrapped an arm round Alex's waist to help take the weight off his ankle. But they were both far too knackered to talk. And their new bond, far too fragile to risk imperilling with words. So they trudged on in silence, until the flying pig flag fluttered into view.

Fred pointed to the lime green tent, with its flickering glow. 'That's my base over there,' he said. 'Do you mind if I nip in to pick up my stuff?'

'Sure. Let's go.'

'Erm… no offence Dad, but it might be best if I go on my own? It's kind of a parent-free zone.'

His manner seemed somehow evasive, but this was no time for a row. Besides, Alex could do with a breather. Close to where they were standing, there was an abandoned luggage trolley, missing a wheel.

'OK fella,' he said, warily lowering himself onto it. 'But don't be too long, OK? Or you may never wake me up!'

*

The tent was lit by a big fat candle perched on a red plastic crate. And despite the Stone Roses pumping out from the speaker beside it, Izzy was fast asleep in the air-bed. Not peacefully though. She was tossing and turning and moaning, as if in the throes of some crazy nightmare. Too much happy dust could do that to a person, apparently. She'd probably appreciate being woken up. Trouble was, her boobs were peeping out over the top of the duvet and the last thing Fred wanted, was for Izzy to think he'd been leching. So best just gather his stuff and make tracks. He could say his goodbyes later, via Joe.

But as he tip-toed across to grab his bed-roll – Izzy's eyes pinged open.

'Freddie!?' she gasped, covering her boobs with a pillow.

'Oh! Hey Izzy! I didn't notice them... I mean *you*... over there...'

There was a sudden movement under the covers and a dark-haired man popped up, his naked torso glistening in the candle-light, his eyes red and dilated, his face rough as toast.

'The fuck are you doing here?' Joe snarled – wiping his mouth with the back of his five-ringed hand.

'I'm sorry Uncle Joe – I...'

'And stop fucking calling me Uncle!'

'Sorry... Joe. I just came by to pick up my stuff. The... the thing is, I had a bit of set-back.'

'*A bit of a shet-back?*' Joe's impression of him was even worse than usual. 'What do you mean – *a bit of a shet-back?*'

'I got... erm... kidnapped.'

Joe blinked at him, unsure how to respond. They were anyway interrupted by a sudden burst of panting outside, which got louder and louder, until a shadowy figure appeared at the entrance. Tall and willowy, with orange hair and a blue boiler suit.

'Bit of a stumbling block I'm afraid,' Kai said, stroking the nasty pink welt on her chin. 'Your little toe-rag of a nephew...'

As her eyes adjusted, she became all too aware of Fred's presence.

'...Talk of the devil!'

Fred was still struggling to join the dots, when a second shadowy figure appeared at the door-flap.

'You really can't take a hint can you?' Alex said, poking Kai in the back with his pen-knife.

As Kai hurled herself to the ground by Fred's feet, Alex clocked Joe and his 'companion' beyond, holding a candle-lit vigil like John and Yoko. It was no real surprise to discover his brother at Glasto, off his face and in bed with a woman half his age. But where did *Fred* fit into that? And *Kai?*

Joe was the first to react. 'Whooooaaah!' he drawled. 'Someone must've spiked my fucking Ovaltine!' He hooked a muscular suntanned arm around the woman's bare shoulders. 'Izzy and I are just… doing the company accounts… Aren't we Izzy?'

'That's right,' Izzy riffed. 'Or we were. Until not one, not two, but *three* auditors showed up, unannounced.'

'Don't worry,' Alex said. 'We'll leave you in peace just as soon as you've answered one question.'

'We're all *ears*,' Joe sniggered. 'Aren't we Fredster?'

Fred was still clutching the bloody tissue to the side of his head, and he didn't appreciate the joke.

'So what's your connection to this piece of shit?' Alex asked, pointing the pen-knife at Kai.

'*That* piece of shit?' Joe tilted his head as if trying to recall some dim distant memory. 'Nope – never seen it before in my life.'

'I see. So it just wondered in here by accident?'

'It would seem so bro, yes.'

'Yeah,' Kai chuckled. 'I totes forgot where I pished my tent!'

Fred was still struggling to keep up. 'But… if you've never seen her before in your life,' he said, 'how would she know I'm your nephew?'

Joe's head flopped onto his chest and rested there,

inert, for a few seconds. Then, without warning, as the Stone Roses erupted into a high-octane instrumental, he leapt out of bed and began cavorting about like a man possessed.

'Alright! I'll be straight with ya,' he ranted. 'This piece of shit works for me.'

And just to prove it, he gave Kai a meaty kick with his bare foot. Her theatrical flinch, however, had more to do with the fact that Joe's crown-jewels were now inches away from her face.

'Whatcha gotta say about that Fredster?'

Fred had no idea *what* to say. It was bad enough seeing a man you'd admired all your life, high as a kite and prancing around in the buff. But the thought that Joe was somehow involved in his kidnap was hard to take in. What was it? A joke that went wrong? An initiation stunt intended to toughen him up, like some Amazonian bullet-ant trial or a Masai circumcision?

'Do you mean it was you who…?'

Joe was slow hand-clapping now. 'Well done! So you're not just a pretty face!'

Fred looked utterly crushed. 'But… why would you do that?'

'Ask yer dad!' Joe sneered. 'He knows.'

'You always talk crap when you're bombed Joe,' Alex said. 'But you're pushing the boat out tonight.'

Joe raised his arms like a rock-star, milking the crowd. Then, just as abruptly, he froze, fixing Alex with a dead-eyed stare.

'OK bro. I'll spell it out in words of one syllable. It's – be – cause – of – the – mon – ey – you – owe – me.'

'What the hell are you talking about? *What* money?'

Joe rested a heavy hand on his brother's shoulder, more to stop himself falling over than as any kind of affectionate gesture.

'How much dough d'you think I got off Dad when he pegged it?'

'None I should think. Same as me.'

'Correct.' He jabbed a desultory thumb towards Fred. 'And how much did *he* get?'

'Also none.'

'Wrong!'

'You know perfectly well *that* money was left in trust,' Alex said sharply. 'For Fred's education. He'd have done the same for *your* kids if you had any.'

'Yeah, right!' Joe moved his face closer until their stubble was touching. 'D'you know how much Dad spent on my education?'

'Same as mine,' Alex said, recoiling from his brother's toxic breath. 'Grammar schools are free – in case you'd forgotten.'

'Only I didn't stay at Grammar school did I?'

'That was hardly Dad's fault. He did his job. He gave us a good home. Unfortunately you fucked it all up.'

'And why *was* that? Why do kids from good homes fuck it up?'

'Because they're pathological narcissists who smoke too much, stick too much stuff up their noses, and can't bear it if they're not in the limelight?'

'Wrong again!' Joe said, swaying back and forth, his glassy eyes struggling to focus.

'Mum and Dad offered you all the love and support

any kid could ever want,' Alex insisted. 'And you just chucked it back in their faces.'

'That's crap and you know it!' Joe brayed. 'They were so *obsessed* with their precious first-born, they hardly even noticed when I came along. And nor did you. I was an after-thought, an irritation, a fly-in-the-fucking-ointment.'

He turned and reeled back to the bed, lashing out at anything that got in his way – a pillow – a pair of trousers – the red plastic crate. And as it went flying, so did the speaker and the candle. But Joe was on a roll and nothing was going to stop him – not even the pungent smell of burning.

'All I wanted was someone to take an interest in me for who I was – not what *they* wanted me to be – a carbon copy of my *model older brother*.'

'That's bollocks,' Alex said. 'And you know it.'

'All I know is – the two hundred thousand Dad gave this little tosser? I want it back!'

A thin plume of smoke was now rising up from the jumble of jackets by the side of the bed. Kai clambered to her feet, seized two plastic water bottles from a cardboard box, then, deciding it was a lost cause, tossed them petulantly at Alex and careered off into the night.

'Jesus – it's going up!' Izzy screamed, vaulting out of bed in a valiant attempt to smother the flames with the duvet – until the duvet itself caught fire. 'Come on Joey,' she yelled, grabbing Joe's hand. 'We need to get out!'

'I'm going nowhere,' Joe railed, jerking his hand away, losing his footing on the soggy groundsheet, and capsizing in a heap.

'The tent's on fire!' Izzy pleaded, trying in vain to drag him to his feet.

'Bring it on!' Joe bellowed, spreading himself out on the floor and basking in the unexpected heatwave. 'I like an all-over tan.'

Fred grabbed his bedroll and furled it round Izzy's naked body. She thanked him, but no squidgy hug was forthcoming this time. Instead, she aimed a last despairing glance back at Joe, and disappeared out through the flap.

'*I am the resurrection and I am the life,*' Joe chanted along with the chorus as the flames flickered above his head.

Alex glanced up at the melting fabric. His first instinct was to grab Fred and pull him out. But in spite of all the hurt, pain and malice that Joe had inflicted, in spite of his brutal attempts to destroy Alex and his family, he couldn't just abandon him.

'Quick Fred!' he cried. 'Grab an arm.'

'Don't you dare fucking touch me!' Joe growled. 'I'm going down with the ship.'

'No you're not Joe,' Fred said firmly.

With that, he and Alex each seized an arm and despite some maniacal resistance, managed to haul him to safety, moments before the whole structure collapsed.

CHAPTER 29

HOLLYWOOD ENDING

By the time they were juddering east through Somerset's waterlogged roads, the epic storm had finally blown itself out and the sky was a glorious confection of orange and purple, worthy of any Hollywood ending. In fact, for a few unguarded seconds, Alex actually caught himself humming the Mission Impossible theme-tune. But as the adrenaline wore off and reality kicked in, he became a jumble of conflicting thoughts and emotions again. His new bond with Fred was gratifying of course – more than gratifying – wonderful – but it was the *only* thing on his doom-list that had changed. And in some ways, it made that looming paternity question even harder to bear. Not to mention the state of his health.

If only his own life could have a Hollywood ending. If only he had the immutability, the durability of Ethan Hunt. And an Aston Martin to go with it. In the event, the Saab's one working wiper was battling with spray from the roads. Its seat-belt alarm was beeping incessantly again. And its three-inch air-gap blasting his face with cold air. But at least these 'quirks' were helping to keep him awake.

Fred, by contrast, had his seat tipped back with his eyes closed and nothing – not even Dire Straits – was going to stop him from falling asleep.

Except, suddenly he was bolt upright again.

'*Shit!*' he cried.

'What's the matter?'

'We need to call Mum.'

'Go on then.'

'I can't. Bastard took my phone.'

'Oh. Well you can't use mine I'm afraid. The battery's dead.'

'So – let's charge it up.' Fred was already checking the arm-rest.

Alex shook his head. 'They didn't have mobiles in 1982.'

'She'll be worried sick.'

'OK. We'll stop at the next services.'

'Thanks.'

'As for the phone, maybe you can get it back off your uncle? Or… whatever he turns out to be.'

Fred stiffened. But Alex wasn't about to drop the subject.

'We can cross that bridge when we get home,' he said. 'I did a test.'

As Fred's eyes burnt into him like lasers, Alex feigned an indifference that would have graced any teen.

'The result's waiting in my inbox,' he said. 'We can open it together if you like.'

Fred was anything *but* indifferent. It was like being dumped – only a thousand times worse.

'No thanks.'

'Sorry?'

'I'd prefer not to know.'

Fred was staring resolutely out of the windscreen now. When he eventually turned back to Alex, he was fighting back tears. They both were. And Alex had his knuckles clenched so tight around the steering wheel, his arms were trembling.

'You're my dad,' Fred murmured. 'Whatever some stupid test result might say.'

Alex was far too choked to say anything. He reached over to squeeze Fred's hand and they sat there in silence for a good half a minute, listening to Sultans of Swing. Which made him remember the *other* thing that was waiting back home. It would be the first thing Fred would see as they walked in. No way could Alex allow that to happen. But how could he avoid it? After what the poor boy had been through, dropping him off at Tesco's on the pretext of buying milk or croissants, and then leaving him to trudge home, just felt plain wrong.

Alex's brain was mullered, but he had to say something.

'By the way,' he confided, 'when Mum called last night to let me know you'd been kidnapped, I was in the middle of… of doing something in the living-room.'

'Doing what?'

'A test-shoot. For the Samaritans.'

Fred shrugged. Whatever. Then he leaned forward and rummaged in the glove box.

'What are you looking for?' Alex asked, relieved to have dodged another bullet.

Fred pointed at the stereo. 'Something a bit less… prehistoric?'

'Ah. You may be out of luck there fella.'

Fred shrugged. 'Well… if you ever fancy an introduction to the 21st century, let me know.'

Ahead of them, the first rays of sunshine were filtering through the mud-splattered windscreen, suffusing Fred's sleep-deprived face with a warm gentle glow.

He tipped his seat back again, closed his eyes, and smiled.

And at that very moment, Alex decided. He was going to have the MRI on Monday.

EPILOGUE

ONE YEAR LATER

Fred and Mikey relaxed their guitars as the fuzz-pedal reverb from their final electrifying chord ripped through the airwaves and bounced off the walls. Felix put down his drumsticks. Rory rested his fingers on the keyboard's edge. Chanel loosened her grip on the hand-mike. And the obligatory applause took over.

Fred's gaze flitted through the small gathering of family and friends and settled on his father. 'So?' he said, a little apprehensively. 'What d'you think?'

Alex looked equally tentative. 'OK. Well. I'm not gonna lie…'

The band were momentarily unsettled. Perhaps it didn't matter what Fred's old man thought of their song. He wasn't Simon Cowell for god's sake. Nor was he exactly *renowned* for his good taste – witness the pervy frieze in Fred's basement! But as the director of Blank Canvas's first-ever music vid, it would obviously be nice if he appreciated their music. They'd put their heart and soul into that performance so naturally they wanted *everyone* to like it.

'Go on then,' Fred said, steeling himself for some negative energy.

They were half way along the graffiti tunnel at Waterloo, with its wraparound urban street art providing the perfect psychedelic backdrop for their funky prog-rock sounds. Alex was filming guerilla-style on his iPhone, not *just* because it was cheap but because a rough-edged, improvised, pop-up vibe seemed a lot more suitable than his usual high-gloss TV ad schtick. What's more, after a career spent prepping and planning and polishing, it felt somehow liberating to shoot from the hip.

Fred couldn't tell if his dad was trying to let them down gently, or merely building suspense like an X Factor judge.

As it happens, it was neither. He was struggling to control his emotions.

'OK. Well…' he continued. 'I… I loved it.'

'*Seriously*?'

'Seriously. I thought it was… awesome.'

There were whoops and high-fives all round. Not just from the band, but from their audience too. Fred couldn't have been more pumped. After everything they'd been through, his dad's opinion really mattered to him now. Especially as the song was a punchy drum and bass cover of Alex's all-time favourite – The House of the Rising Sun.

Ollie and Quentin and Omar and Hestie were filming on their iPhones too, so there'd be a tsunami of footage to edit. But Alex was cool with that. The house-sale had finally gone through, which meant he had time on his hands. And after a course of intensive radiotherapy, his cancer was now in remission, so he felt truly reinvigorated – both physically and mentally. Not quite up to Ethan Hunt's levels of invincibility perhaps – but getting there. Besides, this was also *his* first-ever music vid. So he was as 'pumped' as the band. Most of all though, he felt a deep-seated paternal urge to help Freddie follow his dream.

They already knew who they intended to show it to first of course. With Brian's background and contacts in the music biz, it would have been rude not to. Alex was cool with that too. They'd had a drink at Soho House the other night, just the two of them, and they'd got on surprisingly well. Brian had shown him a photo from the eighties when he had both his own band and his own hair. The shocking pink mohican was certainly a *very* different look to his current shiny bald pate. Alex had at last come to terms with the divorce, and it was important to forge some kind of relationship with Ally's fiancé, not least because Fred had recently moved into their Notting Hill pad.

A few metres from where Alex was standing, a tall elegant woman in a shiny yellow raincoat, was leaning against the heavily graffitied wall. Alex glanced at her quizzically, and she responded with an effusive thumbs up. It had taken a while to forgive Fred for sabotaging her date with Alan Smithee, but although his hand-written note confused her, that bouquet of flowers had melted her heart. And through their shared interest in art, Mo and Fred had become best of friends. Which was just as well, seeing as she and his dad were now living together in Dalston.

'So… shall we do another take before they kick us out?' Alex said, all-too-aware that he hadn't applied for a permit.

'As many as you want Dad,' Fred grinned, tightening a string on his Bullet Stratocaster. 'You're in charge. As always.'

Alex smiled. He was *far* from in charge these days – if he ever really was. He and Ally were merely Fred's pro-tem custodians. And that felt just fine.

Better than fine in fact. It felt right.

ACKNOWLEDGEMENTS

Thank you to Jane, who put up with me while I was living it. To Noemí, who put up with me while I was writing it. And to my mum, my brother and my sons, who have the good grace to recognise that any resemblance to actual persons, living or dead, is (almost) entirely coincidental!

AUTHOR BIOGRAPHY

Jonathan Gershfield is a multi-award winning TV director. He has previously written for the big screen, the small screen, the stage and *The Times*, but *The House of the Rising Son* is his first novel. It was spawned from his own front-line experience as a father grappling with the highs and lows of family life, during the unrelenting blitzkrieg of adolescence.